Book One

Sentence of Marriage

Shayne Parkinson

First print edition published 2006.

Second print edition published 2012.

This paperback edition printed through Createspace.

Family trees and some extra background to the book's setting
may be found at:

www.shayneparkinson.com

1

Beyond the farmhouse the ground fell gradually in a series of low hills and flat paddocks, bright green where they had been planted in grass and darker green where the bush remained. The Waituhi creek wound along the valley floor before disappearing from sight behind a steep bluff. Amy reached the top of a hill and paused, caught as she always was by the beauty of the view.

And beyond the mouth of the valley was the sea. The wide sweep of the Bay of Plenty stretched to the edge of Amy's sight, and straight in front of her ocean met sky all along the horizon, broken only by White Island with its constant puff of smoke. Today she could see the island quite clearly through the crisp winter air. The ocean looked blue and mild. Some days it was grey and threatening; but always to Amy it was fascinating. To her it meant the world outside her valley; it meant excitement and adventure, and the lure of the unknown.

As she always did, she strained her eyes to catch a glimpse of the little steamer that served the coastal settlements, but today there was no sign of it. Her father would be catching it soon, travelling to Auckland to look at the latest in farm machinery. In the whole twelve years of her life, Amy had never been ten miles away from home.

She adjusted her grip on the handle of the basket she carried, and turned away from the view.

The wintry sun shone out of a clear sky, with only a few wisps of cloud near the horizon. It would have been a nice day to find a quiet spot and read a book if she had had the time. The ground was still soggy from recent rain, and Amy had to watch her step in the muddy patches, but she enjoyed the fresh air on her face, blowing away the smell of dust and furniture polish that hung about her clothes. The occasional blast from the bush, where her father and brothers were using gunpowder to split logs, did not completely spoil the peace of the day.

Amy followed the noise as she picked her way along one of the rough tracks carved through the bush to drag out trees. As she got closer to the men, she smelt the acrid smoke of gunpowder.

When she got very close she could hear from their language that they were finding the work heavy going. She smiled to herself, and called out: 'Is that you, Pa?' to give them warning of her approach.

The cursing stopped abruptly as she walked into the little clearing. Jack, Amy's father, managed a smile for her; her brothers, sixteen-year-old Harry and John who was nearly nineteen, were more interested in the contents of her basket.

'Lunch at last—I'm starved,' said John.

'You took your time,' Harry muttered.

'Don't talk to your sister like that,' Jack said, flashing him a look.

Amy ignored Harry's remark; she could see they were all tired out. 'How's everything going?' she asked brightly.

Jack pulled a face. 'Too slow. All this mud is bl… I mean jolly hard to work in. And I think a bit of damp's got into the gunpowder—it smells a bit strange. And your *brother*,' he glared at Harry, 'ruined that trunk.' He gestured over his shoulder at a splintered puriri log lying in a churned-up patch of mud. 'I told you to drill the hole two feet from the end—not half way up the flaming thing. That's no good for anything but firewood now.'

Harry looked sullen. 'I'm sure he didn't mean to ruin it, Pa,' said Amy. 'And you've got plenty more, haven't you?'

'What we haven't got is time,' Jack grumbled. 'I want to get these posts split before I leave, so the boys can get on with fencing that bottom paddock while I'm away. And we've only done half a dozen posts all morning.'

'You'll feel more like doing it when you've had lunch,' Amy said. 'I've made you some currant scones specially.' Jack brightened at the mention of one of his favourite treats. 'Now, where can I spread this cloth?'

They found a pretty spot nearby on the bank of the little Waimarama stream, where sunshine dappled the water as it rushed down to the Waituhi under overhanging tawa trees with their yellow-green foliage. The birds had been driven away by the men's noise, but a few brave bellbirds came back to provide a chorus for them. A large tree stump made a picnic table. Amy set out a meat pie cut into slices, piles of sandwiches, and small cakes and scones, with bottles of her home-made lemonade to wash it all down.

Jack slapped Harry on the back as his son was taking a bite of pie, making him choke on his mouthful. 'Never mind, lad, I remember ruining a few logs myself when I was your age—when I was a bit older than that, now I come to think of it. And it did make an almighty great crack when it split right up the middle like that!' He laughed, and Harry looked more cheerful.

When they had finished eating, John and Harry set to cutting a newly-felled puriri trunk into six-foot lengths with a cross-cut saw. The dense, dark-brown timber was the bush farmers' preference for fence posts, but getting a saw blade through it was heavy work; work for younger backs

4

than his, their father declared.

Amy stayed on with them, glad of the company. Since her grandmother's death a few months before, she had had the house to herself when the men were out on the farm. Jack lit his pipe and puffed away contentedly, and Amy snuggled into the crook of his arm. She closed her eyes and took in the familiar, comforting smell of him, made up of tobacco, the damp wool of his jacket, and a hint of the grassy scent of fresh cow manure.

'Only a couple of weeks now till I'm off to Auckland,' said Jack. 'I should be able to have a week or so there and still get back before calving's really started. And I've got somewhere to stay, too—Mr Craig at the store knows a chap up there he used to be in business with years ago. He's written to this fellow and arranged it all. Says they've got a flash house in Parnell. Better than staying in some boarding house, anyway.'

'I wish I could go with you,' Amy said, the city spreading before her eyes in imagination.

Jack patted her arm. 'I wish you could, too. I miss my little girl when I go away. But you've got to keep these brothers of yours in line, eh? I'll only be gone a week or two—and I'll bring you back something pretty. Would you like that?'

'Bring me a book!'

Jack laughed. 'You and your books. Haven't you got enough yet? All right, something pretty *and* a book, how's that?'

Amy tilted her face for a kiss, and felt the tickle of his beard against her cheek.

'You're not going to get too big for cuddles, are you?' Jack asked.

'Not for a long time.' Amy glanced up at the sky; the sun was now well to the west. 'I'd better go in a minute—I'm doing a steamed pudding tonight, and I need to get it started. Oh, I need to get those rugs in off the line, too.'

Her father let go of her and crouched over his pipe, poking at it to coax more smoke. 'You do a fine job of it all, girl. I know it's a lot to manage on your own.' His mouth made a crooked smile around the pipe. 'I hope I'm looking after you properly, now your granny's not here to do it for me.'

His eyes told Amy he was more troubled over the matter than his light tone suggested. 'Of course you are, Pa. Anyway, Granny taught me all about looking after the house.'

'Maybe there're things I should be telling you—things your ma would, if she'd been spared… ah, well, no use thinking about that.' Jack looked

5

off into the distance for a few moments, then cleared his throat. 'At least you're not wearing yourself out trying to manage that teaching business any more.'

Amy made no answer, not trusting herself to speak calmly about what had been the biggest disappointment of her young life. After nursing her grandmother through the old woman's final illness, Amy had persuaded her father to allow her to work a few days a week at the valley's one-roomed school. The teacher, Miss Evans, had put Amy in charge of the youngest children, and the months she had spent guiding the little ones through their first steps at sounding out words and scratching letters on their slates had been the happiest of her life.

She and Miss Evans had spoken of Amy's intended teaching career as a settled thing. Amy's head had filled with dreams of working in the city; of making her way into the wider world. It had been a time of rushing between farm and school, struggling to get all her work done, and cutting corners where she could.

And it had all come crashing down at three o'clock one morning a little over a week ago, when Jack had come out to the kitchen to find Amy fast asleep in front of a pile of ironing, two flatirons dangerously hot on the range.

'I'm not going to have you working day and night trying to do two jobs,' her father had said. 'You've got to give up one, and you know which it is.'

Amy had seen her dreams dissolve before her eyes, but Miss Evans had managed to comfort her, assuring Amy that she would do her best to persuade Jack to reconsider when Amy was a little older; perhaps next year, she had said. Amy clung to this promise, and did her best not to let her father see her disappointment. They needed her at home, and it was wrong to be selfish.

Harry drilled a hole in one of the lengths of timber, making a show of very carefully estimating two feet from the end, and took the bottle of gunpowder to put some in the hole. 'This look all right, Pa?' he asked. Jack hauled himself to his feet and went to check Harry's work.

Amy stowed the plates and cloth in her basket. She managed to get a fair distance away before the noise of splitting logs began again.

In the winter months Amy was the first person in the house to get up. She rose next morning as soon as a hint of daylight crept into her room. By the time she had dressed, made her bed and brushed her hair, the hills she could glimpse through her window stood out against the pink sky of dawn.

6

She laid her hairbrush on the dressing table, in front of her little bookshelf. To one side of the shelf stood a photograph in a silver-plated frame. The picture showed a dark-haired woman, Amy's mother, holding a tiny baby that Amy had been assured was herself at the age of six weeks. The woman was sitting on the verandah of Amy's house, smiling at the photographer as she held her baby daughter close. Four-year-old Harry stood beside his mother, clutching her skirt and looking dubious, while a young-looking Jack stood on her other side holding six-year-old John by the hand. Jack had an identical photograph on the dressing table in his room.

Amy picked up the photograph and studied it. She had only dim memories of her mother, who had died when Amy was three years old, but they were memories tinged with warmth and affection. She smiled back at the lady in the photograph, replaced it and ran her finger softly along the spines of the row of books that were like old friends to her.

She slipped a black mourning band over her sleeve and went out to the kitchen. The dough she had set by the range the previous evening had risen overnight; she kneaded it and put it into pans, and by the time the range had heated up the bread was ready to go in.

Her father and brothers wandered into the kitchen some time later, attracted by the smell of bacon and eggs. The four of them ate a leisurely breakfast, and the men lingered over second helpings while Amy washed the dishes.

Amy had just gone outside to feed the hens when she saw riders coming up the track. It was her Uncle Arthur, who owned the next farm up the valley, along with her cousin Lizzie and Lizzie's younger brother Alf.

Arthur slipped from his horse and went to have a chat with Jack, eleven-year-old Alf close at his heels, while Amy held Lizzie's reins and the girls exchanged news.

'Have you heard about the whale?' Lizzie asked. 'It got washed up on the beach, Alf heard about it at school yesterday. We're going down to have a look, come with us.'

'I don't think I can, Lizzie, I'm busy this morning.'

'Of course you can, it'll only take an hour or so. Hop up behind me, you don't weigh much and Jessie's strong.' Lizzie patted the roan mare's rump.

'I really can't. I got a bit behind yesterday—I had to take lunch to the men, and I ended up staying a while with them. I didn't even get any baking done. Maybe Pa and the boys will go down later and I can go with them.'

'But I want you to come with me. I tell you what,' Lizzie said, brightening, 'if you come now, I'll give you a hand with your work afterwards. So you can come, can't you?'

Amy laughed. Lizzie was only eighteen months older than her, but as well as being several inches taller and much more sturdily built, she was a good deal more determined. Lizzie usually got her own way in the end; it generally saved time to go along with her from the beginning. 'All right, Lizzie, you win.' She took off her apron and ran back to the kitchen with it before hoisting herself up behind the saddle and putting her arms around her cousin's waist. 'What'll Aunt Edie say about you staying here to help me?'

'Oh, Ma won't mind.' Handling her mother was never a problem for Lizzie.

Arthur and Alf came back and remounted, and they set off down the track at a walk. The sun had climbed above the eastern wall of the valley, promising another bright, clear day. A light breeze ruffled Amy's hair, and there was still a touch of dew on the grass. It was a fine day for an outing.

The steepest of the hills on both sides of the valley were still bush-clad. Many of the tallest trees had been milled over the years, but scattered among the lower-growing manuka were lofty totara, rimu with their drooping foliage, and the darker leaves of puriri. Where the forest canopy had been removed tree ferns flourished, with an occasional nikau palm among them looking like something from the pictures of tropical islands Amy sometimes saw in her father's newspapers.

Nearer the house, the slopes had been burned off and sown with grass years before. Shorthorn cattle wandered among the blackened stumps that had survived the burning, with sheep in the steeper paddocks. The farm's only flat land was in two paddocks edging the creek; here the stumps had been laboriously hauled out and the ground ploughed, so that maize and potatoes could be grown.

They left the farm track and turned on to the road down the valley. Arthur and Alf nudged their horses into a trot, but when Lizzie kicked Jessie into a burst of speed Amy gave a yelp.

'Lizzie, you can't trot with me on Jessie's bare back—it hurts! It doesn't feel very steady, either.' So they had to keep to a walk, which meant the other two quickly got ahead of them.

'Why are you so keen for me to go down with you, anyway?' Amy asked as they slowly made their way down the road.

'Well, I've hardly had the chance to see you these last few months, you were so busy with that teaching business. And… I just thought we

8

might see some people down there.'

Amy gasped as Jessie made a leap over a rut in the road, jolting her against the horse's hard spine. 'What people?' she asked when she had got her breath back.

'Oh, just… people,' Lizzie said vaguely. 'There's that grumpy old Charlie Stewart,' she muttered as they reached the boundary fence. Amy recognised the tall, slightly stooped figure of her father's neighbour standing close to his gate. 'Hello, Mr Stewart,' Lizzie called, sitting up straighter in the saddle to wave. He glared at her; she tossed her head and pressed Jessie into a brisker walk. 'What a horrible man. Did you see how he just stared at me? He's not a bit polite.'

Charlie Stewart lived alone on the farm that bordered Jack's to the north. He seemed to Amy much the same age as her father, and therefore quite an old man, with his long, shaggy beard and sandy-red hair turning grey.

She could remember being frightened of him when she had been younger; he had shouted at her and Lizzie when they had once sneaked over his fence looking for blackberries, and he had complained to her father about the incident. Her father had been amused rather than angry, and her grandmother had thought it so unimportant that she had merely smacked Amy rather than bothering to get out the strap, but Amy could still remember the fury in Mr Stewart's voice, and the wild look in his eyes as he chased them back across the fence. Now she felt those eyes following her as she bumped along behind Lizzie.

'Aren't you scared of him?' Amy asked, slumping down and trying to make herself inconspicuous. 'He always looks so fierce. Don't you remember that time he nearly caught us on his land? I was sure he'd give us a beating if he'd got hold of us.'

'Humph! My pa would have had something to say to *him* if he had.'

'That wouldn't have been much comfort.'

'Yes, it would. Anyway, who'd be scared of him—sour old man like that.' Lizzie dismissed Charlie Stewart with a wave of her hand.

A little beyond Mr Stewart's property was the valley school, set on a pocket of land just big enough for the schoolhouse with its little yard and a small paddock for the horses. It was Saturday, and the school was deserted. Amy gazed at the small wooden building as they rode past, imagining herself working there again. Next year, Miss Evans had said. It did not sound so very long.

There was only one more farm before the valley road met the main road into town. As they went past the Kelly property Amy noticed Lizzie become suddenly alert, straining her gaze up towards the homestead.

'What are you looking for?' Amy asked.

'Oh, nothing.'

'Lizzie, what's wrong with you this morning? You're being very secretive.'

'No I'm not.'

'Yes you are, and you're being argumentative as well.'

'Ooh, what a big word,' Lizzie teased. 'Well, all right, maybe I am. I just wondered if they're both going down to the beach to have a look, and if they've left yet.'

'Who—the Kellys, you mean?'

Lizzie nodded.

'What difference does it make whether it's Frank or Ben or both of them?'

'Well, Ben's no use,' said Lizzie. 'He never even talks to anyone. Frank's nice, though, isn't he?'

'Yes, of course he is.' Frank was seven years older than Amy; she hadn't gone to school with him, but saw him during haymaking and at church. He was quiet, but not as unfriendly as his older brother.

'And they've got a good farm, and they live close.'

'Yes,' Amy agreed.

'I just thought I'd like to get to know him a bit better.'

'Why? Oh!' Sudden realisation came. 'You're after him for a husband!' Amy's voice rose in amusement.

'Shh!' Lizzie hissed, looking around to see if anyone was listening. They were close to the beach now, and there were several other riders plus a few gigs and buggies about. 'Now I didn't say that, did I? I just said I wanted to get to know him a bit better.'

'What's the hurry?'

'I've got to think ahead, you know—these things don't just happen by themselves.'

Amy smiled at Lizzie's serious tone. 'So are you going to walk up to him and ask him to marry you?'

Lizzie pursed her lips. 'I wish I'd left you at home if all you can say is silly things like that.'

'It wasn't my idea to come, you know,' Amy said, bristling a little.

'I didn't make you, did I?'

'Yes, you did actually!'

'Well, we're here now. Let's see if we can find him.' Lizzie slid from her horse and tied the reins to a convenient tree branch. Amy jumped down and followed a few steps behind as Lizzie stalked off in her purposeful way.

A cluster of about twenty people standing below the high-water mark showed where the beached whale lay. Amy glanced at the other onlookers as they drew closer; she saw old Mr Aitken and his son Matt, whose daughter Bessie had been one of Amy's little pupils at school.

'Look,' Amy whispered to Lizzie, 'some of those Feenan boys are here.'

'Trust them. They wouldn't miss an excuse to butt in where they're not wanted.'

'I hope they don't start a fight,' Amy said.

The Feenans were a large Irish family that farmed a rough patch of land about two miles west of the valley where Amy lived. They were what Amy's grandmother had always referred to as 'a bit muddly' about their household arrangements; no one was sure just how many of them lived there nor quite how they were related, but they were all Feenans and as far as their neighbours were concerned they all meant trouble. On this occasion they were represented by three boys whose ages appeared to range from about fourteen to eighteen. Amy was relieved the boys stood on the far side of the group, so that she and Lizzie would not have to pass close to them.

The farmers stood around in small knots, chatting idly now that they had seen all they wanted of the whale. Amy caught snatches of conversation as Lizzie threaded her way through the group:

'Weather's bad, eh?' 'Yes, never seen so much mud—probably still be like this at calving time' 'Lord only knows what the maize'll be like next summer' 'Butter price was pretty low this year' 'It'll be worse next season, you mark my words' 'Hardly worth bothering' 'It's the bloody government—that Colonial Treasurer Harry bloody Atkinson, he doesn't care a damn about anywhere but bloody Taranaki'.

Amy hid a smile and wondered, as she so often did, why they carried on if it was really as bad as all that.

The curser, a farmer from closer to town whom Amy recognised as Mr Carr, was nudged in the ribs by his neighbour as the girls walked past. 'It's the Leith girls,' one of the other men said. Mr Carr looked discomforted, though Amy heard him mutter under his breath something about this being 'no place for women, anyway'. But they were greeted politely enough. 'Morning, girls,' the men said in chorus, touching their hats in greeting. Amy smiled and nodded, but Lizzie had seen her quarry and was oblivious.

'Look, there he is—let's go and talk to him,' she said to Amy in a loud whisper. She walked up to Frank Kelly in what she seemed to think was a casual way.

'Hello, Frank! I haven't seen you in *such* a long time—how are you?'

Frank was a slightly-built youth, with light brown hair and an unfortunate tendency to blush when spoken to, especially by young ladies. He was wearing a battered felt hat that was surely older than he was. Amy, who had three men's clothes to look after, noticed his shirt had a small tear in the sleeve that had been clumsily stitched up in a contrasting thread, and one of his cuffs had lost a button.

'Oh, ah, hello Lizzie… and Amy… yes, thank you… how are you?' He sounded rather confused. He probably remembered seeing Lizzie just the previous week at church, but she was giving the impression they had not met in some time.

'What a huge fish!' Lizzie said. Amy looked away from Frank to take proper notice of the animal for the first time. She had a feeling a whale wasn't a fish, but it was never any use correcting Lizzie. 'What do you think about it, Frank?'

'It's big,' Frank agreed. He fell silent again, having exhausted his conversation for the moment.

Amy stared at the whale. She wondered where it had come from, and how many years it had wandered the seas before ending up lying dead on Waituhi Beach. It was such a huge, powerful-looking creature; it made her think of the grey sea pounding against rocks in a storm. It seemed wrong to her that a being like that should come to such an end: being stared at by an uncaring group of land-bound farmers while half a dozen men sawed large hunks of flesh off it. Amy was surprised to feel tears coming to her eyes; the death of animals was something she accepted as a normal part of her life, but this creature of the sea was different.

'Where are those Maoris from?' Lizzie asked, pointing to the group of men stripping blubber from the whale with apparent expertise.

'From down the coast—they still do a bit of whaling down there,' Frank said. 'They're going to load as much of that fatty-looking stuff as they can into those longboats they came in and cart it home with them, then they boil it up in big iron pots on the beach and get the oil and things out of it.'

'I didn't know that! Fancy you knowing all about that sort of thing,' said Lizzie. Frank blushed deeply at his own boldness, and said no more on the subject.

There was a shout from one of the men working on the whale, and Amy saw the Feenan boys running away from the longboats, one of them clutching a slab of blubber.

'Ooh, they must want to eat that stuff!' Lizzie said. 'Ugh, those mad Irish'll eat anything.'

Something nagged at Amy's memory as Lizzie spoke, but the thought refused to turn into anything clear. She saw the boys throw the blubber to one another, till one of them dropped the slippery lump. They wiped their hands on their sleeves and hooted with laughter, and Amy looked away.

She heard a rasping whistle. 'Hello, gorgeous,' the oldest of the Feenans yelled. 'Want to come home with me?' The other two boys laughed raucously. Amy looked across in horror. 'Yes, you with the dark hair,' the boy called. 'You look as though you'd be good for a bit of fun.'

Amy wanted to sink into the ground. 'Lizzie, can we go home?'

'What a cheek!' Lizzie put her hands on her hips and stared balefully at the Feenans. 'Irish people have got no manners! Look, Pa's going to sort them out.'

Amy saw that Arthur was indeed bearing down on the guilty parties, waving his riding crop in a threatening manner. 'Oh, no,' she groaned. 'There's going to be a fight now. Can't you stop him, Lizzie?'

But there was no need for her to worry; the Feenan boys shrank before Arthur's wrath. It only took a modest amount of shouting and arm-waving on her uncle's part before the boys slunk away out of sight. Arthur called to Alf and walked towards the girls.

'Right, Lizzie, we're going now,' her father said. 'I can't have you two being insulted by a lot of roughs like that.'

'I suppose you were just leaving too, were you, Frank?' Lizzie asked, and Frank was somehow gathered into her wake to walk beside her back to where the horses were tethered.

'How's Ben? And the farm? How *do* you two manage there by yourselves?' Lizzie prattled on, not giving him time to answer. Amy felt rather sorry for him, though she was more amused than anything. Poor Frank didn't know what danger he was in; he was lucky that Lizzie was too young to be allowed to marry for years yet. When they got to the trees Lizzie admired his horse, stroking its neck lovingly as if she had never seen a very ordinary-looking bay mare before, praised the tidy state of his harness, and generally made a fuss of Frank, something he was clearly quite unused to.

'Leave young Frank alone, I want to get home,' Arthur said, interrupting Lizzie in mid-sentence.

Lizzie made a face in her father's direction, though she was careful not to let him see it. 'It's been *so* nice talking to you.' She beamed at Frank. 'I hope I'll see you again soon?'

'Tomorrow at church, I expect.' Frank seemed unsure whether to be flattered or frightened by Lizzie's attentions, but Amy noticed he spent a long time fiddling with his horse's harness; so long, in fact, that the Leiths had mounted and set off while Frank was still adjusting his stirrups, which seemed to need lengthening suddenly for some mysterious reason.

After the trouble with the Feenans, Arthur was obviously feeling protective. He kept his horse to a walk and stayed close to the girls for the first part of the ride, until they were far enough up the valley road to be out of sight of the beach. Amy had to talk quietly to Lizzie so as not to be overheard.

'Lizzie, you're terrible!'

'Why, what did I do wrong?'

'You embarrassed Frank. And I thought you were shameless, throwing yourself at him like that.'

'Rubbish,' said Lizzie. 'Some men need a bit of a push. Besides, he needs a woman—did you see that rip in his shirt?'

'If he needs a woman that badly, you might miss out.'

'What do you mean?'

'Well, he might decide he can't wait years and years until *you* grow up, and he might find someone who's old enough to get married now!' Amy had the satisfaction of seeing a look of shock pass over her cousin's face, then Lizzie turned on her.

'You cheeky little…' She put the reins in one hand and twisted around in the saddle to tug at Amy's hair and tickle her mercilessly. Amy had to keep holding on to Lizzie to avoid falling, but she squealed and tried to wriggle out of her reach. The horse, disturbed by their noise and movement, snorted noisily and shied a little.

'Hey, you girls, settle down back there—stop frightening that horse or I'll lead her home and make you walk,' Arthur said, looking back over his shoulder at them. They composed themselves hastily. A walk of two miles did not appeal.

'Oh!' Amy said when they passed Frank's farm. The thought that had nagged at her earlier had suddenly gelled. 'Oh, you shouldn't have been so rude about the Feenans, either.'

'Me, rude! I like that—after the way they carried on! What do you mean, rude?'

'Not so much what you said about Feenans, but the way you went on about the Irish.'

'It's all true, isn't it? Pa says they're bog Irish, and that's why they fight and cause trouble all the time, and why their farm's so rubbishy.'

'That's what I mean—where do you think the name "Kelly" comes from?'

'I don't know,' Lizzie said with a shrug. 'Oh! Do you think it's an Irish name?'

'I'm sure it is. I remember Granny saying that.'

'Oh.' Lizzie was silent for a moment. 'It doesn't matter,' she said, cheerful again. 'Frank was born here, so he's not Irish, even if his father was. I'm sure the Kellys aren't *bog* Irish, anyway.' As Amy had no idea what 'bog Irish' might mean, she was unable to argue with this.

'I'm staying here till lunch-time,' Lizzie said to her father when they reached Amy's gate.

'Did you ask your ma?'

'Yes, it's all right with Ma,' Lizzie said airily. She turned her horse's head towards Amy's house. 'Ma wouldn't remember even if I had,' she murmured.

'You shake that dress out before you come in my kitchen—you've got sand and horsehair all over it,' Amy admonished when they reached the house. 'You can take those dirty boots off, too.'

'Bossy.' But Lizzie did give her dress a good shake, making quite a cloud of sand and dust, and left her boots at the door.

Lizzie had not worn a pinafore on the outing; when Amy asked if it had been because she wanted to look more grown-up in front of Frank, Lizzie cheerfully admitted that was the case. She followed Amy into her bedroom and with some difficulty squeezed into one of her pinafores.

'It's a bit tight over the chest, but no one's going to see me in it. You'll need a new one when you get a *bosom*,' Lizzie said, all buxom superiority. She straightened Amy's armband. 'How long are you going to wear this?'

'A year, it's meant to be. Pa said I didn't need to—he thinks I'm too young to bother with it. But I want to do the right thing.'

'You always want to do the right thing, don't you? You try a bit too hard sometimes, you know.'

'That's my look-out.'

Lizzie plumped herself down on the bed and patted a place at her side. 'How are you getting on now?' she asked when Amy sat down. 'Still missing your granny?'

Amy nodded. 'It was awful to see her in pain and everything—she didn't even know who I was at the end. But it's strange without her. Granny's always been here.'

'It's a blessed release, Ma says.'

'Everyone says that. I still miss her, though.'

Lizzie gave her a hug. 'You've got bits of leaf in your hair, I think they came off that tree I tied Jessie to. Here, let me.' She picked out a few dried fragments, then stroked the long black curls. 'Your hair is so pretty,' she said, without a trace of envy. 'Ma always says she wishes my hair was wavy like yours.' Lizzie's fair hair, although thick and healthy, was obstinately straight, defying all her mother's attempts at curling it in rags.

'But yours is blonde.'

'That just means I get freckles if I leave my bonnet off for five minutes. Your skin always seems to stay creamy. Ma says you're like a little doll, with your great big blue eyes and all that hair.'

Amy pulled a face at her; 'Little doll' was too much. 'Just because I'm small, everyone treats me as though I'm a baby.'

Lizzie stood up. 'We'd better get on with things. What needs doing first?'

Amy's grandmother had kept to a strict routine; 'Every task has its time and season,' she had been fond of saying; but during her months of juggling her time between the school and home, Amy had learned to be more flexible, fitting tasks in whenever she had a moment. Today the work went quickly, with two of them to share it.

When the cleaning was done, they scrubbed their hands and settled down to a serious bout of baking. Lizzie hummed to herself as she broke eggs into a bowl.

Amy smiled at her. 'You're very pleased with yourself today, aren't you?'

'Mmm.' Lizzie looked smug. 'I think things are going to work out nicely.' Amy knew she didn't mean the biscuits she was making.

'So you're really set on catching Frank?'

'I'm just planning ahead, that's all,' Lizzie said, stirring her mixture vigorously. 'What's wrong with that?'

'Frank's nice, but he's not very… well, exciting, is he?'

Lizzie stopped her work. 'What's that supposed to mean?'

'Oh, I don't mean there's anything wrong with him. It's not so much Frank, it's…. well, he's just the same as everyone else around here. I mean, if you married him you'd move down the road a couple of miles. Apart from that everything would be the same. Why do you want to bother?'

'There'd be a few more differences than that. I wouldn't expect *you* to understand.'

'Don't talk like that, Lizzie! You don't know any more about it than I do!'

'Any more about what?'

'You know what—stop it!' Amy was annoyed to feel herself blushing.

'*I* was just talking about running my own house. I don't know what *you* were talking about, I'm sure. Of course, when I was your age I wasn't very interested in getting married either,' Lizzie said, dropping spoonfuls of biscuit dough onto a tray. 'You're only twelve, after all. You'll have to grow up a bit more before you start being interested.'

'I'm nearly thirteen.'

'Well, I'm nearly fifteen then.'

'You are not! You only turned fourteen a couple of months ago.'

'By the time you're thirteen I'll be nearly fifteen.'

'No you won't! You'll be fourteen and a half, that's not "nearly fifteen".'

'Don't let's argue about it.'

'You always say that when you're losing,' said Amy. 'Not everyone gets married, you know. I don't think I want to.'

'What's wrong with getting married and having babies? Don't you want a house of your own one day?'

'I've *got* one. And I've got quite enough men to look after, thank you. But Lizzie,' Amy put her hand on Lizzie's arm and looked into her eyes, trying to make her down-to-earth cousin understand, 'it's not enough.'

'What's not enough?'

'All this.' Amy gave a wide sweep of her arm, taking in not merely the house but the whole valley. 'Spending all my life in this little place, looking after Pa then getting married and having lots of babies, never seeing anywhere else, never learning anything interesting. Miss Evans says I could be a good teacher. I want to do something useful, not just cooking and cleaning and looking after babies.'

'That's useful enough, isn't it?'

'Not for *me*. Oh, never mind. You know what you want, just let me want something different.'

'You don't want it really,' said Lizzie. 'Just think of all the old maids there must be, stuck at home being bossed around all their lives and everyone making fun of them. That's why I don't want to leave it too late.'

'Who ever bossed you around?'

'Pa does sometimes. Ma tries to, when she thinks of it.'

'I expect husbands can be pretty bossy. And I think there could be worse things than not getting married.'

'Like what?'

'Like marrying the wrong person. Imagine being stuck forever with someone horrible.' Amy gave a shudder. 'I'd much sooner be an old maid.'

Lizzie slid the tray into the range and shut the door. 'That's why you've got to be careful picking a husband. I wouldn't want a bossy one.'

'Mmm, I can't really imagine Frank telling anyone what to do—especially someone like you. I don't know how you do it, though.'

'Do what?'

'Make a spectacle of yourself like you did today, and not get embarrassed.'

'Why should I be embarrassed? And I did not make a spectacle of myself! I was just being friendly.'

'I suppose you'd call it being "friendly" to propose to a man if he was a bit slow off the mark?'

'Oh, no, I wouldn't do that... well, not unless I really had to,' Lizzie answered, so seriously that Amy could not help laughing.

'You're dreadful!'

'No I'm not,' Lizzie said. 'I just know what I want.'

'And you don't care what anyone thinks of you?'

'Not really. Why should I?'

Amy thought there should be an answer to that, but she could not think of one.

2

Jack went off to Auckland, and the house felt empty without him.

It was the quietest time of the year on the farm. There were only three or four cows to milk, just enough to supply the household with milk and butter. Now that she was no longer working at the school, Amy found herself with more time on her hands than she had had for months. She often brought a book from her bedroom out to the cosy kitchen to lose herself in when there was nothing she had to do.

On the first fine morning after several days of rain, Amy felt drawn to more solid company than that provided by books. When she had tidied the kitchen, she went outside to catch up with her brothers who had gone to feed out hay to the cows.

John and Harry had harnessed one of the horses to the sled. It was a rough wooden vehicle with iron runners, made to slip easily across the soft ground of the paddocks where a cart might have foundered in the mud. They put two hay forks on the sled and the three of them took it down to the largest stack, secure behind its fence. Amy laughed to see the cows lined up along the fences, watching them as they passed.

'You won't have to wait much longer, girls,' she called.

She walked around the haystack, waving her arms and clapping her gloved hands in an attempt to keep warm, while her brothers pitched hay onto the sled. Frost crunched under her booted feet. The air was crisp, making Amy's face tingle, and the sky had a clarity to it that only appeared on winter days. She had spent too much time indoors these last few months, Amy realised.

The cows snorted with excitement and rushed up to the gate as Amy's brothers took the laden sled into the first paddock. The hungry beasts were on them at once, nosing at the hay and stealing great mouthfuls of it before John and Harry could get the first forkfuls off the sled. 'Hey, look behind you, you stupid animal,' Harry yelled at a particularly stubborn cow, who seemed to prefer stolen hay over what was thrown to her. 'How about you lead the horse while John and I chuck the hay around,' he said to Amy.

'Where shall I take him?' Amy asked, giving steady old Blaze a rub on the forehead.

'Right around the paddock—if we leave it all in one spot the cows'll tread it into muck.'

'A couple of these girls'll be dropping their calves pretty soon—only another day or so, I'd say,' John said, casting an eye over the cows as they fed. 'I hope Pa gets back before they really get into it.'

'I expect he will,' said Amy. 'He said he'd only be away for a week or two.'

'Depends how much of a good time he's having,' Harry said, but without any real conviction.

A few days later John and Harry came back from feeding out and reported that the first two calves had been born during the night. By the time Jack had been gone a week, a third of the herd had calved. When the calves were a few days old, they were taken from their mothers. Amy taught them to drink from a bucket, which had been one of her tasks on the farm from the age of five. John and Harry were milking more of the cows every day; in a few more weeks there would be enough milk for Amy to start making butter and cheese to sell at the general store.

Lizzie came over one afternoon, just after lunch. 'Come and do some baking with Ma and me. You can do your stuff at our place, and it's more fun to do it together.'

'All right,' Amy said, glad of the change of scene. They walked back to Lizzie's house together.

'I'm making pies,' Lizzie said, as if she were imparting a great confidence.

'That's good.'

'*Apple* pies,' Lizzie said meaningfully.

'Good.'

'*Lots* of them.'

Amy stopped walking. 'What are you getting at, Lizzie?'

'I've been thinking. How well do you think Frank and Ben eat? I mean, two men living together, I bet they just throw a few odds and ends on the table.'

'You're not really worried about what *Ben* eats, are you?'

'Of course not,' said Lizzie. 'But he lives there too, so he'll eat some, I suppose.'

'Some what?'

'Pie, of course.'

'The pies you've been making for Aunt Edie, you mean?' Amy assumed a guileless expression.

'There'll be enough to go round.'

Aunt Edie was sifting flour into a large bowl, Lizzie's baby brother on the floor near her feet, when the girls installed themselves in the kitchen.

'I'll just roll out a bit more pastry,' Lizzie said. 'I think I'll make a couple more of these pies.'

'All right dear,' her mother said. 'Oh, Ernie, what are you up to?' The little boy's mouth and half his face was covered with strawberry jam, which Edie wiped off with her apron.

Edie's kitchen was not as large as Amy's, but there was room on the table for all three of them to work without getting in each others' way.

When Lizzie had her latest pies in the oven, she seemed to see the stack of already-cooked ones for the first time. 'Oh!' she said. 'Oh, I think I've made too many pies, Ma.' Amy stopped her own baking to watch Lizzie's performance.

'They'll all get eaten, I suppose,' Edie said, looking around vaguely to see where Ernie was.

'But I've made *twelve*, Ma.'

'Mmm? Yes, that is quite a pile.'

'Isn't it a shame,' Lizzie said, looking very thoughtful. 'Here we are with all this baking—too much, really—and there are people around who probably never taste a bit of pudding.'

'Who's that, dear,' Aunt Edie asked, a worried look on her kindly face.

'You know, people who don't have women around to cook for them. Like—well, what about Ben and Frank Kelly? I bet *they* never have any pudding.'

'Yes, isn't that sad,' Edie said. She knitted her brows in thought. Lizzie leapt in to help.

'What a pity they can't have one of our pies,' she said, glancing sideways at her mother.

'Perhaps we could give them one,' said Aunt Edie.

'That's a good idea, Ma!' Lizzie said, then looked crestfallen. 'How would we get it to them? Amy and I couldn't really go there by ourselves, it wouldn't be right.'

'I suppose Bill could take it down to them,' Edie said slowly.

'*That's* a good idea!' said Lizzie. 'I'll go and find him right now. Come on, Amy, you've finished haven't you?'

'Not really,' Amy said, her hands deep in scone dough, but she found herself caught up in the whirlwind Lizzie created. She scraped the dough off her hands, pushed it into a heap and resigned herself to being an accomplice.

'Oh, are you girls going with him?' Aunt Edie looked surprised. 'Well, take Ernie with you, then—he'll enjoy an outing.'

'All right, Ma,' Lizzie said sweetly. 'I'll just get ready first.' She whisked Amy into her bedroom. Amy watched while Lizzie brushed her hair and tied a pink ribbon in it. They rushed back through the kitchen, collecting two pies on their way out the back door, too quickly for Edie to notice they had 'forgotten' to take Ernie.

'I don't know why Ma had to go having a baby,' Lizzie grumbled as they went down the path. 'There's ten years between Alf and Ernie— you'd think she'd have more sense at her age. I hope she's not going to do it again.'

'Have babies, you mean?' Amy shrugged. Being farm bred, they had much more idea of the mechanics of reproduction than city girls would have, but they were both rather hazy on the fine details. 'Babies just happen, I suppose. But Aunt Edie must be getting a bit old to have any more, isn't she?'

'I hope so.'

They found Lizzie's older brother cleaning tack. 'Ma says you have to take us down to Kelly's farm' said Lizzie. 'Hurry up and get the buggy ready.'

Bill was happy enough to stop work, though he grumbled as a matter of form. 'What does Ma want you to go down there for?'

'Just a message,' said Lizzie.

She and Amy held a pie each as they rode down to the Kelly farm at the end of the valley.

'Have you ever been to the house before?' Amy asked.

'Ma says she brought me here when Frank's mother was still alive, but I don't remember. I think I was about five when she died. Ma says she was a lovely person.'

'Your Ma thinks everyone's lovely.'

'That's true.'

As they drove past Charlie Stewart's farm Amy said mischievously, 'Don't you feel sorry for Charlie as well? I bet he doesn't get any nice apple pies to eat, either.'

'Humph!' Lizzie said. 'He shouldn't be so grumpy, then.'

The Kelly farm was good-sized, but the paddocks were all full of stumps; too full for maize to be grown even in the flattest of them. Every summer, when the men of the valley got together for the communal task of haymaking, Amy's brothers complained bitterly about how difficult those paddocks were to work.

They turned off the valley road and crossed the Kelly's bridge over the Waituhi; Amy had a bad moment when she noticed some missing planks. The farm buildings they passed all had a neglected look, with doors loose on their hinges and a few rotten boards that needed replacing.

They pulled up in front of the house. It was a good-sized homestead, much like Amy's, but she could see that it was sorely in need of a coat of paint. The iron roof over the verandah sagged drunkenly at one end, weighed down by the creeper that had engulfed much of it. There were a few rose bushes, grown straggly through neglect, but no other suggestion of a garden.

'You'd better come in with us, Bill,' Lizzie said as they got out of the buggy.

'I don't think you'll be in much danger,' Bill said with a laugh, but he walked behind them up to the house when he had tethered the horses.

'We'll knock at the back door,' Lizzie said. 'It's more friendly than using the front as though we were only visitors.'

'So what are we?' Amy asked.

'Neighbours, of course,' Lizzie said briskly. 'We're being neighbourly.'

They went into a porch, where Amy recognised Frank's ancient felt hat hanging from a peg. She looked closely at the back door and decided it might once have been painted green. Lizzie gave the door a firm rap, waited a few seconds, then rapped again.

The door was opened and Frank looked out. When he saw Lizzie his eyes grew wide with something that Amy thought just might have been fear; he looked relieved to see Bill behind them.

'What are you doing here?' he asked. 'Ah, what a nice surprise!' he added hastily, though his face did not quite match his words.

'Hello, Frank,' Lizzie said, flashing him her brightest smile. 'I've baked you something. Can we come in?'

'Ah, yes, of course,' Frank said. He opened the door wider for them. 'Um, I'm afraid it's not very tidy.'

Amy had no idea how many plates the Kellys possessed, but she was sure a large portion of them must be on the table, and most of the rest on the bench. The plates on the table jostled for space with several heavy saucepans, all with spoons or forks inside.

'Haven't done the dishes for a while,' Frank said unnecessarily. 'Would you like to sit down?' He pulled out a chair, then shoved it quickly back under the table, but not before Amy had seen what was obviously a pair of combinations draped over the seat; probably waiting to be mended, judging from the large rent in the back. Another chair was graced with a pair of socks. Frank pulled these off and threw them towards the door, where his boots were lying against each other.

'What about a cup of tea? The teapot's here somewhere.' He lifted the newspapers that were spread over the table among the plates, and sprang with relief on an old enamel teapot.

'That would be lovely,' Lizzie said, to Amy's horror. 'Where shall we put these?' She indicated the pies she and Amy still held.

'Oh, yes, thank you.' Frank took the pies and looked around for a clear space to put them. Lizzie obligingly stacked some plates together on the bench, and Frank put the pies down. 'Hey, these look good!'

'I hope you enjoy them,' Lizzie said sweetly.

'Ah, perhaps you'd rather have it in the parlour,' Frank said, looking anxiously around the room.

'If you like,' said Lizzie.

'Hey, Lizzie,' Bill put in, 'I can't stay here all day, you know.'

'It won't take long,' Lizzie said, casting a threatening look at him.

At that moment the back door opened, and they all turned to see Ben walk in. He stood and stared at the apparition of strangers in his kitchen. There was a long silence; even Lizzie was not bold enough to speak. Then he looked at Frank and said in a tone of utter disgust, 'Women!' With that he turned on his heel and left the house, slamming the door behind him.

'Sorry about that,' Frank said after an awkward pause. 'Ben's not used to visitors.'

'Perhaps we should go,' Amy said hesitantly.

'No, no,' Frank said, looking as though he wished they would. 'You must have a cup of tea first.'

They let him usher them through to the parlour. 'It's a bit tidier in here,' said Frank.

It was indeed tidier, and Amy could guess the reason: the room had obviously not been used in years. It was dim until Frank pulled back the drapes, revealing layers of dust on all the wooden surfaces. Frank opened a window, which disturbed the dust. Amy coughed.

'Sorry, it's a bit dusty in here,' said Frank. 'We don't use this room much.'

'Don't you?' Lizzie asked in apparent surprise. 'But it's a lovely room.'

Amy decided Lizzie was being sincere, so she looked around the room more carefully. Yes, it was rather a nice room; quite large, with a beautiful view down the valley. The furniture was old but solid, and the fine-looking mirror over the mantelpiece only wanted cleaning to look beautiful.

Frank ran his sleeve over a pretty little rimu table, transferring much of the dust to his shirt. 'I'll bring it in, you wait here.'

'Oh, I'll help,' said Lizzie. She was out the door before Frank had a chance to protest. Left alone, Bill and Amy looked at each other, grinned, then burst into helpless laughter.

'Do you think we should go back out there to protect Lizzie?' Amy said between giggles.

'I know who *I* think needs more protecting,' Bill chuckled.

They could faintly hear the sounds of a one-sided conversation until Lizzie returned, carrying a tray with tea things, Frank following at her heels. She poured for them all, clearly enjoying the role of hostess she had appropriated. 'How do you like your tea, Frank?' she asked, looking intently at him as though the question was of vital interest to her.

Frank cleared his throat. 'Ah, just as it comes, thanks.' Lizzie rewarded him with a smile.

Bill drank his tea quickly, then rose to his feet. 'We'd better be going. We really had, Lizzie,' he said, forestalling her protest. 'Pa'll go crook if I'm not back for milking.'

Frank saw them out, and waved from the door. Amy thought he looked relieved. 'Thanks for the pies,' he called as they drove away.

'So you're roping me in to help you manhunting,' Bill said when they were out of earshot. 'You could give me fair warning next time.'

'I don't know what you're talking about, I'm sure,' Lizzie said, looking prim. 'I was just taking Ben and Frank a present from Ma.' Amy saw her prim expression relax into a smug smile.

'It's about time Pa got back,' John said at breakfast the next Friday. Only a few of the cows were still in calf by this time.

'We'll be milking the whole herd by the end of next week, I'd say. That'll be a beggar with just the two of us,' Harry said.

'He won't be away much longer, I shouldn't think,' said Amy. 'I thought he would have been home by now, really.'

The days went quickly, and the following Thursday Amy was surprised to realise almost another week had passed. That morning she went into town with Harry.

They collected the mail from the Post and Telegraph Office while their supplies were being loaded into the buggy. 'There's a cable from Auckland,' Harry said.

'It must be from Pa! What does it say?'

'Give us a chance to open it... damn!'

'What's wrong?'

'He says he won't be back for another two weeks! Damn and blast the old...' Harry remembered Amy's presence. 'I mean, it's a bit rough, leaving the farm for that long, when he knows we're flat out with milking and everything. Damn it, we'll have to organise selling the calves we don't want soon.'

'I hope he's not ill.'

'No, he says he's "very well indeed". See for yourself.'

Amy read the cable and found it was just as Harry had reported. 'That's really strange.'

'I can think of another word for it,' Harry muttered.

John was as dumbfounded as Harry and Amy over their father's truancy. They received another cable at the end of August to tell them Jack would be arriving on the following Thursday.

'He expects us to come and get him, of course,' Harry said.

'Well, he can't walk all this way, can he?' said Amy. 'You'd better go in and fetch him, John,' she added, thinking it might be sensible to put off Harry's reunion with Jack. 'I'll come with you.'

She and John drove in together after lunch on the second Thursday in September. The tide was only an hour past full, so they took the rough inland track instead of going along the beach.

'Should be all right to come back along the sand,' John said as they jolted over the rutted surface.

'Good!' Amy said jerkily.

The day was overcast, with a chilly breeze; when they ascended the last hill before reaching town they saw that the sea looked grey and sombre, with a heavy swell.

'He'll have had a rough trip,' John remarked.

Amy hurried onto the wharf while John hitched the horses. She saw that the *Staffa* had already tied up, and she looked eagerly for a sight of her father, but he was nowhere to be seen among the knot of passengers milling about on the deck.

'Look at that,' John said quietly as he came up behind her. 'That fancy piece waiting for someone to help her along the gangplank.'

Amy followed his gaze. 'Oh, what a vision of loveliness!' she said, smothering a giggle.

The woman who had attracted John's attention was immediately obvious among the other travellers. Not for any particular beauty; her mouth was too thin, her features too sharp and her nose too long for that, though she was tall and slim; almost bony, Amy thought.

But her travelling costume was clearly designed for more sophisticated surroundings than Ruatane Wharf. It was of dark green wool, with contrasting buttons and cuffs in bright red, and it had what seemed to Amy an astonishing number of tucks and gathers. The frill around her hooded cape was of the same red, and it ended in a broad ribbon that came down her back until it rested on a slight bustle. Her hat was trimmed with a green ostrich feather, and red roses that Amy thought might be of velvet. To complete the picture, the woman was looking over her fellow passengers with an obvious sense of her own superiority.

Amy's attention was caught by a new movement on the deck. 'It's Pa!' she said excitedly. 'Pa!' she called out.

Jack recognised them and waved, then to their surprise he took the vision's arm and led her up the gangplank.

'She must have been fluttering her eyelashes at him,' John murmured.

'John! He's just being a gentleman,' Amy said, trying not to laugh. As her father approached them, Amy noticed that the woman's face had a delicate green tinge that toned in with her costume.

'Well, here we are at last,' Jack said, a foolish grin on his face. Amy wanted to throw her arms around him, but she felt awkward under the vision's gaze. 'You're both here, that's good. I want you to meet,' he took hold of the woman's hand and slipped her arm through his,

'Mrs Leith—my wife.'

Amy stared at him, certain she must have misheard.

'Amy,' Jack said, taking her arm and pulling her closer, 'aren't you going to kiss your new mother?'

3

September 1881

The four of them stood on the wharf looking at one another; John and Amy in utter shock, Jack grinning stupidly, and the vision's expression changing from a bright smile to a look of embarrassment. Amy realised that her mouth was hanging open; she shut it abruptly.

The woman turned to Jack. 'You did tell them about us, didn't you, dear? You did say you'd write and tell them.'

Jack shuffled his feet and looked at the ground before meeting his wife's eyes. 'Well, I meant to. But when it came to it... I just couldn't think how to put it. I knew they'd be pleased as anything when they met you, so I thought I'd just let it be a surprise...' He trailed off awkwardly.

'You can certainly see it's a surprise,' the vision said. 'Well, I'm here. You must be John? Surely you're the oldest one?' John looked at her dumbly, still too amazed to speak; when Amy nudged him in the ribs he recovered himself enough to nod. 'And *this* is little Amy.' She turned her gaze on Amy, and her smile wavered. 'You're older than I expected from the way your father spoke.'

She shot a look at Jack, who put his arm around Amy's waist and gave her a squeeze. 'That's because she's my little girl. Come on, Amy, say hello to your ma.'

'Hello,' Amy said dutifully.

'I think you're both a little too old to call me Mama,' the vision said. 'You can call me... well, I suppose you'd better just call me by my name. I'm Susannah.' She removed her arm from Jack's and extended her hand; first John then Amy shook it.

'That doesn't seem right, calling you by your name like that, Susie,' Jack said, frowning slightly.

'It's Susannah, dear,' Susannah said in the tone of one who has repeated the same words more than once. 'I can't have a grown man like this calling me Mother.' She indicated John with a dramatic gesture.

'Well, maybe... but Amy should.'

'Whatever you say dear,' Susannah said, smiling sweetly at her husband.

'Let's get you home, then,' Jack said cheerfully.

'Oh, yes, I'm so looking forward to seeing it all,' Susannah gushed. 'The countryside is so pretty, isn't it? And it's such a relief to be off that horrible ship.' She shuddered, and cast a look of loathing over her shoulder at the steamer.

'Take one of these trunks, boy,' said Jack. 'I'll take this one, and you can come back for the last one.' They hefted the heavy-looking trunks and carried them over to the buggy, along with Jack's modest case.

'You sit in the back, my dear,' Jack said, gallantly offering his arm to help Susannah into the buggy. 'John can drive, then I can point things out to you.'

'I don't think we can fit all this stuff in, Pa,' John said, finding his voice again at last.

'Of course we can,' said Jack. 'Put this trunk in the front, my case can go between you two, there's room for this one behind us... hmm, you're right, we can't fit this last one in. Never mind, we can leave it in the cargo shed overnight and pick it up tomorrow.'

'Couldn't you just come straight back and get it, Jack?' Susannah asked. 'I do need all my things right away.'

'It's a bit far for that, Mrs L.' Jack laughed at the notion. 'It'll be safe enough here, don't you worry.' Susannah obviously was worried, but she said nothing as Jack sent John over to the cargo shed with the last trunk.

Amy had to put her feet on one of the trunks, and it was so high that she found herself perched awkwardly on the seat, but she was too busy trying to adjust to the fact of her father's new wife to take much notice.

'Oh, what a pretty little town it is,' Susannah said as they drove through Ruatane. 'Not many shops, of course, but a few nice little ones—I see a milliner's there—and the gardens around all the houses are sweet. I suppose you come in here most days?'

Jack roared with laughter. 'We'd never get any work done if we came in here every day! No, we come in once a week for supplies, and then on Sunday to church. That's often enough.'

'Twice a week?' Susannah repeated. 'But don't you go visiting, or to the theatre, or—'

'Theatre?' Jack laughed again. 'There's nothing like that here, Susie.'

'Oh.' Susannah lapsed into silence for some time.

'The tide's out enough now to go along the beach, so you'll have a nice, smooth ride,' Jack said.

'Along the beach? Why do you want to go along the beach?'

'You'll know the answer to *that* the first time you go over the inland track. The beach is much easier going.'

'But is it safe?' Susannah asked.

'Now, would I take you somewhere that wasn't safe?' Jack smiled indulgently.

'No,' Susannah answered, but she gave a little shriek when they turned off the road after crossing the Waipara Bridge and went bumping down to the beach.

She seemed to calm a little when they reached the firm sand below the high tide mark and the ride became smoother. 'Are we nearly there yet?' she asked when they had been going about ten minutes.

'Not quite.' Jack caught Amy's eye as she turned her head towards him, and gave her a wink. 'Can't see the island today, it makes a fine sight in clear weather.' He pointed in the general direction of White Island.

'There's some good farms over there,' Jack went on, pointing in the direction of the sand dunes. 'Course you can't really see them from here. This part's called Orere Beach, it turns into Waituhi Beach after the next creek. That's Carr's place we're passing, I got some of my first cows from him. Now, you'll see the difference when we go past this next one—well, you would if it wasn't for those dunes. That's where the Feenan lot live. Half the fences have fallen down, the pasture's more thistles than grass, and they don't have the sense to keep their cows away from the tutu.'

'Tutu?' Susannah echoed weakly.

'Poisonous plant. Cows gorge themselves on it if they get the chance, specially when the pasture's rough as blazes like that lot, then they go into convulsions—they usually die. The Feenans muddle along somehow, but Lord only knows how they feed that tribe of kids, they can't make much out of that place. Now, here's a decent farm again, Forster's place is next, young Bob Forster farms that now the old man's gone.'

He gave a running commentary as they passed each property, and Amy wondered how much it meant to this strange woman. Jack's words to her were still echoing in her head: 'Your new mother.' Words that made no sense.

After another twenty minutes they jolted through a shallow stream where it emptied into the sea, and Susannah interrupted Jack for a moment to say, 'Surely we're nearly there now?'

'About half-way,' said Jack.

'Half-way?'

'Barely.'

'Why didn't you tell me it was so far from town?' Her voice betrayed the effort it cost to appear calm.

'I thought you knew... I didn't think it mattered, anyway. Look, you can see the bluff from here.' He pointed to the hill that marked the end of the Waituhi Valley.

When they turned into the valley road Jack said, 'We're on the last leg now. But the road gets a bit rough from here.'

'Rougher than what we've been on?' Susannah asked in horror.

'A bit rougher, yes. Now this first farm belongs to the Kelly boys, Ben and Frank. Not a bad place. Some of the fences are a bit scruffy, though, and they haven't made much of a job of taking the stumps out of this paddock, see?'

He pointed to the paddock beside the road, and Susannah looked dutifully, though without any interest that Amy could detect. Amy noticed Frank two paddocks away leading his cows in for milking, but she decided not to embarrass him by waving.

The school's horse paddock was empty when they passed it; the children had all gone home for the day. Amy turned away from the sight of the schoolroom and all it meant to her.

'This is Charlie Stewart's place squashed in between my farm and the Kellys'. It's only a hundred acres, two of the old private's allotments joined together.'

'Privates?'

'Yes, after the wars—the soldiers all got a parcel of land, but most of them weren't interested in working it. That's how I got my place, bought it from a captain or major or whatever he was. Got it in July 1866, and we moved out here in September that year.

'Charlie bought his place about seven or eight years ago, there was a couple on it for a few years before that, but they chucked it in and moved up to Tauranga. He lives there by himself—he's a bit of a strange one. He's got some funny notions about the Queen and something called Jacobee—Amy, what's that thing Charlie bailed up the new minister over when he heard Reverend Hill came from Glasgow?'

'The Jacobite Succession, Pa,' Amy answered. 'Mr Stewart thinks…' she struggled to recall a history lesson. 'He thinks someone called James the Third should have been King after James the Second, instead of Mary and William. It's to do with him being Scottish, I think.'

'I'm Scottish, and I don't think that,' said Jack. 'Well, I was born in Dumfries, even if I don't remember living there, so I'm as Scottish as he is.'

They passed the boundary fence. 'This is it,' Jack announced proudly. 'Your new home, my dear.'

Susannah looked more animated for a moment, but as they passed over a particularly rough spot in the road she clutched at her stomach. Jack seemed oblivious to her discomfort.

'You can see we've done a lot of work on the place over the years. This paddock by the road, it was one of the first we cleared—it's a good flat one. Arthur and I broke the two farms in together. His place is next door, I'll take you over to meet him and Edie in a day or two.'

'I can't call on her until she's visited me first,' said Susannah. Amy supposed this must be some mysterious rule of polite society. She could see no reason for it herself; Susannah, she thought, would find country ways rather rough and ready.

Amy wondered how the farm must appear to a city-bred woman like Susannah. To Amy it was all so familiar that she hardly thought about it. She knew that her father looked at each paddock and remembered all the labour that had created it: clearing the undergrowth, felling the larger trees when they could use the timber, burning much of the bush where it stood, pulling out stumps when they had rotted enough, slowly getting drains dug so the paddocks wouldn't turn into mire when stock were grazed.

Amy knew that Jack saw the wilderness it had been, the good farm he had made it, and the even better farm he and his sons would make. Perhaps Susannah would see only a rough road leading through muddy paddocks with the dark green of the bush-clad hills as a backdrop. As they turned off the valley road on to Jack's farm the lowering sky began a drizzle that threatened to turn into rain, and even Amy could see that the farm looked a cheerless place.

'See that building there?' Jack pointed to a two-roomed slab hut with a shingle roof. 'Over by that patch of white pines. We use it for keeping feed in now—well, that was the first house we had on this place.' His eyes took on a distant look. 'Two years we had in that hut, Annie and me and the two boys. The first girl was born in it—died there, too. Amy was born there—she was meant to arrive in the new house, but you came a couple of weeks before you should have, girl.' He ruffled Amy's curls. 'It took Arthur and me a bit longer than we thought it would to get the real houses finished, anyway, so Amy was a month old before we moved in. Can't have been much fun for Annie living in that draughty hut and cooking over an open fire—the roof leaked like a sieve whenever it rained, too—but I don't remember her ever complaining about it. She only had three years in the new house. She deserved better.' He fell silent.

For a few moments nothing was said, then Susannah spoke. 'I'm sure she was a paragon of every virtue. I hope I won't disappoint you too much.' Amy could not tell from her tone whether she was angry or just miserable.

'Eh?' Jack said, jolted from his memories. 'Oh, things are different here now, Susie—you'll never have to live rough.'

Susannah was very quiet for the last part of the drive. When they got to the house and Amy climbed down from the buggy, she saw that Susannah's face was covered in moisture from the drizzle. But Amy did not think it was rain that had made the small trails down Susannah's cheeks from each eye.

'Ohh,' Susannah said as Jack helped her down. 'It *is* a terrible long way, isn't it. Oh, I must sit down—I'd love a cup of tea.'

'I'll make one,' Amy said quickly. She ran on ahead while John went to unharness the horses and Jack took Susannah's arm.

Amy rushed into the kitchen and found Harry sitting at the table. 'Pa's brought a new wife home,' she panted out to him as she filled the kettle and set it to boil.

'What?'

'A new wife—Pa's got married, and he's brought her with him.'

'Are you trying to be funny?'

'Of course I'm not.'

Jack came in, with Susannah leaning heavily on his arm. He pulled out a chair for her and she sank into it with evident relief.

'Harry, say hello to… well, I suppose you can call her Susannah.'

Harry stared from Susannah to his father, then back again. 'Hello,' he said.

'Hello,' Susannah said weakly. She passed a hand over her forehead.

'Would you like to have your tea in the parlour?' Amy asked, anxious to do the right thing.

'Amy, she's not a visitor!' Jack protested. 'This is her home now.'

'I'm sorry,' Amy said awkwardly. But she used the nicest china for the tea.

Susannah drank her tea, but refused any of Amy's cakes. Harry stared at her openly while she drank; John and Amy had at least had the hour's drive to get a little used to the phenomenon of a stepmother.

Amy nudged Harry once or twice, but he ignored her. 'Haven't you got any work to do, Harry?' she asked at last.

'Mmm? Oh, yes, I suppose we'd better go and milk some cows. Are you coming, Pa?' He looked at their father in a way Amy could see was meant to make Jack feel guilty, but her father had eyes only for his new bride.

'Eh? No, I'll get out of my good clothes first, then I might come down later. I want to show the new lady of the house round the place—you'd like that, wouldn't you, Susie?'

'It's Susannah,' his wife said automatically. 'Couldn't we wait till it stops raining?'

'All right, there's no rush, I suppose. I'll take you round tomorrow. You boys can carry those trunks in before you wander off.'

Harry looked rebelliously at his father, but held his tongue and went outside. John helped him carry in the luggage and take it to Jack's bedroom, then went off to his own room to get changed before he and Harry left to get the cows in.

'I'd better start unpacking,' Susannah said, rising from the table. 'Will you show me my—our—room, Jack?'

Jack led her out, and Amy was left alone in the kitchen. She sat at the table, trying to clear her thoughts. The new lady of the house, her father had said. *What does that make me?*

She rose to clear the table and start getting dinner on, reminding herself to set an extra place. It was only later, when she was setting out the plates, that she realised the 'extra' place had better be for herself; her old one opposite Jack at the foot of the table would belong to Susannah now.

Susannah, with a proud-looking Jack at her heels, emerged for dinner in a grey cashmere dress. It had cream lace gathered around the cuffs, and matching lace at the neck above a wide collar trimmed with a dark red fringe. She looked frail but composed.

'What a beautiful dress!' Amy exclaimed.

'This?' Susannah said in surprise. 'It's just a house dress.' Amy looked at her own sensible dress of brown holland under her pinafore, and wondered how Susannah's gown would stand up to a day spread between paddock and kitchen.

Maybe I'll have nice dresses like that one day. Not while I'm on the farm, though.

'I'm afraid it's only chops,' Amy said, wishing she had had time to cook a roast.

'Nothing wrong with chops,' Jack said, illustrating his point by attacking his meal with vigour. 'Sea travel gives you a good appetite, eh?' He turned to Susannah.

'Not really,' she answered, picking at her meal daintily.

'I've made an apple shortcake for pudding—I hope you like it,' Amy said when they had finished the main course. She served the dessert and put a jug of thick cream in front of Susannah before taking her own seat, slapping John's hand away from the jug when he tried to reach for it before Susannah.

'She's a good little cook, eh?' Jack said with his mouth full. 'You can take things a bit easier now, girl,' he said, gazing benevolently at Amy. 'You've got someone to share the work with now.' He beamed at Susannah, but the smile she gave in return was frosty.

'Jack, dear,' Susannah said, 'if all you wanted was someone to help *Amy* with cooking and cleaning, perhaps you would have been better off to hire a servant instead of having all the bother of a wife.'

Amy felt like crawling under the table, but Jack laughed. 'A servant, that's a good one! No one would mistake *you* for a servant, my dear.' He gave Susannah an openly admiring look. 'I just meant it's going to be good for Amy to have a mother again instead of a houseful of men.' Amy and Susannah glanced at each other, then both quickly looked away.

Susannah rose when they had finished drinking their tea. 'I think I'd like to go to bed now. It's been a long day.'

'Good idea,' Jack said. 'You go off, I'll be along shortly.'

'Oh, don't hurry on my account,' Susannah said quickly. 'You'll want to talk to your children.'

Jack's gaze followed her as she left the room, then he turned to meet the three pairs of eyes staring at him.

4

September 1881

'Well, what do you think?' said Jack. 'Bit of a stunner, isn't she?' He looked around the faces of his children, obviously seeking admiration, but puzzled at what he saw there. 'You're all very quiet.'

'We're just a bit... surprised, Pa,' Amy said, taking the lead. 'I mean, you were away so long, I was getting worried about you—we all were.'

'Started to think you weren't coming back,' John put in.

'It wasn't as long as all that,' Jack protested. 'I wouldn't leave you boys trying to run the place on your own for long—I wanted to find everything still in one piece when I got back.'

'We ran it by ourselves for five weeks!' Harry burst out. 'All the calving, and then milking the whole herd with just the two of us.'

'Well, I'm back now, there's no need to go on about it.'

'Yes, you're back all right,' Harry said darkly. 'And with *that*.' He gestured in the direction of the passage.

There was a short silence. Jack stared at Harry, the smile wiped from his face.

'What do you mean by that?'

'It's just that we've never met anyone like her, Pa,' Amy put in quickly. 'I mean, she looks so... well, elegant, I suppose.'

'Wouldn't want to get her hands dirty,' Harry said.

'Doesn't look like she belongs on a farm,' John added.

'She's my wife, so she belongs where I do,' said Jack. He looked around their faces. 'And you'll treat my wife with the same respect you give me. Understand?'

'She's not that much older than I am,' said John.

'What's that got to do with it?' Jack snapped. 'Think I'm too old to get married again, do you? I'm not too old to rule my own house yet.' He glared at his children.

Amy put her hand on his arm. 'Don't be angry, Pa. It's hard for us to get used to, that's all. It's been only the five of us for so long, then only us four since Granny died—I don't even remember Mama properly—it's strange to think there's someone else here now.'

Jack's face softened as he looked at her. 'Maybe I should have let you know. I didn't think you'd all make such a fuss, but I suppose it's only natural you're surprised. Well, you'll get used to it.'

'We don't have much choice, do we?' Harry muttered.

'No, you don't,' Jack said. 'So get used to it.'

'Aren't you going to tell us how you met, Pa?' Amy asked.

'Mmm? All right, then. You know I was staying with this Taylor family, Sam Craig's friend? Well, when I got there what should I find but there's a charming young Miss Taylor as well as Mr and Mrs. And Miss Taylor seemed rather taken with me—*she* didn't seem to think I'm too old to make a good husband.' He shot a look at John. 'Then one thing led to another—'

'I don't want to hear this,' Harry interrupted, getting to his feet. 'I'm going to bed—some of us have been working today.'

'Wait, Harry, please,' Amy said. She didn't like the thought of Harry's going to bed smouldering with resentment at their father, and if a row between the two of them was inevitable they might as well get it over with.

'All right,' Harry grumbled. He sat down again.

'Go on, Pa, we want to hear,' said Amy.

'Well, there's not much more to tell,' Jack said. 'We got married a week ago—didn't seem much point leaving it—then we went up to this place called Waiwera, north of Auckland, for a few days' honeymoon—Susie said it's *the* place to go, fancy hotel there, cost a fortune.' He looked very complacent, Amy thought. 'Then we came back to Auckland just long enough to pick up Susie's things and order the hay mower I fancied—it's coming on the steamer next week—then we hopped on the boat to come down here. And that's it.'

'So she got her claws into you,' said Harry. Amy turned to him in alarm, knowing this was going too far.

'What?' Jack said heavily.

'She saw you and decided you were her last chance, I expect, and you fell for it—then you were having such a good time you forgot about us doing all the work here.'

'Don't you talk to me like that,' Jack growled. 'I'll teach you to—'

'Pa!' Amy interrupted. 'Shh! You'll disturb Susannah, and she looked so tired.'

Jack quietened at once. 'You're right. We'll talk about it in the morning.' He turned to give Harry a threatening look, but his son had already left the room.

'I'm going to bed too,' John said, slipping away in his turn.

'Well, I don't know what's wrong with *them*,' said Jack. 'But you're pleased to have me home again, aren't you?'

'Oh, yes, Pa, of course I am.' Amy hesitated for a moment, then climbed onto her father's lap. She wondered why she felt a little awkward doing so.

Jack stroked her hair. 'And you're pleased to have a mother again?'

'Pa,' Amy said cautiously, 'I don't think she wants to be my mother.'

'Of course she does! Ever since I mentioned you she's gone on about meeting "the dear little girl"—Susie loves children. Anyway, you're my daughter, she's my wife, so she's your ma. That's simple enough, isn't it?'

'I suppose so, Pa.' Amy slipped from his lap and started clearing the table. 'Will you tell me about all the things you saw in Auckland?'

'Not right now, maybe tomorrow. I might as well go to bed myself.'

'Oh,' Amy said, trying not to sound too disappointed. 'I thought maybe you'd stay here for a while and we could talk.'

'There'll be plenty of time for that.' He rose from the table. 'Don't sit up too late, girl.'

'I won't, I just have to tidy up in here then get the bread made for tomorrow.'

'Susie will start helping you with all that soon, she's a bit worn out after the trip today. She was pretty crook on the way down.'

'I don't mind, Pa. I'm used to it.'

'You're a good girl. I'm off, then—see you in the morning.'

'Good night.'

Amy went to bed herself an hour or so later. She tried to read, but found she couldn't concentrate on the book. Through the wall of her bedroom she could hear voices in her father's room, but she could not make out any words.

One of the voices grew louder, then they both fell away into silence. Amy felt tired, but it was a long time before her busy thoughts let her drift off into a troubled sleep, which seemed to be full of the sound of someone weeping.

'Susie's still asleep,' Jack said next morning when he came out to the kitchen. 'She doesn't want to get up, anyway.' He looked perplexed.

'Perhaps she still doesn't feel very well,' said Amy.

'Maybe not. Where're the boys?'

'They've already gone to get the cows in.'

'I'd better catch them up.'

When they returned for breakfast Harry was rather quiet, but Jack seemed cheerful, so Amy decided they must be getting on well enough.

'Susie not up yet?' Jack asked, looking around in surprise.

'No—shall I take a tray in to her while you're having yours?'

'That's a good idea, she'll like that.'

Amy put a plate of bacon and eggs on a tray along with a cup of tea, and carried it through the passage. She knocked softly on the bedroom door, and after a moment she heard a voice say, 'Come in'.

The drapes had been drawn a fraction; Amy's father must have opened them to give himself enough light to dress by. Susannah was lying in bed with her brown hair spread out around her face on the pillow. Her hair was not as long or thick as Amy had thought it when tucked under a hat. There were dark circles under her eyes, and she looked very pale.

'Oh, it's you,' Susannah said, pulling herself up into a half-sitting position. 'I thought it was your father.'

Amy wondered why Susannah would think her father might knock before going into his own bedroom. 'I've brought you some breakfast,' she said, moving to put the tray on a small table beside Susannah.

'What time is it?' Susannah asked, covering her mouth as she yawned.

'Half-past seven.'

'Why did you wake me up so early?' She looked accusingly at Amy.

'It's not early,' Amy said in surprise. 'The men have already finished milking, we've all been up for ages.'

'Oh. I'm not used to getting up till… well, later than this, anyway. Get me that wrap, would you?' She pointed to a pale blue shawl draped over the back of a chair. Amy brought it to her and helped Susannah on with it, enjoying the feel of the soft fabric.

'This is a lot for breakfast,' Susannah said when Amy had passed the tray to her.

'Is it? It's what we usually have.'

'It's not what *I* usually have. I just have an egg and some tea normally.' Susannah ate one of the fried eggs, then pushed the plate away and sipped at her tea.

Without being asked, Amy sat down on one of the chairs and watched. When Susannah finished her tea and pushed the tray away, Amy moved to take it from her lap.

Susannah studied her as Amy leaned across. 'How old are you, Amy?'

'I'm twelve. I'll be thirteen next month, though.'

'Thirteen. And how old do you think I am?'

About twenty-seven, Amy thought, so it was probably safer to say twenty-five. 'Twenty-f—' she began, then decided to be very careful. 'Twenty-three?'

A satisfied smile flashed over Susannah's face for a moment, then she looked troubled again. 'That's close enough. I'm twenty-five. Twenty-five, Amy! That's not old enough to have a daughter of thirteen, is it?'

'I suppose not.'

Susannah sank back onto the pillows. 'I wish I'd known more

about…' she said as if talking to herself, then she noticed Amy again. 'I've finished, thank you. You can take that away now.' She indicated the tray that Amy still held. Amy stood looking at the floor.

'I said you can go now,' Susannah said. 'What do you want?'

'I… I don't know what to call you.'

'Call me Susannah.'

'But Pa wants me to—'

'Never mind what your father wants—I'll talk to him about it. Just don't call me Susie.' She turned away, and Amy left the room, closing the door behind her.

Amy was washing the dishes when Susannah came into the kitchen with Jack later that morning.

'It's not raining today,' Jack said. 'So I'll give you that tour around the place I promised.'

Amy thought Susannah looked less than eager, but her stepmother said nothing. She was wearing the grey cashmere dress again, this time with a dark red mantle that had fur at the neck. As Jack opened the back door for his wife, Amy noticed Susannah's boots. 'You mustn't go outside in those!' she said in alarm, pointing to the elegant things. The boots were black with a high heel; the lower part looked to be made of kid while the uppers were of a strong-looking cloth. To Amy's utter dismay they were trimmed with bows of black silk ribbon near each toe.

Susannah looked affronted. 'What's wrong with my boots?'

'You'll get them filthy out there—it's very muddy with all the rain we've had. Don't you have anything sensible—I mean suitable? Or you can wear mine if you like.' She indicated her own outdoor boots, which were standing in the porch. 'They're a bit big on me, so they'd probably fit you.'

'I'm not wearing those things!' Susannah said, looking at Amy's heavy leather boots in disgust. 'These are perfectly good walking boots—I've worn them all winter in Auckland.'

'They do look a bit flimsy, Susie,' Jack said.

'Don't call me that!' Susannah flared, turning on him. Jack took a step backwards in surprise.

'What's wrong with you?'

'Nothing—I just wish you'd remember my name. And this child fussing over my boots got on my nerves. I—I didn't mean to snap.' Susannah tilted her head a little to one side as she looked at Jack, and he took her arm with a smile. Amy felt as though she were eavesdropping.

'It doesn't matter,' said Jack. 'Let's go—I want to show you the view

40

from the top of the hill before the rain sets in again.'

Jack and Susannah were only gone a short time, just long enough for Amy to finish her dishes and start on the dusting, and when they came back in Amy could see that Susannah was the worse for wear. Her lovely mantle was spattered with mud, and the border of her dress was wet and stained for several inches. Worst of all, when Susannah bent to take off her boots in the porch she gave a cry of distress.

'Oh, look at them! They're just ruined!' She held a boot aloft. It was caked with mud right to the cloth upper, and the ribbon trim was bedraggled and filthy. Tears filled Susannah's eyes. Amy left her dusting cloth on the dresser and rushed to her.

'Let me take them, perhaps I can clean them,' she said, reaching for the boot. 'I could put some new ribbon on for you if you like—I'm afraid that one's ruined.'

Susannah slapped her hand away. 'Leave them alone! And don't you gloat over me.'

Amy dropped her hand in surprise. 'I'm not gloating—I'm only trying to help.'

'No, you're *not*,' Susannah hissed at her. 'You're just trying to say "I told you so"—I won't have it from a child like you. Tell her to stop it,' she said, turning to Jack.

'She doesn't mean any harm, Susie,' Jack said, looking bewildered over all the fuss. Susannah's face turned distraught. She dropped her boot beside its equally filthy mate and ran from the room with a sob. 'What's wrong with her?' Jack asked Amy.

'I don't know, Pa,' Amy said helplessly.

'I'd better try and settle her down,' Jack said with a sigh. He followed his wife out of the room.

Left alone, Amy picked up the sad-looking boots and set about trying to clean them. It took her most of what was left of the morning by the time she had scrubbed them, carefully removed the ruin of the ribbon trim with her tiny embroidery scissors and then put the boots to dry near the range. She thought they would probably be wearable, but would never look quite the same again.

John came in ahead of the other men at lunch-time.

'How did Pa and Harry get on this morning?' Amy asked, looking at the passage door to check they weren't about to be disturbed.

'I stopped them from killing each other.' He saw Amy's worried face and smiled. 'No, they got on all right—I made sure I was between them most of the time.'

'Thank goodness you've got a bit of sense,' said Amy. 'What do you think about it all, John?' She waved her hand in the direction of the passage door.

'I think he's mad. But there's nothing anyone can do about it, so we might as well make the best of it. What about you?'

'I don't know what to think,' Amy admitted. Harry arrived, and the conversation came to an abrupt end.

When Susannah appeared for lunch Amy said nothing about the boots, although she saw Susannah's eyes flick to them then widen a little in surprise. Susannah had changed into a blue woollen dress with a high neck and a darker blue border. Amy gazed at the dress admiringly.

'You have such pretty clothes,' she said.

Susannah seemed pleased. 'I like nice things. It's a pity I've nowhere to wear them now.' She looked at Jack reproachfully, but he was too busy with his meal to take any notice.

Harry paid little attention to Susannah while he was eating, but Amy saw him flash an occasional dark glance at their stepmother when he thought no one was watching.

For her part, Susannah appeared pained when the men reached across the table for butter or salt, or when Jack spoke with his mouth full, and Amy felt ashamed on her family's behalf, even though the culprits were oblivious. Her grandmother's civilising influence had never extended to the men of the family.

'When are you going to get the rest of my things, Jack?' Susannah asked when they were eating pudding.

'Eh? Oh, that's right, we left that trunk at the wharf. You'd better go in and get it this afternoon, John.'

But it was Harry who set off with the cart after lunch, as Amy saw from the parlour window when cleaning that room. She went out onto the verandah and saw John with Jack, working on one of the new fences.

Later in the afternoon she took them down some tea and scones, and Harry drove back up the road while they were still eating. Amy managed to whisper in her brother's ear while Jack was distracted. 'Did you tell Harry to go in instead of you?'

'Mmm, I didn't want to leave him and Pa by themselves until Harry's got used to Her Ladyship,' John answered as quietly.

'I don't think Harry should take the trunk in to Susannah by himself—she's in her room.'

'You're right.' In a louder voice, John said, 'I'll give Harry a hand getting that trunk in.' He and Amy walked back to the house together.

'We can't go on keeping them apart for ever,' Amy fretted.

'No, they'll have to sort it out for themselves. Harry won't have to see that much of her, I guess—neither will I, come to that.'

'I will, though,' said Amy. 'If she ever comes out of her room, that is.'

As if she had heard Amy, Susannah was in the kitchen when they reached the house, looking around. John and Harry carried the trunk in and left again as quickly as possible, leaving Amy alone with Susannah.

'I was just going to get dinner started,' Susannah said. 'I suppose you'll help me?'

'Of course—I'll do it by myself if you want to get your trunk unpacked.'

'No, I'll do it. Don't try to organise me.'

'I'm not—I'm just trying to help.'

'And stop contradicting everything I say!'

'I wasn't... I mean, I'm sorry,' Amy said helplessly.

'You'd better tell me where everything is, then.'

Amy showed her how the dresser was arranged, pointed out her jars of preserves on the shelves that lined one wall, then took Susannah outside to the dairy.

'Is this a larder?' Susannah asked, looking around in surprise. 'Where's the meat?'

'No, it's not a larder, I'll show you that next. It's a dairy, it's where I make the butter and cheese. I keep it on these shelves, see?' She pointed to the neat rows.

'Make it? Why do you make butter and cheese? You can buy it in the shops.'

Amy wondered where Susannah thought the butter and cheese in the shops came from, but she held her tongue on that. 'We've got so much milk, you see. I make it for the house, and I make extra to sell in town. Not in winter, though, there's only enough milk for our own butter this time of year. I'll start making extra again soon.'

'Oh. He needn't think I'm doing that.' There was no need to ask who 'he' was.

It's my job, anyway, Amy wished she could say. 'Come and see the larder.' She led Susannah out of the dairy and over to the large, airy room that held most of the food stores. 'There's not much meat left. Pa usually kills a sheep on a Saturday, so we're nearly out by Friday.'

'Kills it? Himself?'

'Yes,' Amy said, puzzled at the question. She was surprised to see Susannah shudder.

'There's nothing here but chops,' Susannah complained.

'That's because it's Friday, and Pa kills—'

'I know, I know, don't go on about it.' Susannah picked out eight of the cutlets.

'That won't be enough,' said Amy.

'What do you mean? Of course it will—that's one each for you and I, and two each for the men.'

'But those are only little cutlets, we ate all the chump chops the other night. They'll want four each, and I usually have two.'

'Four! They can't want four each! And one's enough for a scrap of a girl like you.'

'They *will*,' Amy said in some distress.

'Don't argue with me, child,' Susannah said, her eyes flashing. 'I'll tell your father you contradict everything I say.'

'I'm only trying to…' Amy gave up, seeing that she was simply making Susannah angrier. She helped Susannah cook the meal, and when the men arrived they set out the plates together.

'Have you run out of meat, girl?' Jack asked, looking at his meagre plateful. John and Harry prodded at their portions in equal amazement.

'No,' Amy said, unsure how to explain without causing trouble.

'Is there something wrong with it?' Susannah asked. '*I* cooked dinner tonight.'

'Ah, no, there's nothing wrong with it, Susie,' Amy saw Susannah close her eyes in frustration, 'there's just not much of it.'

'I thought it was plenty.' Susannah's lower lip quivered slightly. 'It's the first time I've cooked dinner for you, and now you don't like it.' There was a catch in her voice.

'Of course I like it—it's a fine meal—don't get upset. It'll be enough, I wasn't all that hungry anyway.'

'*I* was,' John said very quietly so that only Amy heard. Harry simply stared at his plate in disbelief.

They ate their meat and vegetables, then devoured the custard pudding that Amy had made; she gave silent thanks that she had cooked a huge one. She hesitated before putting the kettle on, but Susannah showed no sign of doing it herself; Susannah did, however, take over pouring the tea from the pot.

Harry drank his tea, then said bluntly, 'I'm still hungry.'

'Hold your tongue,' Jack said, glaring at him.

'Why should I? There's no crime in being hungry.'

'I'll get you some biscuits, Harry,' Amy said. She loaded a plate from her cake tins.

Harry took a handful of biscuits, but he looked at Susannah accusingly. 'It's meat I wanted, not biscuits.'

'Harry,' Jack growled.

'I'm a bit hungry too,' John said, reaching for a biscuit.

'How was I to know you're all such pigs?' Susannah burst out. 'I did my best, and all you can do is complain. And *you*,' she turned to Amy, 'you're just waiting to gloat over me again.'

'I'm not—'

'You're all against me.' Susannah rushed from the room in tears.

'Susie!' Jack called, but she ignored him. 'Now look what you've done.' He glared at Harry and John.

'What?' Harry said. 'All I did was say I'm hungry. It's not too much to ask for a decent meal, is it?'

Jack sighed. 'I suppose it's not. I'd better go and settle her down, though. Blast it, I'm hungry too! Have you got any more of those biscuits, Amy?'

'Plenty, Pa,' said Amy. 'I'll get you some more.'

Jack did not seem to be in any great hurry to soothe his wife; in fact the four of them spent a pleasant evening together. Amy noticed that Susannah's name was not mentioned.

But Susannah could not be ignored for long. Next morning she came out while Amy was cooking breakfast. 'Oh, you've already started.'

'I like to have it ready when they come in,' Amy said apologetically. 'And I didn't know when you were getting up. They're always hungry after milking.'

'I don't want to hear about how hungry they are. Out of my way, I'll finish this. You can set the table.'

The men looked at their plates apprehensively when they saw that Susannah had been involved with breakfast, but appeared relieved when they saw the pile of bacon and eggs. 'Good meal, Susie,' said Jack.

'Susannah,' she corrected him. 'I'm glad you all like it.' She smiled sweetly around the table.

5

September – December 1881

'I popped over to see Arthur this afternoon,' Jack said at dinner on Saturday night. 'I... ahh... mentioned you to him.' He looked awkward, and Amy wondered how her uncle had reacted to the news of his older brother's sudden marriage. 'So they'll all be looking forward to meeting you tomorrow,' he said, looking brighter.

'I'll have to make sure I don't disappoint them, won't I?' Susannah said with a superior smile. It was obvious she did not think impressing country folk would be difficult.

Sunday morning got off to a bad start for Amy. After breakfast she put on her mourning dress and the bonnet she had trimmed and lined with black crepe, then sat in the kitchen with her brothers, waiting for Susannah to finish her toilette. Susannah came in on Jack's arm looking as though she were dressed for a ball; or so Amy thought. The bodice of her dress was stiff silk brocade trimmed with velvet, and the skirts were of heavy bronze silk formed into broad pleats. Her hat was made of bronze velvet trimmed with bronze and dark red ostrich plumes.

'That dress is beautiful!' Amy gasped. She reached out to touch the brocade, then recollected herself and pulled her hand back.

To her dismay, Susannah's eyes narrowed in annoyance. 'Why are you wearing black?'

'Because I'm in mourning for my grandmother,' said Amy.

'Not any more you're not. You can't be in deep mourning when your father's just got married—it looks as though you're mourning *that*.' She looked at Amy as if daring her to admit that very thing.

Amy turned to her father for support. 'But Pa, it's only been six months since Granny died—I should wear this for another six months yet.'

Jack looked troubled. 'No, I think your ma's right, Amy. You can't go around in black when you've just got a new mother. You can wear an arm band instead, that would be all right.'

'You're not wearing your arm band any more,' Amy said, noticing its absence for the first time.

'Of course I'm not—not with a new bride. But you can wear yours for a bit longer if you want. Hurry up and get changed, girl, we haven't got much time.'

Amy went off to her bedroom, determined not to cry even though she felt betrayed. She hunted through her chest of drawers for the previous winter's good dress, and finally found it, rather creased, at the bottom of a drawer. She shook it vigorously to get some of the creases out, then quickly put it on.

To her dismay, she found that she had grown enough during the intervening months for the dusky pink woollen dress to become a little too short, as well as uncomfortably tight under the arms. But it was her only good winter dress, apart from the now-forbidden black one, so she had no choice but to wear it.

Susannah frowned when Amy came back into the kitchen. 'That's rather shabby.'

'It's the only one I've got,' Amy said, still fighting back tears.

'Oh. Well, it can't be helped, then. You'll have to get another one, though.'

'I'm not sure how we're all going to fit,' Jack said, looking round at his expanded family, when John had brought the buggy around to the gate.

'I'll ride,' Harry said just a little too eagerly, and he went off to fetch another horse. 'Don't wait for me to saddle up,' he called over his shoulder. 'I'll catch you up—I'll be faster than you, anyway.'

The church was small, holding around ninety people in its eight rows of pews when it was full; today the congregation was about fifty strong. It had been built fifteen years earlier, and Jack still occasionally referred to it as the 'new' church. Walls, floor and ceiling were all made of broad kauri planks the colour of dark honey, as were the pews, and with the morning sun coming through the high, narrow windows behind the altar (they were of clear glass; Ruatane did not run to stained glass windows) the church felt warm and cosy after the cold drive into town. That meant in summer the church could get unbearably hot, especially when the sermon was particularly long.

They arrived at church just as the first hymn was being sung, and took their pew as quickly as possible. Lizzie's father did not approve of 'pew-wandering', as he called it, so Lizzie could not come and sit with them, but Amy saw her craning her neck to look. Amy noticed heads turning to stare at her father's new bride, and the volume of the singing wavered briefly. No wonder people were looking, Amy thought. The only other person in the congregation who dressed anywhere near as stylishly as Susannah was Mrs Leveston, the wife of the Resident Magistrate; as Mrs Leveston was short, grey-haired and rather plump there was no real competition.

After the service most of the congregation seemed to feel obliged to rush over and speak to the Leiths outside the church. Susannah smiled graciously at them all, and clearly enjoyed the admiring looks given her clothes. Lizzie came over with her family and gave Susannah an appraising glance, then pulled Amy off to one side.

'*Well,*' Lizzie said. 'That's a surprise, and no mistake! I could hardly believe it when Pa said Uncle Jack had come home with a wife—and I didn't expect anything like her.' She looked at Susannah again, and Amy realised that Lizzie was, for once, almost at a loss for words.

'I didn't expect it either,' said Amy.

'What's she like?' Lizzie asked, turning back to Amy with an eager expression.

'She's...' Amy began, then found she was struggling. How could she sum up all Susannah meant in a few words? 'She's twenty-five, she's from the city... she's not used to us yet... she gets upset quite a lot.'

'Why? What's wrong with her?'

'I don't know,' said Amy. 'I... I don't think she likes me very much.'

'She doesn't sound very nice. She's got small eyes, anyway, and that pointy chin! And she's skinny.'

'She doesn't eat much,' Amy said, remembering the argument over the chops. 'She doesn't seem very happy at home.'

'I don't see why not,' Lizzie said. 'She's managed to get a husband, and she must have just about given up. Twenty-five! She looks even older than that.' She cast a disparaging look at Susannah. 'I'll have to get Ma to come over and visit her soon.'

'Why? So you can have a better look?'

'Yes,' Lizzie said simply.

Lizzie had to wait a few days before she could make her visit. Monday was washing day, and for the first time Amy decided there might be an advantage to Susannah's presence: sharing the washing would be a definite improvement.

She had her doubts when Susannah started a stream of complaints. 'Carry water from a barrel!' she said, looking utterly disgusted, when Amy commented on how lucky they were that the rain barrel was full so that they did not have to go all the way to the well to fill the copper and the rinsing tubs. 'We've had running water for three years at home.'

'Have you?' Amy said, wide-eyed with awe. 'That must be wonderful.'

'Yes, it is—it *was*, I should say.' Susannah looked downcast. She carried a bucket or two, wandering along morosely, while Amy scurried back and forth with the bulk of the water.

Running water! Amy tried to imagine what it would be like never to have to haul water again, but gave up the attempt. She mused on what other wonders Auckland might hold. It did not seem worth asking Susannah about the city; it would probably only annoy her, anyway. And she had somehow never had the chance to talk with her father about the things he had seen in Auckland; they hardly ever seemed to be alone together long enough to talk any more.

Susannah might be an extra pair of hands, but she did contribute an awful lot of washing, too. She laundered her own things, but took so long over each one that she did very little of the rest.

She looked with distaste at the state of the men's work clothes. 'Those are disgusting,' she said, wrinkling her nose at a pair of trousers liberally spattered with mud and cow dung.

'Men get dirty on farms,' Amy said, picking up the offending trousers. 'The clothes come clean, you just have to scrub them really well.'

'Don't take that superior attitude with me, child,' Susannah said sharply.

'I'm not—I was just trying to explain...' *Now I'm contradicting again, aren't I?*

But Susannah was distracted when she noticed Amy washing the pink dress. 'I suppose I'd better organise a new dress for you, I can't have you going about as though no one cares how you look.'

'I'll go in on Thursday and get some material—I can make one quite quickly.'

'There is a dressmaker in this place, isn't there?'

'Yes, I think Mrs Nichol does dressmaking—she keeps the millinery shop and drapery. But I always make my own things.'

'I was thinking of my own clothes,' Susannah said. 'I hope some country dressmaker is capable of making wearable gowns. I'm sure you can run something up for yourself.'

'Do you think...' Amy said hesitantly, then plucked up her courage. 'I'd love to have a silk dress.'

'Nonsense, child, you're far too young for silk. You can have *mousseline de laine* or something like that. You'll grow out of a dress in a year, anyway.'

Amy lowered her eyes to avoid looking at Susannah with what she knew must be a rebellious expression.

Tuesday's ironing at least caused no complaints; Susannah was used to the drudgery of that task, and it seemed the city had no magic way to improve on it. On Wednesday morning Amy was cleaning the range while Susannah did some dusting, when Lizzie arrived with her mother and little Ernie.

'Thought we should pop over and say hello,' Edie said, beaming all over her good-natured face. She was puffing slightly from the exertion of the last hill. 'I've brought you a sponge cake.'

'How kind,' Susannah said. 'And you've brought the dear little boy with you, too.' She patted Ernie on the head. 'You will take tea with me, won't you?'

'I wouldn't say no.'

'Amy, make some tea and bring it through to the parlour.' Susannah swept Edie out of the room, Ernie clutching his mother's hand.

Lizzie looked after Susannah in disapproval. 'I don't think much of the way she talks to you. No "please" or "thank you", just "Make some tea". Talks as if you were a servant.'

'I told you, Lizzie, I don't think she likes me.' Amy scrubbed her hands clean, then started making the tea.

'Humph! She must be pretty silly, then—everyone likes you.'

'How are you getting on with Frank?' Amy asked, to change to a more pleasant subject.

Lizzie pulled a face. 'Well, I haven't seen him for a while, except at church, and I don't get much chance to talk to him there.'

'You haven't taken any more pies down to him?' Amy asked with an exaggerated expression of innocence.

'I can't get away with doing that too often, or even Ma would notice. I'm going to have to find some other excuse to see him.'

'You'll think of something,' said Amy. 'I'll be back in a minute.' She picked up a tray with tea and biscuits to carry out to the parlour.

'I'll help you with that—I want to get another look at *her*,' Lizzie said, taking the plate of biscuits from the tray.

They found Susannah was doing most of the talking, punctuated by an occasional expression of interest from Edie.

'Yes, my father is rather well-known in our area,' Susannah said as they entered. 'He has his own building firm, and my brother works with him. He's been quite successful, of course things have been quieter the last year or two.'

'How interesting,' Edie said dutifully.

'My sister is married to a lawyer.'

'Really?'

'Oh, here's our tea. Run along, Amy, I'll pour it.' Lizzie gave Susannah a withering glance, which the latter unfortunately saw. 'Is something wrong, dear—Elizabeth, isn't it?'

Edie laughed. 'Lizzie, you mean—she'd be in bad trouble before I'd use her whole name.'

'Oh, Lizzie if you prefer—I always think names sound so much nicer used as they were meant to be. Anyway, what's wrong, Lizzie dear? You look as though you've got stomach ache.'

'Nothing's wrong with *me*,' Lizzie said haughtily. 'I was just surprised at the way—'

'Lizzie,' Amy took her cousin's arm, 'come and help me in the kitchen.'

'Yes, you can get on with that cleaning while I'm busy, dear,' Susannah said to Amy. 'Oh, your little boy is rubbing a biscuit into the rug.' She looked disapprovingly at Edie.

Edie pulled Ernie onto her lap. 'Don't do that, sweetie.'

'I'll clean it up,' said Amy. She fetched the dustpan and swept the crumbs from the rug before pulling Lizzie out of the parlour.

'Is she much help to you?' Lizzie asked.

'A bit,' said Amy. 'She does a lot of the cooking, and we did the washing and ironing together. She's not very keen on cleaning, though. She said they had a servant to do the "rough" work, whatever that is.'

'You mustn't let her boss you around.'

'What can I do about it? Pa says she's my mother now, so I've got to do what she says, don't I?'

Lizzie looked at her with a troubled expression. 'I don't like to see anyone talking to you like that.'

'I don't mind—not really. It's no more work than before, and I can get away from her quite a bit in the daytime. She often goes to bed pretty early, too. Pa sometimes does, too, since he came home. I suppose they're still tired from that long trip.'

'You're too easy-going. I'll have to think of something.'

'What are you talking about? Lizzie, don't you go husband-hunting for me! Things aren't as bad as all that!'

'Who said anything about a husband? You're too young for that to be much use yet, anyway. I just don't like her manner.'

'Forget it, Lizzie. It's not your problem.' But Amy knew Lizzie would not forget it, and she had a vaguely uneasy feeling when her aunt and cousins left for home.

'She's a pleasant enough woman,' Susannah commented while they were making dinner. 'Empty-headed, but quite agreeable. Her baby's a grubby little creature, though—she looks rather old to have one that young, anyway. And that girl's a sour-faced thing. I hope you don't mix with her too much.'

'She's my friend,' Amy said, stung into defending Lizzie. 'And she's not sour, she's lovely.'

'I see,' Susannah said, looking at Amy through narrowed eyes.

October came in with blustery weather, as if spring was reluctant to

51

show itself. It was much warmer, though, and the grass was growing luxuriantly, so the cows produced plenty of milk for Amy to make into butter and cheese.

She had never resented her tasks in the dairy, seeing them as part of her routine, but now she positively looked forward to her time there as a chance to be alone. She lingered, shaping the butter almost lovingly into perfectly-formed blocks, and when the work was done she lingered a little longer over a book.

At first Amy felt guilty over smuggling a book down to the dairy, but she knew Susannah disliked her company and would not miss her for an extra half hour. So she indulged herself by laughing at Mrs Bennet's efforts to catch husbands for her daughters, or shivering with fear at Jane's discovery of Rochester's mad wife. When she closed the covers of *She Stoops to Conquer*, Amy wondered what it would be like to see a play on stage in a real theatre. Susannah had talked of going to the theatre in Auckland. Amy decided it must be like having a dream come to life.

October the thirteenth was a Thursday, and Amy woke to see sunshine creeping through the gap between her drapes. When she flung them open she could see the valley was bathed in sunlight, and she smiled at the beauty of the scene.

'I'm thirteen,' she whispered to the day.

The weather was so much warmer that Amy decided to put on one of her summer dresses, and the kiss of cool cotton instead of scratchy wool or linsey-woolsey as she slipped the dress over her head made her feel in a holiday mood. She beamed at her father and brothers when they came into the kitchen after milking, and she even felt a warmth towards Susannah when her stepmother came yawning into the kitchen.

'You look very pleased with yourself,' Susannah said, edging Amy aside from the range where bacon was sizzling.

'It's such a lovely day,' Amy said. 'And it's...' she drifted away, shy at telling Susannah what the day was.

'It is nice weather,' Susannah said, looking out the window. 'Even this place looks reasonable in the sunshine.'

'Would you like to take a walk later Susi—annah?' Jack asked. He was learning slowly, Amy noticed. 'The ground's much drier now.'

'I might,' Susannah condescended.

Lizzie came over soon after breakfast, when John and Harry had left the house but Jack was still having his last cup of tea. She carried a bunch of violets and a lace-edged handkerchief.

'Happy birthday.' She gave Amy a hug and presented her with the gifts.

'Thank you, Lizzie,' Amy said, carefully not looking at her father.

'It's your birthday!' said Jack. 'Why didn't you remind me?'

'It doesn't matter, Pa.'

'I always had your ma or your granny to remind me before—you'll have to do that from now on, Susie.'

'I could hardly remind you when I didn't know myself, could I?' Susannah said, affronted. 'Happy birthday, dear.' She planted the lightest of kisses on Amy's cheek.

'I haven't got you anything,' Jack fretted. 'Come to think of it, I didn't bring you anything when I came back from Auckland. Of course I *did* bring you a new mother,' he added, looking pleased with himself. 'You couldn't ask for a better present than that, could you?' Amy and Susannah both pretended they had not heard. 'Make something nice—a cake or something. Then we can have a party at lunch-time.'

When Lizzie had gone home again Amy made a large currant cake as part of the morning's baking. She watched the cake being devoured when the men came back at midday.

'Good cake,' Harry said through a mouthful. 'You should have a birthday more often, Amy.'

'I do wish you wouldn't speak with your mouth full, Harry,' Susannah said. 'It's not very nice, is it?'

Harry glared at her. 'Why not?'

'It's just not nice—tell him not to, Jack.'

'What was that?' Jack said, his own speech muffled by cake. 'What did you say?'

Susannah pursed her lips. 'Really, you're all so *rough*.'

'Airs and graces,' Harry muttered. He left the table abruptly, and Amy felt a shadow had fallen on her day.

I wish she didn't always have to cause trouble.

As November drifted into December the weather grew warmer and more humid. Susannah seemed to become more short-tempered; Amy decided the heat must be getting her down. 'Shall I get a joint to cook for lunch?' she asked Susannah one Tuesday morning in early December. 'Or would you rather have stew?'

'Mutton!' Susannah said in disgust. 'I'm sick to death of mutton. Don't you ever have anything else?'

'We do usually have mutton… would you like to have chicken instead?'

Susannah thought for a moment, her lower lip stuck out like a petulant child's. 'Yes. I want chicken.'

'I'll tell John or Harry to get one of the roosters.'

'No you won't—I'll tell them. This is my kitchen, don't you go giving orders.'

Susannah went to the door and spied Harry not far away in one of the sheds. 'Harry!' she called in a piercing voice. There was no response. 'Harry! Come here right now!' she called even louder, and Harry ambled up.

'What do you want?' he asked ungraciously.

'Get me a rooster, please.' Amy's brothers at least rated a 'please'.

Harry grunted a response and wandered off. When he had not returned half an hour later Susannah became fretful.

'Where has that Harry got to,' she said, looking out the window.

'Perhaps he's had trouble catching a rooster,' said Amy.

'I'm going to see what he's up to.' Susannah marched out of the house.

'I don't think you should,' Amy said, hurrying after her. She had noticed that Susannah found distasteful many of the things Amy took for granted as part of everyday life; killing of animals was one of these.

Susannah turned on her. 'I don't care what you think,' she snapped. 'Don't tell me what to do—you mind your place.'

'You won't like it,' Amy said, but all she could do was scurry after Susannah as her stepmother strode across the garden and out the gate.

As she feared, Harry was just outside the fence with an axe poised above a struggling rooster. Susannah stopped in her tracks, Amy narrowly avoided running into her, and they both watched the axe describe an arc through the air then sever the rooster's neck, triggering a short-lived bloody fountain. For a long moment nothing seemed to happen, then the rooster's body began to twitch violently and Susannah started to scream.

'It's still alive—and you cut its head off—it's still alive!' she shrieked, then picked up her skirts high enough to show a few inches of silk stocking and took to her heels, still screaming.

Harry laughed uproariously. 'That got her going,' he said, nearly choking on his mirth.

'Harry, it's not funny,' Amy said. 'She really got a fright.'

'Serves her right,' said Harry. 'She can move when she wants to—did you see those skinny ankles?' He laughed again, and Amy couldn't suppress a smile at the memory of Susannah's headlong flight.

'It was a bit funny,' she admitted, 'but it's all very well for you to laugh—you won't have to spend the rest of the day with her.'

'Yes, poor you. It's a pity she's such a bitch.'

'Harry!'

'Well, she is.'

'You mustn't say that—she's Pa's wife.'

'She's still a bitch.'

Amy took the unfortunate rooster from Harry and reluctantly went inside to look for Susannah. The kitchen was deserted. She laid the corpse on the table and walked through the passage into the front bedroom.

'Susannah?' she said quietly. Her stepmother was lying face-down on the unmade bed; she rolled over and looked accusingly at Amy.

'Go away.'

'Susannah, I'm sorry you got a fright—I did try to warn you. It's just something that happens when you cut chooks' heads off, they're not really alive, it just looks as though they are. I suppose it does look a bit awful.'

Susannah looked as though she was going to be sick. 'You did it on purpose.'

'No I didn't!'

'Yes you did—it was you who said we should have chicken for lunch.'

'That was only because you said you were sick of—'

'And that Harry *laughed* at me! You did too, didn't you?'

'No! I didn't laugh at you! And Harry didn't mean any harm.'

'You set it up between you, didn't you? So you could make fun of me. You all hate me!' She turned her face back to the pillow and started sobbing.

'No we don't—please don't cry.' Amy went over to the bed and put her hand on Susannah's heaving shoulder, but Susannah pushed the hand away.

'Go away!' she screamed. 'I'm going to tell your father about you two—I'm going to tell him right now! You go and get him.'

'But—'

'Don't argue! Go and get your father.'

'All right,' Amy said with a sigh.

Harry was back in the shed when Amy went outside. 'Where's Pa?' she asked.

'Over in the back paddock with John, they're moving some stock. What do you want him for?'

'Susannah wants him.' Amy sighed. 'You and I are in trouble now.'

'Oh,' Harry said, looking unconcerned. 'What are you in trouble for?'

'The same as you—because she got frightened by the chook. She thinks we did it on purpose.'

'Silly bitch,' Harry muttered.

Jack and his older son were persuading some cattle to go through an open gate when Amy reached them. 'Susannah wants you, Pa,' she said.

'What for—can't it wait? We're busy here.'

'She's a bit upset.'

'What about?'

'She saw a chook being killed, and it gave her a fright. She's having a lie-down.' It sounded a rather feeble reason to summon her father. 'Actually, she's very upset,' Amy amended.

Jack groaned. 'Can't you settle her down?'

'I tried—I made her worse, I think.'

'Well, she'll have to wait until we've got these cows moved. Give us a hand, Amy.'

Amy went over to the far side of the cows and the three of them worked together for a few minutes, then she and her father walked up to the house together.

Amy took the rooster outside to pluck, carefully saving the feathers in a bag to be used for stuffing pillows. She took it back into the kitchen to finish preparing, then when it was in the oven she started the ironing; she was fairly sure she would be doing it by herself that day, and it had been delayed long enough.

'I don't know what's wrong with her,' Jack said when he came into the kitchen again, closing the passage door. 'You two aren't getting on very well, are you?'

'No,' Amy admitted.

'I thought you'd be pleased to have a mother again, not squabbling with her over chooks or whatever she's going on about.'

'I'm trying, Pa, I really am.'

'She's looking a bit worn out, too, you might have to help her more around the place.'

'Help her—Pa, I don't mind doing everything if that's what she wants, I'm used to doing it all. But she gets so annoyed with me when I try explaining anything.'

'Well, you'll have to sort it out between yourselves. You just do what she wants and try to keep her happy.'

Amy sighed. 'I'll try.' She bent over the ironing to hide the irritation she knew must show on her face.

It was unfortunate that Lizzie chose that particular morning to pop over to visit. 'Ma wants to borrow some baking powder. She's making scones and she's run out.'

'Help yourself,' Amy said, indicating the cupboard where she kept baking needs.

'Madam Susannah not helping you?'

'She's having a lie-down.'

'Did I hear my name?' Susannah said, coming into the room from the passage.

'Lizzie was just asking after you,' Amy said quickly. She flashed a warning glance at Lizzie, but her cousin was looking instead at Susannah.

'I was just rather surprised,' Lizzie said very deliberately, 'to see Amy doing all this ironing by herself.'

'What's that to you?' Susannah asked.

'I don't think it's right, that's all.'

'Lizzie,' Amy warned, 'you keep out of this—it's nothing to do with you.'

'She's quite right—what's it to do with you, Miss Lizzie?'

'Amy's too soft to stick up for herself, so someone's got to do it for her. What's she doing ironing all your stuff while you lie in bed?'

'Stop it, Lizzie!' Amy begged. 'You're not helping.'

'It's very interesting to know what you both think of me,' Susannah said. Amy was surprised at how controlled her stepmother sounded. 'I think you'd better go home now.'

'Well, *I* think—'

'Lizzie,' Amy interrupted, 'I want you to go now, too. Go on, go home. I'll come over and see you soon.'

Lizzie looked at her doubtfully. 'Will you be all right?' She appeared to be regretting her outburst.

'Of course I will—just go away.' She opened the door, and Lizzie went out, casting a disapproving glance at Susannah as she did.

'Talking about me behind my back, are you?' Susannah's icy calm was a strange contrast to her earlier near-hysterics.

'No—Lizzie's like that, she always bosses everyone around. We all just ignore her.'

'She seems to think you need protecting from your wicked stepmother.'

'She doesn't mean anything—you mustn't take any notice of her.'

'But *you* take notice of her, don't you?' Susannah hissed.

'Not when she bosses me. She just thinks I need looking after all the time, because I haven't got a... I mean, because—'

'Because you haven't got a mother? Is that it?' Susannah pounced.

'Yes,' Amy admitted.

'I don't count, of course.'

'You don't want to be my mother, do you?'

'Of course I don't.' Susannah sat down at the table. 'I think it's time I told you just what I do want from you—your father seems to think it's my problem to get on with you. Stop that ironing for a minute and listen to me.'

Amy put the iron on the range and sat down herself.

'I'm not your mother. But I *do* want you to show me respect. I expect you to help me around the house—*help* me, I said, don't pretend it's your kitchen all the time and you're only suffering me.'

'I don't do that—'

'Don't interrupt. You've been spoiled—your father's "dear little girl" and such nonsense. Well, you're not my dear little girl, but I'm stuck here and you're stuck with me. We'll get on well enough if you remember that this is *my* house now, not yours. Do you understand me?'

'Yes.'

'Don't think I won't tell your father, either, if you play up for me. And don't ask that girl over here too often. Now, just to show you I'm *not* lazy—'

'I didn't say that!' Amy protested.

Susannah continued as if she had not spoken. 'I'll do the ironing, and you can help me with it.'

When Jack came in for lunch he looked at the two of them working together and beamed in obvious relief. 'Now that's a nice sight—mother and daughter working together. That's better than fighting all the time, isn't it?'

Susannah smiled sweetly at him. 'Of course it is, dear. We're getting on just fine, aren't we, Amy?'

'Yes, *Ma*,' Amy said.

6

December 1881 – February 1882

December wore on towards the end of the year without Amy and Susannah having any more serious disagreements. When Amy paid her promised visit to an anxious Lizzie the week after the rooster incident, she was able to reassure her cousin.

'No, she's not being awful to me. We don't talk to each other very much, no more than we have to, but that saves fights, anyway. She's sleeping in later in the morning, too.'

'Is she bossing you around?' Lizzie asked suspiciously.

'I suppose she is, but it keeps her happy. Lately she's started doing these deep sighs all the time and saying how tired she is, but she seems more annoyed with Pa than me. She gives him such pained looks, as though he's meant to feel guilty.'

'Does he tell her off?'

Amy frowned. 'No, and he doesn't look guilty, either, that's the strange thing. Most of the time he just smiles when she does it, and gives her a pat on the shoulder.'

'He's just humouring her—I bet she nags him when no one's around.'

'Maybe. But he looks, well, sort of proud when he does it.'

'Ahh,' Lizzie said very knowingly. 'Looks proud, eh? I see.'

'What are you going on about, Lizzie?'

'Oh… you'll find out,' Lizzie said, looking smug. Amy let the subject drop; she was just grateful that her father could cope with Susannah's moods so calmly.

By the New Year, though, she could see that her father was starting to find it wearing.

'It's so tiring to work in the heat of this horrible kitchen,' Susannah complained one afternoon.

Jack smiled indulgently. 'You'll be all right,' he said, patting Susannah's arm. But instead of looking soothed she pushed his hand away.

'You don't care if I make myself ill working in this heat!'

'Of course I care.'

'Why don't you do something about it, then?'

Jack looked bemused. 'I don't rightly know what I can do about it—January's a hot month, that's all. You could have a lie-down in the afternoon, I suppose.'

'Yes, have a lie-down,' Amy put in, trying to rescue her father. 'I can finish getting dinner ready.'

Susannah rounded on Amy. 'Don't tell me what to do! And don't you encourage her,' she snapped at Jack.

'She's only trying to help,' said Jack.

'Humph! She's always trying to help, or so she says. And you're always taking her part against me.'

'No I'm not—hey, Susie… Susannah, come back!' But Susannah had stalked out of the room, and they left her alone to have the lie-down of which the suggestion had made her so angry.

Amy was becoming used to accepting instructions from Susannah in what she had thought of as her own kitchen, and she thought she took the directions meekly enough. Susannah, however, complained frequently to Jack of what she considered insolence.

'She's cheeky to me,' she said to Jack one evening in bed. Earlier that day Amy had tried to explain to her that she must be sure to cover the dish of soup she had left on the sideboard, so the horrible huhu beetles wouldn't fall in it.

'What did she say?' Jack asked with a sigh. He knew what was coming.

'It's not so much *what* she says, it's how she says it. She puts on a very superior air with me. It's not right in a child her age. You should correct her.'

'I can't very well growl at her just for having the wrong tone of voice, can I?'

'Humph!' said Susannah. 'You've been too soft on that girl, and that's why she's a burden to me now. It's very wearying, being crossed all the time. As if I didn't have enough to put up with…' Her eyes filled with tears, and Jack reluctantly promised to 'have a word with the girl'.

Having 'a word with the girl' meant that next day he contrived to find Amy when she was alone outside.

Amy smiled as he approached, pleased to see him away from her stepmother, but the moment he spoke her happy mood evaporated.

'Susa… your ma's not too happy with you, Amy.'

'What's she saying about me?'

'She says you don't show her proper respect.' He held up a hand to silence her when Amy tried to protest. 'Now, Amy, don't argue with me. It's not easy for Susannah, you know. She's had to give up a lot of her comforts, coming here to live. So the least we can do is try and make it a bit pleasanter for her, isn't it?'

I didn't make her come, did I? But all Amy said aloud was, 'I don't mean to be… disrespectful, Pa. It's just that everything I say seems to annoy her.'

'Just try a bit harder, then. Make it a bit easier for me, too, girl, for pity's sake.'

Amy saw the weariness and strain in his face. She slipped her hand into his. 'I'm sorry, Pa. I *will* try not to annoy her.'

'You're a good girl.' The smile he gave her made Amy even more determined to do her best.

She did try, but it seemed she couldn't do anything right. If she said nothing she was sullen, and if it meant the food didn't turn out properly she had done it on purpose; if she did try to correct Susannah she was being cheeky. On the whole it seemed safer to be thought sullen.

On a fiercely hot Thursday afternoon in February, Amy and Susannah were working together in the kitchen when there was a knock at the door.

'Run and answer that,' Susannah said, taking off her apron in anticipation of a visitor. Lizzie would not have bothered to knock. Amy found to her surprise that her old teacher, Miss Evans was at the door. She showed her in.

Miss Evans was in her thirties, small and stocky, with a round face framed by brown hair pulled back rather severely from her forehead. The stern effect was softened by her bright eyes, which were turned on Susannah in a friendly smile.

'How do you do, Mrs Leith?' she said. 'We've been introduced in town, I believe, but I'm afraid I haven't had the chance to call on you until now—I'm Ruth Evans.'

'How nice of you to drop in,' Susannah said, with a somewhat glassy smile. 'Yes, of course, you're the school teacher. Won't you have a cup of tea with me? Amy, bring a tray into the parlour, then you can carry on out here.'

'I think Amy should join us,' Miss Evans said. Susannah looked at her in surprise.

'The girl's busy out here, and I hardly think we need her with us.'

'But it's Amy I want to talk about,' Miss Evans said, and Amy felt a sudden leap of her heart, followed by a constriction that was almost painful. *No,* she cried silently. *Don't even try, Miss Evans—not with Susannah. She'll never understand.* She tried to catch Miss Evans' eye, but she and Susannah had locked gazes. Miss Evans was the first to break the silence.

'Now that there's *another*,' and she stressed the word in a way that made Amy want to kiss her, 'woman in the house, Mrs Leith, I imagine

Amy has a little more time. Are you aware that she was intending to train as a teacher under me? She started to, but her responsibilities at home were too heavy at that stage. I think it's time she came back to me.'

Susannah's expression showed that Miss Evans had abruptly changed from being a break in the monotony of her day into an irritation. 'My husband told me about that nonsense of Amy's.' Amy felt a rush of anger. 'He let her do it for a while because she whined at him—he spoils her dreadfully, I'm afraid. But I need her in the house—she is some help to me,' she finished in an injured tone.

There was a few moments' silence. 'So you refuse?' Miss Evans asked.

'I'm afraid I must. I'm sure you can find some other little girl to wash the boards for you, or whatever she did. I'm quite capable of teaching Amy all she's ever going to need. I do expect her to marry eventually, of course.' Amy cringed with embarrassment.

'In that case,' said Miss Evans, obviously holding her tongue with difficulty, 'I won't take any more of your time. Good day, Mrs Leith.' She turned to go.

'Oh, won't you take tea with me?' Susannah asked.

'No, thank you. Perhaps another day.' She walked out the door.

'Miss Evans!' Amy cried in dismay, and made to follow her.

'Where do you think you're going, Miss?' Susannah called sharply. Amy turned to her angrily.

'You were so rude to Miss Evans! I just want to apologise to her.'

'You stay just where you are. What right does she have to come here and say what you should or shouldn't be doing with your time? That's up to me, not her.'

'She just wants to help me!'

'Help you be like her, you mean,' Susannah said with a sneer. 'You should be thanking me for rescuing you from her. Do you want to be a dried up old spinster like her?'

Amy stared at her in fury. She clenched and unclenched her fists, trying to control herself, then her anger boiled over.

'You'd know all about that,' she spat at Susannah, who stared at her in shock. 'Dried up old spinster yourself! Had to take what you could get, didn't you?'

She turned and rushed out of the house. Miss Evans' little gig was already disappearing down the road, too far away for Amy to follow. She heard Susannah call her name as she ran, half-blinded with tears, until she was around the hill and out of sight of the house in a small grove of trees. She flung herself down on the ground and gave way to racking sobs of anger and disappointment.

It was an hour later by the time she had composed herself enough to return to the house and face the consequences of her outburst, and with a sinking heart she recognised her father's boots outside the kitchen door. For a moment she was tempted to slip away again and hide, but she knew it would be more sensible to get it over with. She steeled herself and walked into the house.

Jack was in the kitchen with Susannah. He turned a troubled face towards Amy as she walked in, and she felt a stab of guilt.

'There, you see if she can deny it!' Susannah said to him in a passion. 'She abused me to my face—called me names I wouldn't repeat in front of you—then ran off and left me to do everything by myself—all because I wouldn't let her have her own way about that teaching nonsense. Do I have to put up with that? Or are you going to do something about it?' Her eyes glittered dangerously.

Jack sighed. 'Is this true, Amy?'

Amy looked at her father, at Susannah's wild-eyed face, then back to her father. She thought of the things Susannah had said, and she felt angry all over again. But it would be too hard to try and make her father understand just how much Susannah had hurt her, especially when she was standing full in the glare of Susannah's vengeful gaze.

'Yes, Pa, it's true. I did say...' she realised abruptly just how insulting to her father what she had said was, 'bad things to her. And I ran away, and I stayed away for a long time,' she added, not wanting to spare herself any blame she might deserve.

'You see!' Susannah said in triumph. 'She doesn't even try to deny it.'

'At least she's honest about it,' Jack said in a heavy voice. 'Go to your room, Amy. I'll be along to see you shortly.' Amy went, a feeling of unease joining the hurt and anger.

'What are you going to do to her?' Susannah demanded, sounding almost hysterical.

'I'm going to do what you want me to,' Amy heard her father say as she left the room.

She sat on her bed waiting for her father. It seemed a long time before he came, quite long enough for her to ponder what he had meant by his last words, though in fact it was only a few minutes until he walked into the room and shut the door behind him. He stood with his hands behind his back, looking at Amy in silence for several moments before speaking.

'Why did you do it?' he asked. 'You told me you'd try not to upset your ma, and now see the state you've got her in. She's just about made herself ill.'

'She made me angry,' Amy said, trying to defend herself despite knowing she was wasting her time. 'She was rude to Miss Evans, and she said... she wouldn't... she doesn't think it's worth anything to be a teacher, even though it's what I want...' She trailed away feebly, knowing she had not put up much of a justification for her transgression.

Her father looked at her sternly. 'Amy, I've already said you can't do that any more, and I expect you to obey me. All your ma did was back up what I'd said—that's no excuse for you to upset her. I expected better of you.'

Amy hung her head. 'I'm sorry, Pa.'

'It's your ma you'll have to say you're sorry to, not me. It's not good for her to get that upset, especially in her condition.'

Amy looked up at him in bewilderment for a moment, then in wide-eyed surprise. 'Condition?' she repeated stupidly. 'You mean she's going to—'

'Yes, she is, and there's no need for you to look so shocked over it, either. I'm not as old as all that, you know. Anyway, I don't want to discuss that with you,' he said, clearly embarrassed. 'Don't tell her I said anything about it.

'You've never given me trouble before,' he went on, 'but you've gone too far over this. Your ma says you need correcting. I'd rather she did it herself—'

'She's not my mother!' Amy interrupted, furious at the thought that Susannah might dare to touch her.

'Amy!' Jack shouted, sounding more angry than she had ever heard him. 'She stands in the place of a mother to you, and she has the right to expect obedience, and to correct you if she doesn't get it. But she doesn't want to punish you herself, and I'm not going to make her. She's upset enough without that.

'So I have to do it,' he finished sombrely. 'I've never laid a hand on you—I don't hold with men hitting women as a rule. But I *have* to,' he repeated, pulling his right hand from behind his back. With a sinking feeling, Amy recognised the heavy leather strap. Her grandmother had not used it on her since she was ten.

She stood up from the bed and stretched her right arm out straight in front of her with the hand palm upwards, looking her father straight in the eye as she did so. Remembering punishments from school, she made sure her palm was quite flat, so that the blow would have the maximum effect.

Jack looked from her hand to her face, then looked at the wall.

'I don't think it was your *hand* she had in mind, girl.'

Amy looked at him in alarm, and sat down again on the bed very quickly. 'No, Pa.' She shook her head to emphasise her words. Being punished by her grandmother had been completely different; the idea of exposing her buttocks to a *man*, even her father, was too horrible to contemplate.

Her father regarded her in silence, then his shoulders slumped a little.

'No, you're right. I can't do it. All right, let's have your hand then.'

She stood up and offered her hand as before. To her surprise, Jack took her hand and pressed the palm so that it made a hollow. Didn't he know that meant the strap would make a lot of noise but wouldn't hurt quite as much? All the children she had gone to school with seemed aware of that; unfortunately so was Miss Evans, so Amy had given up trying that trick early on. But if her father wanted to do it that way she would not argue.

Whack! There was a loud noise, but it only hurt a little. Yes, she could bear that in silence. Amy gritted her teeth and fought down the urge to cry out.

'Make a noise, for God's sake!' Jack said in a hoarse whisper. 'She'll be listening!'

After that Amy yelled obligingly at each stroke, wondering if she was overdoing it. Her father did not seem to think so.

After a dozen strokes Jack lowered his arm to his side, and Amy dropped her own arm, rubbing the tender palm. Her father said nothing, but watched her steadily for several moments until she dropped her gaze, unable to endure what she saw in his face.

'Don't ever make me do that again, Amy.' He turned and walked out of the room, shutting the door after him.

Amy collapsed onto the bed and wept bitterly. Not from the pain in her hand, which was nothing; but from the look she had seen in her father's eyes: a look compounded of hurt and disappointment and bewilderment. The knowledge that she was the cause of that look was almost too much to bear.

When she had cried herself out she rolled over on her back and stared at the ceiling, wondering what to do. She wasn't sure if she was allowed to leave her room, and she was in enough trouble without making it worse. She could hear Jack's and Susannah's voices faintly, but she couldn't make out any words, or even tell whether the voices were angry.

The door opened and her father and stepmother came in together. Amy sat up, rubbing the back of her hand across her eyes to clear the leftover tears. She made sure her right palm, with its telltale redness, was hidden in her lap. Susannah looked calmer, but Jack had his arm protectively around her shoulders; the sight made Amy angry, though she knew she had no right to be.

'Amy has something to say to you,' Jack said. 'Don't you, Amy?' He looked pointedly at his daughter. She stood up and looked at the floor.

'I'm sorry I upset you.'

'That's not enough, Amy,' said Jack. Amy shot a glance at him, then looked back at the floor and tried again.

'I'm sorry I was rude to you, and I'm sorry I left you to do the work.' She looked at her father to see if this apology met with his approval. To her relief, he gave a slight nod.

'So you should be,' Susannah said sharply. She was clearly elated at winning the trial of strength, and was going to push her success to the limit. 'You can spend some time thinking about how you should behave in future—you'll have the chance to do that this evening. You're to stay in your room until tomorrow morning, and there'll be no dinner for you, either.'

'Susannah, that's a bit hard,' Jack said. 'I've already punished her.'

Susannah turned on him with her eyes flashing, and pushed his arm from her shoulder. 'You *said* I could punish her.'

'Yes, I did. But you didn't want to, and you made... I did it instead. It seems a bit rough, that's all,' he finished feebly.

'She has to do what *I* say, not just you,' Susannah flung at him. 'Are you going to take her part against me?'

Amy looked from one to the other, wondering if they had forgotten she was there. Jack gave her a helpless glance.

'No, I won't take her part. You do whatever you think is right.'

'I will,' Susannah said triumphantly. 'You heard what I said, Amy, I don't want to see you until tomorrow.'

I don't want to see you at all. But Amy schooled her expression into what she hoped looked like submissiveness and stood with downcast eyes.

'I don't suppose you feel able to sit on a hard chair at the moment, anyway,' Susannah said as a malicious parting thrust before sweeping out of the room, skirts rustling. Amy carefully avoided meeting her father's eye as Jack followed.

She'll have to do everything by herself tonight, Amy thought with some satisfaction. *And I don't care about missing dinner.* She started to reach for her sewing, then abruptly decided against it. Instead she went to her bookshelf and let her finger run along the titles before she selected *Villette*. She snuggled herself comfortably among the pillows and settled in for a long, self-indulgent evening. If she was as bad as all that, she might as well be lazy too.

When the smell of roast meat seeped under the door, her stomach grumbled noisily. The hunger pangs became more insistent as the evening wore on, and Amy began to wish she had eaten a few scraps while baking that afternoon. Thinking about *that* only made it worse. She could see those rows of biscuits looking golden brown and tempting. The faint voices she could hear from the parlour were distracting, too. She wondered if John and Harry had been told why she wasn't there, and if they were all talking about her.

She shut the book in disgust; it was getting too dark to read, anyway, and she didn't have anything to light her lamp with. But after she had undressed and climbed under the covers it seemed a very long time before she drifted off into a restless sleep, and dreamed of roast mutton.

7

February – April 1882

Susannah was not at the breakfast table next morning when Amy served the meal to her father and brothers. She and Jack avoided each others' eyes, and Amy ate in silence; she thought her father and brothers were quieter than usual, too.

Jack ate quickly and left the house as soon as he had finished his meal, but John and Harry seemed to be dawdling over theirs. Her brothers looked at one another, then at Amy.

'You went to bed early last night,' said John.

'Yes,' Amy said, in a tone meant to discourage further comments.

But Harry would not be put off. 'Did you get a hiding?' he burst out.

'Yes, I did.' Amy's hand ached at the memory, and she pressed it against her side.

'What for?' asked John.

'For annoying *her*.'

'Just for that?' Harry said in amazement. 'She annoys me every day, and I've never seen her get a hiding. That's not fair on you—she's always nagging at you.'

'Gee, that's a bit rough, Amy.' John looked concerned. Their sympathy made Amy want to cry, and she rose from the table to hide her emotion.

'It doesn't matter,' she said, making herself busy clearing their plates away.

'Is that why you didn't come out to have tea? Were you bawling?' Harry wanted to know.

'I wasn't allowed to come out,' Amy said, her back to them. 'I had to go without my dinner so I could think about how wicked I am.' *Pa didn't want her to do that—but he let her anyway.* 'And you know what?' She turned around to face them again. 'It didn't work.'

'What didn't work?' Harry looked puzzled.

'Shutting me up like that. I thought about it, all right. I said something I shouldn't have—'

'What?' Harry asked with an eager expression.

'Never you mind—I don't want you repeating it and getting me in more trouble. But it was all true, and she shouldn't have said what she did, and hitting me doesn't change that.'

She stopped, seeing that they both looked mystified. 'Don't mind me, I'm just rambling. I know what I'm talking about, even if I'm not making much sense.'

'So she said something that annoyed you,' John said slowly, struggling to follow her, 'and you said something back, so you got a hiding for it, then you got sent to bed without any tea.'

'That's right.'

'Huh!' Harry said in disgust. 'If she started it, why didn't *she* get the hiding?'

'Because Pa says she's my mother and I've got to do what she says, and because he doesn't want her to get upset.'

'Mother! What a load of crap—she's only a couple of years older than John. What I want to know is—'

'Come on, Harry, let's get moving,' John interrupted. He made a small gesture of warning with his hand. Unlike Harry, who had his back to the door, John had seen the handle turning.

When Harry gave a glance over his shoulder and saw Susannah entering the room, he needed no further encouragement. 'Mmm, better get going—see you later, Amy.' He and John left the house with barely a glance at Susannah.

'Did you have to eat your breakfast standing up, dear?' Susannah asked. 'What a shame. You'll remember that lesson for a while, won't you?' If Susannah had been any more pleased with herself, Amy thought, she would have been purring.

'Can I get you something to eat?' Amy asked very meekly.

'Just an egg, thank you—and some tea, of course.' She lifted the lid of the teapot and looked inside, then wrinkled her nose. 'Make a fresh pot, this looks rather stewed.'

'Whatever you say, Susannah.'

'Well, I must say that's a better attitude from you—I shall have to tell your father you're getting over your haughtiness.'

Amy said nothing as she cleared away the breakfast things. She went into the parlour to start cleaning that room as soon as she could, leaving Susannah still sitting at the table sipping her second cup of tea.

After she had beaten the rugs Amy decided to indulge herself for a while before it was time to make lunch. She took a slim volume from her little bookshelf and slipped quietly out of the house while Susannah was writing letters in her bedroom.

As she walked out of the garden to look for a quiet spot, Amy pondered whether she preferred a calm but vindictive Susannah to a near-hysterical one. Hysteria was very wearing, but at least she could feel a little sorry for Susannah when the woman was so obviously miserable. And she knew it must be hard for Susannah, coming to this dull place after living in Auckland. Amy wondered what it would be like to go to the dinner parties or outings to the theatre that Susannah talked of occasionally, with all the women in such lovely clothes and so many different people there that even if some of them were boring there must always be someone interesting to talk to.

She found a suitable place on the hill behind the farmhouse, where a hedge would put her out of sight of the house but she would still be within earshot if Susannah wanted to call her. She sat under a tree that would shelter her from most of the sun and settled herself comfortably. Amy was soon so engrossed in her reading that she gave a small cry when Lizzie plumped down beside her.

'Lizzie, you gave me a fright! Why didn't you call out first?'

'I thought you'd seen me. I should have known you'd have your nose in a book. I had to ask Madam where you were—she didn't know, she didn't seem very interested, either. Then I just caught sight of you when I was heading back home. What are you doing hiding up here?'

'I'm not exactly hiding, just keeping out of the way.'

'It's a bit much when you can't sit in your own house, and you've got to go under a tree instead.'

'It's worth it for a bit of peace and quiet. It's nice out here, anyway.'

'Yes, it's nice today.' Lizzie stretched her legs out in front of her. 'But what are you going to do in winter? Sit in the cow shed?'

'Maybe,' Amy laughed. 'I don't know, maybe things'll sort themselves out. Susannah's in a better temper today, so Pa will be happier too.'

'Are things pretty bad?' Lizzie asked, searching Amy's face. 'Have you fallen out with Uncle Jack?'

'Sort of. But it's all right now. Don't worry.' Amy decided it would be better not to tell Lizzie about her punishment. 'Susannah's been pretty weepy off and on lately—did you notice anything different about her?'

'What, you mean about her having a baby? I've known that for ages,' Lizzie said in a superior way. 'I wondered when you'd finally catch on.'

'Oh.' Amy said, crestfallen. 'You might have told me.'

'I thought I'd see how long it took you to think of it. What are you reading?' Lizzie asked, peering over Amy's shoulder at the open book.

'It's lovely, Lizzie, listen to this:

> "In Xanadu did Kubla Khan
> A stately pleasure-dome decree:
> Where Alph, the sacred river, ran
> Through caverns measureless to man
> Down to a sunless sea."

Isn't that beautiful?'

Lizzie looked at her dubiously. 'Alf? Like my brother? What sort of name is that for a river?'

'Oh, you're hopeless, Lizzie,' Amy said, shutting her book. 'It's Alph, A-L-P-H.'

'Where's Xanadu, anyway?'

'I'm not sure, it might be a made-up name. Isn't it lovely, though?'

'Not really,' said Lizzie. 'I like poems about *love* and things. You should read some like that, then you might grow up a bit and start thinking about your *future* instead of reading about rivers with stupid names.'

'So what's love, anyway?' Amy asked idly. The day was warm, and she was feeling too lazy to bother being irritated by Lizzie.

'What sort of a question is that? Love's about people getting married and having babies. That's what you should be thinking about.'

Amy pictured her father's face, with the bewildered expression he so often seemed to wear now, and Susannah's alternating smiles and floods of tears. 'Like Pa and Susannah, you mean? I'm not sure I'm very keen on love.'

'It's better than being an old maid—Aunt Susannah seemed to think so, anyway.'

I wonder what she thinks about it now. 'Do you love Frank, Lizzie?'

'Not yet, I don't know him well enough. But I will.'

'What if you don't?'

'I just will, that's all.'

In the face of such certainty Amy admitted defeat.

'I've decided he should come to my house next,' Lizzie said. 'But I haven't quite figured out how to manage it yet.'

'Really?' Amy affected amazement. 'That's not like you.'

'I've started dropping a few hints to Ma,' Lizzie went on, ignoring the interruption. 'You know, lonely men living by themselves and all that, but it hasn't sunk in yet. The trouble is I'd probably have to get Pa to invite him, and I don't know if he would.' She lapsed into silence, pondering the problem.

Jack came into the kitchen while Amy was helping Susannah make dinner. Amy saw his wary expression relax when he observed the two of them working together without apparent animosity. It was so good to see the relief on his face that Amy decided the self-composed Susannah was preferable, even if it meant she had to put up with being exulted over.

'Are you feeling all right, Susannah?' he asked. 'Not too much for you, working in this heat?'

'It's a little wearing,' Susannah said, 'but Amy's being quite a help today. Her manners are really much improved.'

'That's my girl.' Jack gave Amy a look of such gratitude that she felt it was worth being as meek as Susannah wanted. She could put up with a lot if it meant she did not have to see that disappointment in his face again.

'Yes,' Susannah continued as if Amy was not in the room, 'a few more lessons like that and she'll turn into a nice little girl.'

'Now, Susannah, don't go saying that,' said Jack. 'Amy knows she did wrong, she won't do it again, so there'll be no need for anything like that again. You just forget about the whole thing.'

Amy thought Susannah looked disposed to argue the point. 'Well,' her stepmother said rather huffily, 'I'm sure I hope it won't be necessary again, but I don't think you can train a child with one lesson.'

'All right, I've heard enough about it,' Jack said. 'Is dinner nearly ready?'

Susannah started moving plates around in a show of industry, but Amy could see a glitter in the woman's eyes that contrasted with her apparent composure. She wondered how long it would be before the hysterical Susannah returned.

As February wore on Amy kept a wary eye on Susannah's moods, talking to her as little as possible and spending as much time as she could away from her in the garden or the dairy.

For a long time Amy couldn't see that Susannah was looking any different. She began to wonder if she had misunderstood her father, though that would mean Lizzie was mistaken too. By the end of the month she thought Susannah was perhaps lacing a little less tightly, although there was still no discernible bulge.

'What are you looking at?' Susannah asked one day, watching Amy through narrowed eyes, and Amy realised she had been staring.

'Nothing, I was just thinking about what we'd have for dinner.'

'Doesn't take much thinking about—it'll be mutton again, I expect.' Amy resisted the temptation to ask if Susannah would prefer chicken.

Susannah was wearing one of her closest-fitting dresses that day. She pulled at her skirts as though the dress was twisted uncomfortably. 'It's very hot in here,' she complained.

Amy opened a window, but Susannah twitched at the bodice of her dress. 'I think this has shrunk, it's cutting into me. I'll have to get another one made.'

'I could... I mean, would you like me to let it out for you a bit?'

'No. You'll only ruin it, and I want to wear it again next year.'

You won't be able to wear it again if it's shrunk, will you?

Susannah pounced on Jack as soon as he entered the room for lunch. 'I need some new dresses.'

'That's no problem,' said Jack. 'Come into town with me tomorrow and you can get some bits and pieces.'

'I hope that dressmaker's quick with her needle,' Susannah fretted. 'I'm sick of this dress.' She pulled at the bodice again.

'Can't you make something yourself?' Jack asked.

'I don't sew,' Susannah snapped, 'and I haven't the time to learn now.'

'Amy would make something for you, wouldn't you, girl?'

'If you want me to, Susa—Ma,' Amy said dubiously.

'No, I *don't* want something a child runs up in the evenings,' Susannah said. 'Why can't I have something nice?'

'Well, it just seems a waste of money when Amy could do it for you, and you won't wear it for long, anyway.'

'I can't wear my nice clothes any more, and you don't want me to look nice! You want me to look like an old frump!' Tears filled Susannah's eyes.

'Hey, hey, of course I don't... don't cry... hang it all, if it means that much to you you'd better get one made. Just one dress, mind.'

'One's not many,' Susannah said, looking rebellious.

'It'll have to do for now. If you really need any more, get Amy to make one. That dressmaker you're on about can only make one at a time, anyway.'

Susannah gave in, though not graciously. She went into town with Jack to order her new dress, and in another week she duly brought home a gown of soft silk—*foulard*, Susannah said the fabric was called—printed with tiny yellow flowers, with cream lace at the neck and cuffs and yellow ribbon bows around the hem.

Amy could see it was a little larger than Susannah's other clothes, but she wondered how long it would be of any use. She tried to think back to how her Aunt Edie had looked two years earlier when she was carrying Ernie; she remembered Edie had seemed huge to her, and she and Lizzie had had to pretend they knew nothing about the pregnancy even when Aunt Edie was going about the house in what looked like a giant flour sack. Susannah still didn't seem to eat very much, though, so perhaps she would not swell up as much as Edie had.

'She's getting fat,' said Harry. He and Amy were standing together, watching Jack help Susannah out of the buggy after a trip to town. 'It's because she's so lazy, lying in bed half the day.'

Amy looked at Susannah. Yes, she had definitely thickened around the middle. Amy could see that the new dress was now only just wearable; she supposed that meant Susannah would soon be confined to the house. That would probably mean her stepmother's temper would become even more uncertain.

'She's still got a bony-looking face,' Harry said, looking puzzled, 'but she's got a fat belly.' His face fell suddenly. 'Oh, hell, I hope she's not going to have a kid. That's just what I need, a bawling baby as well as a bawling woman. Is she going to, Amy?'

'I'm not allowed to talk about it,' Amy said, feeling her face go red.

'That means she is, then. Blast her! And blast Pa for getting sucked in by her. Silly old—'

'Stop it, Harry, I don't like it when you talk like that.'

'It's true, isn't it?'

'It doesn't do any good complaining about it—it just makes it worse, really. Anyway, it's not your problem if she is going to… if there is a child coming.'

'Huh!' Harry said in disgust. 'You ask Bill some time about what it's like to have a baby crying half the night—none of them got much sleep for a while when Ernie came along.'

'Well, there's no point worrying about all that before we have to,' said Amy.

Amy did not know when the baby was expected, and she was not allowed to ask, but she noticed that Susannah was putting aside all the dresses she had brought from Auckland one by one as they became too small, and Amy could see that even Susannah's new dress was getting tighter and tighter.

At the beginning of April, Amy looked at Susannah one morning when they were making lunch together and she saw that the yellow dress was straining around the middle, with at least one button threatening to pull off.

Susannah looked up from setting the table. 'Why are you staring at me like that?'

Amy hesitated, trying to decide the right thing to do. 'Susannah, isn't that dress hurting you?' she asked abruptly.

'Why should it be?' Susannah turned away from her. 'You mind your own business.'

'Well, it's too tight—Susannah, I'm not trying to annoy you, really I'm not, but you look so uncomfortable with the seams straining like that.'

Susannah turned back to stare at Amy. To her dismay, Amy saw that Susannah's eyes were glittering and her knuckles were white where she gripped the plate.

But it was too late to stop now, so she ploughed on. 'Can't I help you? Please, Susannah. I could let that one out, or I could make you another one—or maybe you could get another one made.'

'A *sack*, you mean—you all want me to wear sacks now. Even that stupid dressmaker wanted to make this dress too big. And your father won't let me have any more dresses made.' She ended in what was very nearly a wail.

'Then let me make you one—you could have it in whatever material you like—it wouldn't look horrible if I made it in nice material.'

'Yes it *would*—everything looks awful on me now—you want me to look horrible!'

'Of course I don't, I love seeing your nice clothes, I just think you should—'

'I don't *care* what you think,' Susannah screamed. With a sudden movement, she flung the plate.

Amy ducked too late, but Susannah's aim was poor, and the plate smashed harmlessly on the floor. They both stared at the fragments of china, and for a moment Susannah looked horrified at what she had done. Then she turned on Amy. 'You made me do that! You and your nasty remarks about what I look like, and what I should wear. You're trying to drive me mad, aren't you?'

'No, Susannah, no! Please don't say that—I just want to help—'

The door opened, and Jack hurried in looking anxious. 'What was that crash? You didn't—oh, it was only a plate.' He looked at the remains of the plate with relief. 'I thought you might have had a fall,' he said to Susannah. He made to put his arm around her, but she stepped backwards out of his reach.

'It's her fault,' she said, pointing at Amy. 'She made me throw it— she's been saying horrible things just to upset me.'

'No I haven't,' Amy said, desperately hoping her father would see how irrational Susannah was being.

'Yes you *have*,' Susannah screamed at her. 'She hates me, and she wants me to look awful so you'll hate me too.' Tears were streaming unchecked down her face, but she pushed Jack away when he moved to comfort her.

'Susannah, no!' Amy begged. 'You know I don't want that—I'm only trying to help you.' She felt tears welling from her own eyes.

'Oh, don't *you* start, Amy,' Jack groaned, and Amy wiped the tears away as best she could with the back of her hand. 'Now, Susannah, tell me just what Amy's done that's upset you so much.'

'She thinks I look horrible, and she wants me to wear a sack. You'll have to beat her again—go on, take her away and beat her! You *have* to!' She gave Jack a push, but he didn't move.

'What are you meant to have done, girl?' he asked Amy.

'I asked if I could make her a dress because that one's too tight. That's all I did, honestly Pa, I didn't think it would upset her.' She looked up at her father, pleading with her eyes for him to believe her.

'Is that what's annoyed you, Susannah? Amy offering to make you a dress?'

'Yes! Yes, she keeps telling me what to do, and I won't have it! You have to beat her so she'll stop it!' She pummelled at Jack's chest.

Jack took Susannah's hands in his, and held them firmly when she tried to pull away. 'Susannah,' he said slowly and deliberately, 'I'm not going to hit my girl every time you get a fit of the vapours. Now, you just—'

'You hate me too! You're taking her part against me!' Susannah screamed. Her body seemed to go rigid for a moment, then Jack let go of her hands and she collapsed into a chair. She flung her arms on the table, laid her head down on them and wept. 'I hate it here… I wish I'd never come… I wish I'd never…' The rest was lost in her sobs.

Jack sat down beside Susannah and put his head in his hands for a moment, then looked at his wife. 'Amy,' he said without turning his head away from Susannah, 'go outside.' Amy went as quickly as she could. Before she closed the door she heard Jack say, 'Now calm yourself, woman, before you do yourself some harm.'

Amy stood by the gate in the hedge, wondering if she should try and find something useful to do outside. But it was nearly lunch-time, so she decided she would just have to wait until she was summoned.

John and Harry arrived a few minutes later, ready for their meal. 'Don't go in there,' Amy said, putting her hand on John's arm. 'Pa's talking to Susannah and he doesn't want anyone else around.'

'What about lunch?' John asked.

'You'll just have to wait.'

'They're having a row, are they?' Harry asked.

'Not exactly. Susannah's got in a state and Pa's trying to settle her down, I think.'

'Do you think he's going to give her a hiding?'

'Of course he's not, Harry, don't be stupid. No, she's really miserable.' She looked at the house and thought about the distraught woman at the table. 'She's annoyed at me again, too.'

'What about?'

Amy sighed. 'I don't really know. I always seem to upset her when I say anything.'

The door opened and Jack looked out. 'Amy,' he called. 'Come here, girl.'

'I'm in trouble again,' Amy said, trying to sound more confident than she felt as she turned to walk back up the path.

'Do you want us to come with you?' John asked. 'I mean, you shouldn't get in trouble over nothing, maybe we should talk to him.'

'Yes, that's right,' Harry agreed.

Amy was touched by their support, but she shook her head. 'I'll be all right,' she said, hoping it was the truth. 'You two just wait out here a bit longer.'

She felt her heart beating faster as she entered the house and closed the door. Susannah was no longer in the room. 'Yes, Pa?' she said, trying to gauge her father's mood from his expression.

'You'd better finish getting lunch on, I—' He stopped when he saw the look on her face. 'Amy,' he said, and she thought he sounded hurt, 'why are you looking at me like that? You're not frightened of me, are you?'

'I just thought…' She could not think how to finish.

'You are frightened. Amy, listen to me.' He put one hand on her shoulder, and with the other tilted her chin so that she was looking up into his face. 'Didn't you hear what I said to Susa—your ma before you went out? I'm not going to hit you just to please her. I'm not sure I should have done it that other time, either.'

He let go of Amy and sat down heavily. 'I don't know what's wrong with her, and I don't know how to make her happy. She's in a bad way—to tell you the truth, girl, I'm starting to think I didn't do the right thing by her, bringing her here. But what can I do about it? She's my wife now, and I've got to do the best I can for her—whatever that is.' He sighed. 'I don't know, it's beyond me. Your ma—your real one, I mean—was never like that.'

He looked so troubled that Amy's heart went out to him. She put her arm around his neck. 'Pa, I know I'm not meant to talk about this, but… well, I remember Lizzie saying Aunt Edie was sort of strange when Ernie was coming. Do you think that's the trouble with Susannah?' She did not add that Edie's strangeness had consisted of being even vaguer than usual, threatening to faint once or twice, and having one fit of weeping in late pregnancy when she was worn out by the February heat.

77

Jack looked more hopeful. 'Maybe you're right—though I don't remember your ma being that bad. Of course it's a long time since I had a broody woman around. Well, what do you think I should do about it?'

'Perhaps if Aunt Edie had a talk with her? She's the most likely one to be any use.'

'That's a good idea!' Jack leapt at it. 'I'll mention it to your uncle, he'll get her to pop over. What would I do without you, girl?' He squeezed her hand.

'You'd get your own lunch, for a start,' Amy said, pulling her hand away. She went to the door and called her brothers; seeing that they looked at her with concern, she gave them a smile and whispered as they walked into the room, 'It's all right'.

8

April 1882

Susannah stayed in bed the rest of that day. Neither Jack nor Amy was keen to disturb her, so they both kept away until the evening. When the table was set for dinner and Susannah still had not appeared, Amy asked her father what she should do about Susannah's meal.

'Shall I put something on a tray for her?'

'I suppose you'd better. Yes, take it in to her.'

'Ah… Pa, I think it might be better if you took it to her. She won't want to see me.'

'Well, she's got to put up with seeing you. I'm not carrying her meals about for her.' Amy could see that her father was very aware of John's and Harry's eyes on him, and she wished she had brought it up before her brothers had come in. Reluctantly she took the tray herself.

'Excuse me, Susannah, I've brought your—'

'Go away,' came a muffled voice from the bed.

'I've brought your dinner.'

'I don't want it. Take it away.'

'You might want it later. I'll just leave it here.' Amy put the tray on the bedside table.

Susannah's head emerged from under the sheet, and she reached a hand out to the tray. 'Take it away or I'll push it onto the floor.'

'No, you won't.' The voice came from behind Amy. She jumped, and Susannah stared, as Jack entered the room. 'You'll sit up properly and eat that, and thank Amy for bringing it to you.'

'I don't *want* it,' Susannah insisted.

'You've got to eat, Susannah, and you've had nothing since breakfast. Now you get that down you.' He walked past Amy and lifted the tray, then sat on the bed. 'Come on, sit up.'

Amy waited for Susannah to shout, but instead her stepmother sat up very meekly and took the tray onto her lap. 'Now thank Amy for bringing it in.' But Amy was already walking quickly through the doorway. She had no intention of giving Susannah a fresh grudge against her.

Jack lingered in the kitchen with Amy after her brothers had left the room. 'She says she doesn't want to get fat,' he said, frowning. 'She's got a bee in her bonnet about those dresses of hers. I hope Edie can talk some sense into her.'

'So do I,' Amy agreed.

*

Edie bustled in the next morning soon after breakfast, with Lizzie and Ernie in tow. There was a gleam in her eye and no trace of her usual vagueness; she was clearly a woman with a mission. 'Where's your ma?' she asked without preliminaries.

'Still in bed,' Amy said. 'I'll tell her you're here.'

'No, don't worry about that, I know where it is. Don't you girls disturb us. You can keep an eye on Ernie for me.' She hurried down the passage.

'Ma's all fired up today—she loves anything to do with babies. She's come to sort Aunt Susannah out,' Lizzie explained.

'I know,' Amy said. 'It was my idea.'

'Oh, was it just?' Lizzie was taken aback.

'Yes. You're not the only one who ever gets any ideas, you know.'

'I never said I was. You're not usually any good at getting people to do what you want, that's all.'

Edie came out again after half an hour. 'Well!' she said. Amy thought her aunt looked tired out. Edie looked at the girls, chewing her lip as though she was struggling with a decision, then seemed to make up her mind. 'Go outside and play with Ernie, Lizzie,' she said. 'I want to talk to Amy.'

Lizzie looked at her in amazement. 'Why can't I stay?'

'Because you're too young.'

'I'm older than her! I'm fifteen, she's only thirteen.'

'Don't argue with me, girl. Just go outside.' Lizzie was so stunned at her mother's unusual manner that she went without further argument.

When she had gone, Edie continued. 'Amy, you're a bit young for this, but your ma's going to need your help, so I'd better tell you. She's going to have a child.'

'Really, Aunt Edie?' Amy hoped she looked sufficiently surprised.

'Yes. I'd say it'll be around the beginning of August, so she's got about four months to go yet. She's keeping well enough, as far as I can tell, but she's pretty nervy.'

'I know, Aunt Edie. She gets very upset.'

'That's because she's scared stiff.'

Amy no longer had to pretend surprise. 'Scared? What of?'

'Scared of having a child. Now, it's nothing to be scared of, it's the most natural thing in the world. She'll know that after she's done it once, but for now she's frightened. I've told her a few things about what'll happen and she's calmed down a bit, but you'll have to try not to let her

80

get upset.'

'What should I do, Aunt Edie?'

'Don't let her tire herself out, that's the main thing, especially now she's getting big. Most of all don't let her lift heavy things. Has she had any fainting spells?'

'I don't think so. No, I think Pa would have told me if she had.'

'Good. She admitted to me she'd kept lacing herself up pretty tight as long as she could bear to, I thought that might have made her prone to faints. Now, what else? She mustn't go out any more, I've told her that. She grizzled about it a bit, but I think she sees the sense in it. I want you to tell your pa I said she's to stay home, he's the only one who can make her if she decides to be uppish.'

'Aunt Edie, will I have to help her when… when the baby comes?' Amy blurted out.

'Look at that serious face of yours!' Edie said with a laugh. 'Bless you, child, of course you won't—you'll be kept well out of the way. No, she'll have a nurse out from town to stay for a week or two. I'll pop over too if she wants me. There, now you look happier.'

'I do want to help Susannah. She seems so unhappy sometimes.'

'She'll be all right once the baby's come. That'll take her mind off her troubles. That's a while away yet, though, and she's got one more problem, Amy.'

'What's that?'

'She's nothing to wear. That's why she hasn't got out of bed since yesterday morning, but she can't stay in bed till August. She should have got something organised before, she's been a bit silly about it.'

'She didn't want to stop wearing her pretty dresses.'

'I told her they'll still be hanging in the wardrobe next year and she can wear them then. But she needs something to wear now.'

'I could make her something, but she doesn't want me to. She got really upset when I offered.'

'She won't go crook at you now, she knows she's got to put up with not looking flash for a while. You talk to her about it this morning. Now what's wrong, child?'

'I don't want to talk to her about it. I'm scared, Aunt Edie.'

'What have you got to be scared of?'

'You didn't see the way Susannah acted when I offered before. She screamed and screamed. She even threw a plate at me.'

'Did she, indeed?' Edie looked shocked. 'What did your pa say to that?'

'He was pretty unhappy. He worries about her when she gets in a state

81

like that.'

'Unhappy? She's a lucky woman to have an easy-going husband like your pa. Not every man would put up with that nonsense, even if she is with child.' She looked closely at Amy. 'You've had quite a time of it, haven't you?'

Amy shrugged. 'I suppose so.'

'Right.' Edie rose from her chair. 'You come with me.' Amy found herself being hurried along the passage and into the bedroom, where Susannah was sitting up in bed.

'Now, Susannah,' Edie said briskly. 'You know what we were talking about before—you need something else to wear. This child's handy with her needle, she can sort something out for you. Isn't that right, Amy?'

'If you want me to, Ma.' Amy was glad of Edie's solid presence beside her.

'Of course she wants you to. Don't you, Susannah?'

Susannah looked from Edie to Amy, then at the wall. 'All right,' she said in a small voice.

'That's the girl, now you're being sensible. You tell Amy what you'd like and she can come into town with me tomorrow to buy what she needs. You'd better make a couple, Amy, that should do her.'

'Do I have to stay in bed till that's done?' Susannah asked.

Amy was amazed at how docile Susannah had become. It gave her the confidence to suggest, 'I could let one of your other dresses out.'

She cringed a little, waiting for Susannah to shout at her, but under Edie's watchful gaze Susannah just said, 'If you want to. Take that one, if you like.' She pointed to the yellow dress, which was lying across a chair.

Amy picked it up and was relieved to see that it had deep seams; she guessed that the sharp-eyed Mrs Nichol had noticed Susannah's state. 'Oh, yes, I can easily let this one out. I'll do it right now, then you can wear it this morning if you want.'

'Now, aren't you lucky to have a good little daughter like Amy?' Edie said. That, Amy thought, was asking too much of Susannah even at her most docile. She took the dress out of the room before Edie decided to press the point.

Amy went into Ruatane the next day with her Aunt and Uncle, and of course Lizzie came too. Edie helped Amy choose material that as nearly as possible matched what Susannah had asked for: 'She said it had to be dark,' Amy reported, 'and with little stripes if we can get it, and the stripes have to go up and down, not sideways.'

They chose a navy blue woollen fabric with fine black stripes, and a plain dark green *mousseline de laine*. Amy was grateful for Edie's advice on how much to buy; to her it seemed a vast amount for each dress.

'Would you help me cut it out, please, Aunt Edie?' Amy asked. 'I don't quite know what sort of… well, shape to make the dresses.'

'No shape at all, that's the most important thing,' Edie said. She glanced at Lizzie, who affected a profound lack of interest in their discussion. 'Yes, you come home with us now and I'll get you started.'

As they passed the Kelly farm Amy could see a short slash of freshly-turned dark earth running through the green of one of the roadside paddocks. When she looked more closely she noticed Ben and Frank working away with shovels, slowly extending the new drain. Lizzie nudged Amy as they drew level with the two men. 'Watch this,' she whispered. 'Look, Ma, there's Frank and Ben,' she said in a normal voice. 'Don't you think Frank looks a bit thin?'

Edie tut-tutted. 'Poor boy, yes, he does a bit. I don't suppose they eat very well.'

'What do you think of that drain they're digging, Pa?' Lizzie asked. 'It doesn't look quite like the ones you do.'

'Hopeless,' Arthur agreed, glancing at Frank and Ben working. 'That'll cave in as soon as the rain gets heavy. It's not even very straight.'

'You know, Pa,' Lizzie said, sounding very thoughtful, 'I just happened to be talking to Frank after church last Sunday, and he was saying how much he's always admired you—especially the way you run the farm.'

'Was he, indeed?' Arthur looked over his shoulder at Frank with more interest. Amy thought back to the previous Sunday; she was quite sure Lizzie had managed no more than a brief exchange of 'hellos' with Frank.

'Oh, yes, he was saying how he wished he had someone like you to ask for advice about things to do with the farm. He was just a boy, really, when his father died, and Ben doesn't even talk much to Frank.'

Arthur gave a snort. 'Ben doesn't know anything about running a farm—you can see that by looking at the two of them working.'

'No,' Lizzie said with a sigh. 'It's a shame, Frank would really like to do things properly, but he hasn't got anyone to ask. He doesn't even get much to eat, so I suppose he's tired half the time.' Amy thought that was stretching things a bit far, but Arthur and Edie both looked thoughtful. Lizzie nudged Amy again, and both girls waited eagerly for Lizzie's efforts to bear fruit.

'Perhaps I should drop in and visit Frank some time, point out a few things to him,' Arthur said, and Lizzie shut her eyes in frustration. Amy had to smother a giggle; Arthur visiting Frank might well give Frank some useful advice he didn't even know he needed, but it would not be much use to Lizzie.

'That's a good idea, Pa,' Lizzie said. 'I just wonder, though… you know how unfriendly Ben is, maybe he might be a bit funny about it.'

'Humph! I won't bother, then.'

'No, I see why you can't. Poor Frank, what a pity—I know he'd love to talk to you. And he's so thin,' Lizzie added, somewhat irrelevantly in Amy's opinion.

Edie stirred in her seat as an idea slowly penetrated her mind. 'Perhaps you should ask Frank to come over for lunch some time, Arthur.' Lizzie raised her eyes heavenwards in silent gratitude. She held her breath for a moment to see if her father would react in the right way.

'That's not a bad idea. It's only neighbourly to give the lad a bit of advice if he's got the sense to want it. All right, I'll drop in next time I'm passing and ask him over.' Lizzie was too much of an artist to spoil things by making any indication of approval, but she smiled triumphantly at Amy.

Edie helped Amy cut out the blue material into what looked like a small tent, then they bundled up both lots of fabric together and Amy started back home.

Lizzie walked with her to the boundary, and as soon as they were out of earshot Amy said, 'You must have had a very quick talk with Frank last Sunday, Lizzie, for him to say all that about your father—I only heard him say hello.'

'He asked how I was, as well. Frank's very quiet, you know that. He would have said that about Pa if he wasn't so shy.'

Amy reflected, not for the first time, that Lizzie had her own very individual attitude to the truth. 'I hope you'll invite me over as well when Frank comes? I'm looking forward to seeing him have this useful little chat with your father.'

'Ahh. You don't really want to come, do you?'

Amy saw to her astonishment that Lizzie actually seemed a little embarrassed. 'I won't if you don't want me to—it's a bit hard for me to get away at meal times, anyway. Don't you want me there?'

'I wouldn't exactly put it like that, but… well, no, not really.'

'Why not?'

'Because I don't want Frank to take any notice of anyone else—this lunch is going to be important. Much more important than when we went to his house.'

'He'll have to take notice of Uncle Arthur when he gets all this advice.

Anyway, I don't think Frank would pay any attention to me with you there.'

'That depends whether he does more *listening* or *looking*. I can take care of the listening all right, but when it comes to looking... well, I'm never going to look like you, am I?' Lizzie touched Amy's dark curls admiringly.

'Don't talk silly, Lizzie.'

'It's true. It doesn't worry me, I'd just rather not shove it in Frank's face until he's got the message a bit better.'

'Unless he's very slow, Lizzie, that's not going to take long.'

9

April 1882

'It's a beautiful day!' Amy said as they drove along the beach into town that Sunday. The sun was shining out of a sky that was crisply blue after the morning's frost, and the sea sparkled. As they drove through a dip in the sand that made the buggy lurch, Amy laughed aloud.

Jack smiled at her fondly. 'You're in a good mood today.'

'I am!' Amy leaned across the seat and gave her father a hug. She felt a lightness of heart that she recognised came only partly from the beauty of her surroundings. It was so good to be sitting beside her father with her brothers behind them, all of them laughing and joking together. *Just like the old days.* None of them mentioned Susannah, sitting by herself in the parlour wearing the newly-altered yellow dress.

Amy sang her heart out in all the hymns; today it was easy to give thanks. She was aware of people staring at her family, and she knew they were speculating on the reason for Susannah's absence.

Mrs Carr bore down on Jack after the service, trailing her two unmarried daughters, giggly Martha and the almost-silent Sophie, in her wake. 'Is your wife not well, Jack?' Mrs Carr sounded concerned, but Amy saw the gleam in her eye and she knew the news would be all around the Orere Beach farms within days.

'She's feeling a little poorly,' Jack said. 'She'll be staying home for a couple of months.'

'Ah, I thought as much. Now, you take good care of her.'

'Good on you, mate,' Mr Carr said to Jack as he walked past, so quietly that Amy only just heard him. Martha tittered, and Sophie gave Amy a shy smile.

'Hey, Frank!' Amy heard her Uncle Arthur call. She looked over and saw Arthur striding towards Frank while Lizzie stood with her mother at a discreet distance. 'Don't rush off, lad, I want a word with you.'

Frank appeared to be wondering what misdeed he had been caught in. 'Yes, Mr Leith?'

'Why don't you pop up and see me sometime soon? You could come over for lunch if you want—Mrs Leith wants you to. Come next week, maybe Wednesday or Thursday. Ben too, of course,' he added.

'That's very nice of you.' Amy saw Frank's eyes flick to Lizzie, then quickly away. She could see he was screwing up his courage. 'I'd like to come,' he said in a rush. 'I don't think Ben will, though, he's not much on company.'

'Never mind him, then, you come by yourself. My wife thinks you need feeding up.' Arthur clapped Frank on the shoulder and laughed. 'So you'd better bring a decent appetite. Come good and early, then we can have a proper talk.'

'What do you want to talk about, Mr Leith?' Frank asked, glancing at Lizzie once again.

'About farming, of course, what did you think?'

'Oh! Oh, yes, of course, that's what I thought.'

'Good. Then we'll see you Wednesday week, shall we? Will that suit?'

'Yes, that'll suit very well. Thank you very much, Mr Leith.' He managed a smile.

'That lad's scared of his own shadow,' Arthur muttered to Jack as he walked back past Amy and her father. 'Anyone would think I was threatening to hit him instead of inviting him for lunch. What did he think I was asking him over to talk about?' He shook his head over the foolishness of the young.

Amy met a smug Lizzie's eyes for a moment, then turned away to hide her own smile.

'Come on,' Jack said to Amy, looking around to see where his sons had wandered. 'It's time we got going. We can't leave your ma by herself too long, can we?' Amy came down to earth again with a thump.

Frank tried to raise the subject of Arthur's invitation with Ben all that week and half the next, but though he waited and waited for the right moment it didn't seem to come. Before he knew it the appointed day had arrived, and he could put off his confession no longer.

As he and Ben did the milking that morning Frank tried out different words in his head, but none of them sounded right. When they were walking back to the house together he took the plunge.

'Arthur Leith asked us to come up for lunch today,' he said, carefully not looking at his brother.

There was a moment's silence, then: 'Why?'

'Just to be friendly.'

'Uh.' That obviously surprised Ben. 'We won't go.'

'I... I thought I might.' Frank was aware of Ben's eyes on him, glowering.

'What the hell do you want to do that for? What's wrong with having your lunch here—you don't want to go wandering off visiting strangers.'

That was an unusually long speech for Ben, and Frank knew his brother must be quite agitated to have come out with it. 'I just thought it'd be good to get to know them a bit better,' he said. 'Arthur wants to be friendly, and they're neighbours, sort of. He's asked me—us, I mean, so I should go, really.'

'Humph. Suit yourself, then.'

'There should be a good feed, too—remember those pies Lizzie brought down? They were pretty tasty.'

Ben eyed him suspiciously. 'You're not getting keen on that girl, are you?'

'Who—Lizzie, you mean?' Frank affected disbelief. 'Of course I'm not. What do you think I am, stupid?'

'Just watch yourself.'

Frank pondered for some time over what he should wear for his visit. It was such an honour to be asked out for lunch that he thought perhaps he should wear his one and only suit. But then he would get it dirty on the road; there was still plenty of mud in places for the horse's hooves to throw up if he went beyond a walk, and he needed it for Sunday.

No, he decided, he had better wear his work clothes and hope he didn't cause any offence. His trousers weren't *too* muddy, and he could get the worst of the morning's cow dung off from around the hems with a damp rag. He made sure he was out of Ben's sight as he went outside and rubbed down the trousers, and gave his jacket a thorough brushing at the same time for good measure. He knew he was just trying to look decent to be polite, but Ben might get some silly ideas about it. He took the old felt hat from the kitchen table and went off to catch Belle, the bay mare.

Lizzie was a nice girl, Frank reflected as he rode up the valley, but he had no intention of getting keen on her. He and Ben got on well enough; he knew Ben would never accept a woman in the house, anyway.

No, he'd have a good lunch and a chat with Arthur; maybe he'd ask the older man for a bit of advice about that drain they were struggling with. There was no need for Ben to look so disapproving about it all.

It was a funny thing about Lizzie, he mused as he passed the school. She seemed to have turned almost overnight from a plump little girl with fair pigtails sitting in the front of the class into… well, into a young woman. She was so friendly, too; always interested in how he was and what he was doing. He smiled at the thought of Lizzie's beaming face. What a good-natured girl she was. There was no harm in being friendly back.

'Frank! Good to see you,' Arthur said when he caught sight of Frank reining in Belle. 'Right, you can let that horse out in this paddock with mine and we'll have a look around the place. I'll show you a few things—what do you want to see specially?'

'Me? Ah, whatever you want to show me,' Frank said as he loosened Belle's girth and took off her bridle, wondering if he had missed part of the conversation.

'That's the idea,' said Arthur. 'You're interested in everything, aren't you?'

Arthur's oldest son, seventeen-year-old Bill, waved a friendly greeting from beside the pig sties where he was pouring whey into troughs, but made no move to join them. Eleven-year-old Alf, though, had no intention of being left out, and he attached himself uninvited to Frank.

'What are you doing here, Frank?' Alf asked.

'He's come because I asked him to,' Arthur said before Frank had the chance to reply. 'Frank wants to see how to do things properly around a farm.'

'Oh.' Alf sounded disappointed. 'I thought you might have come to help pull some of those stumps out of the north paddock.'

'I… I will if you want me to,' Frank said, looking questioningly at Arthur. He was glad he had decided not to wear his Sunday best after all.

'No, of course I don't—who asked you, Alf?' Arthur leaned across Frank to Alf and aimed a half-hearted clout at his son that came nowhere near its target. 'Go on, get out of here if you're going to butt in where you're not wanted.' Alf continued trailing along beside Frank, but he moved a little further out of his father's range.

Arthur led Frank a short way down the track the younger man had just ridden up, until they stood beside a wooden gate leading into one of the paddocks. 'Now, Frank,' he said, 'you see this gate?'

'Yes,' Frank said, looking closely at the gate and wondering what special significance it had.

'What do you notice about it?'

Frank studied the gate. 'It's a good, solid-looking one,' he offered, somehow feeling that more was wanted.

'It's that, all right. But you watch this.' Arthur unhooked the loop of wire that held the gate. He swung it open, then closed, then open again, then he closed and re-fastened it. Frank watched carefully.

'Now, you'll have seen,' Arthur said, 'how well this gate opens. I'm not one to criticise, Frank, but I can't help noticing that gate you've put in between your two road paddocks has slipped a bit on its hinges, so you've got to lift it a foot off the ground to get it open at all. Do you know what that means?'

Frank thought of the guilty gate, with the ever-deepening hole it gouged every time it was dragged open. He had had a bad feeling about that gate as soon as he and Ben had started on it, but Ben had gruffly shrugged off his concerns. 'It means it's not much of a gate, doesn't it?' he said, avoiding Arthur's eyes.

'Well, I wouldn't say that,' Arthur said kindly. 'But you should think about putting a better lot of hinges on it—that set you've used wouldn't hold up a cupboard door.'

So *that* was the problem, Frank thought, storing away the information. He was so busy thinking that he forgot to answer Arthur, and he didn't notice Arthur looking at him quizzically.

'Did you follow what I said, Frank?'

'Mmm? Oh, yes, of course—thank you, Mr Leith, I'll remember that.'

'I hope so. Now, come and look at this fence—you see these battens? What do you make yours out of?'

'Just whatever there's plenty of—I think it was rewarewa last time.'

'I thought as much. Rewarewa's all right, but the best thing's kohe. It's tough, but it splits well. You remember that.'

'Kohe. Right, yes.' Frank stored the information away carefully. He followed Arthur around several more paddocks, listening to the older man's opinions on raising cattle and pigs, and growing potatoes and maize.

'You should get on and pull a few of the stumps out of one of your flat paddocks and get some maize in there—it's fetching a good price, and it's easier than milking cows.'

Maize sounded a good idea to Frank, but he knew how much Ben hated change, and they had never grown maize before. So he nodded and smiled, and said nothing.

Arthur finished the tour by showing Frank one of his drains. He was pointing out the carefully-shaped angle of the walls when Bill joined them.

'Lizzie says it's time for lunch. And she says to hurry up before it gets cold.'

'She can wait till we're ready,' Arthur said, but he turned in the direction of the house and started walking, with his sons and Frank around him. 'Never let yourself be ruled by women, Frank—they'll do it if you let them get away with it.'

Frank thought of his own gentle mother, who had never tried to rule anyone, and had always seemed in awe of her husband.

'Oh, and one more thing,' Arthur said, breaking into Frank's reminiscences, 'I want you to take a good look at that drain.'

'Drain?' Frank repeated stupidly, still thinking about his mother.

'Yes, Frank,' Arthur said very deliberately, 'that drain just behind you, the one we've been looking at. There's something else for you to take note of—it's straight.'

Frank looked at the drain. 'Yes, it is,' he agreed. 'It's very straight.'

'And doesn't it look better than if it was weaving all over the paddock? Drains are meant to be straight—you remember that.'

'I'll do that,' Frank promised. He was vaguely aware of Alf sniggering behind him as the four of them walked up to the house together.

And there was Lizzie, standing in the doorway looking out for them. 'Here you are at last,' she said. 'I thought you were never coming.' But she gave Frank a warm smile. She had her Sunday best on, a pink cotton dress with a wide white collar and a white sash, and a matching pink ribbon in her hair.

'Frank and I had a lot to talk about,' Arthur said, looking at his daughter's finery in some surprise. 'Didn't we, Frank?'

Frank pulled his eyes away from Lizzie. 'Eh? Oh, that's right, Mr Leith. It's been really interesting—I've learnt a lot just talking to you.'

'Well, now you're here hurry up and sit down,' Lizzie said briskly. 'I've dished the soup up, and I don't want it to get cold. Frank, you can sit here.' She pointed out the chair at her father's right hand. It was Bill's place, but her older brother took his seat next to Frank with no more than a quizzical grin and a slight raising of his eyebrows at Lizzie, who studiously ignored him. Alf sat on Bill's other side, next to his mother at the foot of the table.

'I'll give thanks,' Arthur said just as Frank was reaching for his soup spoon. Frank felt hot at the thought that he had nearly disgraced himself. He bowed his head and closed his eyes, guiltily conscious that he and Ben never said grace; sometimes, remembering his mother's attempts to teach him, Frank would say a few words silently to himself, but most of the time it was just a bit too difficult to feel grateful for the sort of meals he and Ben produced.

Lizzie sat directly opposite Frank, sharing her side of the table with little Ernie. 'Do you like vegetable soup, Frank?' she asked, looking at him intently.

'Ah, yes, I like it a lot,' Frank assured her. 'Hey, this is really nice,' he said when he tasted the soup.

Lizzie beamed at him. 'That's good. I made it specially—I thought maybe you don't bother with soup at home.'

'No, we don't. I don't think I've had soup like this since Ma died. This is just like she used to make.'

'Do take another slice of bread, Frank,' Lizzie encouraged. She held the plate out to him.

'Mmm, thanks. It's nice bread—really fresh.'

'I just made it this morning.' Again Lizzie smiled warmly at him.

'Excuse me, Lizzie,' Arthur said loudly. 'Do you think anyone else could have some of that wonderful bread of yours? Perhaps Frank doesn't need it all.'

Frank reddened, and he quickly passed the plate of bread to Arthur. 'I'm sorry, Mr Leith, I didn't mean to—'

'Forget it, Frank.' Arthur dismissed Frank's apology with a wave of his hand, and took a slice of bread. 'My daughter seems to have forgotten there's anyone else eating here.'

'I'm just trying to be a good hostess,' Lizzie said tartly, but she lowered her eyes at a sharp look from her father.

When they had finished the soup, Lizzie carried a roast shoulder of mutton to the table, along with dishes of roast potatoes, boiled beans, and a large jug of gravy. Frank's eyes opened wide in appreciation, and when Arthur had carved the meat and the plates were piled high Frank attacked the meal enthusiastically.

'Do you like everything, Frank?' Lizzie asked superfluously, and Frank stopped eating for a moment to assure her that he most certainly did. 'Oh, that's good, I hoped I was cooking things you liked.'

'Did you have anything to do with this meal, Edie?' Arthur asked.

'Mmm?' Edie looked up for a moment from her task of cutting Ernie's food into small pieces and encouraging the two-year-old to eat. 'Oh, no, nothing at all—Lizzie shooed me out of the kitchen. She wanted to do it all by herself so I could have a rest this morning while the little fellow was having his sleep. Isn't she a good girl?' She beamed at her daughter, who sat with her eyes modestly downcast.

'Yes, she's a very good girl,' Arthur said, looking at his daughter in amusement. 'I'm really quite impressed with you, Lizzie.'

'Thank you, Pa,' Lizzie said demurely. 'Oh, Frank,' she said, noticing that his plate was empty, 'would you like some more meat?'

While Frank hesitated, torn between politeness and hunger, Alf reached his fork towards the platter of meat. Lizzie's hand snaked out and slapped his wrist away.

'Hey, what was that for?' Alf asked indignantly.

'Guests first,' Lizzie said. 'You can have some more when Frank's had another helping.'

'Why should I wait for him?'

'Shut your mouth, Alf,' Arthur growled. 'Your sister's right, have a few manners.' Lizzie smiled smugly, and Alf scowled at her and muttered under his breath. 'What was that, Alf?' Arthur asked.

'Nothing.' Alf looked at his empty plate disconsolately.

'Good. I thought I was going to have to teach you how to behave in front of visitors for a minute there.' He stared hard at the boy, and Alf glanced at him then looked away at once.

'I'm sorry,' Frank said awkwardly. He piled some more meat onto his plate, then pushed the platter towards Alf.

'Do you like steamed pudding, Frank?' Lizzie asked when the meat and vegetables were finished and she had cleared the plates away.

Frank had to make an effort to remember what steamed pudding was like. 'I think so.' In a burst of courage he added, 'Everything else is so nice, I'm sure it'll be lovely.' Lizzie rewarded him with a glowing smile. She dished him up a huge helping of pudding and handed him a jug of cream.

'I like it too, Lizzie,' said Arthur. 'How about giving me some?'

'Of course, Pa,' said Lizzie. 'I was just going to, but I wanted to see that Frank was all right first.' She smiled at Frank again.

After two helpings of pudding and a cup of tea Frank sat back in his chair feeling deeply content, then he reluctantly said, 'I suppose I'll have to go now. That was a wonderful meal,' he added with feeling. He looked at Lizzie in admiration, then, remembering his manners, turned to her mother. 'Thank you very much, Mrs Leith.'

'No need to thank me, Frank,' she said, looking away from wiping Ernie's face. 'I didn't have anything to do with it, you thank Lizzie. But I'm glad you came,' she added, smiling at Frank in a way that reminded him for a moment of Lizzie. 'You come again—soon, too. Arthur, you should ask Frank again soon. He needs a few more good meals.'

'Yes, you'll have to come again, lad,' Arthur said, clapping Frank on the shoulder. 'We'd all be pleased to see you, wouldn't we, Lizzie?' He looked at his daughter with a slight smile, and she stared straight back at him.

'Yes, Pa,' she said very innocently. 'It's nice to have visitors.'

Arthur and Bill walked Frank back to the horse paddock, and Bill helped him catch Belle and put her tack on. As Frank mounted, Arthur said, 'Now I meant that, Frank, you'll have to come again soon.'

'Thank you, Mr Leith, I'd like that—I'd like it a lot.' He started Belle off at a gentle walk, and his eyes slipped away from them. Arthur followed Frank's gaze to see Lizzie standing in the doorway waving and smiling.

What a nice family, Frank thought as he guided Belle towards home. He kept the horse to a walk, feeling too pleasantly full to want to trot. Anyway, he was in no hurry to get home; he was enjoying the memory of his visit too much. Arthur had been so friendly to him; Frank was still a little puzzled as to why Arthur had wanted to give him all that advice, but a lot of it was interesting. Edie had said she wanted him to come again, too, and she seemed to mean it.

And Lizzie. He remembered Lizzie, and felt something he couldn't put a name to. She had made such a fuss of him, as though he was someone special. She was really quite pretty, especially when she smiled at him like that. And what a cook she was! What a meal. He belched contentedly.

'Well, Lizzie,' Arthur said when he walked back into the kitchen. Lizzie was clearing the table, and she looked up at him as he spoke. 'Did you enjoy your visitor?'

'My visitor, Pa?' Lizzie said in apparent surprise. 'But you invited him.'

'You were very pleased to see him, I noticed—you got dressed up, too.'

'I just wanted to be polite. You'd gone to the trouble of asking Frank, so I thought I should make an effort to make him feel welcome.'

'You certainly did that.' Arthur gave her a hard look, but Lizzie went back to her work and seemed unaware of his scrutiny.

'He's such a nice boy,' said Edie. 'So polite. He enjoys his food, too— I like to see a boy enjoy his food. Did you get on well with him outside?'

Arthur sat down in the chair next to his wife and took Ernie onto his lap. 'He's heavy going sometimes.' He noticed Lizzie watching him out of the corner of her eye, for all she was pretending to be wrapped up in her work. 'I wasn't always sure if he understood what I was saying, though he seemed to be paying attention.'

'Poor boy,' Edie sighed. 'It must be hard for him with no father—a boy needs a father, and he was only fourteen when he lost his.'

'So, Edie, do you think that's what he's after?'

'What, dear?' Edie looked puzzled.

'Do you think young Frank's looking for a father... or something like that, anyway?'

'I'm sure I don't know what you're talking about, Arthur—what's "something like" a father?'

Arthur looked thoughtfully at Lizzie. That girl, he decided, was growing up faster than he had realised. She wasn't quite as grown-up as she liked to think, though; how old was she? Barely fifteen. 'Well,' Arthur said, 'Frank hasn't got a father, so perhaps the next best thing would be... a father-in-law?' He had the satisfaction of hearing Lizzie bang a plate down heavily on the bench, as though for a moment her grip had slackened.

10

August 1882

Darkness closed in early on the winter evenings. As Amy worked in the kitchen one afternoon in mid-August she knew the sun would dip below the steep hills that walled the valley before dinner was over.

Amy was enjoying the peace of having the kitchen to herself. Her father and brothers were still out working, and Susannah had taken to having a lie-down every afternoon since she had found that her ankles swelled uncomfortably if she stayed up all day. As Susannah now also stayed in bed late in the morning, with Amy bringing breakfast in to her, Amy could imagine herself once again mistress of the house.

Poor Susannah, Amy thought. Her stepmother was far too tired now to be bad-tempered, and when she did get out of bed she moped around the house in lethargic misery. Most days she had at least one fit of weeping, and everyone in the house was very aware Susannah had backache, Susannah's legs hurt, and Susannah was generally uncomfortable and unhappy. And now it seemed the baby was a week or so late, at least by Edie's reckoning. It seemed unfair that Susannah should have to put up with the whole wretched business for longer than the appointed time.

But Amy could not deny to herself that her stepmother's condition had made life easier. Her brothers had become more cheerful, too, now that Susannah played such a small part in their lives. Jack sometimes showed signs of weariness from spending his nights with a querulous and restless woman, but Amy sensed he, too, found a weepy Susannah easier to cope with than a snappish one.

Amy decided to make the lemon curd tart Susannah always seemed to enjoy, hoping that might cheer the poor woman a little. She already had stew simmering gently on the range and the vegetables sliced ready for cooking. When the tart was assembled and ready to be popped into the oven, Amy had time to read a few pages from her slim volume of Shakespeare. She closed the book and daydreamed briefly of actually going to the theatre and seeing a real play, then stood to give the stew a stir.

She was halfway across the room when she was transfixed by a piercing scream. She was at Susannah's bedside before she had time to think.

'What's wrong, Susannah?' Amy asked breathlessly.

Susannah was sitting bolt upright in bed. Her eyes were wide and she looked about her wildly, then clutched Amy's arm. 'I felt a pain *here*.' She put her other hand on her abdomen. 'The baby's coming!'

Stay calm, Amy told herself. *She needs me to be sensible now, she's so frightened.* 'I'll go and tell Pa.' She dashed from the room.

'Hurry!' Susannah wailed after her.

Where are they? Amy fought down panic. Where had her father said they were going to work that day? Then she remembered: they were fencing in the gully paddock. She set off down the hill at a run.

'Pa!' she called as soon as she was within hearing. 'The baby's coming, you've got to hurry!'

Jack dropped the hammer he was holding. 'It's started? It's about time. Right, one of you boys will have to go into town for the nurse. You'd better do it, Harry, you're lighter, so you can ride a bit faster.' For once Harry did not look disposed to argue; he ran up the hill towards the horse paddock.

'Hurry up, Pa,' Amy urged, taking hold of her father's arm and trying to pull him along.

'No, I'm too old to run,' Jack said; though he walked briskly beside Amy, leaving an unconcerned John to carry on by himself. 'There's no real rush, anyway.'

'Yes there *is*,' Amy said. 'The baby's coming!'

'They don't come as fast as all that, girl. When did it start?'

'Just now—I ran straight down.'

Jack nodded. 'That means it'll be a long while yet. We shouldn't leave her alone for too long, though. You run on ahead and tell her I'm on my way and so's the nurse.'

Amy hesitated, torn between wanting to do as her father asked and fear of what she might have to be part of. 'You're... you're sure it won't have come yet?'

'It'll be the fastest child ever born if it has,' Jack said. 'I've fathered five children—six now—I should know a bit about it by now. Go on, off you go.' He gave her a gentle pat on the bottom and Amy obediently broke into a run.

Despite her father's confident assurances, Amy was apprehensive as she went back into the bedroom. She was relieved to see Susannah sitting up in bed looking less wild. 'Pa's coming, and Harry's gone for the nurse,' Amy reported, then collapsed into a chair to catch her breath. 'Are you all right?'

'It hasn't hurt again, but the nurse won't be here for hours!'

'No, it won't take that long—they'll canter along the beach, so it'll only take about half an hour each way.'

'It's still going to be ages before they get here, and Edie said the nurse would give me something to stop the pain if it gets bad—what am I going to do?'

'Will it hurt a lot?' Amy asked anxiously.

'Yes... no... I don't know. Edie said it wouldn't hurt much because of the chloroform, but if the nurse doesn't get here I can't—oh!' Susannah suddenly clutched her middle, and for several seconds she looked panic-stricken again. 'That was another pain—it was stronger this time!' Amy went to her and put her hand on Susannah's arm, but her stepmother pushed it away. 'You're no help! Standing there looking terrified like that—you're making it worse.'

'I'm sorry.' Amy sought desperately for anything that might help. She recalled an incident two years before when John had injured his foot with an axe, and what her father had done while they waited for the doctor. 'Shall I get you some whisky? That might stop the pain.'

'Whisky!' Susannah's voice was almost a scream. 'I'm nearly out of my mind worrying about the pain and you offer me whisky! I suppose you think that's funny. Get out of here—go on, get out of my sight.'

'I was just trying to help—and I can't leave you alone, Susannah.'

'I don't want you here. Get *out*.' Her voice rose even higher, and Amy left the room helplessly.

Jack looked surprised when he saw Amy standing in the doorway waiting for him. 'Why aren't you with your ma?'

'She doesn't want me there—she said I made it worse. She's frightened of the pain.' The pain must be very bad, Amy thought, for Susannah to be so afraid.

Susannah's voice came down the passage. 'Jack? Is that you?'

'I'd better go to her, then.' Jack went in the direction of the voice.

Left alone, Amy looked around for something useful to do. She cooked the rest of the meal so it would only need reheating. She doubted anyone would be interested in eating it very soon, but she couldn't bear to do nothing. Then she drifted aimlessly around the kitchen, tidying things that did not need tidying and wiping down an already spotless table, listening the whole time for any more cries of pain from Susannah, but all was quiet.

Jack came out a few minutes later. 'She wants a woman with her. I'd better go and get Edie.'

Amy leapt at the chance of being helpful. 'No, let me go, Pa— please. What say Susannah needs something? She doesn't want me to go in to her again.'

'All right, I'll sit with her till Edie gets here—I'm better than nothing,

I suppose. You're faster on your feet than I am, anyway—there's no need to run all the way, though,' he called after Amy, who had already set off at a brisk pace.

Despite her father's advice, Amy ran most of the way across the paddocks. She was almost out of breath when she burst into Edie's kitchen, where Edie and Lizzie were preparing dinner. 'Aunt Edie, the baby's coming!' Amy gasped out. 'Please could you come over—Susannah wants a woman with her.'

Edie had her apron off in a moment. 'Right, I'll walk back with you—Lizzie, you'll have to finish this by yourself. You can tell your pa where I've gone.'

'Is Aunt Susannah having a baby?' Lizzie affected innocent amazement.

'Never you mind. Tell your pa I'll be back as soon as I can, but it mightn't be tonight. Come on, Amy.' Edie put her boots on and they set off together, at a walk this time.

'How long since the pains started?' Edie asked briskly.

Amy was again amazed at the difference in her aunt's manner from her usual vagueness. Babies were definitely Aunt Edie's favourite subject. 'About half an hour, I think. Harry's gone for the nurse.'

'Good. Nothing much is going to happen before morning, though.' Edie slowed her pace, and Amy slowed with her. It was a relief to have Edie's stolid, confident presence alongside her, and she was sure her aunt knew everything there was to know about having babies.

Edie went into the bedroom as soon as they reached the house, shooing Jack out of the room unceremoniously. 'It's no place for men in here,' she announced.

Amy thought her father looked relieved at being dismissed. John had come up to the house by this time, and the three of them sat in the kitchen. Twice in the next half-hour they heard a cry from Susannah and the murmur of Edie's voice. As dusk began to set in Jack said, 'We might as well have dinner. You can keep Harry's warm for him, but I'm hungry now.'

Amy looked at her father in disbelief, amazed he could even think about eating when Susannah was going through this mysterious and terrifying experience. 'You want to have dinner? What about Susannah?'

'She won't want anything,' Jack said, oblivious.

'Oh.' Amy was briefly lost for words. 'Oh, what about Aunt Edie, though? She's had to rush over here without her dinner.'

'That's right—you go and ask her if she wants any.'

'Me?' Amy asked doubtfully, but she went into the passage and stopped just outside the bedroom door. 'Aunt Edie?' she called.

'What do you want, child?' came the reply.

'Do you want any dinner? Pa's going to have his now.'

'Dinner? I am a bit peckish, now I think of it. I'll wait till the nurse comes, though, she won't be long now.' A long wail came from Susannah. 'Steady, girl, that's nothing to yell about. Those aren't real pains—you've only just started.'

Amy heated up the food. She was just dishing up the meal when they heard the noise of hooves outside. 'Thank goodness,' she breathed. 'It'll be really dark soon.'

A few moments later Harry came in, carrying a large cloth bag for the tall, thin woman of about forty who followed him. This was Mrs Parsons, one of the three maternity nurses Ruatane boasted. She had grey-streaked dark hair scraped severely back from her face, and she wore a very plain brown dress under a navy blue cloak. Amy thought she looked like someone for whom even Susannah would have to behave.

'Well,' Mrs Parsons said, looking at them all disapprovingly. 'I wish I'd known how far out the back of beyond you people live before I agreed to follow that young man at such a breakneck pace. That was a most unpleasant journey. Now, where is she?' She took her bag from Harry.

'I'll show you,' said Amy, helping Mrs Parsons out of her cloak. She led the nurse down the passage, then pointed at the door that she still felt was forbidden to her.

When the nurse had gone into the bedroom, closing the door firmly behind her, Amy went back to the kitchen to finish dishing up. Her father and brothers wolfed down their food while Amy toyed with her own, wincing every time she heard a muffled cry.

The men had almost finished when they were joined by Edie. 'I'll leave it up to the nurse for a while. I feel like a good feed,' Edie said, sinking into a chair with obvious relief. 'Susannah's not the easiest of women.' None of them had anything to say to that.

'Won't Susannah want anything?' Amy asked, fetching another plate for her aunt.

'No, nothing in her stomach from now till it's all over, whenever that is. Mrs Parsons said she had a bite to eat before she left, so she won't need anything till later—keep her something, though.'

'Poor Susannah. I made her favourite pudding, too.'

'Food's the last thing on her mind right now,' Edie said, helping herself to some potatoes. 'You make her another pudding in a couple of days, she'll be grateful then.'

'Everything all right, Edie?' Jack asked.

'Yes, the nurse had a good look, and she says everything's normal but nothing's going to happen before morning.'

'That's good.' Amy was amazed at how unconcerned he sounded.

Jack and his sons got up from the table soon afterwards and went off to the parlour, leaving Amy alone with her aunt.

'Aunt Edie?' said Amy.

'Yes, child?' Edie looked up for a moment from her pudding.

'Will the nurse give Susannah something to take the pain away?'

'She will when it gets bad. She's already had an argument with Susannah—your ma wants something now, but the nurse says she'll have to wait till she's further along. That won't be till after midnight, I expect.'

'But she's really bad now!'

'No, she's not. She's just making a fuss, but the nurse can deal with her. Come on, let's go through to the parlour and see what they're up to. I'll have to give Mrs Parsons a break in a couple of hours, so I want to have a nice sit down first.'

Amy went to the other room with her aunt, but it was even worse in the parlour than it had been in the kitchen. Susannah's bedroom was just across the passage, so her cries were more audible. John and Harry looked uneasily at the door once or twice, then took the lead from their father and seemed to forget about the drama being played out a few feet away.

Mrs Parsons emerged from the bedroom around nine o'clock, and Edie took her place while Amy dished up some food for the nurse. She wanted to ask how Susannah was, but Mrs Parsons looked too forbidding to be questioned, so Amy went back to the parlour and left her to eat in peace. The nurse disappeared back into the bedroom as soon as she had eaten, and Edie stayed there with her.

'It's about time we turned in,' Jack said soon afterwards. 'John, you're sleeping with Harry tonight.'

'Eh? Why?' John asked.

'Because I'm sleeping in your room—I can't sleep in there, can I?' He indicated his own bedroom. There was clearly no point in arguing, so John and Harry went off to their shared bed with only minor grumbling.

Amy went to her own room, undressed, and got into bed. Despite being tired from all that had happened she could not get to sleep. She tried putting her head under the covers, but she could still hear Susannah's cries through the wall. Even when she put the pillow over her head, the sounds penetrated faintly.

Later she wondered if she had nodded off briefly between yells, then she decided the cries were closer together. *It must be getting even worse*, she thought in growing distress. The thought stabbed through her: *What if Susannah dies?* For the briefest of moments Amy felt a longing for the life she had had with her family before Susannah arrived, then she was overcome by a rush of guilt. How could she even think such a thing with Susannah suffering on the other side of a thin wall, having Amy's own brother or sister? Amy sobbed into her pillow over her wretchedness and guilt, finally exhausting herself enough to fall asleep in spite of the noise.

When she woke a few hours later she lay very still for some time, wondering what was strange, before realising it was the silence. What did that mean? Why wasn't Susannah making any sound? Her heart started to beat faster. Hardly knowing why she did so, Amy slipped out of bed and made her way carefully across the room through the darkness until her outstretched hands met the door. She opened it as quietly as possible and felt her way along the passage until she stood pressed against the wall just outside Susannah's room. The door was open, and now she could hear voices murmuring; there was another noise that didn't sound quite human. Without thinking what she was doing, Amy walked through the door.

A lamp glowed, so that the bed was in a circle of soft yellow light. Susannah lay inert in the centre of the bed with her legs sprawled awkwardly; there were patches of blood on her thighs. Edie and Mrs Parsons stood on either side of her, and in her hands the nurse held a dark, wrinkled mass that was blotched with blood and mucus. Something that looked like twisted rope hung from the thing and disappeared between Susannah's legs. Amy hardly glanced at the other women; it was Susannah who held her gaze. Her stepmother was unnaturally still; far too still to be asleep. Her face had a ghastly pallor in the lamplight. Her mouth hung open, a small trail of saliva running from one corner, and her breathing made a horrible, gurgling sound. Amy was suddenly quite sure that Susannah was going to die.

Amy gave a small cry, and Mrs Parsons looked up. 'What's that child doing here?' she said sharply. 'Get out of here—this is no place for you.'

Amy fled back to her own room, flung herself into bed and hid her head under the covers to muffle the sound of her weeping. *She's going to die. I kept upsetting her all the time, and now she's going to die. I said she was an old maid and she had to take what she could get—Pa said it was bad for her to get in a state, and I upset her. I made her cry. And I thought it was funny when she got a fright about the rooster. And I wished she'd never come, and I kept thinking how nice it used to be without her. And now she's going to die.*

Amy sobbed until she had no strength left to cry, then she pushed the covers back so that she could breathe and lay exhausted and miserable, wondering when the women would wake her father to tell him about Susannah.

She heard a noise in the passage, and Edie came into her room holding a candle. Her aunt put the candle on Amy's dressing table, then sat down on the bed. 'Poor child, you got a fright, didn't you?' she said, stroking Amy's hair, and her kindness made Amy start crying again. 'Now, you just put it all out of your head and go to sleep—it's all over now.'

Amy sat up against the pillows. 'You mean she's dead?' *Dead.* The finality of the word seemed to drop like a stone.

'Dead? Of course she's not—is that what you thought? No, she's sleeping quietly now, and when she wakes up she'll find she's got a fine son to cuddle. What put that idea in your head?'

'She was so still, and she looked so… horrible. And… that's how my real mother died, isn't it?'

'Who told you that?' Edie frowned at her.

'No one told me, but I've heard them talking sometimes—Pa and Granny specially. She had a baby, didn't she, and then she died.'

Edie sighed. 'Well, if you've got the wrong idea I'd better tell you all about it or you'll fret.'

Her voice took on a different quality, and Amy felt that her aunt was seeing again something that had saddened her deeply. 'It wasn't having the baby that killed your ma. She took a chill when she had about two months to go, and she didn't seem to get better. Then she got a terrible, racking cough that made it hard for her to breathe sometimes.'

'Couldn't the doctor help?'

'Your pa had him out a couple of times, but he just said she had a bit of bronchitis and she'd get better when the weather warmed up. All the time she was getting bigger and bigger, and what with the cough keeping her awake at night she was just plain worn out by the time the baby came. She had a terrible time having that baby. It was a little girl.' Edie smiled sadly at Amy. 'She named her Edith, after me. The little one only lived an hour or so. Your granny said the baptising words over her while your pa went for the minister and the doctor—she was right, too, the baby was gone before they got here.' Edie stopped, seeing the stricken look on Amy's face. 'I shouldn't be telling you all this.'

'Yes, please Aunt Edie—I want to know, and I don't think Pa will ever tell me.'

'No, he won't. It's not something that's easy for him to think about. The doctor said your ma had consumption and he couldn't do anything for her. Your granny and I had to stop your pa from hitting the stupid man when he said it—he made it sound as if he was talking about whether it might rain tomorrow. But he gave her some things to take the pain away, and she didn't suffer much after that. You came and stayed with me then, do you remember?' Amy shook her head. 'No, of course you don't, you were only a little thing of two or three. I had you for three months. Your ma died two months after the baby, and… well, your pa wasn't too bright for a while after that, so I kept you a bit longer. My Alf was only a year old, so Lizzie kept an eye on you for me. I remember she said you kept crying for your Mama at night, and she had to cuddle you and kiss you till you stopped. She thought you were her little sister, I think—you both cried when you went home at last.'

Edie stopped, and Amy saw that her aunt's cheeks were wet with tears. She realised that her own eyes were streaming unchecked.

'There, now I've made us both miserable,' said Edie. 'I'm a fine one, aren't I? But there's nothing wrong with Susannah—she's strong as a horse, that one.'

'But why does she look so horrible, Aunt Edie? She doesn't look as though she's just asleep.'

'That's the chloroform. It puts you out soundly, but she'll wake up right as rain in an hour or two. Don't you worry, in a couple of days she'll be growling at you as good as ever.'

'Really and truly?' Amy asked, desperately wanting to believe her aunt.

'Cross my heart. Now, you go to sleep and in the morning you can see your new brother.'

'Is the baby all right?' Amy remembered the ugly mass. It hadn't looked wet and shiny like new-born calves did.

'Right as rain. Babies don't look too lovely when they're just born, but we've cleaned him up and he's all pink and nice now. Your pa's going to be proud. Now, off you go to sleep.' She gave Amy a kiss, and Amy put her arms around her aunt's neck in grateful affection. She was asleep with minutes of Edie's going.

11

August 1882 – February 1883

Amy woke the next morning eager to make amends for her guilty thoughts by being helpful to Susannah. She dressed and started making breakfast, then knocked timidly on Susannah's door.

Mrs Parsons came to the door, looking weary. 'What do you want?' the nurse asked.

'Is Susannah allowed breakfast? I'm just making it now.'

'No, I don't want her to have anything solid before lunch. You can bring her a cup of tea if you like.'

By the time Amy had made the tea Edie and Mrs Parsons had appeared in the kitchen, both yawning. She poured them a cup each before going back to Susannah's room.

Despite her aunt's assurances, Amy was nervous at the thought of seeing Susannah, but her stepmother was propped up against the pillows with a healthy colour in her face. Her hair had been brushed and her face washed; she looked drowsy but was clearly alive.

'Susannah,' Amy said quietly, 'do you feel all right now?'

'I feel sick, and I hurt all over,' Susannah said, slurring her words. 'That's the most horrible thing that's ever happened to me.'

'I'm sorry. Would you like some tea?'

'I think so. I'm very thirsty. Help me sit up better. Ow!' Susannah gasped as she tried to shift her position. 'No, that hurts too much. I'll have to try and drink it like this.'

Amy held the saucer for her and took the cup after each sip until Susannah had finished. 'Go away,' Susannah said. 'I want to go back to sleep now.'

'Can't I see the baby?' Amy asked, looking at the cradle on the far side of the bed.

'If you must. Don't wake it up.'

Amy walked as quietly as she could around to the cradle, and looked at the sleeping infant. All she could see was the top of the baby's head peeping out of a blanket. He was bald apart from a light fuzz of dark hair. 'He's beautiful,' she said dutifully, then on impulse she knelt beside the bed so that her face was close to Susannah's. 'You'll feel better soon, Susannah. I'm going to look after you.'

'No you're not,' Susannah said, a little of her old snappishness coming through her drowsy tone. 'You're going next door—I think I've earned a rest from having you annoying me for a while.'

Amy's vision of redeeming herself by good works evaporated instantly. For a moment she was too stunned to speak. 'But… I won't annoy you! I just want to help you till you feel well again—can't I stay? Please?'

'It's bad enough having that Parsons woman poking and prodding at me and ordering me about—I don't want you nagging at me and grizzling to your father all the time. He can take some notice of *me* for a change.'

'I don't know what you mean, Susannah,' Amy said, standing up and shaking her head in confusion. 'I thought I could make you nice things to eat, and help you look after the baby, and—'

There was a noise from the doorway, and Amy looked up to see her father erupt into the room. 'It's all over and no one called me! I went out looking for my breakfast and those women calmly tell me I'm a father again—where's my son?' He walked over to the cradle, crouched down and carefully pulled the blanket back to look at the baby's face. 'He's a fine boy,' he said proudly. He replaced the blanket, sat beside the bed and took Susannah's hand between both of his. Amy, feeling out of place, made to leave them alone.

Jack noticed her movement. 'Amy's going to enjoy having a baby around to look after, aren't you, girl?'

'I… I would like to.' Amy winced at the look in Susannah's eyes.

'You're lucky to have the girl, she'll be a real help to you,' Jack said, smiling at Susannah.

'You haven't forgotten that Amy's going to stay with Edie for a little while, have you, Jack?' said Susannah.

'Oh, that's right, that nurse has to sleep in her room. Still, Amy could sleep there as well, couldn't she?'

'You can't expect Mrs Parsons to share a bed with the girl! It's hardly fair on the woman. Please don't upset me, Jack, not when I'm so ill.'

'All right, if that's what you want,' Jack conceded. 'You don't mind, do you girl?'

'I… can I come and visit?' Amy asked, reluctant to lie.

'Of course you can! You come over every day—I'll miss you if you don't. You'll want to see the baby, anyway.'

With that Amy had to be content, and she went out to the kitchen to finish making breakfast.

John and Harry were waiting at the table by now, apparently more concerned with their breakfast than with hearing about a new brother. By the time Amy was ready to dish up the bacon and eggs her father had also joined them, having seen Susannah off to sleep, and they all ate together. 'Now mother and baby are settled I'd like to have a few hours sleep,' Mrs Parsons said when she had finished her meal. 'Where's my room?'

'My wife said you're to have Amy's room,' said Jack. 'Can Amy stay with you, Edie?'

'Of course she can.' Edie beamed at her.

At least she *wants me*, Amy thought dejectedly. She plucked up her courage to make one more attempt. 'Mrs Parsons, won't it be a lot of work for you to look after everything here? Couldn't I do the cooking and things for you?'

'And where would you sleep?' Mrs Parsons said curtly. Then, seeing Amy's hurt face, her manner softened a little. 'Well, if you're that keen to help... Mr Leith, how would it be if I only stayed a week instead of the ten days? That would give me long enough to see that the baby's thriving and your wife's all right, then this girl could look after her until she's able to get up. I've another patient near her time, anyway.'

'Of course Amy wants to look after her ma,' said Jack. 'If you think it's all right, Mrs Parsons, that's good enough for me.'

Amy showed Mrs Parsons where everything was in the kitchen and the larder, then took the woman into her own bedroom and folded back the coverlet for her. Amy bundled up the few clothes she would need and took them out to the kitchen, leaving Mrs Parsons to her well-earned rest.

'You must be tired too, Aunt Edie,' she said, noticing that her aunt's eyelids were drooping as she sat cradling a half-empty cup between her hands.

'Hmm? Yes, I suppose I am.' Edie looked around the room as if unsure how she had come to be there. 'I think I'll go home soon—after the nurse gets up, anyway. I'll have to keep an ear open for your ma until then.'

'I could do that if you want to have a lie-down,' Amy said eagerly.

Edie smiled at her. 'You're a good girl, but you wouldn't be much use to her. I'll have to show her how to feed the baby when he wakes up—you can't do that, can you?'

'No,' Amy admitted, with a deep sense of her own uselessness. She made herself busy around the kitchen, doing what preparations she could towards lunch so Mrs Parsons would have less to do, but at the same time trying not to make any noise that might disturb the sleepers. Edie sat at the table, somewhere between sleep and wakefulness but apparently content.

They both looked up startled when the back door opened half an hour later to admit Lizzie, leading Ernie by the hand. The little boy rushed to his mother as soon as he laid eyes on her and clambered onto her lap. 'Pa wants to know when you're coming home,' Lizzie said. 'Ernie's been playing up, he wouldn't go to sleep for hours last night because you weren't there to put him to bed.'

'Poor little fellow,' Edie crooned. 'Did you miss your Mama?'

'Pa gave him a smack, but that made him worse,' Lizzie said. 'He really yelled then, and I had to take him to bed with me. He still bawled for ages, though. You *are* coming back today, aren't you? Pa said you're to come home,' she added quickly. Amy wondered if her uncle really had said it, or if Lizzie was merely 'sure' he would have.

'Yes, now the baby's arrived safely I'm not needed. I'll come back with you in a bit. Not just yet, though.'

Amy put the kettle on again, and they were halfway through drinking another pot of tea when Edie abruptly turned towards the open passage door. 'The baby's awake,' she announced, though neither girl had heard any sound, and a moment later they heard Susannah's voice coming faintly down the passage. Edie put her cup down and disappeared from the room, with Ernie trailing after her.

'So, what is it?' Lizzie asked.

'A boy.'

Lizzie pulled a face. 'Another one. We're not very good at girls in our family, are we?'

'No. It doesn't make much difference yet, anyway.'

'It will, though. Boys just make more work, a girl would be a help around the place.'

'I suppose so.'

'You don't sound very cheerful—what's wrong with you?' Lizzie asked, looking at Amy's set expression.

'Nothing. I'm coming to stay with you.'

'That's nothing to look miserable about! I can tell you about me and Frank. Why are you coming?'

'Because Susannah doesn't want me around.'

'Oh. That's lucky—I thought she'd want you fetching and carrying for her.'

'So did I.'

Lizzie took a last gulp from her cup and stood up. 'I'll go and have a look at this baby.'

'Susannah mightn't want you to.'

'Of course she will. Women always want to show off their babies.'

Amy followed Lizzie down the passage and into the bedroom.

Susannah was sitting up with the baby at her breast while Edie sat on the bed close to her, adjusting the way Susannah held her new son.

'What are you doing here?' Susannah said, frowning at the two girls. 'I'm not on display, you know.'

'Now, Susannah, don't get upset—they just want to see the baby. He's had enough for now, anyway, I'll put him down again.' Edie took the baby in her arms and Susannah quickly buttoned her nightdress. 'Come and have a look, Lizzie,' Edie invited, and Lizzie stared at the child with mild interest as Edie laid him in the cradle.

'You've had a look, now go away—and take *her* with you,' Susannah said, indicating Amy.

'I think I'll go home now, Ma,' Lizzie said as if it had been her own idea. 'I'll tell Pa you'll be home for lunch.'

'All right, dear,' said Edie. Lizzie pulled Amy out of the room before her mother had time to tell her to take Ernie with her.

The girls were awake late that night, sharing whispers in the darkness as they lay close in Lizzie's bed. Amy was distracted from her sense of hurt by Lizzie's chattering. 'Frank came for lunch again on Saturday,' Lizzie said, and Amy could hear the smug satisfaction in her voice. 'That's the third time Pa's asked him now.'

'He's starting to be quite a member of the family, isn't he?' Amy said, trying hard not to giggle.

'He's getting there. He hardly says a word to me—'

'I don't suppose you give him much chance.'

'Of course I do, but he's so shy, if I said nothing he'd be embarrassed. Don't interrupt all the time. He doesn't say much, but he *looks* a lot—and he enjoys a good meal.'

'So is he going to come regularly now?'

Lizzie gave a snort of annoyance. 'I don't know yet. It's up to Pa to ask him—so far, anyway—and I don't like talking to Pa about it.'

'Why not?'

'Well, when I did just casually mention it, he started making smart remarks about how there's no need for me to panic, I won't be an old maid for a year or two yet, and I don't need to run after Frank because he won't run away very fast, and—what's so funny?' she said, sensing Amy's smothered giggles.

'You, that's what. Uncle Arthur's a bit sharper than you gave him credit for, isn't he?'

'Humph!' Lizzie said in disgust. 'He certainly *thinks* he's very clever. Anyway, the main thing is he's getting used to seeing Frank around the place. Frank'll stop being scared of me if I give him time.'

'And you've got plenty of time,' Amy said, trying to sound serious. 'Like Uncle Arthur said, you won't be an old maid for at least another year.'

'Careful, girl, none of your cheek,' Lizzie growled in a fair imitation of her father's voice, and she gave Amy the gentlest of slaps on the arm. 'It's a pity that baby's a boy,' she said, switching subjects abruptly.

'It doesn't matter,' Amy said with a shrug. 'I'm used to brothers.'

'I suppose it doesn't, really. Now I come to think about it, it'd be at least five years before a girl would be old enough to be any use to you, and you'll probably be married by then.'

'Don't start that, Lizzie. You worry about yourself, leave me out of it.'

'Oh, I'll definitely be married by then. Good grief, I'll be twenty! Even if Pa gets really stupid about it and wants me to wait, I'm sure he'll let me get married when I'm eighteen. Your father's so soft-hearted, he'd probably let you when you're sixteen.'

'Lizzie! Don't go on about it, I'm not very interested.' *I want to be a teacher.*

'Hey, maybe we could get married together!' Lizzie said in a new burst of enthusiasm.

Amy decided to play Lizzie at her own game for a change. 'What a wonderful idea—are you going to organise Ben for me when you get Frank sorted out?'

'Ben? I didn't know you were interested in Ben—it won't be very easy to talk him round… are you trying to be funny?'

'Yes,' Amy admitted. 'Figuring out how to court Ben would be a bit much even for you. But can't you just see the two of them side-by-side at the altar waiting for us? Frank'd be trying to figure out if it was too late to run away and hide, and Ben—'

'Ben would be saying you'd be all right as long as you stayed in the kitchen day and night and never said a word,' Lizzie interrupted, her voice rising in mirth.

The two of them dissolved into fits of giggles, until they were silenced by a thump on the wall. 'Settle down, you two,' they heard Arthur call, and Amy pressed her face into the pillow to muffle her laughter.

Susannah had decided her son was to be called Thomas James, after her own father and brother, and Jack seemed happy to let her please herself over the names. When Thomas was three weeks old and Susannah had taken her first tentative excursions out of the bedroom, she announced that she wanted to have a tea party to show off her new son. Amy made the nicest cakes and biscuits she knew how to, and Jack was given the job of delivering Susannah's invitations to the chosen women.

On the appointed afternoon, Amy helped Susannah settle herself comfortably in the best armchair, Thomas on her lap, before the guests arrived. It was a small group that assembled in the Leith's parlour. Edie was there with little Ernie, and Lizzie had invited herself. Bessie Aitken's mother Rachel brought her younger two children (Bessie was at school); Amy, whose eyes had grown sharper to the signs, thought Rachel might be expecting a fourth baby. With Rachel came her friend and neighbour Marion Forster, with her own two-year-old son.

After serving the tea and cakes, Amy and Lizzie took over the task of supervising the four toddlers in a corner of the parlour, where the women soon ignored their presence. The girls plied the children with cakes, which kept them remarkably quiet if not clean. Amy resigned herself to giving the rugs an extra-good beating later.

'He's a fine, healthy-looking boy,' Rachel said, brushing Thomas' cheek with her hand. 'You must be relieved it's all over.' She smiled at Susannah with the sympathy of shared pains.

'Oh, yes,' Susannah said with feeling. 'I had a terrible time of it—I thought I was going to die.'

'Worst pain in the world, soonest forgotten,' Edie said complacently. 'The pain's nothing much with chloroform, anyway—having Ernie was no trouble, not when I think about Annie and me delivering one another's babies with nothing to help. Now *that* was pain.'

'I didn't have any till it was nearly over,' Susannah said huffily.

'You had it as soon as it was safe—you don't know how long it was after that, you were asleep, you silly girl.' Edie smiled at her, but Susannah did not return the smile.

'We're lucky there's things to help nowadays,' Marion agreed. 'Things are much easier for women now.'

Thomas started to cry, and Susannah opened her bodice and put him to her breast. 'I'll be glad when this part's over and he can eat solid food. When will that be, Edie?'

'Well, you can start giving him a bit of milky gruel when he's five or six months old, but you'll want to keep feeding him yourself for a year.'

'A whole year! Oh, no, I can't put up with that,' Susannah said firmly.

'I always feed mine for at least a year,' Rachel said in her shy way. 'I think it's better for them—and it's certainly better for me.'

'I fed Bobby for a year and a half,' Marion chimed in. 'It's no bother, really.'

'Ugh! It's so… well, undignified. It'll ruin my figure, too, a child dragging at me like this.'

'There's one thing that'd ruin your figure faster than that, Susannah—that's having a child every year. Best way of spreading them out is to keep on feeding him yourself as long as you can.' Edie sounded very certain.

'Really?' Susannah looked more interested. 'Is that how it works?'

'Oh, yes. You hardly ever hear of a woman getting with child while she's still feeding the last one.'

'That's how I've put off having another one this long,' said Marion.

'It's how I've got two years between all mine, too,' Rachel added.

'Oh. Well, I suppose I can put up with it, then.'

'Of course you can slow them down a bit by fiddling about with calendars and dates,' Edie said vaguely. 'It's no good young women like you trying that, though. Wait until you've been married a few more years, Susannah, and I'll tell you about that.'

Edie leaned towards the other women and spoke more quietly. 'I had a bit of a fright myself last month,' she said in a conspiratorial tone. 'The bleeding was a couple of weeks late—I'm never sure exactly when it's coming, I always forget to make a note of the date when I get it, but I know it was late. It gave me quite a turn, I can tell you—another baby at my age.'

Lizzie's eyes opened wide at her mother's words, and she turned to Amy with a horrified expression. 'Oh, no!' she mouthed silently.

'I'd be nearly forty when it was born. Of course, I wouldn't mind too much myself.' She smiled fondly at little Thomas, who was still sucking greedily. 'Arthur would've gone crook, though—he reckoned he was a bit past putting up with babies when Ernie came along. Not that he isn't sweet with the little fellow most of the time.'

'You're not, are you?' Susannah asked, looking rather disapproving.

'No,' Edie said, and it was hard to tell if she were more relieved or disappointed. 'The bleeding turned up in the end. No, I think it meant the opposite, really—I'm about finished with having babies, and I won't be getting the bleeding much longer.' Lizzie gave an exaggerated, though silent, sigh of relief.

'I've got another child coming,' Rachel said shyly. 'I think I'm going to have a big family—I'm only twenty-four now.'

'You must have married very young,' Susannah said, turning to her with a slight frown.

'Yes, I was only seventeen. That's too young, really, I think eighteen's soon enough. Matt was older, he was twenty-five, so at least one of us was grown up.' She smiled ruefully. 'I don't think he'll let our girls get married before they're eighteen.'

Lizzie pulled a face. 'That's just what Ma needs to hear, I *don't* think,' she whispered to Amy.

'She'll have forgotten by the time she gets home,' Amy whispered back.

For a time Susannah appeared to enjoy the status a new baby gave her among other women, but the novelty of the baby soon seemed to wear off. Amy found there were unpleasant tasks involved in caring for a child, and as nasty smells and messes upset city-bred Susannah far more than they did Amy, the girl took on much of the napkin-washing and cleaning up of vomit that Thomas generated. Susannah seemed to be tired most of the time; even when Thomas started sleeping through the night, when he was four months old, he still woke much earlier in the morning than his mother would have chosen. Amy now always brought Susannah a cup of tea when Jack had got up, and she got into the habit of taking the baby out to the kitchen with her after Susannah had given him his first feed of the day so that her stepmother could doze for an extra half hour. Thomas seemed content to gurgle to himself in the nest of blankets Amy made for him in a warm corner of the kitchen until his mother emerged to take charge of him again.

Susannah's mother had sent parcels of beautifully embroidered baby gowns, more ornamental than useful, when Susannah had written to let her parents know they had a new grandchild. One day in early December, while Amy was holding Thomas and Susannah was having her morning tea, Jack brought home another parcel. Susannah was at first delighted over the delicate lacy shawl that emerged, but when she read the letter that had been tucked into the shawl she made a sound of dismay.

'Oh no! It's not fair!'

'What's wrong?' Jack asked. 'Not bad news from your mother?'

'Yes... no... oh, it's just not fair. Constance and Henry have got a new house—in Judges Bay!'

'Is that bad?' Amy asked.

'It's just the nicest part of Auckland, that's all,' Susannah said, obviously close to tears. 'My sister living in Judges Bay, and I'm in this dump.' Thomas stirred in Amy's arms and began to cry, and Susannah snatched him up to carry him off to the bedroom, where she could feed him in privacy. 'I'm turning into an old frump, stuck out here with this little parasite draining my strength and ruining my figure,' she flung over her shoulder as she stalked out of the kitchen. Amy and Jack looked at each other, then went about their work. An unspoken agreement had evolved between them not to discuss Susannah's more unreasonable outbursts.

Even Susannah now considered the elaborate dresses she had brought from Auckland too fussy for the country during the height of summer, and she had taken to wearing plainer cotton ones around the house. She found the hot, dusty trip into town too much to bear more than once a week, and on particularly humid Sundays she even felt unable to go to church. Throughout January Amy thought Susannah seemed worried about something, but she knew better than to pry. One February morning when Amy went into Susannah's room to bring her cup of tea and take Thomas away, she found Susannah standing in her nightdress in front of her open wardrobe, stroking her dresses and looking at them with an expression that was almost hungry.

Amy put the cup on Susannah's bedside table and went over to stand beside her. 'Those dresses are really beautiful,' she said softly. 'It'll be nice to see you wearing them again this winter.'

'I hope so,' Susannah said. There was a catch in her voice that puzzled Amy, but Susannah's feelings were so often a mystery that she thought little of it. 'They're all I've got left.'

'You could get some more.'

'That's not what I meant. They're all that's left from how I used to be, before I got like this.' There was a silence between them, then Susannah got back into bed and picked up her teacup.

Amy picked Thomas up and carried him from the room. She was not sure why Susannah seemed so desperately unhappy, but she thought perhaps she understood just a little of her stepmother's longing for the life she had led in Auckland.

Amy was playing with Thomas, who was just learning to push himself up on his hands to look around, in the kitchen after breakfast when Susannah came out. 'Look after him for me, I'm going out for a little while,' she said.

'Where are you going?' Amy asked in surprise, but Susannah went to the porch and put her boots on without a word, then closed the door firmly behind her.

'Where's your ma?' Jack asked when he came in for morning tea. He took his little son onto his lap. 'Not still in bed, is she?'

'No, she got up quite early and went out—I don't know where she's gone, she didn't say,' said Amy.

Jack sighed. 'I wonder what's got into her now—she's not usually much of a one for taking walks, especially in this heat. Oh well, the fresh air might do her some good—she's inclined to spend too much time inside moping.' He sniffed. 'The air's not too sweet in here, what's that?' He felt gingerly at Thomas' napkin. 'Hmm, I think this little fellow needs cleaning up.'

'I'll change him, Pa.' Amy scooped up the baby and took him to Jack and Susannah's room. When he had a clean napkin on she thought he looked sleepy, so she laid him down in his cradle and crept out of the room, closing the door softly.

She was almost back at the kitchen when she heard the outside door open and close. Amy could tell from the tread that it was Susannah, and she stopped in the passage near the open door, unsure whether to go into the kitchen or not.

'Where've you been?' she heard her father ask. 'Amy said you rushed off somewhere and wouldn't tell her where you were going.'

I didn't say it like that, Amy thought in mild irritation.

'I don't have to ask that child's permission to step outside the door, do I?' Susannah sounded barely in control, and Amy's heart sank.

'Of course you don't, we just wondered where you were—have you been crying, Susannah?' Amy heard her father's step as he crossed the floor.

'Don't touch me!' Susannah flung at him, but she went on more quietly. 'I've been to see Edie to ask her about what's happening to me. Things didn't seem right, not like how she said they'd be. And they're not right. All that talk about how it couldn't happen while I had all the unpleasantness of feeding him myself—it wasn't true.' She fell silent for a few moments. 'I'm with child again.'

'That's nothing to be upset about!' Jack said, delight in his voice.

'Yes, trust you to think that,' Susannah said bitterly. 'Just like one of your cows, regular as clockwork every August. Well, I'm not one of your cows, and I don't want to be treated like one. I'm not going to put up with it, do you hear?'

'Now, Susannah, there's no need to talk like that. It's a bit sooner than you thought, but that just means the little ones will be good playmates for each other. You would've had another one soon enough, anyway— what difference does it make whether there's one year between them or two?'

'Take your hands off me!' Susannah screamed. She rushed from the room, too abruptly for Amy to make a dash for her own bedroom.

Susannah came face to face with her and stopped in her tracks.

114

'Listening at keyholes, were you?' she said, her voice raw with suppressed weeping, then she pushed past Amy and disappeared into her bedroom. She slammed the door after her, and Amy heard Thomas start crying, but the baby's wails were soon drowned by his mother's.

12

February – December 1883

It seemed to Amy that the remaining months of Susannah's second pregnancy were like living the previous year all over again. With this baby being due just a year after Thomas's birth, Susannah was at the same stage each month as she had been exactly twelve months beforehand.

There were differences, though. This time Susannah went into her sack-like dresses and stopped leaving the house in her fifth month with only minor complaints. And of course this year Thomas was there. Susannah weaned him at six months; when she announced this to Edie, the older woman sighed and agreed.

'Yes, you've got to, really. It's a bit early for the little fellow, but you'll need all your strength for the new baby.'

'That's got nothing to do with it,' said Susannah. 'I'd be giving up that unpleasantness anyway, even if I did have the strength to do both. I don't see why I should put up with it if it's not going to do me any good.'

Thomas continued to grow and thrive, even without his mother's grudged milk, and Amy enjoyed playing with him as he became more responsive.

'Makes me feel young again, having a baby around the place,' Jack would say as he bounced the child on his knee.

'It makes me feel old,' was Susannah's muttered reply.

There was something different about Susannah this year, Amy thought. She still had tantrums and fits of weeping, but far fewer than when she was carrying Thomas. As her pregnancy wore on, Susannah was more and more inclined to wear an expression of grim determination, as though screwing up her courage to make a difficult decision. Amy decided Susannah was probably frightened again about the birth, even though Aunt Edie had said her stepmother wouldn't be nervous after she had had one baby.

Amy was confirmed in May that year, when the Bishop made his annual visit to Ruatane. Lizzie had delayed her own confirmation so that the cousins could be confirmed together, which meant Lizzie was the oldest of the ten candidates. Two weeks before confirmation Mrs Leveston, the wife of Ruatane's Resident Magistrate and the self-appointed arbiter of style for the town, invited the girls of the confirmation class to her house for a Thursday afternoon tea.

'She thinks she's giving us wild colonial girls a taste of civilisation,' Lizzie said, with more truth than she knew. But both girls enjoyed the prospect of an outing and seeing the inside of what was probably the most elegant house in Ruatane.

Arthur dropped the girls off at the Leveston's house in good time on the appointed day. 'I'll pick you up in a couple of hours when I've finished in town. Watch yourselves, don't disgrace the family,' he said as he drove off.

'As if we would,' said Lizzie. She led the way up the drive with a determined stride.

The house was not large, no bigger than Amy's home, but the garden had a manicured perfection that betrayed the fact that Mr Leveston employed two gardeners. Dotted about the lawn were rose beds, unfortunately without roses at this time of year, but filled with marigolds and violas to give colour. Other beds were planted in lavender, which gave off a sweet scent as the girls walked past, or in tall larkspurs and mignonette with lobelias and alyssum around the edges. A huge lilac tree had pride of place in the centre of the lawn, with several rhododendrons and camellias around it. The gravel drive ran around the edge of the garden, right up to the front door, with a border of petunias all along its length.

When Lizzie rapped on the door it was opened by a maid wearing a dark dress and a white cap and apron. Both girls stared at her, never having seen such a thing as a uniformed servant before. 'Come through to the drawing room, ladies,' the maid said, and Amy very nearly looked around to see where the 'ladies' were. But she collected herself, and with Lizzie followed the maid a short way down a wide passage then into a room that overlooked the beautiful front garden.

'You're the first ones to arrive,' the maid said. 'I'll tell the mistress you're here,' she added as she left the room.

'I told Pa he was bringing us too early—he never takes any notice of me,' Lizzie grumbled, but Amy hardly heard her. The room was taking her whole attention.

'Did you ever see such a place,' Amy said in a voice little above a whisper. 'It's just so *elegant*. Look at these things.' She walked over to the fireplace with its marble surrounds, and looked at herself in the ornate gold-framed mirror that hung above the mantel. An elaborate clock with the figures of young women either side of it and a glass dome over the whole, was in the centre of the mantelpiece, with a heavy silver candlestick on either side. Silver-framed photographs and several porcelain vases shared the rest of the mantelpiece.

Amy turned from the fireplace and looked around the rest of the room, exclaiming over the delicate china figures that sat on a small table around a vase decorated with painted flowers and gold leaf, then studying a painting of a young woman who bore an expression of rapture as she rose from a man's lap. 'Isn't that gorgeous?' she said at the sight of a magnificent candelabra that hung from the ceiling.

'Mmm,' Lizzie said dubiously. 'It looks nice, but what an awful thing to dust.'

'Don't be so *practical*, Lizzie,' Amy scolded. 'Oh, look at this beautiful piano!' She rushed over to the Brinsmead that dominated one corner of the room and ran her fingers lightly over the polished wood. 'Wouldn't you just love to have beautiful things like these?' she asked, turning a glowing face towards her cousin.

'What's the point in hankering after things you're never going to get?' Lizzie said, in a down-to-earth way Amy found maddening. 'It only vexes you. Let's face it, Amy, we're not from the sort of family that has pianos.'

'There's no harm in dreaming, is there?' The piano drew Amy to it. She raised the lid and laid her fingers very gently on the exposed ivory keys, too softly to make a sound.

'It's a lovely instrument, we brought it out from Home,' came an English-accented voice from close behind her. Amy quickly put the piano lid down, took a step backwards and turned guiltily. Mrs Leveston had entered the room without the girls noticing; despite her plumpness she could move very quietly. 'Do you play, my dear?'

'Ah, no, I don't,' Amy said, feeling her face reddening. 'I've never learned.'

'Oh, you should,' Mrs Leveston said. Her elegant voice and dumpy figure seemed oddly mismatched. 'Look at those lovely graceful fingers of yours, I'm sure you must be musical.' She took Amy's unresisting hand in her own, and turned it over to expose the palm. Amy felt the cream lace at the cuffs of Mrs Leveston's lilac silk dress brush against her wrist. 'But look at the state of it,' the woman exclaimed, seeing Amy's rough, broken skin. She took the other hand as well and put the guilty palms side by side. 'You're not looking after your skin properly, my dear. These hands of yours are spending too much time in water.'

'Well, there's the washing, you see,' Amy said. 'Especially now we've got the baby. And the dishes. And all the scrubbing, of course.'

'Don't you have a servant for the rough work?' Mrs Leveston asked.

'No, only me,' Amy said. 'And Susa... I mean my stepmother,' she added hastily.

'Hmm. Well, if you must get them wet all the time, make sure you dry your hands thoroughly. And every night you should rub glycerine and lemon juice into them. That will keep them soft and white. Do you understand?'

'Yes, Mrs Leveston, thank you. I'll try and remember.'

'Good. Now—' But Mrs Leveston was interrupted by the maid announcing the arrival of more girls, and any further advice she might have had for Amy was forgotten.

The next two hours passed in a succession of cups of tea, tiny sandwiches and dainty cakes. 'These things don't fill you up unless you have half a dozen of everything,' Lizzie muttered to Amy, but Amy frowned her into silence. Then the visitors were given a tour around the gardens, with Mrs Leveston explaining each tree and shrub to them in great detail.

Arthur tilted his hat politely to Mrs Leveston when he arrived to collect the girls. 'Good day, ma'am. I hope they've behaved themselves?' he asked, earning a scowl from Lizzie.

'Oh, they've been a pleasure to have,' Mrs Leveston assured him. She gave the girls a delicate wave as the buggy moved off.

'It must be wonderful to live in a place like that,' Amy said dreamily as they jolted along the inland track. 'All those beautiful things to look at.'

'Mmm, and nothing to do except give orders and watch other people work,' said Lizzie.

'You'll have to find someone fancier than Frank Kelly to set your cap at if you want to be one of the idle rich,' Arthur put in from the front of the buggy, startling the girls, who had almost forgotten his presence.

'Who said I wanted it?' Lizzie said tartly, and they heard Arthur chuckle to himself.

The new baby arrived in August, just as Thomas had the previous year, and to complete the pattern it was another boy, this time given the name George. Susannah did not want a tea party this year, but Edie came to visit, with Lizzie at her heels, when George was a few days old and Susannah was still confined to bed.

'Another boy,' Edie said, looking at the tiny figure in his cradle. 'Jack'll always have a houseful of sons at this rate.'

Little George started to make a mewling cry. 'He's hungry, pass him to me, would you, Edie?' Susannah said, unbuttoning her nightdress. Edie laid the baby in Susannah's arms and watched as he began to suckle.

'Now, you will feed this one for a whole year, won't you?' she said.

'You stopped a bit soon with Thomas. I know you had to, but you should be all right this time.'

'No,' Susannah said flatly. 'I'll feed him till he's old enough for ordinary food, that's all.'

'But Susannah, you're sure to have another one next year if you don't feed him yourself, and you made enough fuss over this one coming so fast.'

'I'm not going to have any more children.'

'That's easy to say,' Edie laughed. 'They come along whether you plan them or not—especially if you're so set on not feeding him.'

'It didn't work last time, did it?' Susannah flung at her. The child stirred in her arms, and she transferred him to her other breast. Susannah's eyes went to her wardrobe, then back to Edie. 'My dresses are still hanging up in there, Edie, just like you said they'd be—hanging there getting out-of-date. Well, next winter they're not going to just be hanging up—I'm going to wear them. I'm not going to be fat and frumpy. I'm not going to have any more babies, and that's that.'

'We'll see,' said Edie.

Amy and Lizzie left the room unnoticed and went out to the kitchen. 'What do you think she means about not having any more babies?' Lizzie asked. 'Ma doesn't seem to think she can get out of having them.'

Amy shrugged. 'How should I know? Susannah seems pretty certain about it.'

Even if she had wanted to, Susannah could not accompany Jack on his weekly visits to town for supplies before George was content to be fed less frequently. One Thursday morning in October when Jack had gone to town, Susannah sat in the kitchen, drumming her fingers absently on the table top while Amy prepared lunch. The babies were both asleep in the bedroom; George in his cradle and Thomas in his little bed under the window. Amy glanced at her stepmother from time to time, puzzled at the woman's strange silence. Susannah's eyes had an odd, inward-looking expression, as though she were having a silent conversation with herself, and Amy found it disconcerting.

It was a relief when her father arrived home. He was carrying an armload of parcels, plus a letter that he put on the table in front of Susannah. Amy took charge of the food her father had brought home and started to put the things away while Jack sat down beside Susannah.

'You all right, Susannah? You're very quiet today,' he said, putting his hand over hers.

She pushed his hand away and reached for the letter. 'I'm tired. I'm

120

always tired. Oh, it's a letter from Mother.' She roused a little as she opened the letter. 'Constance has had another daughter,' she said when she had reached the bottom of the first closely-written page. 'Of course she has Mother there to help her when she has babies,' she added bitterly. 'She doesn't live at the back of nowhere. She has a nursemaid to look after her children, too.'

'Well, you've got Amy,' said Jack, and Susannah flashed him a look that would have warned a wiser man into silence. 'Amy's better than some stranger.'

'That's a matter of opinion.' Susannah went back to her letter. 'Oh!' she said when she had read on a little further. She put the letter down and looked at Jack with a softer expression. 'Oh, Jack, Mother says James would like to come down and stay with us this summer. Could he? Please? I'd *love* to have him come and stay.'

'Your young brother, eh?' Jack said. 'I don't see why not, we can always use a bit of extra help over the summer, what with haymaking and everything. He could bunk in with one of the boys.' He put his arm around Susannah's shoulders, and she made to push it away, then seemed to change her mind and let it stay there. 'Do you think it might cheer you up a bit to see him?' Jack asked.

'I'm sure it would,' Susannah said, looking positively happy. Amy tried to remember the last time she had seen Susannah so animated; not since before Thomas was born, she was sure. 'It'll be wonderful to hear all the news and catch up on the latest fashions and things. I've missed James so much, too, we were always specially close. I'm going to write to Mother straight away to tell her you've said James can come.' She rewarded Jack with a radiant smile, then slipped out from under his arm and went off to the bedroom with the letter to write her reply.

Jack followed her with his eyes, a soft smile playing around his mouth. 'That's brightened her up, hasn't it?'

'Yes, Pa.'

'She's been crook since George arrived, it really seemed to take it out of her, even worse than Tom did. Jimmy seemed a pleasant enough lad when I was staying at their house, he should fit in with us all right. It's worth it to see her happy, eh, girl?'

'It's only one more to cook for, that won't make much difference,' Amy said, but she couldn't help feeling apprehensive about what it would be like to have a male version of Susannah to put up with all summer. *I hope he's better tempered than she is. And I hope he doesn't decide to hate me like she seems to.*

*

121

'Guess what?' Lizzie said when she came over to see Amy the following week. The two of them were leading Thomas up the hill behind Amy's house, walking slowly to keep to the toddler's hesitant pace. 'Frank and I went for a walk together when he came over on Saturday—that's the first time!'

Amy laughed. 'Well done! I expect you'll be announcing your engagement any time now. Where did you go?'

'Well,' Lizzie said, 'it wasn't very far, really—but it was still a walk.'

Her evasiveness made Amy suspicious. 'Go on, Lizzie, tell me—where did you go?'

'Oh, if you're going to nag about it—we went down to feed the pigs. Frank carried the slops bucket for me, though,' she added quickly. 'Stop laughing.'

'I can't help it,' Amy said, hardly able to speak for laughter. 'You're so funny. Did he give you a kiss by the pig sty?'

'I won't answer that,' Lizzie said with a toss of her head.

'That means he didn't. I expect he was too shy with all those pigs watching.'

'Humph! I suppose you think that's funny. We're not up to kissing yet, I'll have you know. It'll be a while before I'll let him do that. I don't want Frank to think I'm a loose woman.'

'I don't know about *letting* him, Lizzie—you might have to do it for him.'

'I don't think so,' Lizzie said, suddenly thoughtful. 'On Saturday I caught him looking at me, and I sort of got this feeling he wanted to... I don't know, hold my hand or something.'

'Hmm, you'd better watch him, then,' Amy said with mock seriousness. Thomas let out a cry; Amy looked down and saw that he had bumped his foot against a stone. 'Oh, Tommy, poor baby.' She snatched him up and cuddled him until he stopped crying. The little boy seemed tired, so Amy decided to carry him the rest of the way.

'Aunt Susannah didn't seem as grumpy as usual today,' Lizzie said. 'What's cheered her up?'

Amy grimaced. 'Her brother's coming to stay in December. He's going to be here all summer.'

'Ugh,' Lizzie said. 'Fancy having two lots of Susannah around. You'd better come and stay at our place.'

'I can't do that, I've got too much to do here. It'll be even worse with another man to feed. Anyway, you'll probably be too busy with Frank to want me around.'

'Maybe. I'll still have time to keep an eye on you, don't you worry.'

'It's you who'll need an eye kept on if Frank's going to go wild,' Amy said. She screamed as Lizzie made a grab at her. 'No, Lizzie, don't tickle me, not when I'm holding Tommy—I'll drop him.'

'Don't be so rude, then,' Lizzie growled.

Susannah became more and more excited as her brother's arrival drew closer. Jack watched her in fond indulgence. 'You're like a child waiting for Christmas,' he said.

'I haven't had anything nice happen for so long, of course I'm looking forward to it,' Susannah answered. Amy looked at her father to see if that had hurt him, but he was still smiling affectionately.

'It's next week!' Susannah said at the end of November. 'I'm going to make all his favourite cakes. He especially likes gingerbread—and currant cakes, too.' She bustled about, taking more interest in the kitchen than she had for many months.

'It's tomorrow!' she said the following Tuesday at breakfast. 'Now, where's he going to sleep?'

'He can share with me, I don't mind,' John said, surprising Amy. John had become steadily more silent around the house over the last two years, as Susannah became more difficult.

'Oh. That's good of you, John, thank you,' Susannah said. 'Though perhaps it would be nice for James to have a room to himself?' She glanced at Harry, and he glared back with a look of such open hostility that she quailed before it. 'I suppose it doesn't matter, really,' she added hastily.

The next afternoon Susannah was ready to leave for town long before she needed to be, and she kept casting anxious glances at the clock as Jack lingered comfortably over his pudding. 'Are you sure it's not time to leave yet?' she asked repeatedly.

'Don't worry, the lad won't go anywhere till we get there,' Jack said as he finished his cup of tea. 'The boat won't be tying up for a couple of hours yet, anyway.' But to humour Susannah he agreed to leave an hour earlier than he thought was necessary. He helped Susannah into the buggy, where Amy placed a sleeping George on her lap, then Amy held Thomas and encouraged him to wave as the buggy disappeared down the road.

'They've gone to fetch your uncle,' Amy told Thomas as she carried him back inside, and the oblivious toddler chortled at her.

Jack and Susannah were gone all afternoon. Amy had the table set and the roast keeping warm by the time she heard the buggy rattle up the road. She steeled herself to be polite to the intruder.

123

The back door opened, and Susannah walked in clutching her brother's arm with one hand while she held George in her other arm. Jack came in at their heels. 'Here we are!' said Susannah. 'Oh, this is Amy,' she added carelessly. 'Amy, this is James.'

'Jimmy,' he said quickly. 'I prefer "Jimmy". You and Mother—and Constance, of course—are the only ones who call me James, and I've given up trying to get you to change.' The fond smile he gave Susannah took any sting out of his words.

The next moment Amy found his smile turned on her, and it was such an infectiously friendly smile that she found herself returning it. Jimmy was tall and slim, like Susannah, and like his sister he had dark brown hair and blue eyes. He was much younger, though; probably about twenty, Amy decided. She had assumed he would be in his late twenties, like Susannah.

'Hello, Amy,' Jimmy said, putting down his Gladstone bag. He waited politely for her to offer her hand before extending his own to shake it. 'You're older than I expected—they talked about you as though you're six years old!'

'Everyone always does,' Amy said with a rueful smile.

'And this fine little fellow must be Thomas.' Thomas had decided to be shy, and he hid behind Amy's skirt, peering out cautiously. Jimmy crouched down to the little boy's level. 'Don't you want to say hello to your Uncle Jimmy?'

'Come on, Tommy,' Amy coaxed, and Thomas emerged to study the stranger more carefully. After a few moments he broke into a happy smile and let Jimmy hug him.

'I'll show you your room, James,' Susannah said, unloading George into Amy's arms. 'I'm afraid you'll have to share it with John.' She led Jimmy out of the room.

'I've had my ear bent all the way home,' Jack said, sitting down at the table. 'The two of them talking non-step—well, mainly your ma talking and Jimmy listening.' He smiled fondly. 'She's been a different woman since she knew young Jimmy was coming—I think she's starting to get her strength back.'

Amy soon saw what her father had meant. During dinner the conversation was completely dominated by Susannah asking questions about her family and her old acquaintances, with Jimmy doing his best to answer between mouthfuls. When Susannah stopped to take a breath Amy would leap in to offer Jimmy more food, and she was pleased to see that he seemed to enjoy the meal.

After dinner Susannah led Jimmy off to the parlour on her arm, and

Jack and his sons soon followed. Amy cleared the table and washed the dishes, then mixed the bread dough for the morning's baking and left it near the range to rise. She collected her sewing box from her bedroom and went through to the parlour, where she sat opposite Susannah and Jimmy, who were sharing a sofa. Her father smiled at her from his armchair, then buried his nose in the *Weekly News* again.

Amy pulled out the embroidered pillowslip she was working on and stitched away while she listened to Susannah and Jimmy talking about people she had never heard of. Susannah was in a lively mood, and she even laughed once or twice, something Amy could not remember ever hearing her do before. Jimmy had a pleasant voice, low-pitched and somehow always sounding as though there was laughter bubbling not far below the surface.

'I went to rather a good play the other week,' Jimmy said when Susannah had briefly run out of questions.

Before she had time to think, Amy burst out, 'A play! Oh, what was it?'

Susannah turned a disapproving stare on her, and Amy shrank back against the sofa, furious with herself for having spoken out of turn.

'It was—' Jimmy began, but Susannah interrupted him.

'Amy, it's time you went to bed. You've got to be up early in the morning, and you seem a little over-excited.'

'But it's only half-past seven!' Amy protested. 'I don't usually go to bed till—'

'Never mind that tonight you're going to bed at half-past seven. Off you go, be a good girl.'

Amy could see it was no use arguing. She put away her sewing, went to her father and gave him a goodnight kiss, then exchanged the barest brush of cheeks that passed for a kiss between Susannah and herself. 'Good night,' she said to Jimmy as she walked past him, and he gave her a smile that she thought just might be sympathetic.

'She's rather a spoiled child,' she heard Susannah say to Jimmy as she left the room. 'Take no notice of her.'

13

December 1883

On the morning of Jimmy's first full day on the farm, Amy came out to the kitchen to find him sitting at the table. He yawned dramatically and gave a rueful smile.

'Slept in too late to help with milking, I'm afraid,' he said. 'I think John gave me a nudge, but I was enjoying being asleep too much to take any notice. I'm not used to country hours yet.'

To her annoyance, Amy felt tongue-tied and shy. She wanted to make a good impression, but she would seem a real bumpkin if she just stood stupidly and looked at him.

'Would you like some breakfast?' she asked. He accepted, and even offered to help, which rather shocked her. She tried to refuse as graciously as she could, but Jimmy insisted on setting the table for her.

'If I can't be any use in the cow shed, at least I can give you a hand in the kitchen,' he said with a laugh, and Amy found herself laughing with him. It was pleasant to have company while she worked, and Jimmy was easy to talk to once she got over her initial hesitation. He seemed interested in the mundane details of her daily routine of house and farm work, wanting to know how she made butter and how many hens she had.

She served him breakfast and ate her own with him, then stacked their dishes on the bench while she prepared food for the men.

'Where's that lazy sister of mine?' asked Jimmy. 'Why isn't she out here helping you?'

'Oh, Susannah never gets up before eight,' said Amy. 'The babies wake her up in the night, so she gets very tired,' she added quickly, not wanting to appear critical of Jimmy's sister.

'And what about you—don't you get tired, getting up so early and working hard all day?'

'I'm used to it,' Amy said, a little embarrassed but at the same time flattered.

'Could you show me around the farm later?' Jimmy asked. 'I want to see it all and learn all about it.' He gave another of his engaging smiles. 'As much as I'm capable of learning, anyway.'

'I'd love to,' Amy said, her cheeks pink with pleasure.

So later that morning they explored the farm together. She showed him the cow shed and the barns, pointing out the wagons and machinery and explaining their uses. She prattled away, describing the haymaking that would soon start.

'First there's Christmas, there's usually a party just before that with everyone there, babies and old people and all. Then Boxing Day they start getting the hay in. Everyone works together, especially with the stacking. The men go around all the farms working on the haystacks. It takes weeks to do them all. There's often a dance after the haymaking's finished—a real one, with music and proper dancing and no children. I've never been to a hay dance, but Pa said I could this year.'

'Never been to one?' Jimmy asked, surprised. He looked at her more closely. 'How old are you, Amy?'

'I turned fifteen in October,' she said proudly.

'Only fifteen? And practically running the house, and you know so much about the farm—I thought you were seventeen at least,' Jimmy said. Amy glowed.

They walked up the hill behind the farmhouse. They had to climb over a gate on the way, and Jimmy put his hands around her waist to lift her down from it, holding her for a moment longer than was strictly necessary when he had put her back on the ground. He was puffing from the climb by the time they reached the top, and Amy had to slow her pace so he could keep up with her.

The day was brilliantly fine. From their vantage point they could see down the length of the valley to the broad sweep of the bay spreading out on both sides into the haze of distance.

'Don't you love the view?' Amy said. 'I feel as though I can see the whole world from here. I look out and pretend I can see all the way to America.'

'Yes, it certainly is a lovely sight. I suppose you can see all over the farm from here. Where does your property end?'

Amy dragged her gaze away from the inviting distance to point out the northern and southern boundaries. 'Uncle Arthur's farm starts beyond that row of trees there. On the other side, over here, Ch... I mean Mr Stewart's farm starts just where you can see that bend in the creek. You can't really see the other boundaries, one's over there in the bush, and the last one's on the far side of this hill. Oh, look!' she said excitedly, pointing down the valley at the blue ocean sparkling in the sun. 'There's the steamer just turning in towards the harbour. It's come from down the coast, and it goes all the way to Tauranga, then there's another boat that goes to Auckland. Oh, you know that, don't you?' she trailed off, feeling foolish. 'You came down on it just yesterday.'

'Yes, and I'm not a particularly good sailor, I'm afraid,' Jimmy said, wincing at the memory. 'Don't let that calm sea fool you—the wind can whip it up quick as a flash. I must admit I'm not really looking forward to the trip back.'

'You'll have to stay for ages, then,' Amy said, flashing him a smile. 'I hope you won't get bored, though—it'll seem dull here after Auckland.'

'I'm not finding it dull at all, with you looking after me,' Jimmy said, smiling back. 'And I think I'll stay here for quite a while. Perhaps I could go with you and your brothers to that dance you were telling me about?'

'That would be lovely,' said Amy.

She glanced at the sky; the angle of the sun told her the morning was nearly over. 'I need to get back to the house, there's lunch to get on,' she said, reluctant to end the moment. 'You can carry on looking around by yourself if you like.'

'No, I'll wait until you're not so busy,' Jimmy said, to her delight. 'I'll come down with you. I'd better spend some time with Susannah now, anyway.'

Susannah was bustling around the kitchen when they got back to the house.

'James, there you are!' she exclaimed. 'I wondered where you'd got to. Oh, how nice of you to keep Amy amused.' Amy felt her cheeks burn at being referred to as if she were a small child who needed entertaining. 'James and I want to talk now, dear, perhaps you could just finish things off for me here? That's a good girl. Come along, James, we'll sit on the verandah.'

Susannah swept off, dragging Jimmy in her wake, leaving Amy to make the lunch; she soon found Susannah had barely started on it. *That Susannah!* she thought angrily. Jimmy was being so nice, and he wouldn't want anything to do with her if Susannah made him think she was just a baby. She took her frustration out on the vegetables, and when the family assembled for lunch they found the eyes of the potatoes had been gouged out with particular savagery.

After lunch Jimmy went off with the men to move some stock, while Susannah and Amy worked on their weekly baking. The silence between them was even stiffer than usual, but they were busy enough with chopping, mixing, rolling and baking for the scene to appear companionable to anyone who didn't know them. Little Thomas played at their feet, from time to time begging for currants and scraps of dough, while Georgie had his afternoon sleep.

When the last batch of scones was in the oven Susannah sighed, took off her apron and hung it on a hook behind the kitchen door.

'I'm so tired, and it's too hot to be in here, anyway. Clear things up, please, Amy—I'm going to have a lie-down while George is asleep. Keep an eye on Thomas for me, would you?'

Amy gave a curt nod in acknowledgment. When she had put the kitchen in order she took Thomas out to the garden and picked some peas for the evening meal while the little boy played in the dirt, making hills and roads. He laughed in delight as he kicked down the highest of his hills, and Amy could not help smiling with him. He was a sweet child.

When the men came up from milking, John and Harry were each carrying two pails of milk while Jimmy and Jack had one large pail each. Jimmy's face was red and shining from the exertions of the afternoon, but he looked cheerful. Jack put his milk can down on the grass, picked Thomas up and threw him in the air, making the child chortle with glee.

'We'll make a farmer of this lad yet,' Jack said, slapping Jimmy on the back. 'He's got a good touch with the cows.'

Jimmy smiled in reply. 'No, I don't think I'm really cut out for a farmer, but it certainly is a good, healthy life. A month or two of this'll clear the smut of the city out of my lungs.'

'These two cans are for butter,' Jack explained to Jimmy, indicating the large pails. 'Take them to the dairy, would you? Amy will show you where they go, won't you, girl?'

She would, and gladly. Jimmy walked beside her to the cool, dark room a short way from the house, and poured the pails full of milk into a wide, shallow dish she pointed out to him.

'When are you going to make it into butter?' Jimmy asked as they walked back to the house.

'First thing tomorrow, before the day gets hot. If the weather's too warm the cream froths up in the churn and makes an awful mess, and the butter can take hours to come, so at this time of year I start it around six o'clock.'

He raised his eyes heavenward in mock horror at the notion of starting work so early, then broke into a chuckle, and Amy laughed with him. She seemed to be doing a lot more laughing since Jimmy had arrived.

The next morning when she went out to the dairy, she was astonished to find Jimmy there before her.

'I still didn't manage to get up early enough for milking,' he said, 'but I thought I could watch you make the butter, if you don't think I'll be in the way.'

'Of course not—I'd like to have you here. I haven't got all that much to make today, I made the extra for selling on Tuesday.'

'Selling?' Jimmy repeated. 'You mean you have time to earn money for the family as well as all the work you do around the house? You keep this whole place going single-handed, don't you?'

'Not really.' Amy smiled at the outrageous suggestion. 'There's money from potatoes and maize, and we sell calves for meat. Pigs sometimes, too. The butter and cheese I make only fetches a few shillings a week, but it all helps. I enjoy doing it, really.'

'You're quite a girl, aren't you?' Jimmy said, and Amy felt a warm glow from his admiration. She had never thought of herself as anything special.

Jimmy watched as she carefully skimmed off the cream that had formed overnight and put it into a churn. She cranked the handle until it was turning over steadily. The turning of the churn was a rhythmical motion that took strength but not much concentration, and left her mind free to wander. Amy was used to doing a lot of her thinking during her twice-weekly butter making, but today she had Jimmy to talk to instead.

'Granny always said the more you try and hurry butter or men, the more of a muddle things get into,' Amy said, smiling at the memory. 'She was right about the butter, anyway. You just have to be patient.'

Jimmy watched her turn the handle for some time, then asked if he could try. He was clearly surprised at the effort needed to work the churn. He grunted away at it for a few minutes, then Amy gently pushed his hands off the handle.

'Let me,' she said. 'It takes a bit of getting used to.'

Jimmy sat down heavily on a bench against the wall, took a handkerchief from his jacket pocket and mopped his brow.

'It certainly does. You must be strong, for all you look so small and dainty.'

Amy was unsure whether this was a compliment or not. Being dainty sounded nice, but being strong was not particularly ladylike.

'I suppose we seem a bit coarse to you,' she said wistfully, 'after all the fine people you mix with in the city.'

'Oh, no.' Jimmy got to his feet and walked over to her. 'Not you, anyway—there's nothing coarse about you, little lady.' He stood looking down at Amy with such an openly admiring stare that she felt a blush creeping up her face. She lowered her eyes from his gaze, aware of a surge of pleasure mixed with embarrassment; she tried to hide her awkwardness by turning the churn furiously. For once she was disappointed that the butter came quickly.

Jimmy helped her turn the butter out onto a marble slab, and she began working away at the mass with a pair of butter pats.

'This takes ages,' she warned, 'and you're probably getting bored, anyway. Don't feel you have to stay here with me.' *Please don't go away*, she begged silently.

'I can't think of anywhere I'd rather be,' he said, again fixing her with that disconcerting stare.

So Jimmy stayed with her while she worked at the butter, removing every trace of buttermilk from the mass and afterwards washing and salting it. He carried the shallow dish of skimmed milk to the pig sty, with Amy at his side, and poured it into the trough. They leaned over the rails and laughed at the pigs' excitement as the animals pushed their snouts noisily into the milk. Back at the dairy Jimmy poured the buttermilk into one of the milk cans. This time Amy insisted on helping, so they put one hand each on the handle and carried it between them.

'What do you use the buttermilk for?' Jimmy asked.

'Haven't you ever tasted buttermilk?' He shook his head. 'Well, you're in for a treat, then. Buttermilk's lovely, especially on a hot day. I'll pour you a mug when we get this inside, and you can see how you like it, then I might make some buttermilk scones later if I have time.'

Jimmy's hand slid along the handle as they walked, so that it rested against Amy's. She held hers very still, savouring the contact. When they reached the kitchen and lifted the pail onto the table he gave her hand a tiny squeeze, so slight that she was not sure whether it was deliberate. She poured him the promised mug of buttermilk, and he pronounced it delicious.

'What are you going to do now?' he asked.

'Make you some breakfast first of all!' Amy said with a laugh. 'I left plenty keeping warm on the side of the range before I went down to the dairy, but those greedy pigs must have eaten it all when they came back from the cow shed—they haven't left us any! Then I'll do the rugs, Friday's my day for cleaning them, and after lunch I'll sweep the floors and wash some of the windows.'

As she spoke she cut slices of bacon and placed them in a frying pan. The big loaves of bread had finished baking while she was in the dairy; she put them on the table to cool, then cooked eggs to go with the bacon. She set the kettle on the range, then sat down with Jimmy to eat. The house was quiet; Susannah had not yet appeared, and her father and brothers had gone off somewhere on the farm after breakfasting. It seemed very cosy with just the two of them.

'It makes me tired just hearing about your day,' Jimmy said. 'How do you clean the rugs?'

Amy pointed to a carpet beater standing ready against the wall.

'I hang them over the clothesline and give them a pounding with that.

It really gets the dust jumping,' she said with housewifely pride.

'Oh, yes, I've seen Mother's servant use one of those on our rugs. I thought you might have some special country method!'

'No,' said Amy, 'I suppose dirt's dirt, in the country or the town.'

Susannah chose that moment to appear on the scene. She poured the tea and sat down at the table with them, refusing Amy's offer to cook more food for her.

'No, my head is just *too* bad this morning. I'll just have some tea.'

'No wonder you're so thin,' Jimmy remarked, startling Amy.

Susannah gave him a disapproving look. 'Don't make personal remarks, dear. I do hope you're not picking up rough country manners.'

Jimmy smiled at her, and Susannah's expression softened. 'Hurry up and drink your tea, James,' she said, putting down her own empty cup. 'I thought it might be rather nice if you took me into town this morning, but you'll have to get changed first.' She walked towards the door into the passage, not waiting for Jimmy's reply. He rose to follow.

'Are you coming, Amy?' he asked.

'No, Amy can look after the boys for me,' Susannah answered for her. 'George shouldn't need another feed for a few hours, give him some boiled water if he seems hungry.'

'All right,' Amy said, trying unsuccessfully to keep the irritation out of her voice. She did not particularly want to go into town with Susannah, but she resented being ordered about by her in front of Jimmy.

Later that morning Amy rolled up the heavy rugs and dragged them out to the yard. When she had them slung over the clothesline she closed her eyes and pretended it was Susannah before her, rather than a set of blameless rugs. She wielded her beater more vigorously than usual.

Jack came up behind her while she was lost in the task. 'You'll wear that carpet out if you pound it like that,' he said, making Amy jump. He patted her on the shoulder. 'You'll wear your arms out, anyway. Where's your ma?'

Amy wondered for a moment if he had guessed her thoughts, but his face held its usual bluff expression. 'Gone to town.' She left the rugs in peace while she went to make lunch for him.

Susannah and Jimmy were out till well into the afternoon. The following day Amy and Susannah were busy all morning with cleaning the kitchen, and Amy spent much of the afternoon giving the rest of the house a thorough dusting and polishing the furniture, so she had little chance to talk to Jimmy. But all that Saturday she hugged to herself the thought of going to church the next morning and showing him off to everyone she knew, especially Lizzie.

On Sunday morning Amy took her good dress out of the wardrobe and looked at it critically, hoping it was smart enough. She had made it out of pink and white striped cotton, with a deep flounce around the hem and a white lace collar. She had been delighted with it the previous summer, but now when she put it on and tweaked the collar in front of the mirror she wondered how it would look to Jimmy, who must be used to seeing women in the latest fashions.

Well, it was the only smart dress she had, and it would have to do. At least her boots were stylish, the finest Ruatane's shops could offer, even if they did not compare with any of Susannah's. They were of fine brown kid leather, and as she did them up with her buttonhook she admired them all over again. She pinned the cameo brooch her grandmother had given her below her left shoulder, tied a pink ribbon around her hair, then gave the folds of her dress a final shake.

Jimmy looked wonderful, and Amy had to make herself look away when she realised she was staring. He was wearing light-coloured trousers of a much slimmer cut than she was used to seeing, a white shirt with a high starched collar, and a striped tie. His short jacket and waistcoat were dark, and he had a gold watch chain across the front of the waistcoat, with a smart silk top hat completing the effect.

Jack laughed when Jimmy appeared.

'Oho, a fine swell we have here! Careful when you sit down, lad, you don't want to split those trousers!' John and Harry laughed with him, and Amy felt embarrassed and annoyed at the same time. She flashed Jimmy a silent plea, begging him to understand that she wasn't part of the laughter. He smiled at her in return, rewarding her with an admiring glance at her own appearance.

'Really, Jack, where are your manners?' Susannah snapped, and for once Amy agreed with her.

Of course Susannah insisted on sitting beside Jimmy in the buggy, and Amy had to ride next to her father on the front seat while her brothers went in on horseback ahead of them. She found it disconcerting to be directly in front of Jimmy, not knowing if he was looking at her, and unable to turn and look at him. When she tried to peep around, all she could see was Susannah's face turned towards Jimmy. Amy found the hour very long.

They arrived at church barely in time to take their seats. To her delight Amy found herself sitting beside Jimmy, who had Susannah on his left hand. It felt wonderful to be sitting next to this man who so obviously outshone all others there. Amy had trouble concentrating on the service, and felt guilty when she realised it was nearly over and she could not remember a word of the sermon. She was aware of Lizzie in her pew a few rows behind, craning her neck to catch a glimpse of Jimmy whenever they rose to sing.

After the final hymn was sung the congregation spilled out of the church, and Lizzie rushed to Amy's side, soon followed by her parents and most of the neighbours. Jimmy had to be introduced to them all, with Susannah proudly taking that role.

'This is my brother James, yes, down from Auckland for the summer... yes, that's right, he works at our father's firm.' She kept a proprietorial grip on Jimmy's arm as she repeated her speech. Amy had to admit they looked well together. Susannah was no beauty, but she was tall and carried herself admirably, and Jimmy was several inches taller than her. In her green flowered silk, Susannah outshone the women in style almost as much Jimmy did the men. Jimmy made a better partner for her than Jack, who was now nearly fifty and quite portly.

Amy and Lizzie went a little aside from the main group to talk.

'What do you think?' Amy asked eagerly. 'Isn't he just *so* elegant? And such manners.'

Lizzie gave Jimmy a keen stare. 'He certainly dresses well. And he's very tall, and he's got a friendly smile. His eyes are a bit close together, though.'

'Lizzie!' Amy said, irritated that Lizzie could dare feel anything negative towards Jimmy. 'What a silly thing to say! You'll be saying his trousers are too tight next. His eyes are as far apart as anyone else's, I'm quite sure.'

'Well,' Lizzie said, 'I've always heard people with their eyes too close together aren't all that trustworthy. But maybe that's not true. And you're right, he does look very smart. There's nothing wrong with his trousers. What's he like?'

'Just wonderful.'

Lizzie looked at her doubtfully. 'Is he any good on the farm?'

'Oh, yes,' said Amy. 'Well, he's not really used to it yet... well, I suppose he finds it all a bit strange after life in the city, and he's not used to heavy work.'

'Hmm,' said Lizzie. 'And what does he do in Auckland?'

'Works with his father.'

'Yes, but doing *what*?'

'Oh, I don't know, something to do with building things, I think.'

'And what prospects does he have?'

'Prospects?'

'Yes—you know, does he have a house, what's his income, will he inherit the business?'

Amy realised she had done a good deal more telling than asking in her conversations with Jimmy, and had very little idea just what he did. Her guilty awareness made her answer sharply.

'Honestly, Lizzie, he's not a prize bull I'm thinking of buying! I haven't asked him all those personal questions.'

'Well, it doesn't hurt to know these things,' Lizzie said, rather primly Amy thought. She wondered if Lizzie was perhaps a little jealous of Amy's sophisticated house guest, though it seemed unlikely. She and Lizzie had never been jealous of each other before.

Anyway, he isn't really my visitor, it's Susannah he's come to see.

But over the next few days Jimmy continued to seek out opportunities to spend time with her. Most days he somehow contrived to cross her path when they were both alone, especially when she was working away from the house. Early morning was the best time for these meetings, when the men were milking and Susannah was not yet up. By now it was accepted that Jimmy just couldn't seem to get up in time for the morning milking; Jack had teased him about it, but good-naturedly. On one of these occasions Amy plucked up her courage to ask him what he did in Auckland.

'Just a boring desk job in Father's building firm, I'm afraid. I'm called assistant manager, but it just means when my father says jump, I jump.' He smiled ruefully. 'Actually, I had a bit of a spat with the old man— over nothing in particular, really, but that's the main reason I've come down here for a while.'

Amy immediately pictured a bad-tempered and unreasonable man who did not appreciate his son. Susannah must take after her father, at least in being hard to please. But she was, nevertheless, grateful to the 'old man', as Jimmy called him, for inadvertently sending Jimmy to her. She did not feel able to question him about his prospects. It was enough just to have his company.

When the following Friday came around, Amy was startled to realise she had only known Jimmy for one week. It already seemed like much longer. Jimmy joined her again for her butter making, and afterwards they breakfasted together. She was about to suggest a walk to the northern end of the farm, where he had not yet been, when Susannah surprised them both by appearing much earlier than normal. She gave Amy a sharp look when she found the two of them chatting away happily.

'Perhaps you wouldn't mind spending a *little* time with me this morning, James?' She sounded hurt. Jimmy tried to hide a sigh, and smiled at his sister by way of reply.

'Good,' she said. 'Bring your tea out onto the verandah, and we can sit together for a while. I won't keep you *too* long.' Jimmy followed her out, with only time for a brief glance at Amy, but she thought he shaped the word 'Later' to her as he left.

Later will have to look after itself. She wondered if she would get the chance to talk to him again that morning. Well, she had plenty to keep herself busy with. It was time to shake out the rugs again, for one thing.

After clearing away the breakfast things Amy went through to the parlour, intending to start on the rugs there. She noticed that the door out to the verandah was slightly ajar; if she listened carefully she would be able to hear Susannah and Jimmy. She knew she should leave the room straight away so as not to overhear their conversation; instead she crept closer to the door and pressed her back against the wall, standing very still.

'I do wish you wouldn't keep wandering off without telling me where you're going, James,' Susannah said in an injured tone. 'It's such a long time since I've had anyone to talk to. I've missed you especially. I've been so looking forward to having you come, and now you seem to be hanging around with that girl all the time.' *'That girl' indeed!* 'I didn't know you were so fond of children,' Susannah added, rubbing salt in the wound.

'Hardly a child, Susannah,' said Jimmy. 'Quite a young lady, I would have said.'

'She's still in pinafores,' Susannah said dismissively. Amy looked down at her clothes in dismay. She did still wear little-girl dresses that only came to her calves, with a white pinafore over the top to keep them clean.

'Yes, and filling them out delightfully,' Jimmy retorted.

'James,' Susannah said sharply. 'These country girls are very bold and forward, and Amy probably seems older to you than she is. But it's just rudeness masquerading as maturity—she really *is* just a child.' There was a moment's silence while Susannah let her words sink in. 'And a vexing child, at that. Now don't be tiresome, James. You've no idea what my life is here.' Amy could imagine the tears forming in Susannah's eyes to go with the slight catch in her voice. 'No culture, no society. Just mud in the winter and dust in summer, and drudgery all the year round. I did so hope you'd help me take my mind off things for a while.'

Amy heard sudden steps on the verandah and had a moment of panic, thinking one of them might burst through the door and catch her listening. But it was only Jimmy crossing to Susannah's chair.

'Of course I'll keep you company whenever you want,' he said in a much softer voice. 'And you're quite right, I've been neglecting you shamefully. It must be lonely for you here. I'm afraid I've been very selfish—enjoying all the fresh air and sunshine, and forgetting about you stuck here by yourself with no one to talk to. I tell you what, why don't you and I go for a nice walk after supper when the heat goes off, and I can tell you about the ball I went to at the Fowler's in September. Would you like that?'

'Oh, yes, darling. And you *must* tell me absolutely everything about it, who was there and what they all wore. But tell me, is Catherine Fowler still walking out with that army officer?'

Their conversation became full of names that meant nothing to Amy. She slipped away to sit by herself in her bedroom.

'Eavesdroppers never hear any good of themselves,' her granny had always told her, and had reinforced the lesson with a strapping when she had once caught Amy listening at a door. Well, she had learned the lesson all over again today. So she was being bold and forward, it seemed. Jimmy had not argued with Susannah about that; in fact he had fallen over himself to be nice to her.

She would have to be more reserved with Jimmy. She would hate him to think she was pushing herself on him when she wasn't wanted. A sad face looked back at her from the mirror. It wasn't going to be easy.

14

December 1883

Amy barely spoke to Jimmy the rest of that day. She was busy with her own work in the house, while he helped around the farm, spending most of the day outside. He glanced at her from time to time during lunch and dinner, apparently noticing her silence, but she avoided his eyes.

Susannah spoke enough to cover any lack of words on Amy's part. As soon as dinner was over she and Jimmy set off for the promised walk. Just as he reached the kitchen door, Jimmy turned and looked across the room at Amy with a questioning gaze. She dropped her eyes quickly and stared in apparent fascination at the dirty dishes she was stacking until she heard the door close.

Jimmy came out when Amy was alone in the kitchen on Saturday morning. She made a show of busyness as she prepared breakfast. 'Can I help you with anything?' he asked.

'No, thank you,' Amy said shortly. 'I'll get it done faster by myself.'

'Oh. Well, if I'm in your way I'd better leave you alone.' He sounded hurt, and Amy turned to apologise, but he was out the door before she had the chance to say anything.

I hope I'm not being rude now, she fretted. It was so hard to know what was the right way to behave. Still, at least no one could accuse her of being 'forward'.

Amy again sat at Jimmy's right hand at church that Sunday; it would be too obvious a snub if she avoided sitting beside him. She was also very aware of Lizzie watching them, and she didn't want to have to answer a lot of silly questions about whether she and Jimmy had 'fallen out'. Besides, she had to admit to herself that she enjoyed sitting next to Jimmy, even if she couldn't talk to him anymore.

After church she stood at a small distance from the circle around Jack, Susannah and Jimmy. She smiled as she watched Lizzie walk with Frank to the horse paddock, then Lizzie walked up to her grinning broadly.

'Did you see the way Frank waited for me?' Lizzie said. 'He takes it for granted now that I'll walk over there with him.' She turned and waved to Frank as he rode off.

'Mmm,' said Amy. 'Have you been for any more romantic walks down to the pig sty?'

'I'd hit you if it wasn't Sunday—I might anyway.' Lizzie gave the lie to her words by taking Amy's arm as they strolled back towards their families. 'How are you getting on with Jimmy?'

'Just fine,' Amy said in what she hoped was a casual manner. 'He's a very pleasant person to have around.'

'Oh. I thought you were a bit keen on him.'

'Of course I'm not! We're just friendly, that's all. I'm not very interested in men, you know that.'

'That's all right, then. I don't want you getting keen on someone from the city.' Having dismissed Jimmy, she went on. 'Hey, what do you think I should wear to the Christmas do? Ma's helping me make a new dress, but I don't know whether to save it for the hay dance or not. What do you think?'

I'm not keen on him—not like Lizzie means, anyway. I just enjoy talking to him, and he's nice to me. That's all.

'Amy? Are you listening to me?'

'What?' Amy said, startled out of her thoughts.

'Should I wear the new dress or not?'

'Oh. What new dress?'

'You're not taking the least bit of notice of me, are you? Aren't you interested?'

'I'm sorry, Lizzie, I was thinking about something else for a minute. Tell me again? Please?'

Lizzie did not need much persuading, and the girls were soon too deep in discussing the pros and cons of Lizzie's new dress for Lizzie to wonder about Amy's lapse of attention.

Jimmy slept in even later than usual the next day, and the men had come back from milking before he appeared. *That's good*, Amy told herself. *I won't have to worry about whether I'm being rude or forward or anything.* But the kitchen seemed lonely rather than peaceful without Jimmy to laugh and joke with.

Amy was filling the copper for the weekly wash, lost in her thoughts as she tipped in a bucketful of water, when Jimmy spoke behind her.

'Amy?'

'Oh! You made me jump—I nearly dropped the bucket.'

'I'm sorry. Put that bucket down for a minute, I want to talk to you.' He took the bucket out of her hand as she made no move to obey him. 'Have you been avoiding me?'

'Of course I haven't. I'm just busy all the time, that's all. Give me back my bucket, please.'

'No.'

'Please, Jimmy. I've got to get this washing started, there's an awful lot of it.'

'Even more now I'm here. I'll carry the bucket for you, then you'll have to talk to me. Where do you get the water from?'

Amy led him over to the rainwater tank, but she said nothing as he filled the bucket, carried it back and emptied it into the copper. Jimmy stood back from the tubs, put the bucket on the ground and studied her. 'What's wrong, Amy? Have I upset you? I can't make it up to you if I don't know what I've done.'

'You haven't done anything, it's just… well, I don't want to take up all your time. It's Susannah you've really come to see, not me. Anyway, I don't want you to think…' She trailed off into an awkward silence.

'Don't want me to think what?' Amy stared at the ground. 'Come on, Amy, you have to tell me. What don't you want me to think?' He put his hands on her shoulders, and she reluctantly tilted her face up to look at his.

'I don't want you to think I'm *forward*,' she said in a voice little above a whisper. 'But I don't really know what that means.' She felt tears pricking at her eyes. She twisted out of Jimmy's hands and turned away from him.

There was a moment's silence. 'Susannah's been talking to you, hasn't she?' said Jimmy. 'That's what's brought this on.'

'No, she hasn't—honestly she hasn't. But I'm sure there's lots of things you'd like to be doing, you'd better go now.'

She kept her face turned away until she was sure he had gone. A little later she heard a horse whinnying, and she looked up to see Jimmy riding off down the road. Amy wondered where he was going, but Susannah joined her at the tubs soon afterwards with Thomas at her heels, and after that the washing took all Amy's attention.

Amy rose early for her Tuesday morning butter making. She made breakfast and left the bacon and eggs to keep warm, then went out to the dairy. Something told her she would have it to herself that morning. It seemed terribly quiet in the cool room, despite the noise of the churn turning over and over.

When she got back to the house she saw that Jimmy's boots had disappeared from the porch. He must be with her father and brothers somewhere on the farm; he was, after all, meant to be earning his keep.

There were four dirty plates on the table to show where the men had been. Amy ate her own breakfast alone, then went to change her buttermilk-splashed pinafore for a fresh one before starting on the ironing.

She stepped into her bedroom and immediately felt something was strange. Looking about for the reason, she saw a length of velvet ribbon in a rich, deep shade of blue coiled on her pillow. She rushed across to her bed and picked up the beautiful thing, then ran it through her fingers, feeling its softness. *That's what he went to town for! To buy me a present. He doesn't think I'm forward at all—he likes me!* She rubbed the ribbon against her cheek, then quickly pulled it away before any of the tears she could feel spilling out of her eyes could fall on it.

Amy spent the rest of that day alternately basking in the warm glow of Jimmy's kindness and fretting over how she could show she appreciated it. It would be too much of a risk to wear the velvet ribbon when she and Susannah were going to spend the whole day ironing, flung together more closely than on any other day of the week. But she saw Jimmy look at her when the men came home for lunch, and the disappointment in his face sent a pang through her.

By the time dinner was ready she decided she would have to hazard Susannah's sharp eyes, and she slipped off to her room to tie the ribbon around her hair. They had barely sat down to the table when Susannah glanced at Amy and said with a slight frown, 'Where did you get that ribbon, Amy? I don't remember seeing it before.'

'It was a present,' Amy said, hoping that would be enough to satisfy Susannah's curiosity.

'A present? Who from? Oh, that girl, I suppose.' Susannah's lips compressed into a disapproving line. 'It's a little fancy for the dinner table,' she added, but said no more on the subject.

Amy breathed a sigh of relief, and risked a peek at Jimmy. He was looking back at her with a tiny smile playing on his lips, and Amy decided it had been worth the risk. But after dinner she put the ribbon away safely in her top drawer with her underwear.

To her delight, Jimmy came out next morning in time for them to breakfast together. 'Thank you for that lovely present,' she said, looking up from setting out their plates. 'It's the most beautiful ribbon I've ever had.'

'Then it suits you, because I think you're the prettiest girl I've ever met.' Amy was too flustered at such an extravagant compliment to be able to speak. 'Have you got those silly ideas out of your head?' Jimmy asked. 'All that nonsense about being too forward?'

'I think so.' She smiled shyly at him.

'Good.' Jimmy reached across the table and put his hand over hers. 'You're natural and unspoiled, Amy, not full of a lot of false airs. That doesn't make you forward—it makes you charming.' He gave her hand a gentle squeeze, and Amy felt a strange, quivery sensation. She wondered if she should pull her hand away, but the feeling of Jimmy's on hers was so nice that she left it where it was. A few moments later the back door opened, and they quickly let go of each other's hands.

The Saturday before Christmas saw the nearby families gathered for a party in Aitken's barn, just outside the valley. It was a casual affair; the men wore their Sunday-best suits, but left the jackets undone, and the women wore pretty but plain dresses, generally of cotton, with simple bonnets. After much soul-searching, Lizzie had decided to save her new dress for the hay dance. Susannah was the only one in silk, but it was the plainest of all her silk gowns, grey with cream lace at the cuffs.

The party soon divided into distinct groups. The young children (apart from baby George, who at four months old was too small to be abandoned to the toddlers) played in a corner of the barn, getting steadily grubbier as the evening wore on but ignored by their mothers except when squabbles broke out. The women divided their time between bringing plates of food from the kitchen and sitting on the chairs Matt Aitken had carried out for them, taking turns at holding little George and talking rapidly all the while. Their husbands discussed the hardships of farming with mournful pleasure, while the young people found the corner remotest from all the other groups to enjoy each other's company. Thirteen-year-old Alf wandered somewhat morosely between his father's group and his older brother's, feeling out of place in both, but reluctant to miss anything.

Frank arrived a little after the two Leith families. He stood twisting his hat between his hands and looking about uncertainly, trying to decide whether he belonged in the farmers' group or the young people's, till Bill, after a nudge from Lizzie, good-naturedly put him out of his misery by calling him over. They all chattered away happily, even Frank losing his shyness with so many friendly faces around him. Amy was pleased to see how well Jimmy fitted in, despite being the only stranger there. He seemed interested in everything and everyone.

'You live alone, do you, Frank?' Jimmy asked.

'Just me and Ben—that's my brother. He's not much on company, that's why he's not here tonight.'

'Two bachelors, eh?' Jimmy said, a twinkle in his eye. 'You want to watch out, Frank—you'd be a good catch for someone.'

Frank scuffed his feet in the thick layer of dust that covered the floor, and carefully avoided Lizzie's eyes. Jimmy turned his smile on Lizzie, but she gave him a rather cold look in return. Jimmy raised his eyebrows at

Amy, then dropped his arm across Frank's shoulders. 'Come on, Frank, let's fetch the young ladies a drink.' They set off to the table where large bottles of lemonade and ginger beer stood, with Harry walking beside them.

Amy pulled Lizzie a little to one side, out of John's and Bill's hearing. 'What did you scowl at Jimmy like that for?' she asked indignantly.

'He's got no right to make fun of Frank.'

'But Lizzie, everyone makes fun of Frank. Anyway, all he said was Frank'd be a good catch, and that's what you think too.'

'I don't say it to his face, do I? And people shouldn't make fun of Frank, it embarrasses him. Especially not strangers. He likes himself, that one—picking on Frank just because he's quiet.'

'Jimmy's not a stranger, he's family, sort of. And I don't think he said anything so terrible. Don't be so grumpy, and don't talk about Jimmy like that.'

'I thought you didn't like him,' Lizzie said, her eyes narrowing.

'I didn't say that! We're friends, I told you that.'

'Suit yourself,' Lizzie said haughtily. She turned a glowing smile on Frank as he and Jimmy returned with their drinks.

'Who's that?' Jimmy murmured in Amy's ear. She glanced over to see Charlie Stewart trudging towards the group of farmers.

'That's Mr Stewart, from the farm next to ours. He just turns up for the free beer—that's what Pa says, anyway,' Amy replied softly. 'He's not very friendly the rest of the time.'

As if to vindicate her, Charlie soon picked up a mug and approached the beer barrel. When he walked back with his full mug he gave the laughing group of youngsters a baleful stare. Amy shivered a little, despite the warmth of the night.

'I don't think he approves of frivolity, do you?' Jimmy said to the group, grinning.

'Nah, just serious drinking,' Harry replied, and they all laughed.

'You'll be around when the haymaking starts, won't you Frank?' Jimmy asked.

'Oh, yes, we always do that together. We usually start up at Lizzie's… I mean Arthur Leith's place, then work our way down the valley.'

'That's good,' said Jimmy. 'Maybe you'll show me the ropes? You must be a real expert, having your own place. I'm going to be pretty hopeless, I'm afraid.' He smiled ruefully.

'Yes, no trouble—I'd be glad to. There's nothing to it, really.' Frank looked bemused at being considered an expert.

The party broke up around nine o'clock. Horses were saddled up or harnessed, sleepy children bundled into buggies and carts, and the guests set off for home in the moonlight. Amy sat beside her father, with Jimmy once again behind her and next to Susannah. Thomas snuggled in Amy's lap, while Susannah held George.

Both children were asleep within minutes of leaving the barn, rocked by the motion, but as soon as they drew up to the buggy shed George woke and became fractious. Susannah carried him off to the house, Jack following soon afterwards with Thomas in his arms.

Amy hung back while Jimmy exchanged a few words with her brothers, who assured him they did not need his help dealing with the horses. She and Jimmy walked towards the house as slowly as they could, talking in low voices.

'I don't think your cousin likes me very much,' Jimmy said. 'That was quite a look she gave me tonight!'

'Take no notice of Lizzie—she's always been a sort of mother hen to me, and now she's getting the same way with Frank. She doesn't like to see anyone upset him, that's all. You and Frank seemed to get on all right after that.'

'Mmm, he seems a decent sort of fellow, even if he hasn't got much to say for himself. I must say I've always thought blushing suited pretty girls better than grown men, but I'm sure he has a heart of gold. He and Lizzie will make a fine match.'

'They will if Lizzie has any say in it!'

'From what I've seen of Lizzie so far, she'll have a big say in it.' A morepork, the small native owl, hooted softly from the trees; Jimmy looked around, then moved closer to Amy. 'Susannah seemed to have quite a good time tonight—and she gave me a bit of peace for a change.'

'That's why Pa said you could come down this summer, you know, so you could cheer Susannah up a bit. I'm taking up a lot of your time now, I hope she won't get too upset about it.'

'Now don't start that again, Amy—I'm allowed to enjoy myself while I'm here as well as wait on Susannah, aren't I?'

'Of course you are.' She smiled up at him. Under cover of the dim night he took her hand and held it until they had reached the house.

Christmas Day fell on a Tuesday, which Amy knew would throw the rest of the week into disarray with ironing moved one day out of place. She finished making her presents very early on Christmas morning by lamplight, since Monday had been devoted to washing and sewing was, of course, forbidden on Sunday. The purse she was making for Susannah had taken the most time, but she was determined to give Susannah something beautiful.

After the service, which saw the little church full to overflowing, the family returned home to a large meal. They lingered over their roast lamb and vegetables, followed by hot plum pudding with cream, until well into the afternoon, when the heat of the kitchen drove them out to the verandah to drink tea. Susannah went off to the bedroom to settle Thomas for his afternoon sleep and to feed George before putting him back in his cradle. She returned with a long, thin package wrapped in tissue paper.

'Here's your present, dear,' she said, passing the package to Amy before taking her seat again. 'It's from your father and I.'

'Your ma chose it, though—it was her idea,' Jack put in.

'Thank you.' Amy smiled at them both, and wondered what it might be. The previous year they had given her some coral beads, the sort little girls wore, and to add injury to insult the string was too short to go around her neck comfortably. The beads had lain discarded in the back of a drawer ever since. She hoped she would not have to make too much of a show of pleasure this year.

She gave a gasp as she opened the parcel. 'A parasol! It's beautiful—I've never had such a lovely thing!' She carefully opened out the parasol, running her fingers along the handle from the mother-of-pearl hook all the way up the smooth wooden stick. The cloth was cream satin, with bands of pale lemon silk and a fringe of the same lemon colour. Amy twirled the parasol, making the fringe fly out prettily, then she placed it reverently on her chair, impulsively rushed over to Susannah and flung her arms around her stepmother's neck. 'Thank you,' she said, planting a kiss on Susannah's cheek. She stood back, suddenly shy.

'I... I'm glad you like it.' Susannah looked a little dazed. She recovered herself and added in something closer to her usual tone, 'I like you to look smart when you come out with us—it reflects on me when you're untidy.'

Jack beamed at them both. 'That was a good present you picked, Susannah,' he said, and Amy embraced him, too.

She darted off to her bedroom to fetch her gifts for the others. 'They're nothing much, just things I made myself.' She handed small parcels to the men first; they opened them to reveal handkerchiefs she had made from fine cotton, each with the initial of the recipient embroidered in one corner. 'So many "Js",'—you nearly got a "J" too, Harry, I realised just in time.' Then she handed Susannah her package. 'I hope you like it,' she said anxiously.

Susannah gave a smile that didn't reach her eyes, then opened the parcel. 'Oh,' she said in surprise. She carefully lifted the purse from its wrapping. It was of bronze satin (scraps Amy had begged from one of Edie's dresses, though she had no intention of telling Susannah that), and Amy had used soft-coloured silk threads to embroider delicate leafy stems twining around tiny flowers. She had made a carrying band for the purse out of mauve ribbon left over from a bonnet she had helped Lizzie alter. 'Oh, Amy, this is really rather nice. And you made it yourself? It must have taken you a long time. Thank you, dear.' Susannah offered Amy her cheek, and Amy brushed her own against it.

Jimmy produced a pair of gloves for Susannah, bought in Auckland before he left, which she exclaimed over delightedly. He turned to Amy. 'I... ah... I haven't got you a real present, Amy. I thought you might like these, though.' He handed her a small tin of toffees.

'Oh,' Amy said, trying unsuccessfully to look pleased. 'Thank you, I'm sure they'll be very nice.' She sat silent while the others chatted around her, then excused herself as soon as she politely could and went off to her room, where she sat on her bed. *Lollies—just as though I'm a baby. He does think I'm just a little girl. I thought he liked me. He even held my hand. He must have thought I needed minding, like a baby.*

There was a soft tap on her door; she looked up to see Jimmy standing in the doorway. He put his finger to his lips and beckoned her. 'Do you want something?' she asked, her voice cool.

'Yes,' he said quietly. 'Come for a walk with me.'

'No, thank you. I don't want to.'

'Come on, Amy, don't be difficult. Susannah wanted to come with me, and I had to make her think I was just going out to... you know. If she hears us talking she'll make a fuss.'

Amy was too used to doing what she was told to argue. She went with Jimmy down the passage and through the kitchen to the back door.

She was determined to be aloof. When Jimmy made to help her climb down from the first fence she pushed his hands away. They walked side-by-side in silence until they were around the hill and out of sight of the house. Jimmy stopped abruptly and stepped in front of her. Amy looked at the ground until he put his hand on her chin and forced her to look up into his face.

'I've hurt you, haven't I? I'm sorry, little one—I should have warned you, but I didn't think of it in time. Don't you see—I couldn't give you something special in front of everyone.' He grinned at her. 'Your father and Susannah think you're too young for men—I don't think it's the right time to let them know they're wrong, so I've got to pretend I haven't noticed you've...' his eyes flicked to her chest briefly, then returned to her face 'grown up... either. But I have.' His smile was replaced for a moment by a more earnest expression that sent a shiver through Amy.

Jimmy took hold of her hand, then reached into his pocket with his free hand and pulled out a small box. He placed it on Amy's palm and closed her fingers around it. 'How could you think I wouldn't have a real present for you?' he said, the slightest hint of reproach in his voice.

'I... I'm sorry, I was silly and thoughtless.'

'No, you weren't. You're never thoughtless. Aren't you going to see what's in it?' He let go of her hand.

Amy lifted the lid of the box. Lying on a bed of white velvet was a gold brooch in the shape of a letter 'A'. She touched it in disbelief, and looked up at Jimmy with wide eyes. 'For me? It's gold! I've never had anything gold before. Oh, it must have cost you a lot of money.'

Jimmy shrugged. 'Father's still paying my allowance into the bank while I'm down here. And I can't think of anything I'd rather spend money on than making you happy. You like it?'

'I love it!' Her face dropped. 'What'll I tell Susannah about it, though?'

'Don't tell her anything. I'm afraid you won't be able to show anyone—at least not for a while. Can't you wear it somewhere no one will see it?'

Amy nodded. 'I can wear it under my dress. I'll wear it every day.' She gave him a radiant smile.

'Could you put it on now, just for a minute, so I can see it?'

'Of course.' She tried to fasten the brooch at the front of her collar, but it was awkward without a mirror. Her fingers fumbled with the catch.

'Let me.' Jimmy took the brooch and pinned it deftly, but when it was done instead of dropping his hands he slid them on to her shoulders. He leaned towards her till his face was only a few inches from hers and caressed her shoulders with his fingers. 'Don't I get a thank-you?' he asked, looking into her uptilted face.

Amy opened her mouth, but before she could get any words out Jimmy's mouth was on hers, and she gave a little mew of surprise. He raised his head and smiled down at her.

'I'm afraid we'd better go back now,' he said, letting his hands drop from her shoulders. 'They'll miss us soon. Happy Christmas, little one.'

'It's the best Christmas I've ever had.' Amy took off the brooch, slipped her hand into his and walked back to the house at his side, clutching her brooch in a blissful dream.

15

December 1883 – January 1884

Amy woke next morning with the brief softness of Jimmy's lips on hers still fresh in her memory.

When she looked out her bedroom window she saw that this year the weather was not going to allow the Boxing Day start to haymaking that was tradition in the valley. There was no rain falling, but the sky was overcast, not the clear blue her father always insisted on before he would allow the hay to be cut. Unless they could be sure of four or five sunny days in a row, there was a risk of producing piles of rotting grass instead of sweet-smelling hay.

Amy went out to an empty kitchen to start making breakfast. While she was sawing slices of bacon she heard the passage door open, and she turned an eager face to see Jimmy entering.

'I hoped it would be you,' she said. He strode across the room and stood smiling down at her, then he bent and gave her a kiss so gentle she could only just feel the tickle of his moustache on her lips. The noise of a baby crying came faintly down the passage, Jimmy took a step backwards, and they both turned guiltily at the noise.

'Not very private in here, is it?' Jimmy said ruefully. 'I don't suppose there's any chance of disappearing for a while after breakfast?'

'Not really. We've got to do the ironing, that'll take all day. It might rain later, too, so no one would believe you wanted me to take you for a walk and show you some more of the farm.'

'Mmm. I suppose that means we'll all be stuck inside. There's not a lot to do here when it rains. Ah, well,' he sighed, 'I'll do my duty and talk to my sister. Are you wearing your present?' he added with a twinkle in his eye. 'Where is it?'

Amy smiled shyly at him. 'It's here.' She pointed to the place between her breasts where she had pinned the brooch to her chemise.

'I'll have to take your word for that, won't I?' Jimmy said, his eyes dancing.

The sky soon broke into drizzle and occasional downpours. Amy and Susannah spent the day ironing, an exercise that did not normally put Susannah in the best of tempers, but Jimmy sat in the kitchen with them for much of the time, feeding Susannah's insatiable desire for news of Auckland.

The weather showed no sign of improving over the next few days. Jimmy joined Amy in the dairy on Friday morning, but she could tell from his restlessness as he wandered around the room that he was tired of being trapped inside so much.

'What would you do if you were home and it got rainy like this?' she asked as she formed the butter into pats.

'Oh, there's always something to do. Visit people, maybe go to the theatre.'

'The theatre! Do you go there much?'

'Quite a lot. I went to a Shakespeare play a couple of months ago, it was… what was it? That one with the girl and her old father stuck on a island—do you know anything about Shakespeare?' he asked, looking at Amy doubtfully.

'That's *The Tempest*,' said Amy. '"I might call him a thing divine, for nothing natural I ever saw so noble." That's what Miranda says when she first sees Ferdinand, because she's never seen anyone like…' She trailed off, seeing Jimmy's surprised expression. *I hope he doesn't think I'm showing off.*

'There's more to you than meets the eye,' he said. 'So you're keen on plays, are you? Where on earth do you manage to see them?'

'I've never been to a play,' she admitted. 'I just read them sometimes.'

'Do you think you'd like to see one?'

'I'd love it.' For a few moments Amy was so lost in contemplation that she forgot to work the butter. 'But they don't ever come to little places like Ruatane, and I never go anywhere else.' She gave him a sad smile.

'Would you like to go somewhere else? Maybe Auckland?'

'It's what I'd like more than anything in the world,' Amy said fervently. 'I used to think I might be able to when I was…'

'When you were what? What were you going to say? Tell me, Amy.'

But she shook her head and fought down the tears that came at the memory of how her teaching had been taken away from her. 'Not now. Maybe I'll tell you another time.' She washed the butter patters and put them away neatly. 'I've finished now, I'll just wash my hands then we'd better go inside.'

'What about a kiss first?' Without waiting for her reply he put his arms around her waist and kissed her, a longer embrace this time. She held her buttery hands out awkwardly, anxious not to brush them against his sleeves.

'You should have let me wash my hands first,' she scolded when her mouth was free.

'No, I shouldn't,' he said with his infectious grin. 'This way you couldn't push me away.'

'Why on earth would I want to push you away?' she asked in bewilderment.

She got an even broader grin in return. 'Why indeed?' he echoed.

'Grey sky again,' Jimmy said in disgust when he joined Amy for breakfast on Saturday morning. 'How long do you think it's going to carry on like this?'

'Not much longer, I shouldn't think,' Amy said, trying to sound encouraging. 'January's usually really sunny.' She frowned, searching for something he might enjoy. 'Would you like to see Pa kill a sheep?'

'Oh. All right, I suppose it'd be a change. What are you going to do this morning?'

'I'll come and watch, too—I haven't done that for years.'

'You're not serious, are you?'

'Yes,' Amy said, surprised at his look of disbelief. 'I used to when I was little—I've only got brothers, you know, so I was always hanging around with them, and they were always hanging around Pa.'

'Well, as long as you think you'll be all right. I'll be there to keep an eye on you, anyway.'

'Why wouldn't I be all right?' she asked, puzzled, but Jimmy just smiled at her.

After the other men had breakfasted, Amy led Jimmy out to the killing area. 'There's Pa now.' She pointed to where her father was half-riding, half-dragging an unwilling sheep to the slaughter.

Jack brought the sheep close to the base of a big, old karaka tree near where Amy and Jimmy stood. 'Come to see the fun, eh? You can give me a hand in a minute, Jimmy.' He pulled a large knife from his belt as he spoke. Keeping a tight grip on the sheep with his legs, he hooked one arm under its chin and forced its head back. He slashed the blade across the animal's throat and the sheep's struggles abruptly stopped. Jack threw the knife, now thick with blood, onto the grass, then wrenched the sheep's head back with a jerk. 'That's broken her neck,' he said as he let the carcass drop to the ground. 'Faster than just cutting her throat.'

Amy glanced from the sheep to Jimmy to see if he was finding it interesting. She was surprised to see that he looked rather pale; she supposed it must be the heat. Although the sun was hidden, the day was becoming uncomfortably humid. She looked back to see that her father already had the sheep half-skinned, and had attached the rope slung over a branch of the tree to the sheep's back legs.

'Give a tug on this rope,' he said to Jimmy. 'Your arms are younger than mine.'

150

As if in a daze, Jimmy moved to obey him. He hauled on the rope until the carcass was swinging free, and Jack took the rope from his hands to tie it.

Jack retrieved his knife from the ground and made a long cut down the front of the carcass, then he reached into the cavity he had made and pulled at something. A mass of offal spilled out through the cut and landed in a bloody heap on the ground. Amy glanced at it, then back to where her father was finishing off skinning the sheep.

'This is a good bit, when he pulls the skin right off.' She turned to see if Jimmy was watching carefully. 'Jimmy, you've gone a funny colour. Do you want to get out of the heat?'

Jimmy turned a horror-stricken face to her, but instead of answering he turned away, leaned over and vomited, then walked rather unsteadily towards the house.

'Jimmy?' Amy called after him. 'Pa, Jimmy's not very well.'

'Weak stomach,' Jack said. 'City folk, girl—he's not used to this sort of thing. How about you tie this rope for me when I've hauled it a bit higher?'

Amy fastened the rope securely, then rushed back to the house to check on Jimmy.

She found him sitting on the back steps, his face still somewhat green. He looked up at her approach and grimaced. 'I made a fool of myself then, didn't I?'

'No, of course you didn't,' Amy protested. 'It's my fault, really—I know Susannah doesn't like things like that, but I didn't think you'd mind, because you're a man.'

'I'm *meant* to be a man,' he muttered. 'That sort of thing doesn't make you feel sick?'

'No—I'd never get anything to eat if Pa didn't kill animals, so why should it worry me?'

'Well, you must despise me now,' he said dejectedly. 'You watched it without turning a hair while I lost my breakfast.'

'That's only because you're not used to it! If you'd seen hundreds of sheep killed like I have it wouldn't worry you, either. Anyway,' she looked at him shyly, 'I don't think I could ever despise you.'

'You know what, Amy?' Jimmy said, smiling at her. 'You're not only the prettiest girl I've ever seen, you're the sweetest one, too. And the one with the strongest stomach!' He laughed, and Amy joined in his laughter.

Haymaking began on the last day of the year. Arthur cut his hay first, and on Wednesday morning while Amy was taking her loaves of bread out of the oven Jimmy set off with Jack and his sons to help with raking the hay.

'That's hard work,' Jimmy told her when he came home just in time for dinner. Jack had returned earlier with John and Harry to do the milking. 'I'm going to have some aches and pains tomorrow! It's good to get out in the fresh air again, though.'

'Did you see Lizzie?'

Jimmy laughed. 'I certainly did! Every time I turned around she seemed to be there with food and drink, then she'd hang around to watch Frank eat it. She'll get some fat on him when she's got him to the altar.'

On Friday Amy decided to go and see for herself how the haymaking was going. Late in the afternoon, when her father and brothers had already come home, she walked over to her uncle's farm. She could see the haystack from some distance away, and when she got closer she saw Jimmy working beside Frank, pitching hay onto the stack. Lizzie seemed to have found some excuse to stand around watching the work, and Amy went up to her.

'Hey, Amy,' Jimmy called. 'Look at this—I'm getting good at it!' He hurled a forkful of hay to the top of the stack. The hay landed almost in the centre of the flat top. 'Frank's a good teacher, eh?'

'You're getting better at it than I am,' Frank said, sending up a forkful that only just reached the top.

'Skite,' Amy heard Lizzie mutter. 'Showing off like that—Frank can't help it if his arms are six inches shorter than that one's.'

'Beginner's luck! And I bet you won't be stiff and sore like I will tomorrow—you're used to this sort of work.' Jimmy clapped Frank on the back.

'He's not skiting, Lizzie,' Amy scolded. 'You've got to stop going crook if anyone even looks at Frank the wrong way. I think Jimmy's being really nice to him.'

'Humph!' Lizzie said in disgust. 'You're a fine one to talk—you're quick enough to jump down my throat if I say a word against His Lordship.' She gave Amy a hard look. 'You are getting a bit keen on him, aren't you?'

'Maybe I am,' Amy admitted. 'Just a little bit.' Her hand crept towards the hidden brooch. 'He's so nice to me all the time. And he's interesting to talk to—not like the people round here. He doesn't just talk about cows and drains all the time.' She watched Jimmy, admiring the strength she could see at work in his long, lean body.

'What's wrong with cows and drains?' Lizzie demanded. 'That sort of thing's important, isn't it?'

'It's not *interesting*, though. Don't let's talk about it, you'll only get grumpy. Haymaking's a good excuse for you to have Frank around every day.'

'I suppose so. I don't get to see much of him, though—not by ourselves, I mean. Never mind,' Lizzie said, brightening. 'We'll have the hay dance next month, I'll have Frank to myself there. I suppose he'll be coming with you?' She indicated Jimmy with her thumb.

'Of course he will—he'll come with John and Harry and me.'

'Mmm.' Lizzie looked about as if to see if anyone was listening. 'I might even let Frank kiss me after the dance,' she said to Amy in a conspiratorial tone.

'Haven't you yet?'

'Don't you think I would have told you if I had?'

'I… I didn't really think about it. I just thought you would have got up to kissing by now, that's all.'

'Well, he hasn't proposed to me yet, so I've got to be a bit careful.'

'Just a kiss, though, Lizzie—there's no harm in that, is there?'

'No—that's why I think I might let him.' She looked superior. 'Of course I wouldn't expect you to understand about all that—you're two years younger than me, after all.'

'One and a half,' Amy corrected absently, watching Jimmy as she let Lizzie's words fall in her ear barely heeded. Lizzie wasn't such an expert as she tried to make out, Amy thought. She gave a tiny smile as she wondered how Lizzie would react if told about Jimmy's kisses.

'That's it,' Jimmy said, walking up to the girls. 'The slaves have finished for the day. Are you coming home with me, Amy?'

'Of course.' She turned to say goodbye to Lizzie, but her cousin was already scurrying over towards Frank.

Jimmy caught Amy's hand when they had climbed the boundary fence and she was about to take the most direct route to the house. 'There's no rush, is there?' he asked. 'Couldn't we take the longer way back—maybe through those trees?' He pointed to a clump of uncleared bush to their left.

'Well… I expect we could take a bit longer without anyone noticing. They won't have finished milking yet.'

As soon as they had entered the grove Jimmy took her hand. After a few steps they both stopped, as if by unspoken agreement. 'A bit of privacy at last,' Jimmy said. 'We've hardly had any time to talk lately.' He held out his arms and she allowed herself to be enfolded in them. 'Mmm,' he said, running one hand up and down her back. 'You're so nice and soft to hold, not all stiff with whalebone.'

Amy laid her face against his chest and savoured his touch. 'I won't start wearing grown-up dresses till I'm seventeen or eighteen.' *Will I feel all stiff and hard to you then? Will you still like me?*

He nuzzled at her hair. 'You know what, Amy? All day long I've been thinking about you, wondering when I'd see you—I had trouble keeping my mind on the work—and then you turn up like magic just in time to walk home with me.'

'I've been thinking about you all day, too.'

'You are a bit magic aren't you?' he said fondly. 'A bit of a changeling, anyway. You're so different from all the other people around here— they're nice enough, but a bit... well, rough and ready. Not you, though. You don't belong in a place like this—you should be at a ball in Auckland, dressed in a beautiful gown and turning all the men's heads.' He tilted her face up with one hand. 'You've turned mine,' he said softly, just before he kissed her.

A thrill ran through Amy at his words and his touch. She flung her arms around his neck and kissed him back. The kiss went on for a long time, and when Jimmy lifted his face away from hers she could see amused surprise in his eyes.

'You liked that, did you, little one? I'll have to find some other things you'll like.'

She smiled back rather uncertainly, hoping she hadn't done anything she shouldn't have. But then he kissed her again, and she lost herself in the pleasure of his embrace.

His hands moved across her back. She became aware that one of them had slipped through the wide armhole of her pinafore and was inching across her dress towards her breasts. She disengaged her lips from his with difficulty, but he kept his hand where it was. 'What are you doing?' she said in alarm.

'Just checking if you're wearing my present.' He slid his hand closer to one breast.

'Yes, I am. Don't do that, Jimmy.' She tried to pull away from him, but his other arm held her firmly.

'You like it really, don't you?' He cupped her breast in his hand.

'No, I don't—you mustn't touch me there! Please stop.' She put her hands on his shoulders and pushed hard, but he gave a chuckle and squeezed her breast harder. 'If you don't stop I... I'll yell for help,' Amy said in desperation, tears welling up in her eyes. 'I will!'

He took his hands off her suddenly, and now that she was no longer being held Amy took an involuntary step backwards. She found that she was shaking.

'I'm sorry,' he said in an oddly flat tone. 'There's no excuse for what I just did.' He turned away from her and leaned his arm against a branch, then let his head fall onto the arm. 'I'd better go.' His words came muffled through his sleeve.

'We'll both go—it's time for me to help Susannah with dinner, anyway.'

'That's not what I meant.' Jimmy lifted his head and turned to face her. 'I'd better go right away from here. I'll go into town tomorrow and find out when the boat's leaving next.'

'No!' Amy reached her hand out towards him, then let it drop awkwardly to her side. 'Please don't go,' she begged. 'I don't want you to go away.'

'I've got to. If I stay, I know something like that's going to happen again—I can't help myself.' He looked at her with something like torment in his face. 'I thought you were encouraging me. That's still no excuse. Goodbye, Amy.' He turned away and walked towards the house, leaving Amy with tears streaming down her cheeks.

'Don't go,' she whispered, but he was already almost at the edge of the trees. Being touched in that way suddenly didn't seem so terrible, not compared with losing him. 'Jimmy,' she sobbed, then she picked up her skirts and ran to him, catching hold of his sleeve. 'Please don't leave me. I couldn't stand it if you left me.'

Jimmy turned to her and slowly enfolded her in his arms. 'I thought you might hate me after what I just did.'

She shook her head emphatically. 'I'll never hate you, no matter what you do. Jimmy, I… I think I love you.' She hid her face against his chest, but he cupped her chin in his hand and made her look up at him.

'I think I love you, too.' He lowered his face to hers and kissed her, at first gently then more urgently. The words echoed round and round in Amy's head: *I love you. I love you.*

16

January 1884

Jack and Susannah were sitting on the verandah with Jimmy the next afternoon, and Amy had just brought out a tray with tea, when Harry returned from a visit to Bill bursting with news. 'Hey, guess what? There was a fight at the Masonic Hotel last night, and someone got stabbed! Bill went in to town this morning and everyone's talking about it.'

'That's terrible!' Amy said. 'Is he all right? Who was it?'

'Some bloke from Tauranga. He got off the boat yesterday—there were a few of them, looking for work I think. They went drinking in the Masonic, then a row started.'

'Don't tell me,' said Jack. 'Feenans?'

Harry grinned. 'You guessed it.'

'Who are the Feenans?' Jimmy asked.

'A mad Irish lot—they live down by Orere Beach,' Jack explained. 'Whenever there's trouble, you can be pretty sure the Feenans won't be far away.'

'Really, this is such a *rough* place,' Susannah said, pursing her lips, but the others ignored her.

'What about the man who got stabbed?' Amy persisted. 'Is he all right?'

'Bill said they got the doctor to him—he was pretty bad, but people were saying he'd most likely get over it.' Harry looked a little disappointed, but then he brightened. 'There's a bunch of them in the lock-up now—the other ones from Tauranga and a few Feenans. They'll all be up before Leveston next week. If that fellow dies, Gerry Feenan'll hang! He's the one that had the knife.'

'Oh,' Susannah said, slumping back in her chair. 'Oh, I don't feel very well.'

'Course, they all probably had knives, but Gerry Feenan's one had blood on it,' Harry went on with relish. Susannah gave a groan.

'That's enough about it,' said Jack. 'You're upsetting Susannah. Haven't you got any work to do, boy?'

'Oh, all right,' Harry grumbled, casting a dark look at Susannah. 'I'll go and give John a hand getting the cows in.'

'I'll come with you—I've spent enough time sitting around doing nothing,' Jimmy said. 'I can't let you do all the work, Harry.' He and Harry strolled off together out of sight around the corner of the house.

'Well, at least that'll be a few less Feenans around for a while,' Jack said. 'Ruatane should be a bit quieter.'

'I think there's still plenty more of them, Pa,' said Amy. 'There seem to be so many Feenans.'

'That's true enough,' Jack said.

Amy looked at Susannah, trying to gauge her mood. She seemed calm, and Jimmy had spent most of the afternoon with her, so she was probably in as good a mood as Amy was ever likely to find her. 'Susa— Ma,' Amy corrected herself, aware of Jack's watchful presence, 'the hay dance is next month—it's only about four weeks away now.'

'I know,' said Susannah. 'It seems to be the only dance you ever have around here, and I can't go to it.' She looked resentfully at Jack, but he smiled back at her.

'Now, Susannah, we talked about that. No one takes babies to the dance.'

'Why can't *she* look after the boys for me?' Susannah waved her hand towards Amy.

Amy felt a stab of alarm. 'Pa, you did say I could go this year.' She winced under the look Susannah turned on her. 'But I'll stay home and look after the babies if you say I have to.' She saw her longed-for outing with Jimmy evaporate as she spoke.

'Yes, I said you could go—and I meant it, too. Susannah, it's the girl's first dance—you don't want to take that off her, do you? Anyway,' he went on, not giving Susannah time to answer, 'the dance is for the young ones, really—us old folk should stay home and let them get on with having a good time.' He laughed at his own humour, but Susannah looked less than amused.

'I'm only twenty-seven. *I* don't think that's old.'

Jack smiled at her. 'No, of course you're not. You're still a young thing—you'll keep me young, too, you and the little fellows. But you couldn't leave Georgie all that time—what if he needed a feed?'

'I'm going to wean that child,' Susannah muttered. 'He's taken my strength for long enough.' She cast a defiant look at Jack. 'I'm going to that dance next year.'

'If that's what you want.' Jack put his hand over hers, but she pulled her hand away. 'Unless you've got a new baby by then.'

'I won't have a baby—I told you I'm not going to have babies every year.' Susannah glared at him, and Amy tried to make herself inconspicuous.

'Hey, Susannah, no need to talk about that sort of thing in front of the girl.'

'Humph! She's heard it all before—she listens at keyholes to find things out.'

'I don't,' Amy began, then gave up the attempt to defend herself. She wondered why Susannah had told Edie she wasn't going to have any more babies ever, while Amy's father only seemed to have been told that she wasn't going to have another one this year, but it was none of her business.

Well, the conversation had got off to a bad start, but she could hardly make it worse. She ploughed on. 'About the dance—could I have a new dress for it?'

'All right,' Susannah said, indifference in her voice. 'You must be due for a new smart dress.'

So far, so good. The next part would be harder. 'I'm fifteen now, I don't think I'm going to grow much more. Do you think…' she gathered her courage. 'Do you think I could have a silk dress this year?' she said in a rush.

Susannah looked at her doubtfully. 'I don't know, you're a little young for silk, really—'

'Oh, go on, Susannah,' Jack broke in. 'Let the girl have a silk dress if her heart's that set on it. It's her first dance, you know.'

'So you keep saying,' Susannah snapped. 'Well, if you want to waste the money it's up to you.'

The next week saw haymaking start on Jack's farm, and because Charlie Stewart's farm was so small his solitary hay paddock was mown at the same time. Amy took morning tea, lunch and afternoon tea to the workers, which meant she got to see Jimmy often during the day, but they had no chance to be alone. The obvious route for the short distance from Jack's hay paddocks to the house lay across cleared ground, so there were no quiet walks home together. Instead Amy trudged to and from the haymaking by herself, and Jimmy came up with her brothers at the end of the day.

That Thursday Jack took Amy into town with Susannah and the two little boys, leaving John, Harry and Jimmy to turn the hay. Thomas was entrusted to Jack, and Susannah led the way into the draper's shop. Mrs Nichol ushered Susannah to a tall stool in front of the counter, and lifted down bolts of fabric for their inspection. Amy stood by the rolls of silk, gazing at the beautiful fabric in delight.

'Your first silk dress, dear,' Mrs Nichol gushed. 'What do you think you'd like?'

Amy tore her eyes away from the silk with difficulty. 'Oh… I suppose I have to choose one, don't I?' She looked back at the fabric. 'There're such a lot of them. Well… what about this one?' She pointed to a plain silk in pale pink. She usually seemed to have pink dresses, so it was probably a safe choice.

'No,' Susannah said decisively. 'You're not having that—it wouldn't do a thing for you. No, I think *this* one.' She indicated a bolt of blue silk. When Mrs Nichol unrolled it on the counter, Amy saw that the light seemed to play across the silk in waves, sometimes paler and sometimes darker. It reminded her of sunshine on the sea. Amy thought she had never seen a more beautiful fabric.

Mrs Nichol held it up against Amy. 'Oh, yes, with your colouring this will look beautiful. You certainly have good taste, Mrs Leith. Now, dear,' she smiled at Amy, 'how much do you think you'll need? What sort of dress are you going to make?'

'She's not making it,' Susannah interrupted, and Amy turned to her in bewilderment. Was Susannah going to take the dress away from her after all?

'But Susannah, I thought you said I could have it.'

Susannah silenced her with a wave of her hand. 'If your father's to spend all this money on a silk dress for a child, it's up to me to see it's not completely wasted. I'm not going to have you spoil this material. Mrs Nichol, I want you to make a dress for Amy.'

'Of course, Mrs Leith, it'll be a pleasure.' Mrs Nichol took out her tape measure and noted down a bemused Amy's measurements. 'You'll look *beautiful* in this,' she said effusively. 'She's such a pretty girl,' she said to Susannah.

'She's very small,' said Susannah.

'She's dainty. What style did you have in mind, dear?' Mrs Nichol asked, turning back to Amy.

'I thought I'd make it plain, maybe with a frill at the bottom?'

'That wouldn't do justice to the fabric,' Susannah broke in. 'Mrs Nichol, I want it narrow in the bodice, then flaring out over the hips and very full around the hem. Loop the upper part over her hips, then the rest will look like an underskirt, except in the same material. Narrow sleeves, too, with a frill around the cuffs—this lace is rather nice.' She picked up some wide ivory lace from the counter. 'What do you think of this for the cuffs?' She was talking to the dressmaker rather than to Amy.

'Very pretty,' Mrs Nichol agreed. 'Now, around the hem a pleated organdie frill would be nice. I could attach this lace to it—see, it goes nicely with the wide lace for the cuffs.'

They were ignoring her, but Amy broke in timidly. 'Wouldn't that lace around the hem be a bit hard to wash?'

'I'll attach the frill so you can easily take it off for washing, then sew it on again,' Mrs Nichol explained.

'Yes, the organdie frill is just right,' Susannah agreed. She pursed her lips. 'I suppose this is rather foolish, having such an elaborate dress made for a girl her age.'

'The style is perhaps a little old for her—but if I put on a good, deep hem she can lower it when she goes into adult clothes. She should get several years of wear out of it that way.'

'Hmm. That seems sensible enough.' Susannah stood up. 'Is that all you need to know? When can I collect the dress?'

'I should have it ready in two weeks. Bring her in for a fitting next week, I'll have it cut out and pinned by then.' It would be finished in plenty of time for the dance, Amy was relieved to realise.

'Susannah,' Amy said when they were walking back to meet her father. 'About my dress...'

'What are you nagging about now? You're not having anything else—that dress is going to cost quite enough money.'

'No, I just wanted... I just wanted to say thank you. I mean, about saying I could have the dress made and everything. It's going to be beautiful, and you picked such nice material and lace and things—'

'Don't fuss,' said Susannah. 'You had no idea what you wanted—you're too young to have any idea of style, anyway. I didn't want to see you looking ridiculous, that's all.' But Amy could see that Susannah was gratified by her praise.

The following day the hay was ready to be stacked, and again the men of the valley gathered for the laborious work. Amy had to make piles of sandwiches and pies, along with cakes, scones and tarts, to feed them all. It was difficult for her to carry four baskets full of food and drink, and she was grateful that the hay paddocks were so close to the farmhouse.

When Amy was gathering up the plates and mugs from lunch, her father ambled over in her direction. 'We'll be finishing up this paddock in a couple of hours, then we'll go over and stack Charlie's bit of hay,' he said. 'So you'd better bring the afternoon tea over there.'

'All right, Pa.' Although she knew it was irrational, Amy felt a reluctance to go on to Charlie Stewart's farm. She said nothing of it to her father. Lizzie was right: Charlie was just a grumpy old man, and there was no reason to be frightened of him.

But when she carried down the afternoon tea things Amy felt annoyance rather than fear. It really was a long way to struggle with her heavy baskets, and every time she climbed a fence it meant putting them down, scrambling over, then hauling the baskets after her.

She was hot and flustered by the time she reached the hay paddock where the men had just started building a small stack, but she felt better when Jimmy greeted her with a warm smile. He was the first to reach her, and Amy knew it was not just eagerness for the food.

'You look worn out, sweetheart,' he said, too quietly for the other men to hear as they approached. 'You sit down and I'll set these things out.'

'No, you mustn't—it's my job. Anyway, they'll all laugh if they see you doing that,' Amy protested. But Jimmy insisted on helping her, and to her surprise Frank helped too when he came up to them.

Charlie took his food in silence and went a short distance away from the others. When Jack walked over to Amy she saw him frown at his neighbour. 'Bad tempered so-and-so,' Jack muttered as he loaded his plate. 'Amy, when you go home again you'd better go around by the road.'

Amy's heart sank. 'But that's quite a bit further, Pa, especially with all these baskets. Why do I have to do that?'

'Because Charlie says he doesn't want you wandering around his farm—he says you'll frighten the cows in that paddock by the fence because they're not used to skirts.' He scowled in Charlie's direction. 'Load of rubbish, but it's his farm so he can say who comes and goes on it. Flaming cheek—I notice he's happy enough to eat the stuff you brought.' Charlie was, indeed, tucking greedily into a slice of mutton pie.

'Oh. All right.' Amy resigned herself to the unpleasant trek. She glanced at Jimmy, and was startled to see anger on his face, but he spoke very calmly.

'I think that's a bit far for Amy to carry all these things. There's not that much hay to pick up here, how about I take them for her? It won't take me long to get there and back.'

'That's a kind thought. Yes, you take the girl home—there's no need for you to come back afterwards, but you can start getting the cows in if you want.'

So when they had all finished eating, Jimmy gathered up Amy's baskets and they set off down the road.

'That was nice of you, Jimmy,' Amy said as soon as they were out of earshot.

'I can't have my little sweetheart wearing herself out like that, can I? I wish I'd thought about you bringing all this down in the first place—I should have carried it for you then.' Jimmy glanced over his shoulder. 'No chance of a kiss, I'm afraid—we're still well in sight of the workers.'

161

'It's nice just to be with you,' Amy said. 'You must be getting sick of the sight of hay by now. Stacking's hard work, isn't it?'

Jimmy grinned at her. 'Not as hard as entertaining Susannah. Oh, I suppose I shouldn't say that—I wouldn't have come down here if it wasn't for her, then I never would have met you. It's no harder than trying to keep Mother happy.'

Amy felt a burst of gratitude towards her stepmother. Susannah might be difficult, but she had brought Jimmy to the farm, and that covered a multitude of faults.

'What's your other sister like?' she asked.

'Constance? I suppose she's a lot like Susannah, really. She's two years younger than her—five years older than me. They both used to boss me around when we were all young—it should be against the law for a boy to have older sisters!' He laughed at the thought.

'Constance is prettier than Susannah, though. Not that that makes her a beauty—nothing like you—but she's always been rather fond of herself. She was a bit of a flirt when she was a girl, Mother was quite relieved when Henry proposed to her. Constance got married when she was nineteen, just after Henry qualified as a lawyer.'

'What did Susannah think of that?'

'Just what you'd expect. Constance didn't help by going on and on about how nice it was to be getting married before she was in her twenties. And there was Susannah, twenty-one and never been asked. She didn't mind so much when Henry was still struggling and Constance had to make do with two or three dresses, but when he started to get on... well, you can imagine.'

'Yes, I think I can. Poor Susannah.'

Jimmy warmed to his subject. 'Then you should have heard Constance when Susannah told her she was getting married—"Oh, darling, how wonderful. At your age, too—you're so lucky to have found a *mature* man". Susannah was so proud of herself, and all Constance could do was be patronising. Of course when Susannah was out of earshot Constance didn't call him mature—he was Susannah's old farmer. "At least the poor dear shouldn't have to put up with him for too many years, he's so old"—'

Jimmy stopped abruptly and looked at Amy. She felt her face burning. 'Amy, I am an insensitive idiot and I deserve to be kicked, repeating that about your father. I'm sorry—can you forgive me?'

'It's all right,' Amy said when she could trust herself to speak. It's not as if you said it yourself. And Pa is an awful lot older than Susannah.'

'Well, if it's any consolation, I think your father's the fittest man for

162

his age I've ever met. He'll probably live to be ninety.'

Amy was thoughtful for some time. 'I'm glad you told me that, Jimmy,' she said when they had turned off the valley road and were back on Jack's farm. 'It sort of helps me understand Susannah a bit better—why she gets difficult sometimes.'

'She certainly gives you a hard time, doesn't she? Sometimes when she snaps at you I feel like snapping back at her, but of course I can't say a word. We don't want her getting suspicious.'

'Oh, Susannah hasn't been difficult since you came—not like she was before, anyway. She used to go really strange, especially when the babies were coming. She'd cry all the time, then she'd yell and scream, at me mostly—she threw a plate at me once. And one time she even made Pa...' she stopped, unwilling to relive that particular memory.

Jimmy looked at her in astonishment. 'Really? I didn't know she was in that bad a state. She used to be quite a lively sort of person—your father was taken with her as soon as he arrived at our place. Of course she *was* making an effort to impress him—it worked, too, didn't it? Poor old girl.' He gave a shrug. 'Ah well, she got what she wanted. She's no one but herself to blame if it's not what she expected.'

'I suppose not,' Amy said doubtfully.

When they reached the farmhouse, Jimmy put down the baskets in the porch and looked around. 'No sign of Susannah. What about slipping off for a minute?'

'Well,' Amy said, torn between duty and the desire to be with him, 'I probably should start getting dinner on—and Pa said for you to get the cows in.'

'Just for a minute. Come on.' He took her hand and tugged. She went with him around the hill to where a small grove of trees sheltered them from prying eyes.

'I can't stay long,' said Amy.

'Neither can I. Let's not waste time.' He put his arms around her, and Amy raised her face willingly for a kiss. 'I love you, Amy,' he whispered as his mouth came down on hers.

'I love you, too,' she said when he released her mouth.

Jimmy stared at her with a yearning expression. 'You are so beautiful.' He kissed her again, more passionately this time, and Amy felt herself responding. She slid her arms around his waist and pressed her body hard against his.

She became aware that her breasts were rubbing against his chest and that the contact gave her pleasure. She wriggled a little, enjoying the feeling. *Is this wicked? I wouldn't let him touch me like this, and now I'm sort of doing it myself. But it's just a cuddle—surely that can't be too bad?*

Jimmy gave a low moan. He lifted his mouth from hers and whispered her name raggedly. 'Amy, Amy. I want you so much. I want to be with you forever. Amy!' He kissed her almost roughly, and for a moment he held her so tight that Amy could hardly breathe. Then his grip slackened enough for him to slip a hand between their bodies. Amy found one of her breasts being very gently caressed.

For a moment she went rigid, then she relaxed into his arms. He was being so gentle, and he loved her. Maybe it was all right to do this? Even if it wasn't, she didn't want him to stop. She felt a stab of disappointment when he dropped his arms.

'I've done it again, Amy.' He gave her a rueful smile. 'I'm not very good at controlling myself around you. Are you going to send me away? You can if you want—I'll go if you say the word.' His eyes pleaded with her for forgiveness.

'No! I don't want you to go—I don't want you to ever go away.' She flung her arms around him.

'And you forgive me for doing that?'

Amy hid her face against his chest and nodded. 'I don't think it's such a terrible thing to have done,' she whispered. 'Not bad enough for me to send you away for, anyway. But you shouldn't do it again.'

'I'll try,' he said. 'I'll try really hard.'

17

February 1884

When Amy got out of bed on the eighth of February, the first thing she did was put a cross through the '7' on her calendar. She looked with satisfaction at the red-circled '8': the day of the hay dance had arrived.

Despite all the activities of her day, the hours until dinner seemed to drag. Although the dance wasn't to start till seven, Amy looked at the clock many times as she helped Susannah prepare and serve the evening meal, and she was too excited to do much more than toy with her food.

Lizzie and Bill arrived soon after dinner, Lizzie carrying her new dress wrapped in paper, and the girls went off into Amy's room to help one another get ready. Amy pulled the silk gown from her wardrobe with a flourish.

'What do you think of it?' She had the pleasure of seeing Lizzie's eyes grow wide in surprise.

'That is just gorgeous,' Lizzie breathed. 'However did you talk Aunt Susannah into letting you have a dress like that?'

'I didn't talk her into anything—she decided it all, what material to use and how the dress was going to look. Susannah really does have good taste, you know.'

'Mmm. No one could argue with that. Let's get ready, those boys will start complaining if we take more than five minutes.'

They took a good deal longer than five minutes by the time they had put on their new dresses and then fussed over each other's hair. Lizzie's dress was of pale pink silk covered in tiny flowers of a deeper pink, with white cuffs and collar and a wide white sash. Her fair hair and pink cheeks completed the picture of a rosy girl just crossing into young womanhood.

'Have you got anything for your hair that would go with the dress?' Lizzie asked.

'Yes!' Amy pulled her beautiful blue velvet ribbon from its place in the drawer, and Lizzie tied it around Amy's dark curls.

'That's just right,' Lizzie said. 'When did you get it?'

Amy was silent for a moment, then she decided to share the small secret. 'Jimmy gave it to me.'

'He's giving you presents, is he? What does that mean?'

'It means we're friends. Don't pry. Do you think my dress is sitting right over the hips?'

That distracted Lizzie. When Amy's dress had been tweaked and puffed out to their mutual satisfaction, Lizzie stepped back and gave Amy a long, admiring gaze. 'Turn around,' she ordered. Amy twirled on the spot, making the silk rustle. The dress fitted like a dream. Amy thought that no princess could ever have had a more beautiful gown. 'Well, everyone's certainly going to be looking at you tonight,' said Lizzie.

'Not Frank, Lizzie. He's only interested in you.' *And I'm only interested in Jimmy.*

'It's such a nuisance that his house is the other side of the school— I'd like him to walk me home. Fancy having to walk home with my brother.' Lizzie gave an exaggerated sigh. 'Ah well, I'll just have to make the most of the time while we're at the dance.'

'I hope you're not going to make a spectacle of yourself, Lizzie.'

'What's that supposed to mean? We'll have more chance to talk than we usually get, that's all. Do you think I'd let him kiss me in front of everyone?'

'That's all right, then.' Amy gave a small giggle. 'Just don't get Frank too excited.'

'Maybe I want him to get just a little bit excited,' Lizzie said thoughtfully. 'I don't know why I'm talking about it with you, though, you're much too young to understand.'

'Oh, am I just?' Amy retorted. 'Maybe you don't know everything, Elizabeth Leith.' She regretted her small outburst at once.

Lizzie looked at her through narrowed eyes. 'What are you talking about?'

'Nothing. It was just a joke—I was sick of you showing off, that's all.'

'You sounded pretty serious to me. What's going on, Amy? Have you got an understanding with Jimmy? You might have told me.' She sounded hurt.

'There's nothing to tell. We're friends, I've already told you that.'

'You're keen on him, you told me that, too. Has he been taking liberties with you?'

'Liberties!' Amy scoffed. 'Don't be so prim.'

'I'm not prim—I'm careful, and you should be careful too. Has he proposed to you?'

'Of course he hasn't. We've only known each other for two months.' *He said he wanted to be with me forever.* Amy smiled at the memory.

'Amy, stop grinning like that and listen to me. I don't want you to go and live in Auckland, but if Jimmy can provide for you and it's what you want, well, I suppose that's all right. I'd miss you, but you've always gone on about living in the city. But does he want to marry you or what?'

'Don't be so silly!'

'It's not silly.' Lizzie took hold of Amy's wrist. 'Tell me the truth, now—have you let him kiss you?'

Amy thought of the caresses that had gone with the kisses, and felt herself blush at the thought of Lizzie's reaction to being told about those. *Maybe I shouldn't have let him touch me like that.* Guilt made her speak more sharply than she had intended. 'What if I have? It's none of your business.'

'You mustn't! Not until you know what his intentions are.'

Amy snatched her arm away. 'Stop telling me what to do! You're just jealous—jealous because I've got Jimmy and you've only got Frank.' The moment the words were out Amy wished she had bitten her tongue.

Lizzie looked as if she had been struck. 'I'm not jealous,' she said very quietly. 'I just care about you, that's all.' For a moment Amy thought her cousin might cry.

'Lizzie, I'm sorry. I didn't mean that. It was a stupid thing to say. I like Frank, you know I do—I just get a bit tired of you bossing me around.'

'I don't boss. I was trying to make you see sense. I'll stop trying if that's what you want.'

'Yes, it is. Come on, let's go or the boys will go without us.'

They walked out to the kitchen where the rest of the family were assembled. Jack's eyebrows shot up when he saw them. 'Well, look at you! You girls look like you've stepped out of a picture—look at them, Susannah, pink and blue and good enough to eat.'

'You look very sweet together,' Susannah agreed. She gave Amy an appraising look. 'The frill isn't sitting properly around the sleeves—here, let me.' She fussed over the lace, then puffed out the overskirt. 'That dress really does suit you, Amy.'

Jimmy said nothing in front of the others, but the admiration Amy saw in his eyes gave her a thrill of pleasure.

'I've never seen you look like this, girl,' Jack said, gazing at Amy. 'You look like your ma—not that I could ever afford a fancy dress like that for her.' He cleared his throat noisily. 'You boys take care of her for me tonight—there's plenty of you, she should be safe enough.'

'Can we get going?' said Harry. 'The dance'll be half over before we even get there at this rate.'

The girls loaded the young men with their share of the supper, then they donned their walking boots, carrying their dancing shoes in their hands as they set off from the back porch.

'Now, if Amy gets tired one of you can bring her home—I don't want her walking home by herself,' Jack called from the doorway, much to

Amy's embarrassment.

'I wish he wouldn't talk as though I'm a baby—why should I get tired before anyone else?' she complained to Lizzie, but her cousin was unusually quiet.

The sky was still a rich blue; sunset would not be for another half hour. Jimmy walked beside John until they were well out of sight of the house; Amy knew he was aware of her father standing on the porch watching them all. The impatient Harry, with Bill for company, was soon a short distance ahead of them, leaving Amy and Lizzie in the rear.

It was not in Lizzie's nature to let herself or Amy be neglected, and she soon complained. 'Hey, you boys are meant to be *escorting* us, you know—how about waiting for us instead of rushing off like that?' Amy was relieved to hear Lizzie being bossy again; a quiet Lizzie was unnatural.

'Can't wait all night for you,' said Harry, but Jimmy slowed for the girls to catch up, while John joined Harry and Bill.

'You're quite right—fancy ignoring two such lovely ladies,' Jimmy said, flashing his infectious grin. Lizzie did not smile back at him, and Amy hoped she was not going to be difficult. Jimmy took his place on Amy's right-hand side, just as Lizzie looped her arm through Amy's. Lizzie's familiar gesture of affection suddenly struck Amy as possessive, but she was relieved that her cousin seemed to have forgotten Amy's earlier cruel words.

'Will it be the same people who went to the Christmas party?' Jimmy asked.

'Some of them,' said Amy. 'Not so many old people, though.'

'What about your charming neighbour?' They were walking past Charlie's farm as he spoke.

'Humph,' Lizzie said in disgust, abandoning her haughty silence for the moment. 'He'd better not be. He wouldn't dance or talk to anyone.'

'There'll be us, of course,' Amy put in. 'And maybe the Aitkens— they've got a lot of little ones, though, so they mightn't be able to. Frank will be there—'

'How could he bear to stay away?' Jimmy said, again without raising an answering smile from Lizzie.

'And some of the others from Orere Beach, and from further down Waituhi Beach, too. Maybe fifteen or twenty people altogether—it's quite a big dance. Oh,' she gave him a wistful smile, 'I suppose that doesn't seem very big to you at all.'

'Well, I've been to bigger ones,' he said. 'But I'm sure I've never been to one with better company—or prettier girls.' Lizzie gave a snort. She dropped Amy's arm and caught up with their brothers.

'What's wrong with her?' Jimmy asked quietly. 'She hasn't had a row with Frank, has she?'

'Oh no, nothing like that. No, it's sort of my fault—I said something horrible to her.'

'You? I can't imagine you saying anything horrible.'

'Well, I did this time, I'm afraid. Lizzie doesn't really approve of… you and me.'

'What did you tell her about us?' Jimmy asked quickly.

'Nothing—I didn't tell her anything. She guessed a bit, though.'

'Hmm. Never mind, take no notice of her. I don't think I've ever been to a dance in a school before.'

'It's the only place around here that's big enough. Pa and the others built the school, so we get to use it for the dance.' She sighed. 'It's going to be strange being there again.'

'Why strange, sweetheart? It can't be all that many years since you went to school.'

'No. Not many at all.' Amy was quiet for some time.

'What are you thinking about, little one?'

'The school. It makes me sad when I think about it. Jimmy, do you remember one day you asked me if I'd like to go to Auckland?'

He looked thoughtful. 'Yes, I do. You said you used to think you'd go there, but you wouldn't tell me about it. Will you tell me now?'

'Yes. I don't want to have secrets from you. I was learning to be a teacher for a little while.' She glanced at him, worried that he might laugh at the idea, but he was staring at her in astonishment. 'Why are you looking at me like that?'

'You mean with all the work you do, you found time for a job?'

'Well, I was pretty busy while I was doing it.' She sighed. 'Too busy, really. Pa made me stop, then when Susannah came Miss Evans—that's the teacher—thought maybe I could start again.'

'My sister didn't agree, I gather.'

'No.' Amy was pleased at how steady her voice sounded. 'Everyone seemed to think I was mad to even want to be a teacher. They all talked about old maids and things. Do you think it's silly for me to want to *do* something?'

'I think you'll never stop surprising me. Trust you to be different from other women. And trust you to want to be useful. You're certainly clever enough to be a teacher, I'm sure of that.'

'You're the only person except Miss Evans who's ever understood! Oh, Jimmy, I do love you!'

'Shh,' he warned. 'Save that till later—there're too many ears about.' Amy saw that Lizzie was indeed looking over her shoulder at them.

They rounded the last corner and saw that a few buggies had pulled up outside the schoolhouse and several horses were in the school's grazing paddock. Frank was standing in the road; as soon as he saw Lizzie his face lit up. He hesitated for a moment, then walked over to join the Leiths. Lizzie at once manœuvred herself to Frank's side, and they mounted the steps ahead of the others.

Amy hung up her cloak in the school porch. She put her boots at the end of a neat row that had formed, and replaced them with light kid shoes, far too impractical for outdoors.

'Now I get to walk in with the prettiest girl in the room,' Jimmy said, offering her his arm.

'You haven't seen them all yet,' Amy laughed as she looped her own arm through his.

'I don't need to.'

The schoolroom looked very different from the last time Amy had seen it. All the desks and benches had been pushed against the walls, leaving a clear space for dancing, and the room was decorated with nikau and fern fronds. 'Oh, isn't it pretty?' she said in delight.

'Mmm. Very pastoral.'

Rachel Aitken saw Amy and rushed over to her. 'Hello, Amy. Do you like the room? The children and I decorated it this afternoon.'

'It's lovely. Is your mother looking after your little ones tonight?'

Rachel gave a broad smile. 'Yes! This year I haven't got a tiny baby, so I'm having a night out. It'll be the first time Matt and I have danced for... oh, I don't know, years and years—I hope we still remember how!' She noticed the plate Jimmy was holding. 'Let me take that, the supper table's over there, but I've put a cloth over the food so you men can't start on it too early. Thank you, Mr... Amy, I'm afraid I've forgotten your young man's name. You'll have to introduce me again.'

Amy was flustered at hearing Jimmy referred to as her young man, and before she had the chance to say anything Jimmy answered for himself. 'I'm Jimmy—Jimmy Taylor. I remember you, Mrs Aitken, you've got that nice little girl—Bessie, isn't that her name?'

'That's right, Bessie's my oldest. Amy used to teach her at the school. Fancy you remembering her name. Well, I'd better finish setting out this food, I hope you enjoy yourself tonight.' Rachel went over to the supper table.

'That's her husband, you met him at the Christmas party.' Amy pointed to the tall, thickset Matt Aitken who was setting up a barrel of beer in one corner, beside a table loaded with empty mugs and bottles of lemonade. 'That's Bob Forster with him. Over there are the Jenners,' she indicated a couple in their mid-twenties standing next to a man of about thirty, 'they live east of the valley. I don't know them very well, but that's Dick Jenner and his sister Mabel. Dick's talking to Sam Collins, they're neighbours. And there's Marion Forster, I wonder what they've done with their little ones. I don't know that lady with her, though.' She led Jimmy over to introduce him.

It took a moment to attract Mrs Forster's attention. Marion was indulging in her favourite activity, talking excitedly while waving her arms around to emphasise her point. As her companion seemed as keen a talker, their small corner was by far the noisiest part of the room. Marion eventually paused for breath, glanced around and saw Amy.

'Amy, how are you?' As always, Marion's mane of rich brown hair with its hint of red looked barely contained under her hat. She rushed on without giving Amy time to answer. 'Rachel and I are the chaperones tonight—what a responsibility!' she laughed. 'Mrs Carr's looking after my two wild creatures—she'll be worn out tomorrow. Now, who's this young man of yours—Bob, come over here and meet Amy's young man,' she called, and Bob wandered over from where he had been talking to Matt Aitken.

'This is Jimmy, Susannah's brother. He's visiting Susannah this summer.' Jimmy shook hands with Bob.

'Do you know my sister?' Marion asked. 'This is Jane, she's the baby of the family. She's the only one Ma and Pa have still got at home in Te Puke. Jane's staying with us for a few weeks.' Amy could see the family resemblance, though Marion was in her mid-twenties while her sister looked to be about eighteen. Jane Neill had the same brown eyes and luxuriant hair as her sister, but in her case the hint of red had become a definite auburn. She also had the same lively tongue.

'Marion's dragged me along to help with the singing,' Jane said. 'She told me there aren't enough women, either, so I expect I'll be danced off my feet!' She laughed merrily.

'Hey, Bob,' Matt Aitken called. 'How about you and Marion start working—some of us want to dance, you know.'

Bob took his fiddle from its case and tuned up, evoking groans from the others in the room. 'That cat's not dead yet, it wants its guts back,' Dick Jenner called, but Bob soon had sweet notes coming from the fiddle. Marion's rich contralto soared with his music, and all around the room people took their partners.

'May I have the pleasure of this dance?' Jimmy asked, and Amy found herself being swept around the floor in his arms. Jimmy was a wonderful dancer; he moved smoothly and with confidence, and Amy felt sure the others were all impressed by her handsome partner. She noticed Lizzie standing beside Frank; Lizzie was swaying to the music, but she had obviously been unsuccessful in persuading Frank to take the floor.

Amy drifted round in a dream, but after the first two songs she felt sorry for John, Harry and Bill, who were partnerless. 'I'd better dance with one of the others—there aren't enough girls.' She went over and took John's arm, leaving Jimmy talking to Bill and Harry. This time Lizzie managed to get Frank onto the dance floor. Amy looked at Frank struggling not to fall over his feet and she had to hide a smile, especially when she saw Lizzie wince as Frank trod on her toes.

She was about to ask Harry if he wanted the next dance, but before she had the chance her brother had led Jane Neill onto the floor, so she danced with Bill instead. Lizzie talked Frank into a second dance, then the first set of songs ended and Bob and Marion took a well-deserved rest.

'Come on,' Matt called when five minutes had passed since the last song. 'Start playing again—I want to dance with my wife.' He put his arm around Rachel's waist.

Marion pointed at her throat. 'Not till I've had a decent rest—I'll lose my voice if I'm not careful.'

'That'd be a miracle,' her husband retorted. He ducked as Marion aimed a mock punch at him.

'Jane, you sing a couple,' Marion said. Her sister stood beside Bob and began to sing. She had a sweet soprano voice strong enough to be heard easily over the fiddle.

Amy felt she had done her duty by the partnerless men for a while, so she willingly let Jimmy take her by the hand, and abandoned herself to the pleasure of gliding around the floor in his arms.

Frank let Lizzie persuade him to dance once more, but when the next song started he looked at the other couples whirling confidently around and decided to give up the struggle. 'I think I've had enough dancing for now, Lizzie,' he said. 'Your feet must be getting sore, too—I've stood on them enough.'

'Have you? I hadn't really noticed. I'm getting tired, anyway, let's sit down. It's so hot in here, too.'

Although there were plenty of seats, Frank thought the bench Lizzie chose didn't seem to be quite long enough for the number of people sitting on it, but the two of them managed to squeeze on at the end.

Lizzie fanned herself with her hand. 'It's terribly hot in this room.'

'I'll get you a drink.' Frank returned with a glass of lemonade for Lizzie and a beer for himself.

Lizzie downed her lemonade quickly. 'Oh, I think I might faint, I'm so hot.'

Frank felt a surge of alarm; mostly out of genuine concern for Lizzie, but also in part from fear of everyone staring at them if she were to collapse. Lizzie slumped against him a little, increasing Frank's nervousness. 'Do you feel crook? Do you want to go home?'

'No, I think I'll be all right if I get some fresh air. I'll go outside for a minute.' She stood up. 'Oh, will you take my arm, Frank? I do feel a bit dizzy.'

Frank put down his beer and took hold of Lizzie's arm. They walked to the porch and outside into the dim night. The moon had not yet risen, and their eyes took some time to adjust to the darkness. The silk of Lizzie's sleeve felt smooth under his hand; he was aware of her soft flesh just a thin layer of fabric away. Out of sight of the others he felt suddenly brave. 'Lizzie, you look nice tonight. You look really nice.'

'Thank you, Frank.' He could hear the smile in her voice. 'It's much cooler here, shall we sit down for a bit?'

There was a low wooden seat against the outside wall of the school, just around the corner from the door. They made their way to it, walking carefully to avoid stumbling in the darkness. When they sat down Frank kept hold of Lizzie's arm; he wondered if she would pull it away, but she made no move to.

'How do you feel now, Lizzie?' he asked.

'Much better. Isn't it lovely and peaceful out here? It's so hot and noisy in that room. I was tired of dancing, too.'

Frank felt keenly his own lack of skill in that area. 'I'm not much good at dancing—you should have a go with one of the others. They're all better than me. What about Jimmy? He's a really good dancer, you'd enjoy it with him.'

'No!' Lizzie said, startling Frank with her vehemence. 'I don't want to dance with someone else, especially not him.' She was quiet for a moment. 'I'd much rather talk with you than dance with anyone else.'

'Would you?' Frank studied her closely. His eyes had adjusted enough for him to be able to make out the pale oval of her face, with her hair even paler around it. She was looking at him very seriously, and for a moment he wondered if she was upset about something. But then she smiled.

'Yes, I would. I really like talking with you, Frank, I wish we had more

173

chance to. Pa sort of takes you over when you come to our place.' She shivered a little, and moved closer to him on the bench. 'It's a lot cooler out here.'

Frank could feel her thigh pressing against him, and she looped her arm more tightly through his. 'Are you getting cold? Do you want to go back inside?' he asked, trying to hide his reluctance to return to the noisy room.

'Not just yet. Let's talk a bit more.'

Her face suddenly seemed much closer; he wondered which of them had moved. He stroked the silk of her sleeve, aware of his hand's roughness on the smooth fabric. 'I'm not much good at talking, Lizzie. I think about things, but I can't find the right words.'

'Sometimes you don't need words,' Lizzie whispered, so quietly that he had to bring his face even closer to hers to catch what she said.

Now they were only inches apart. Lizzie's lips were parted slightly, and he could hear her breathing fast. A wisp of blonde hair had escaped from its ribbon to lie against her cheek. He brushed it away very gently before touching his lips to hers.

He pulled away, astonished at what he had done and half expecting Lizzie to slap him, but when he dared look at her again he saw that she was smiling. 'Was that all right—you don't mind?' he asked unnecessarily. Lizzie nodded, and he could see her eyes shining. For a few moments nothing was said, then Frank asked, 'Can I do it again?'

'Yes, please,' she murmured.

Lizzie tilted her head just as Frank moved towards her, and their noses collided. 'Aw, gee, sorry Lizzie—I'm not much good at this.'

'Neither am I.' There was a hint of laughter in her voice, but Frank was somehow sure she wasn't laughing at him. 'We'll get better.' Her eyes invited him to practise.

This time there were no mishaps, and when Frank finally lifted his mouth from Lizzie's to take a gulp of air he realised he had been holding his breath for some time.

'I think we'd better go inside now,' Lizzie said, a slight tremor in her voice. 'We don't want people talking.'

'No,' Frank agreed, despite his reluctance to end the moment. He helped Lizzie to her feet. 'I hope we can... talk some more soon,' he said as they rounded the corner of the building.

'Me too.'

18

February 1884

Frank was just stepping aside to let Lizzie walk up the steps into the porch ahead of him when a burly figure pushed past with barely a grunt of recognition.

'That's Charlie Stewart!' Lizzie said. 'What's he doing here?'

Frank shrugged. 'Anyone's allowed to come, I guess. I bet he hasn't come for the dancing, though.' They laughed together, and Frank felt a warm glow as he walked into the room behind Lizzie.

'What have you two been up to?' Bill said with a smile when they rejoined the group.

'I didn't feel very well, the heat was getting me down, so Frank took me outside for a minute.' Lizzie challenged Bill with her eyes to say any more about it.

Bill laughed. 'Frank looks as though he got a bit overheated himself.' Frank felt his face burn, and he looked studiously at the floor.

'I suppose you think that's funny,' Lizzie said indignantly.

'Well, I'm supposed to look after my little sister,' said Bill. He slapped Frank on the back. 'Looks like I don't need to bother if you're going to do it for me, Frank.'

Marion Forster had relieved Jane of her singing duty. When the next dance started Harry again claimed Jane as his partner, while Jimmy led Amy onto the floor once more. 'I see your skirt-hating old neighbour's turned up,' Jimmy said.

'Yes,' said Amy. 'He hasn't talked to anyone, just sort of grunted at a couple of the men and helped himself to some beer, then plonked himself down in that corner. I suppose he's come for the free beer.'

'Hmm. That and a look at the pretty girls, I'd say. He's been having a good stare at all the women—especially you, of course. At least he's got good taste.'

'He makes me a bit nervous,' Amy confessed. 'He looks so grumpy all the time.'

Jimmy held her more tightly. 'You're safe with me, darling.'

'I know.' For the next few minutes Amy was aware of no one in the room except the two of them.

When supper time came at ten o'clock she was amazed at how quickly the evening had passed. The supper table was attacked with vigour, and the food was rapidly demolished.

'Gives you a good appetite, all this dancing, eh?' Harry said through a mouthful of cold chicken.

'So does courting.' Jimmy gestured with his eyes towards Frank, who was devouring a slice of pie as though it was the first edible item he had seen all day; but he spoke too quietly for Lizzie to hear.

After supper the dancing was about to start again when there was a noise at the door. Amy glanced over to see what was going on. 'Oh, no,' she said as four young men, all in their early twenties, sauntered into the room. 'It's some of the Feenans.'

'The mad Irish?'

'Yes. Oh, I do hope they don't cause any trouble.'

Bob Forster and Matt Aitken walked over to the uninvited visitors. 'You fellows can only stay if you behave yourselves,' Matt said sternly. 'Understand?'

'Course we will,' Mike Feenan, spokesman for the group, said. 'You won't know we're here.' They walked a little unsteadily over to the supper table and picked disconsolately at the chicken bones.

'Kicked out of the hotel, I'd say,' Jimmy murmured in Amy's ear.

'Hey, red, you going to sing?' one of the Feenans called, seeing Marion standing by Bob.

She looked at her husband questioningly; he shrugged and picked up his fiddle. Marion began to sing, and the various couples took the floor.

Amy ignored the Feenans as best she could, though every time she and Jimmy danced past the supper table one of them would whistle at her, and occasionally they called out to one another, 'Here comes the good-looking one again'. It spoiled her pleasure in dancing. When the song ended she was about to ask Jimmy if they could sit down for a while when she felt a hand on her shoulder. It made her jump, and she was even more startled when she turned around to see that it was Mike Feenan standing behind her.

'What about a dance with me now?' He pushed his face close to hers so that Amy got a whiff of beer-sodden breath.

'No, thank you.' She stepped away from him. He made another grab for her shoulder, misjudged the distance and stumbled, then lunged again, this time making contact. Amy tried to twist away, but he held her tightly. She jerked her head around towards Jimmy in fright.

'Come on, gorgeous, you want to dance with me, don't you?'

'You heard the lady,' said Jimmy. His mouth smiled, but his eyes glittered. 'She doesn't want to dance with you. Take your hands off her.'

'What's it to you?' Mike Feenan jeered. 'You in your fancy clothes— let the girl dance with a real man.'

'I *said* take your hands off her.' Jimmy knocked Mike's hand off Amy's shoulder.

Despite the amount of alcohol he had obviously consumed earlier that evening, Mike moved fast. His fist snaked out and caught Jimmy on the chin, and Amy screamed as she heard the crack of bone on bone. Jimmy's head was jolted to one side. He recovered himself and looked at Mike in naked fury for a moment before swinging his arm to connect with his opponent's jaw. Before Mike had recovered from the blow Jimmy followed it with another, then a third which saw Mike sink almost gracefully to the floor.

There was a yell of rage from the other Feenans, and they converged on Jimmy hot for vengeance. He faced the three of them with his fists up looking almost eager. Amy thrilled at his courage while at the same time she trembled with fear, but before the adversaries got within a few feet every other man in the room (even Charlie abandoned his mug of beer for the moment) had gathered round Jimmy.

Even in their drunken state the Feenan boys could see that three against ten was not a sensible proposition. They backed off, muttering darkly.

'Get out of here,' Matt ordered. 'Don't come back, either, if you value those lousy hides of yours.'

'What about Mike?' one of them demanded.

Bob Forster brought a jug of lemonade from the table and emptied it over Mike Feenan's head. Mike coughed and sputtered, then rose to his feet even more unsteadily than before. One of his companions walked over to him and Mike leaned heavily on his shoulder.

'Go, on, get out,' Matt said, giving the nearest youth a rough shove to punctuate his words. The Feenans stomped out of the room, casting black looks over their shoulders.

'We'll see them on their way,' Bob said. He and Matt, with several of the other men, walked out after the trouble-makers.

Amy saw a small trail of blood forming at the corner of Jimmy's mouth. 'Oh, you're hurt.' She brushed his mouth with her fingers.

'You should see the other fellow,' Jimmy said with a wry grin. 'That's one thing they teach you at a good grammar school, anyway—how to fight.' He wriggled his lower jaw experimentally, and Amy saw him wince. 'Don't worry, it's nothing much—it's my own fault, I should have seen that punch coming. I thought he was too drunk to move that fast. What about you? Are you all right?'

'Yes, I'm fine. I was frightened for you, that's all.'

'You look pale. Come on, let's sit down.' He led her over to one of the benches and Amy sank onto it. She realised she was shivering despite the warmth of the room.

'You got a bad shock, didn't you? You sit there quietly, I'll get you a cool drink.' Jimmy brought her a glass of lemonade, and she drank it gratefully. Her hand shook as she held the glass.

Jimmy looked at her in concern. 'You really are very pale. I think I'd better take you home.'

'No! I'll be all right, and I don't want to spoil your evening.'

'Well, I'm not sure I feel much like dancing any more tonight—this would slow me down a bit, anyway.' He showed her his right hand, and Amy saw that the knuckles were grazed. 'I did that on his bony jaw. It was worth it, though.' He gave a grim smile, then rose to his feet. 'Come on, no arguing. I'm taking you home.'

'All right. I do feel a little bit sick.'

Lizzie watched Amy and Jimmy walk towards the door. 'What's he doing with her?' she murmured to Frank.

'Taking her outside for a talk, maybe,' Frank replied with a grin, but Lizzie frowned in thought.

As Amy was putting on her boots in the porch, John came back with the other men who had seen off the Feenans. 'John, I'm taking Amy home, she's a bit upset after all that,' Jimmy said, lifting Amy's cloak from its hook as he spoke.

'Good idea,' said John. He walked with them as far as the school gate.

When Lizzie saw John going out through the porch with Amy and Jimmy she relaxed. 'It's all right, John must be going home with them. Amy got a fright from that trouble.' She allowed herself to forget about Amy and Jimmy, and instead concentrated on Frank. 'I hope you can come around to my place again sometime soon.'

'So do I. I like it at your place, it's a real family. Ben gives me a hard time over it, though. I keep telling him it's nothing to do with you... I might have to stop saying that now.' He smiled.

'Take no notice of him.'

'Well, he is my brother, Lizzie.'

'No reason to let him boss you around.' Lizzie glanced across the room, and it took her a moment to register the significance of John's presence at the beer barrel. Then she rushed over to him. 'John, where's Amy? I thought you were with her.'

'Jimmy's taken her home.'

'By themselves?'

'Yes—what's wrong with that?'

Lizzie was quiet for a moment. 'Nothing… I hope.'

Amy walked along the road at Jimmy's side, savouring the night's coolness after the noise and heat of the schoolroom. The moon had risen, giving them enough light to see their way clearly. The silence was broken only by their footsteps and the occasional mournful hooting of a morepork.

'It's so quiet here,' Jimmy said. 'It never seems to get really quiet in town. Even in the middle of the night there're always a few people rushing about.'

'It's a beautiful night.'

'And a beautiful girl beside me.' Jimmy glanced over his shoulder to check that they were out of sight of the school, then put his arm around Amy's waist. 'Your dress is lovely—it's the first time I've seen you in anything that does you justice.'

She snuggled against him. 'I had such a nice time tonight until all that trouble. I didn't want it to end.'

'Neither did I.' He bent and placed a kiss on the top of her head. 'Let's make it last a bit longer.'

'What do you mean?'

'We don't need to go straight home, do we? Let's have a bit more time together first. You're always so busy in the daytime, I hardly get a chance to see you.'

Amy hesitated for a moment. 'I suppose it would be all right, as long as we don't stay too long. There's a nice place up the road a bit, I'll show you.'

Just before the track that turned off to Amy's house, she led Jimmy away from the road into a small patch of bush. 'They haven't cleared this yet, even though it's quite flat, but there's an open bit just through here.'

They walked a little further until they came into a small clearing. Some large puriri had been chopped down there, and the second growth had not yet taken over, so that among the ferns there were patches of grass. The bush surrounded them on all sides, and the silence of the night seemed even deeper here.

'Mmm, this is nice,' Jimmy said. 'Put those down for a minute.' Amy placed her dancing shoes carefully on the ground. Jimmy held out his arms; she nestled into them and tilted her face up for a kiss. He kissed her very gently, then harder, but just as she was starting to enjoy herself he pulled away from her.

'Ow, that hurts a bit,' Jimmy said, touching his mouth gingerly. 'I would've hit that ass harder if I'd known he was going to spoil my time

179

alone with you.'

'You poor thing,' said Amy. 'You were so brave, the way you faced them all. I was really frightened for you.'

'When I saw him touch you I was so angry I almost wanted to kill him. Amy, I can't stand the thought of anyone else touching you.' He kissed her again, more carefully this time, but then to Amy's surprise he turned away and began pacing around the clearing.

'You're being fidgety again, like you are when you're stuck inside,' she scolded gently. 'What have you got to be restless about now?'

Jimmy looked startled. 'Am I? Yes, I suppose I am. I get like this when I'm trying to make up my mind to do something, too. Amy, what happened tonight with that fellow—it made me think about how I'd feel if I lost you.'

'You won't lose me,' Amy said. 'I love you.'

He crossed to her and took her in his arms. 'Let's do something about it. I want you to belong to me.'

'What do you mean?'

He was still restless. He pulled away and paced back and forth for a few more moments, then stopped and turned to face her. 'Amy, let's… no, I want to do this properly.' He put his arms around her waist and picked her up, making Amy squeal in surprise, then he sat her on a large stump.

'What are you doing?' she said through her giggles.

Jimmy went down on one knee and took her hand between both of his. 'Miss Leith,' he said very solemnly, 'will you do me the honour of giving me your hand in marriage?'

For a moment Amy's heart was too full for her to make a sound. Jimmy looked at her with apprehension growing in his eyes. 'Amy, please don't turn me down. Please say yes.'

'Yes! Yes! Yes!' Amy said, half-laughing in delight while at the same time she felt tears of happiness fill her eyes.

'Thank you!' He snatched her up from the stump and kissed her again. This time his sore mouth did not seem to trouble him. 'Oh, Amy, I love you so much.' He planted kisses all over her face, finally coming back to her mouth. 'Let's sit down,' he murmured. 'We've got a few minutes.'

'All right.' Amy slipped off her cloak and spread it out for them both. She sat down beside Jimmy in a rustle of silk, and snuggled against his side.

Jimmy gently pushed her back to lie on the cloak with her arms around his neck. He stroked her shoulder, then slid his hand down to the space between her breasts till he found the hard lump of her brooch.

'I've found my present,' he said, smiling.

'I told you I'd wear it every day.'

'Now I know you were telling me the truth. You'll be able to wear it on the outside soon, when we've announced our engagement.' His hand slipped across to fondle her breasts. This time Amy did not struggle. *He's asked me to marry him. It must be all right now, just a little touch like this.*

'You are so beautiful, and you're going to belong to me.' Jimmy gave a moan as he lowered his mouth to hers. His embraces became more urgent, and Amy felt herself responding, pushing her own body against his. His hand stroked her leg softly over and over through the silk, then he seemed to be fiddling with something on his trousers. Amy raised her head to look, but he pushed her down with another kiss.

The night air was suddenly cooler against her legs. When she glanced at her dress, she saw that it had somehow ridden up as Jimmy stroked her. She tried to reach down to straighten it, but his chest was pressed too closely against hers for her to slip her hand between them.

Then suddenly he had his leg between hers, then both legs. 'What are you doing?' she said in alarm. He silenced her with a kiss. She tried to twist her face away, but his mouth had hers firmly captured. 'Please stop it.' But her words were muffled by his mouth, so all that came out was an unintelligible mumble. His hand was pushing the two sides of her drawers apart. Then she felt a sharp, tearing pain, and she knew it was too late to struggle.

19

February 1884

Jimmy rolled away from her to lie on his back. Amy straightened her drawers and pulled her petticoats and dress down over her knees as well as she could with her hands trembling so violently, then she lay weeping silently, wondering what to do next. Jimmy was still for so long that Amy began to wonder if he had gone to sleep, but at last he stirred and rolled onto his side, raising himself on one elbow to look at her.

'You have just made me a very happy man, Amy.' He reached out to stroke her face, and pulled his fingers away wet with tears. 'What's wrong, little one? Why are you crying?'

'We've d-done a t-terrible th-thing,' Amy choked out through her sobs.

'Terrible? I thought it was rather good myself.' He gave a low chuckle. Amy was too stunned to cry for a moment, then she was racked with weeping.

'Oh, sweetheart, I'm sorry.' Jimmy slipped an arm under her shoulders. 'I'm so happy that I just didn't think about how you might be feeling. Come on, sit up and tell me why you think it's all so terrible.' He raised her and sat with his arm around her, but when Amy tried to speak all that came out was more sobs.

Jimmy pulled out a handkerchief and wiped her eyes, then held it over her nose. 'Blow,' he ordered, and she blew her nose noisily into the handkerchief. 'There, do you feel a bit better now?'

Amy's sobs slowly subsided. 'A little bit. Can I keep the handkerchief?'

'Only if you promise to give it back later—it's the one you gave me for Christmas. Now, tell me what's so bad.'

'We've done *that*, and we're not married. Isn't that wrong?'

'But we're going to get married, so it doesn't really matter.'

'Doesn't it?' Amy asked doubtfully, desperately wanting to believe him.

'Oh, I admit we've put the cart before the horse a bit, but what difference will that make once we're married? You're almost my wife already. Now, listen. First thing in the morning I'll have a talk with your father—'

'He'll be really angry with you.'

'Hey, I'm not going to tell him about *that*! There wouldn't be much left for you to marry after he'd finished with me. No, I'm going to ask him for permission to marry his beautiful daughter. How do you think he'll take it?'

Amy chewed her lip. 'He won't be very happy. I'm sure he'll say I'm too young.'

'Hmm. Well, I'll have to talk him round somehow. I don't think I can wait till he finally notices you've grown up.'

'I'd like to get married soon,' Amy said. 'It'd make me feel better about what happened.'

'Me too. All right then, I'll ask him first thing tomorrow. Now up you get and I really will take you home.' He helped her up and placed the cloak over her shoulders. 'We'd better get moving—if I'm not in bed when John gets back I'll have some explaining to do.' He laughed, and Amy smiled with him, though she was still shaken. Jimmy sounded so confident about it all, and he didn't think they'd done anything wrong. *If only Pa says yes, then everything will be all right.*

The house was in darkness when they crept up the passage and exchanged a last, brief kiss before going into their separate rooms. Amy undressed and put on her nightdress in the dark, leaving all her clothes piled on a chair rather than making any attempt to put them away. She slipped between the sheets and lay staring towards the invisible ceiling. *We're going to get married*, was her thought one moment, and a warm glow crept over her. Then *Pa might say no*, came the thought, like a hand clutching at her heart. *What if he finds out what we did? He mustn't—he just mustn't.* She tossed and turned as the thoughts chased one another around in her head. She thought she would never get to sleep, but finally she was exhausted enough to drop off.

Amy woke feeling like a wrung-out rag. It took an effort of will to get out of bed rather than roll over and go back to sleep. She stood in the middle of the room in her nightdress, trying to summon the energy to get dressed and start the day. Then she remembered that she wanted her father to be in the best possible mood when Jimmy asked for her hand; that gave her the impetus to hurry. She wanted to have plenty of time to prepare breakfast before her father came in from milking.

When she picked up her silk dress, she saw to her dismay it was badly creased. It even had some grass stains around the hem, where the dress had not been protected by her cloak. Her drawers had a small patch of blood on them, and Amy recalled that sharp pain. She anxiously checked her dress; there was no sign of blood, though one of her petticoats had a few spots.

She shook the dress out, but it was obviously going to need washing. That would mean explaining to Susannah how she had got the dress in

183

such a state; she did not look forward to that conversation. There was no time to worry about it now, however. She hung it in the wardrobe, shoved her soiled underwear in a drawer and hurriedly dressed.

As she brushed her hair, Amy was surprised that the sleepy face staring back at her from the mirror looked the same as ever. She felt so different within herself that she had thought it might show on the outside, too. Her eyes fell on the photograph of her mother. She picked it up and looked at the woman who was almost a stranger. *Did you feel like I do, Mama? Did you love Pa like I love Jimmy? I think you must have, you look so happy. I think he still misses you,* she realised for the first time, and she felt a pang for her father.

When she had splashed cold water on her face Amy felt more alert, and she hurried out to start preparing the meal. She was already in the kitchen before she remembered that her brooch was still on yesterday's chemise, tucked into a drawer; she considered going back to put it on before deciding she did not have time.

Breakfast was almost ready by the time Jimmy appeared. She abandoned her frying pans to rush to his arms.

'How's my little wife this morning?' Jimmy said, nuzzling her hair as he spoke.

'Tired. And I'm not your wife yet,' she said, trying unsuccessfully to sound stern.

'Yes you are, as far as I'm concerned. You belong to me now, little one—it's just a matter of convincing one or two other people.'

'Pa, you mean.'

'My father too. He could be even more of a problem, he can be difficult when it suits him. I've been thinking about that—' They were interrupted by the noise of the back door opening, and Amy went to the range just as Jack and his sons came in.

'Well, lad,' Jack said in his booming voice, 'what's this I hear about what you've been doing for my daughter?'

Jimmy glanced from Jack to Amy with a look of terror, which she returned with interest, then he managed to look calm again and spoke to Jack with no more than a quizzical note in his voice. 'What do you mean, Jack?'

'These boys of mine have been telling me what happened last night.'

'Ah, what in particular?' Jimmy probed cautiously.

'No need to be modest about it.' He bore down on Jimmy and raised his arm. Amy cringed until she saw that her father had merely extended his hand to shake Jimmy's. 'So one of those Feenans tried to take liberties with my daughter, eh? And you laid him flat on the floor! I wish

184

I'd been there to see it. I wish I'd been there to do it myself, come to that.' He crossed to Amy and gave her a bear hug. 'Of course, I might have killed him,' he said in a conversational tone. 'Laying a hand on my little girl. I'd have broken his arm, at least—probably both arms.'

'Pa,' Amy said weakly, 'please don't talk like that, I don't like it.'

'All right, sorry girl, didn't mean to upset you. Anyway, I'm grateful to you, Jimmy.'

'It was nothing, I just didn't like to see Amy upset, that's all.'

Amy distracted them by serving breakfast, but once she had got over the shock of misunderstanding her father's words she felt a glow of happiness. He was in such a good mood with Jimmy, this morning would be a perfect time to ask him. She caught Jimmy's eye once or twice during the meal and he smiled back encouragingly.

After they had finished eating, Amy was clearing away the plates when Susannah flung open the door from the passage. They all looked up in surprise, and Amy felt a stab of alarm when she saw that Susannah had the blue dress draped over one arm.

'What on earth have you done with this?' Susannah cried. She spread the dress out with a dramatic flourish. 'Just look at it—creased as if you'd slept in it for a month, and you've got stains around the hem. How did you get it in such a state?'

She gave Amy no chance to respond, even if the girl had had an answer, before she turned to Jack. 'I told you the child was too young for a silk dress—I told you, but you never take any notice of me. No one takes any notice—especially not *her.*'

'Calm down, Susannah,' Jack said, his cheerful smile replaced by a look of weary resignation. Amy felt a surge of anger at Susannah for spoiling her father's mood.

'Don't tell me to calm down. Just look at this dress—she's worn it once and it's ruined!'

'Give it to me!' Amy snapped, giving in to her anger and snatching the dress away. 'What right do you have to go poking around in my room?'

'Do you hear the way she speaks to me?' Susannah demanded. 'All I did was go in to see if she'd hung the dress up properly, and I get abused for my trouble! I suppose you're going to take her part like you always do?'

'Amy, that's no way to speak to your ma,' Jack admonished. 'Your ma's got the right to go anywhere she wants in this house, and she was only seeing that you were taking care of your clothes. It looks like you weren't, either.'

Amy remembered her secret brooch, lying in the drawer where

Susannah could have found it if she had decided to explore a little further. 'Why is she allowed in my room? I don't want her going in there! It's my room, isn't it?'

'Hey, you settle down, girl—there's no need for you to carry on like that. You just do as your ma tells you, and keep a civil tongue in your head. What's got into you this morning?'

'You'd better get that strap out again,' Susannah said, her eyes glittering. 'She's far too full of herself—it's because you let her go to that dance—she's too young for outings like that, as well as too young to have decent clothes.'

Amy was aware of Jimmy looking helplessly from her to Susannah. She felt tears of frustration spilling from her eyes. 'I'm not! I'm *not* too young! You say that every time I want anything.'

'Do I have to put up with this, Jack?' Susannah demanded. 'Are you going to make her treat me with respect or not? You'll have to beat her again.'

'You leave my sister alone!' Harry roared, erupting from his chair and startling them all. 'You nag at her all the time, then you let her do all the work while you sit on your backside.' Susannah gave a gasp. 'Don't you touch her, Pa,' he warned.

'Don't speak to me like that, you young—'

'What are you going to do about it?' Harry interrupted.

'I'll show you who runs this house.'

'You'll have to show us both,' John said, getting up from his own chair and crossing to stand beside Amy. 'Don't touch Amy—she's put up with enough the last few years.'

Jack looked at his two sons, both of them taller than him and almost thirty years younger, and he seemed to shrink a little before Amy's eyes. 'I wasn't going to hit her,' he said dully.

'So she's allowed to talk to me like that?' Susannah's voice rose to a near-shriek.

'No, she's not. I think *she'll* still do what I say, even if no one else in this house will. Apologise to your ma, Amy.'

'I'm sorry,' Amy said, but it was her father's forgiveness she sought, not Susannah's. 'I'm sorry I got the dress dirty, I just—'

'It's my fault,' Jimmy put in, the first time his voice had been heard since the trouble erupted. Amy turned to him in fear. She was quite sure this was the worst possible moment for him to confess.

'I brought Amy home last night. There was a bit of a fight at the dance—nothing serious, but unpleasant. Amy was very shaken, and I wasn't looking after her properly—she tripped in a difficult part of the

186

road and I didn't catch her in time. Don't be angry with her, Susannah, she's too young to be blamed.' He crossed to his sister and put his arm around her shoulder.

'That's no excuse for her to talk to me like that,' Susannah said, her eyes flashing. 'She's allowed to say whatever she wants to me, and *he,*' she flung out her arm in Harry's direction, 'uses language like that to me and his father does nothing.'

Susannah's fury abruptly subsided into weeping, and she collapsed into Jimmy's arms. 'Now do you see what I have to put up with? They all hate me—none of them want me here—his children hated me from the day I arrived, and he always sides with them against me.'

'Shh,' Jimmy said, patting her gently on the back as she sobbed against him. 'Don't talk like that, Susannah, you'll make yourself ill. How could anyone possibly hate you? You're tired and upset—you need a nice rest and something to cheer you up. Why don't you and I go somewhere quiet and have a talk, and maybe we can think of something you'd like to do today? Shall we do that?'

'Yes,' Susannah said, her voice muffled against Jimmy's neck.

'Is that all right with you, Jack?' Jimmy asked.

'I'd take it as a kindness, lad,' Jack said, sounding wearier than Amy had ever heard him before. Jimmy led Susannah out of the room, and the rest of them stood in silence, avoiding one another's eyes.

Amy made herself go over to her father. She put her hand on his sleeve. 'I'm sorry about all that trouble, Pa, I really am.' Her father patted her hand absently, then walked out of the house without so much as a glance at his sons.

'Thank you for sticking up for me,' Amy said, turning to John and Harry. 'We've upset Pa, though.'

'Too bad,' Harry said, but Amy thought both her brothers looked shaken. 'If he wants to let that bitch boss him around it's his business, but he needn't think she's going to tell the rest of us what to do.'

'I think maybe you two should leave him alone for a while,' Amy said.

'Mmm, you're right,' said John. 'C'mon, Harry, let's get out of here before Her Ladyship comes back.'

Amy found herself alone in the room. The kitchen seemed strangely quiet after the uproar. She wiped away the last traces of her tears and started on the dishes, puzzling over how the day could have gone so wrong so suddenly. *Now he won't be able to talk to Pa this morning*, she fretted. *I don't think Pa would even listen just now—if he did listen he'd go crook. And now Jimmy's gone off to look after her.* She sighed deeply. It seemed Susannah was always involved whenever there was trouble in the family.

But I wouldn't have Jimmy if it wasn't for Susannah. Why does it all have to be so complicated?

Jimmy slipped out half an hour later, when Amy was part-way through making a batch of scones. He had changed into one of his suits, and Amy thought he looked wonderful. It made her very aware of her dowdy brown holland dress. 'I've settled her down—it wasn't easy. I'm going to take her visiting, so that's my morning written off.' He rolled his eyes melodramatically. 'She certainly gets in a state, doesn't she?'

'Yes. Especially when I do something to annoy her—and I'm always annoying her somehow. I honestly don't mean to, Jimmy, but everything I say makes her angry. And then Pa looks so miserable when she gets upset.'

'I'm afraid my sister is the sort of person who wants everyone to suffer with her. I can understand why your father looks worn out.' He planted a quick kiss on Amy's forehead; she had to resist the urge to hug him with her doughy hands. 'Susannah's getting ready now. I hope we'll have a chance to talk later, it depends how much visiting Susannah wants to do. You understand why I won't be able to talk to your father for a while—maybe not today?'

'Oh, yes—it would be silly for you to even try.'

'Right now your father's probably wishing he'd never even heard of my family. We'll just have to wait for a better time.'

Susannah came back out to the kitchen, resplendent in green flowered silk. Little George, enveloped in a flannel gown, looked incongruous in her arms. She ignored Amy's presence and spoke to Jimmy. 'I've a letter to Mother to post, we can go to the Post and Telegraph first. Do you want to write a few lines before I put it in the envelope?'

'No, I won't bother. I'm sure you've told her all the news.'

'Really, James, Mother would love a note in your hand.'

'Would she? Oh, you know how I hate writing letters, that's why I never do it. I never know what to say in them, anyway.'

'Yes, you've never written to me in all the time I've lived here.' She sighed. 'Ah, well, I suppose most men aren't much use at writing. I'll tell Mother you send your love.' The baby in her arms reached up to tug at Susannah's hair; she tilted her head out of his reach. 'I'm not sure whether to take George with us or not, it depends how long we're going to be.'

'Bring him,' Jimmy said decisively. 'Then we can stay away as long as you like, and you won't have to worry about rushing home. He's such a handsome little fellow, too, you must enjoy showing him off.'

'I suppose I do, a little bit. Not that we do much visiting. I would've rather had a girl this time, though.'

'There's not much difference at that age, before they're in trousers. Tom and George could both be little girls, really. Look at George with those big blue eyes and all that hair. You'd better bring him, Susannah.'

'All right, I'll put a pretty gown on him. *She* can look after Thomas and give me a rest for once. Come with me, James, while I get them both dressed.' Jimmy raised his eyebrows to Amy behind his sister's back, but he said nothing as he followed Susannah from the room.

Left to herself again, Amy divided her time between housework and entertaining the lively eighteen-month-old Thomas, until she was interrupted by the back door being flung open to admit Lizzie. Amy could not recall ever before having been reluctant to see her cousin.

'How are you?' Lizzie demanded, advancing on Amy.

'I'm fine,' Amy said, annoyed at the defensive note in her voice. 'Why shouldn't I be?'

'Did you get home all right last night?'

'I'm standing here, aren't I? You can see I got home.'

'You didn't have any trouble?'

'I don't know what you're talking about, Lizzie.' Amy was aware of the pitch of her voice rising. She made an effort to speak more calmly. 'All I did was walk home from the school to here, what could happen?'

'All right, there's no need to bite my head off. I was worried about you, that's all. John shouldn't have let Jimmy take you home by yourselves.' She peered closely at Amy. 'You're sure you're all right?'

'I've already said I am.'

'You look sort of… muddled.'

Amy sighed. 'We had a big row this morning.'

'You and Jimmy? What was it about?' Lizzie's eyes widened. 'Was it something he tried to do last night?'

'No, not Jimmy! He was the only one not fighting. It was all the rest of us—it was a terrible row, Lizzie.'

That distracted her cousin. 'What was it about?' Lizzie asked, looking eager.

Amy hesitated, as reluctant to explain to Lizzie how her dress had got soiled as she had been to Susannah. 'Oh, it was just Susannah getting annoyed with me. She really upset me, and I shouted at her. Then she wanted Pa to beat me, and Harry and John said they wouldn't let him, so they had a row with Pa, then Susannah had a row with Pa… it was awful.'

'Gosh! What did Uncle Jack do? He didn't beat you, did he?'

'No, of course he didn't. You know Pa never beats me.' *Except that once. That wasn't a real beating, though.* 'He just sort of looked confused, then he wandered off by himself. Poor Pa, I think he felt everyone was against him.' She sighed. 'I'd better make something he specially likes for lunch.'

'Well, if you're really sure you're all right—now, don't snap at me, I won't talk about it any more. I want to tell you what happened to *me.*' Lizzie gave a broad grin. 'Frank kissed me!'

'Did he? That's good, you wanted him to,' Amy said distractedly, pulling Thomas away from the flour bin he was about to put his face in.

'Yes. He kissed me three times, the first wasn't very long, then the next one didn't really work properly, but the third one—'

'Lizzie, I don't think I want to hear every little detail of what Frank does to you,' Amy cut in, remembering again vividly everything that had happened with Jimmy under the stars. 'I hope you're not going to tell me every time he touches you.'

'Well, I do beg your pardon!' Lizzie said haughtily. 'I thought you'd be interested, that's all. Of course you're such an expert, aren't you? I shan't tell you when we get engaged if it's all so boring. I suppose I'd better go home if I'm annoying you.'

'Oh, don't be like that, Lizzie. I just don't like hearing all those personal things—I think you should keep it a secret, just between you and Frank.'

'Like you do? We never used to have secrets, Amy.'

Amy picked up Thomas and carried him to the other side of the kitchen, using him as an excuse to avoid meeting Lizzie's eyes. 'I suppose it's just something that happens when you grow up… when you fall in love,' she added quietly, her back to Lizzie.

'Love? Are you in love?'

Amy turned to face her. 'Yes. I love him, and he loves me. And that's all I'm going to tell you, Lizzie, so it's no use prying.'

'Suit yourself. I'll go home, then.'

'Don't go off in a huff, Lizzie.'

'I'm not in a huff.' Lizzie dropped her haughty manner. 'No, I should go home really, I'm meant to be helping Ma. I just came over because I was worried about you, but you say you're all right. I suppose I'll see you tomorrow.' She opened the door, but when she was half-way through it she turned to face Amy once more. 'Amy, you will tell me if anything happens, won't you?'

'What are you talking about now?'

'I don't really know. I suppose I mean… oh, I don't know, if anything horrible happens and you're worried about it. Promise you'll tell me?'

190

'Nothing horrible's going to happen.'

'But if it does,' Lizzie pressed her. 'Promise me.'

'No, I won't promise. Do stop going on, Lizzie. If you're going home, get on with it.'

Lizzie gave her a last searching look. 'All right.' She pulled the door closed after her.

Susannah and Jimmy had not returned by lunch-time, and Amy dished up the meal to an unnaturally quiet roomful of men. She was grateful for the distraction Thomas provided as she cut up his food and helped him spoon it messily into his mouth. Jack took the little boy onto his lap and let him help himself to handfuls of pudding from Jack's own bowl, something Susannah did not allow. Thomas's frock got steadily grubbier, and the white tablecloth acquired sticky blotches of Jack's favourite caramel pudding during the exercise, but it was worth it to Amy to see her father smiling at his little son instead of glowering at his grown ones.

It was mid-afternoon, and Amy had put Thomas to bed for his afternoon nap, when she heard the buggy rattle up the road. When Susannah came into the room ahead of Jimmy, Amy could see that her stepmother was in an animated mood. She hoped that meant the family would have a peaceful evening. Perhaps Jimmy would be able to talk to her father the next morning if there were no more fights.

'That was a lovely outing,' Susannah said. 'Mrs Leveston is quite a charming woman, really. I'll put George down for his sleep. I suppose he'll need changing again,' she said, wrinkling her nose in distaste.

'Can I do that for you?' Amy asked, eager to prolong Susannah's good mood.

'I'm quite capable of looking after my own son,' Susannah said, barely glancing at Amy. 'You get on with whatever you're doing.' She sailed out of the room.

' "Whatever you're doing" is making dinner for us all, I see,' Jimmy said. 'The outing's cheered her up, but it hasn't made her any more polite to you.'

'I've given up hoping for that,' said Amy. 'You've been out an awfully long time.'

'I know! I had trouble keeping awake, I don't mind telling you. Mrs Leveston's husband was out when we called, so I sat in her drawing room drinking tea from ridiculous little cups and looking at my hands while she and Susannah talked as though they were both taking a vow of silence tomorrow—now there's a good idea,' he said, looking so serious that for a moment Amy almost believed him. 'I wonder if Susannah's ever considered joining a silent order of nuns.' He gave her his infectious grin, and Amy giggled.

'Isn't their house lovely, though,' she said, remembering the treasures in Mrs Leveston's drawing room. 'All those beautiful things.'

'The most beautiful thing I've ever seen was right here, and I thought about you all the long, weary day.' He looked over his shoulder, then gave Amy a quick kiss. 'We were asked to stay for lunch, Mr Leveston came home in time for that, and afterwards I had to walk around the grounds with him and hear his opinions—he's got one on every subject. "A magistrate is a father figure to the community, my boy," ' Jimmy said in an imitation of Mr Leveston's pompous tone. ' "It is a great responsibility, but also a great privilege." ' Jimmy gave a groan, then laughed, and Amy laughed with him.

'What a terrible day you've had,' she sympathised.

'It's certainly been a long one. Still, at least Susannah was sweet-tempered all the way back. She didn't go on about how much she hates it here like she did on the way into town.'

'Did she talk about me on the way in?'

'Well, yes, she did. I think you're better off not hearing the details, though. I wish I hadn't. Now, let's talk about us for a minute—'

'What are you talking to her about?' Susannah asked from the doorway, making them both jump.

'I was just telling Amy what a nice day we've had,' Jimmy said. Amy was amazed at how smoothly he covered his confusion. 'I'd better get changed, they'll be getting the cows in soon.'

'You don't have to help with that. Sit out here with me while I get dinner on.'

'No, I'd better earn my keep. You know, Susannah, you look rather worn out after all the excitement we've had today. Why don't you have a lie-down? I'll bring you a cup of tea, if you like. You shouldn't have to cook all the time. Here, take my arm.'

'You're so thoughtful, James. Perhaps I will have a rest, and a cup of tea would be very nice.' She smiled at her brother as they went out into the passage together, and Amy went to put the kettle on.

Jimmy came out a few minutes later in his working clothes to collect Susannah's cup. 'I'm sorry I've made you cook dinner by yourself, but I wanted to get her out of the way for a while.'

'Oh, I don't mind—I'd much rather do it by myself than help Susannah,' Amy assured him. He smiled, kissed her, and took the cup away.

'There, that's her settled for a bit,' Jimmy said when he came out once more. 'Lying in state against a heap of pillows, looking pale but not very interesting. Now, how about we go for a little walk before I go off to help milk those cows?'

'I'd love to, Jimmy, I've missed you all day, but I can't really leave all this,' Amy said, pointing at the stew-pot she was filling. 'Couldn't we just talk here for a bit till you have to go?'

'Well, all right then. Susannah's at the other end of the house, so she won't hear unless we shout at each other.' He moved to stand close to Amy as she worked. 'I've had a lot of time to think today—there certainly hasn't been anything else very interesting to do. Amy, what do you think your father's going to say when I ask if I can marry you?'

'He'll say I'm too young,' Amy said with conviction.

'Yes, I'm sure he will, but that's not so bad. I've heard of girls getting married at fifteen, we'd be able to talk him round on that, though he might say we have to wait a while. No, as soon as he gets over my cheek for wanting to marry you, he's going to say, "How are you going to provide for her?"'

'Oh. Yes, I suppose he will.'

'I'm sure of it. And what am I going to say? "Well, I sort of work for my father, except I had a row with him before I came down here, and he gives me my keep and a small allowance"? I don't really see your father giving his precious daughter to someone with those prospects.'

'But he's got to say yes!' Amy said, turning to him in alarm and forgetting about the carrots she was slicing.

'Hey, stop waving that knife around! You don't need to threaten me—I *want* to marry you. It's your father who needs convincing.'

'I'm sorry.' She put the knife down carefully. 'What can we do to make him let us? Will we have to tell him what we did last night? I'm sure he'd want us to get married if he knew about that.'

'I expect he would, and you'd get to watch him break both my arms first—those brothers of yours would join in, too, they're both very fond of you. You don't really want that, do you?'

'Of course I don't. What are we going to do, then?'

'I think I should get things straight with my father first. I've got to have his permission to get married, anyway, I won't be twenty-one for months. If I can talk him into paying me a proper salary, that might be enough to set your father's mind at rest.'

'Do you think your father will agree?'

'Well, he must know he's got to start paying me one day, especially once I've got a wife to support. He's a bit of a tyrant sometimes, but most of the time he's not as bad as all that.'

Another thought struck Amy. 'If you've got to talk to your father, does that mean you're going away? I'll miss you if you do.'

'I hope not. I was thinking I might write to him and explain everything—well, not everything,' he amended with a smile. 'He'd probably disapprove of last night. Why are fathers so difficult, Amy?'

'Pa's not difficult, he just thinks I'm still a baby. I suppose that does make him a bit difficult. When are you going to write to your father?'

'As soon as I get the chance. Maybe tomorrow. Then I'll have to get the letter into town and on the boat without Susannah noticing what I'm up to, she knows I never write to anyone. I'll have to try and do that this week.'

'Then we'll have to wait for your father to reply. Oh, it's all going to take such a long time! I wish we could get married soon. I wish we were married already.'

'So do I, sweetheart,' Jimmy said, giving her one last kiss before he went outside.

20

February 1884

'There's a lot of mushrooms in some of the paddocks,' Harry mentioned at breakfast the following Thursday. 'I haven't had mushrooms for ages.'

'Mmm, I just fancy some mushrooms with lunch,' said Jack.

That was enough of a hint for Amy. After breakfast she took a large basket and prepared to set out on a mushrooming expedition. She was in the porch putting on her boots when Jimmy came through the gate.

'Have you got another basket?' he asked. 'I'll come and help you.'

'Shouldn't you be working somewhere?'

'Oh, they won't miss me. Anyway, we can pick more if we both go.'

Amy did not need much persuading to fetch another basket, and they set off together.

'Have you written to your father yet?' Amy asked as soon as they were safely out of earshot of the house.

'I haven't got any notepaper. I'm not sure what to do, I can't ask Susannah for any, because I don't want her to know I'm writing.'

'Her paper's pink and scented, anyway,' Amy said, remembering letters she had seen Susannah write to her mother. 'That wouldn't impress your father!' They both laughed at the thought.

'You don't have any, do you?' Jimmy asked.

'No, I never write letters—who've I got to write to? Except sometimes I help Pa if he has to order things from Auckland or write to the bank, things like that. I don't see how I can ask Pa for any of his notepaper, though. He'd want to know what I wanted it for.'

'I'll have to buy some in town, then. If I can get in there without Susannah wanting to come, that is. Yes, I'll try and find some excuse to ride in by myself this week.'

They found mushrooms in the low-lying paddocks, but they had to cover a large area before their baskets were half-full. They worked their way along the bank of the Waimarama until they reached the point where the stream emerged from the bush.

'Are there any mushrooms in there?' Jimmy asked, indicating the trees.

'Not many. There might be a few in the clearings.'

'Let's go and see. We've about cleaned out this paddock.'

Amy hesitated, torn between the desire to be alone with Jimmy and the fear of what might happen if she was. 'I don't know if we should.'

'Oh, come on,' Jimmy said, pulling at her hand. 'It won't be for long. I can't kiss you out here in the open.'

'Well…' Amy said. 'I'd like to, but—'

'Please?' Jimmy gave her a beseeching smile. 'I haven't kissed you for days—not properly, anyway.'

'All right, then.' *That thing's not going to happen again, though—not until we're married*, she told herself firmly. The last time they had both got over-excited; this time she was prepared.

When they came to the first sunlit clearing Jimmy put down his own basket, then took hers out of her hand and placed it on the ground. 'Now let's not waste any more time.' His mouth came down on hers. Amy flung her arms around his neck and kissed back enthusiastically.

Jimmy slid his arms down her back and held her close, then pushed her gently so that she lost her balance and would have fallen if he hadn't been holding her so tightly. Instead Amy found herself being lowered gently to the ground, and in a moment Jimmy was lying close beside her.

She moved her hands to his shoulders and pushed, at the same time twisting her mouth away from his. 'What are you doing?'

'Showing you I love you,' Jimmy said, reaching out to fondle her breasts. 'You do love me, don't you?'

'Of course I do, but I don't think we should lie down like this.'

'It's a bit hard to do it standing up,' Jimmy murmured in her ear as he nuzzled at her hair. 'Just relax and enjoy yourself.'

'No!' Amy said, pushing harder at his shoulders. 'No, we mustn't—not till we're married.'

'But we'll be married soon—what's the difference? Why wait? We're as good as married now. Come on, Amy, it's even harder to resist you now I know what you're like.'

'We're not married yet. Please stop, Jimmy. I don't want to.'

'I know what's worrying you!' Jimmy said. 'It's because I hurt you, isn't it? That's because it was the first time—I was a bit rough, too, because I was so desperate for you. It won't hurt any more, I promise. You might even enjoy it.' He tried to slip his leg between hers, but Amy kept her thighs pressed tightly together.

'I'll be careful,' he said. 'I promise I'll be careful. Don't you trust me?'

'No… yes… I don't know… I don't want to. I don't want to!' Amy felt tears starting from her eyes.

Jimmy let her go abruptly. He sat up and moved away from her a little. 'So that's how it is,' he said flatly. 'I hurt you the other night, and now you want to get back at me. Ah, well, I suppose it's only natural.'

'I don't understand—how am I hurting you?' Amy asked, sitting up quickly.

'I wish I didn't have to tell you this, Amy.' Jimmy seemed unwilling to meet her eyes. 'It's not easy for a man to think he's going to be made happy, then be turned down. It's… it's *painful*.'

'I'm sorry,' Amy said helplessly.

'I didn't think you were that sort of girl.' He turned away from her as he spoke, sounding deeply hurt.

'What? What sort of girl? I don't know what you mean.'

'I don't want to say it, but what else am I to think? You let me the other night, and now you say you don't want to. I didn't think you were a tease, Amy.' He still had his back to her.

'I'm not! I don't want to be a tease.' Amy was unsure exactly what a 'tease' might be, but was certain it was something unpleasant. 'I didn't mean to do that the other night, it just sort of happened.'

Jimmy turned to face her again. 'I suppose you didn't mean to say you'd marry me, either. Well, I won't hold you to it if you've changed your mind. Do you want to break off our engagement?'

'No! I want to marry you more than anything in the world!' Amy reached out to put her arms around his neck, but he sat still and unresponsive. She let her hands drop to her lap.

'Maybe you'll change your mind about wanting to marry me like you have about making me happy.'

'I'll never change my mind. I love you, Jimmy.'

'I thought you did. Until today I was sure you did.'

'What have I done wrong?' Amy pleaded. 'Why don't you believe I love you?' He said nothing, just stared at her reproachfully.

Amy looked at him helplessly through the tears spilling out of her eyes. She was desperate to see that reproach turn once again into happiness. *Maybe it doesn't really matter. We've done it once, and we're going to get married soon. I don't want to… but he looks so unhappy…*

She lay back on the ground, her eyes tightly closed and her teeth clenched against the pain she was certain would come in spite of his assurances, and waited for him to lie down on top of her. When several seconds had passed and nothing had happened she opened her eyes again, to see Jimmy looking at her with a mixture of amusement and sadness.

'You must think I'm a monster,' he said. 'I wish you could see yourself, lying there like a sacrificial lamb, determined but terrified. And I'm the man with the knife. Forget about it.'

'Don't you want to now?' Amy asked in confusion.

'Not like that. I want *you* to want it. Just forget about it for now and let me tell you how much I love you.'

'But—'

'Shh,' he ordered. He silenced her with a kiss, then lay down beside her once again. 'My beautiful little one, how could I force you to do anything against your will? I'm just impatient for you, that's all. I've been thinking about what it's going to be like when we're married. You'll be with me in Auckland—you'll like that, won't you?'

'Oh, yes.'

'We'll have our own little place, and I'm going to see that you have a servant to help. You shouldn't be washing and scrubbing all day. You can sit and do embroidery while I'm out, and watch someone else do the cooking and cleaning.'

'No,' Amy said firmly. 'Not the cooking. I'm not going to let anyone else cook for you—I want to do that myself. I'll make all the things you like best.'

He laughed. 'Whatever you want, darling. You're a wonderful cook, anyway. On the weekends I'll take you out visiting, and walking in Albert Park, and I'll see all the men wishing they had a beautiful wife like you. I'll have to get a carriage so I can show you off in style.' Amy giggled in delight. 'And lots of beautiful dresses for you, too. Like your new dress, only even prettier.'

'You'd better get a couple of horses for your carriage. I'm going to cost you a lot of money,' Amy said, enjoying the fantasy.

'Well, maybe I won't buy all those things just at first. Will you wear the blue dress for our wedding?'

'I don't think I'll have much choice. I got in such trouble over getting it dirty the other night, I won't be allowed another new dress for a while. Not a silk one, anyway.'

'Good. You're pretty enough in your pinafore,' he ran his hand over the white cotton pinafore as he spoke, until his palm cupped one breast, 'but in that blue dress you're a princess. It's like a wedding dress already, because you were wearing it when you said you'd marry me.'

'I don't suppose I'll be wearing pinafores much longer after we get engaged—officially engaged, I mean. I'll have to start wearing grown-up clothes.'

'And corsets.' Jimmy wrinkled his nose in disgust. 'I'd better make the most of you now, then.' He held her close and kissed her, then ran both hands over her chest and stomach, down her legs and back up again. Amy shivered at his touch, and pressed her body against his hands.

'Now, where was I?' Jimmy murmured. 'Let's see, in the evenings I'll take you to the theatre—I know you'll enjoy that.'

'I'll love it! What will we see?'

'Whatever you want—we'll go as often as you like.' He lifted her pinafore to fondle her more easily. Amy felt her dress ride up above her knees as he stroked her, but she was too happy to worry about it.

'It'll be like a fairy tale,' she said dreamily.

'It'll be true,' Jimmy whispered in her ear. 'Then the best part will happen. We'll go home, and we'll be all alone in our soft bed. No more lying in the grass for you, little one. Then I'll take you in my arms—'

'Like this?' she murmured.

'Just like this. Except more comfortable. Don't interrupt.' He placed a finger on her lips. 'I'll take you in my arms and kiss you,' he fitted his action to his words, 'and tell you how much I love you,' his hand ran down her leg, 'then I'll show you how much.' He lifted her dress and nudged his legs between her now-limp ones. Instead of struggling, Amy put her arms around his neck and pulled his face down to hers to kiss him. A few moments later she found he had been right: this time it didn't hurt a bit.

When Amy took Susannah's early morning cup of tea to her a few days later she found her stepmother pacing around the floor with a crying George in her arms, while little Thomas slept on undisturbed.

'What's wrong with him?' Amy asked.

'How should I know? He can't tell me. He can't be hungry, I fed him an hour ago. Then he was sick all over my nightdress. He woke me in the night, grizzling like this.'

'I know. I heard him through the wall. Shall I take him for a while?'

'All right.' Susannah passed the baby to Amy. 'See if you can get a bit of porridge or something into him, perhaps he is hungry after all. He was sick last night after I gave him his bottle, too.'

'Do you think maybe he's not well.'

Susannah shrugged. 'Edie says I'm weaning him too quickly. I weaned Thomas at this age, though, and he wasn't sick all the time. He's growing, so he must be all right.'

Amy made a secure little nest of blankets for George in a corner of the kitchen and mixed up some milky porridge for him while the adults' breakfast was keeping warm on the range. She sat him on her lap and spooned food into the eager mouth. 'You really are hungry, aren't you, Georgie,' she murmured. 'Poor little thing.'

She was rocking George on her lap and singing to him when she became aware that she was no longer alone in the room with the baby. She looked up to see Jimmy smiling at her. 'You look sweet with him.' He sat down beside her. 'You look like someone in a painting.'

'He's a lovely baby. Both Susannah's little ones are sweet.'

'They don't take after their mother, then.'

'Jimmy, you shouldn't talk about your sister like that,' Amy scolded. 'Would you like to hold George for me while I dish up your breakfast?'

'Well, I don't know,' he said dubiously. 'He won't break, will he? I'm not used to babies.'

'Don't be silly. Here you are.' She put George on a reluctant Jimmy's lap. 'He can hold up his head nicely. You just put your arm behind him like this, then he'll be quite steady.' She took Jimmy's hand and curled his arm around the baby.

George looked up at Jimmy and broke into a broad smile. 'Oh, you like your old uncle, do you?' Jimmy said, looking gratified. The next moment George gave a lurch, and the porridge returned to cover his own front and Jimmy's. 'Maybe you don't like me after all.' Jimmy looked helplessly from George to Amy.

'Oh, I'm sorry.' Amy snatched up the baby from his lap. 'I didn't think he'd be sick again—wait a minute, I'll get you cleaned up as soon as I've sorted Georgie out.'

'Don't worry about me, I can clean myself up. I'll just put another shirt on.'

He disappeared from the room. By the time he came back, Amy had mopped up the vomit from the front of George's gown and had started changing his napkin.

'Phew! What's that awful smell?' Jimmy asked.

'It's the smell of babies. It is horrible, isn't it? Much worse than cows and things. This is worse than usual,' she said, looking at the runny mess in the soiled napkin. 'I think he might have an upset tummy. I'm sorry I've got to do this in the kitchen, but Susannah's having a sleep and I don't want to disturb her.'

Jimmy opened the back door and a window. Once Amy had put the dirty napkin outside, the air soon freshened. 'I'm a little bit worried about Georgie,' she said, frowning. 'Susannah said he was sick last night and first thing this morning, now he's done it again.'

'Is Susannah worried?'

'No, but she doesn't know he's been sick again. Well, she knows more about it than I do,' she said, looking at the baby now dozing contentedly among the blankets.

'She should do, she's got two of them. Now, do you think we could manage a little walk in the bush today? Ever since last time I've been thinking about it.'

'I don't notice you wanting to do much walking once we're among the trees,' Amy said with a smile. 'You seem to want to lie down all the time.'

'Well, it's very tiring, this farming life.' Jimmy returned her smile. 'What about this walk, then?'

'Not this morning, I've got a lot of cleaning to do. Maybe I could slip away this afternoon for a bit, if you're not too busy working.'

'I'll find some excuse. I'll make sure I'm hanging around after lunch.'

But when lunch-time came Amy had other things on her mind. George vomited several more times during the morning, and Susannah began to look concerned. 'Amy, you go over and ask Edie what she thinks about it,' she said at eleven o'clock when George had produced another runny napkin.

Amy trotted across the paddocks. She was soon back with her aunt's message, to find her father in the kitchen with Susannah and both children. 'Aunt Edie looked worried,' she reported. 'She said you should take him to the doctor, because he's too little to go without anything to eat all this time. She said take him today or tomorrow.'

'Oh. It must be bad for Edie to worry. I suppose I'd better go in this afternoon, then. Jack, will you take me?'

'I'd rather not today,' said Jack. 'I want to get some of those early potatoes harvested this afternoon while the weather's holding. One of us will be going to town in a day or two, anyway, me or one of the boys, can't it wait till then? He looks well enough, he's just bringing up a bit of food.'

'Jack, don't you care about my baby?' Susannah looked accusingly at Jack as she clutched George to her. 'My poor little baby's ill, and all you can think about is potatoes!' She sounded on the verge of tears.

'Hey, don't get upset, Susannah. If you're really worried, Amy can take you in today.'

'Me?' Amy said in surprise.

'Yes, you know how to drive the buggy.'

'I haven't for a while, Pa,' Amy said, struggling to remember the last time she had sat beside her father on the front seat and held the reins.

'It doesn't matter. Those horses know the way by themselves, anyway. I'll get one of the boys to harness them up for you after lunch.'

As soon as they had eaten, Amy left the dishes unwashed and they set off towards town. Susannah sat at her side holding George, and Thomas was between them. Amy was nervous for the first few minutes, and she jerked the reins awkwardly several times, but she soon found it was easiest to let the horses have their heads. Her father was right, the animals really did know the way.

The jolting of the buggy soon put both little boys to sleep, which made the silence between Amy and Susannah all the more obvious. Amy made an effort to break it.

'It's a lovely day,' she said when they had been travelling for ten minutes.

'It's terribly hot.' Susannah adjusted the angle of her parasol to protect herself and George a little better.

'Well, yes, but it's nice and sunny. The sea's going to look beautiful today.'

'I hate this long drive in to town. Why is everything so ugly here?'

'I don't think it's ugly! I think the bush looks lovely in the sunshine, and the sea's always beautiful.'

'I'm not interested in what you think. What would you know about anything? You're just an ignorant farm girl.'

Amy bit back the retort that came to her lips. 'I've never been anywhere, I know that. I'd like to see other places. I still think it's pretty here, though.'

Susannah sighed. 'You wouldn't if you'd ever lived somewhere interesting. I suppose it would be easier to put up with a place like this if I didn't know any better.'

Susannah had dropped her habitual wounded expression, and a look of genuine sadness had replaced it. 'What was it like, where you lived?' Amy asked.

'Lovely. We had a lovely house in Parnell. Everything was—is, I should say, the house is still there, even though I'm not. Everything is so nice. Nice furniture, nice carpets, a nice little garden—only half an acre, not a great wilderness. I must have been mad.' Amy could think of nothing useful to say, so she kept silent.

'It's almost worse in a way, since James came.' Susannah sounded as if she were talking to herself. 'It's made me miss Mother and Father more—even Constance. And James will have to go home soon, he can't stay here much longer. Then I'll be all by myself again.'

Amy could understand Susannah's sadness at the thought of not seeing Jimmy again. 'Maybe… maybe he'll come down again some time,' she said, wanting to share a little of her own happiness.

'No, he won't. Not for a long time like this, anyway. Father's getting older—he's even older than your father, though Constance wouldn't believe that,' she said with more than a touch of bitterness. 'He'll want James to take over properly in a year or two, James won't be able to leave Auckland for months on end then.'

'So Jimmy's going to run things?' Amy probed delicately, pleased to be given the opportunity to find out about Jimmy's prospects without having to interrogate him.

'Of course he is. He's Father's only son—he'll inherit the business. Long before that happens he'll be in charge of it. He's going to be quite a wealthy young man. Not that he doesn't deserve to be, he's very clever.' Her mouth curved in a fond smile.

'Does that mean—'

'Stop being so nosy,' Susannah cut in. 'It's nothing to do with you, it's my family. You just think about your driving and give me some peace for a change—I don't want you tipping us over in one of these streams.'

I wouldn't do that. But Amy was happy enough to keep silence for the rest of the journey while she mulled over what Susannah had told her. Jimmy's prospects sounded wonderful to her, and she was sure her father would be impressed by them. That meant he would say yes! She hugged her happiness to herself.

Amy walked up and down the street with Thomas while Susannah was seeing the doctor. She did not have to wait long before Susannah came out again, clutching a wailing George.

'That stupid doctor's upset him, poking and prodding at him. George was sick again while he did it—at least he managed to be sick over Doctor Wallace's coat. I'm going to have a terrible time settling him down now.'

'He'll probably go to sleep again when we start moving. Are we going home now?'

'Yes. Get on with it.'

Amy held George while Susannah climbed in the buggy, then she handed up the baby and helped Thomas onto the seat. She unhitched the horses and they were soon on their way.

'What did Doctor Wallace say about George?' she asked.

'None of your business.'

'What?' Amy said, shocked. 'Why won't you tell me what he said? I want to know.'

'It's personal.'

'How can it be personal? Georgie's just a baby. Please tell me what the doctor said—is it something really nasty?' she asked anxiously.

'It's nothing to do with you!' Susannah snapped.

Amy was stung into arguing. 'Yes, it is! He's my baby brother, and I care about him. Tell me what the doctor said—go on, tell me!'

'You're getting very full of yourself lately,' Susannah said. 'I'd tell your father you're being cheeky, except he never takes any notice. Well, if you're going to plague me I'll tell you—not that you'll understand.'

She was silent for so long that Amy thought Susannah must have changed her mind. 'Please, Susannah. Maybe I can help look after him.'

'Humph! I know you think you're terribly clever, but you can't help with this. That stupid doctor says George can't tolerate solid food and cows milk yet. He says I've got to feed him myself until he's at least nine months old.'

'Oh. What's wrong with that?'

'I *hate* it, that's what's wrong!' Susannah flung at her. 'It's uncomfortable and undignified, and it'll ruin my figure. I don't want to be a cow. Oh, why am I bothering to try and explain to you? You're just a stupid child.'

'I'm not stupid!' Amy snapped. 'And I'm not a child, either.'

Susannah looked at her through narrowed eyes. 'You really are getting full of yourself. Whatever's got into you lately?'

'Nothing,' Amy said, wondering if the difference she felt in herself really was visible on her face.

'You've got a lot to say for yourself these days.'

'Maybe I'm growing up.' Amy concentrated on the road ahead of them to avoid meeting Susannah's eyes.

'It's certainly high time you did. You've been awfully cheerful lately, too. What's making you so happy?'

'Why shouldn't I be happy?'

'No, I suppose it doesn't take much to make a girl like you happy,' Susannah said.

A tiny smile formed on Amy's lips. *Oh, yes it does.*

21

February 1884

Amy was well through her buttermaking the following Friday before Jimmy joined her in the dairy.

'I thought you weren't going to come this morning,' she said, abandoning her churn to return his kiss.

'I slept in—well, I always sleep in compared to you, I know, but I slept in even later this morning. I think it's this weather,' he said, looking gloomily out the open doorway at the drizzling rain. 'That's the trouble with only being able to get a bit of privacy by going up in the bush—as soon as it rains we're stuck inside.'

He paced restlessly round the dairy, looking out the door every few minutes to see if the sky had suddenly cleared. 'You're a terrible fidgeter,' Amy scolded, looking up from where she was working the butter. 'Why don't you just sit still and enjoy having a rest?'

'You sound like my mother,' he teased. '"James, why don't you sit quietly and read a book?" She was always saying that to me before I was old enough to go out and please myself. I know, I'm hopeless when I'm stuck inside.' He flopped down on a stool against one wall; it was far too low for him, and his long legs looked uncomfortably doubled up.

'I'm a bit scared of meeting your mother and father,' Amy admitted. 'Actually I'm very scared.'

'Why? They'll love you.'

'Will they? They might think I'm not good enough for you.'

'Well, they'd be wrong. Anyway, of course they'll like you—who could help liking you?'

'Susannah doesn't like me.'

'Susannah's different. She doesn't like anyone very much these days. Take my word for it, Mother and Father will love you.' He brushed the subject aside with a wave of his hand. 'Listen, Amy, you know I went in to town with Harry yesterday to get the supplies? I managed to get some notepaper and things, too.'

'That's good! I don't suppose Harry was interested in what you wanted it for.'

'No, his mind was on other things. You know that red-headed girl who sang at the dance?'

'Jane Neill, you mean? Mrs Forster's sister?'

'That's the one. She was at the store with her sister, and Harry was too busy staring at her—not to mention exchanging the odd cheeky

205

remark—to take any notice of what I was doing.'

'Was he just? I didn't know Harry was even interested in girls.'

'I don't think he knew either until he saw Miss Neill.'

'So, have you written the letter yet?'

'I've started,' Jimmy said. 'I did a couple of lines before I came out here. It's not easy, though. I'm no letter writer, and I want to make a good job of it. I'm not going to get much chance to write it, either, what with working in the daytime and sitting in the parlour with Susannah in the evenings.'

'Mmm. And you can't write at night, because you're sharing John's room. That's hard.' She frowned in thought.

'I'll get it written, don't you worry. It just might take me a few days, that's all.'

'You should be writing it now.'

'I know. I'd rather be with you, though.' He rose from his stool and came to stand behind Amy. He slipped his arms around her waist and squeezed while he planted a kiss on the top of her head. 'I don't see enough of you, I don't want to waste my chances.'

'You'll see plenty of me when we're married.' Amy tried to ignore his embrace and carry on shaping the butter into pats. But when he slipped his hands higher to fondle her breasts she gave up, wiped her hands on a towel, and wriggled around so that she could put her arms around his neck and pull his face down for a kiss.

'I thought you didn't approve of people making spectacles of themselves,' Lizzie said, cutting into Amy's thoughts as the two girls stood together outside the church that Sunday. Lizzie had grabbed Amy by the hand and pulled her over to a quiet spot under a tree as soon as the service was over.

'What?' Amy dragged her gaze reluctantly away from Jimmy, whom Susannah was holding by the arm in her usual proprietorial way. 'What are you talking about?'

'Your tongue's just about hanging out, you're staring at him so hard. People will notice.'

'I'm not!' Amy said , but she felt herself blush. 'Was I really, Lizzie?'

'Well, I suppose other people wouldn't notice as much as I do,' Lizzie allowed. 'At least I know you're mad on him, even if you refuse to tell me anything about what's going on.'

'There's nothing to tell. It's a secret, anyway,' Amy said, avoiding Lizzie's eyes.

'What's a secret?' Lizzie pounced.

'Nothing. Oh, I'll tell you as soon as I can, Lizzie, really I will.' *As soon as Pa knows, as soon as he says yes, we'll be able to tell everyone.*

'Why can't you tell me now, Amy? Is it something you're ashamed of?'

'No!' *Jimmy says it's nothing to be ashamed of. We've just started a bit early, that's all. I wish we could get married soon.* 'Please stop prying, Lizzie—oh, there's Frank.'

Frank stood just outside the church porch, looking about uncertainly. He glanced at Lizzie's family, but it was obvious he had not seen what he wanted there. When he caught sight of Lizzie his face lit up.

'Go on, Lizzie.' Amy gave her a small push. 'Go and talk to him.'

Lizzie looked from Amy to Frank, and chewed her lip distractedly. 'I suppose I might as well, you won't talk to me.' She walked briskly over in Frank's direction.

Amy followed more slowly. She stood close to her own family group, but carefully avoided looking at Jimmy. *I wonder if people really are noticing.* But her father and stepmother had shown no sign of being suspicious, and they were the only ones she really needed to worry about.

Lizzie somehow managed to lead Frank over to her father without actually taking his hand. Amy was glad of the distraction her cousin provided. There was no chance of Amy's giving herself away by paying any conspicuous attention to Jimmy when she had Lizzie's performance to watch.

'Pa,' Lizzie said very sweetly, 'weren't you going to ask Frank to come for lunch today?'

'No, I wasn't,' said Arthur. 'But you can come if you want, Frank.'

'I don't want to be a nuisance,' Frank said.

'Lizzie'll be a nuisance if you don't—she'll plague me to ask you next week. Oh, stop looking as though you wish the ground would open up and swallow you,' Arthur said, but the hint of irritation in his voice was more than balanced by amusement. 'Edie, have you got plenty for lunch?'

'Mmm?' Edie relaxed the tight hold she had on Ernie's hand. The toddler took advantage of his freedom to rush over to Rachel Aitken's children, where he was soon involved in a mutual shoving match. 'Oh, yes, I think there's quite a lot. Lizzie seemed to want to get an awful lot ready yesterday.'

'Well, isn't that fortunate?' said Arthur. 'So you think we could make room for Frank today?'

'Oh, he's always welcome,' Edie said. She beamed at Frank. 'He's almost one of the family now.'

'Almost,' Arthur echoed. 'Well, you'd better come and help us eat all that food, Frank.'

'Thank you, Mr Leith. I'll see you later, then.'

Lizzie walked him over to the horse paddock, and flashed a triumphant grin at Amy as she walked back. When she caught sight of her father looking at her, she replaced the grin with a poor attempt at a detached smile.

Amy noticed a loose thread hanging down under her petticoats when she was changing into a work dress after church. She recalled that she had caught her finger on the hem of her drawers that morning while dressing. She hitched up her petticoats to check, and saw that the hem of one leg was trailing, with ripped stitches for several inches. At first she decided to ignore the tatty hem for the rest of the day; after all, no one was going to see it. Then the thought struck her that someone just might. Just maybe she and Jimmy would manage to slip away today, and if they did… well, it was best to be prepared.

She pulled off the unsatisfactory drawers and put them in her washing pile, then rummaged through her underwear until she found the prettiest pair she owned: extra-fine lawn, with three deep layers of lace around each leg and two rows of ribbon above the lace. They felt soft against her skin, and she knew they looked pretty. *Is this shameless? Is it shameless to hope Jimmy will like my underwear, Mama?* she asked the photograph. But her mother smiled out of the frame at her, and Amy felt comforted. For the first time, she was glad she did not have a photograph of her grandmother.

Friday's drizzle had disappeared as though it had never been, and the afternoon was fiercely hot, drying the last of the rain from the paddocks. The family ate early, and after dinner the heat of the day subsided into a soft warmth without a breath of wind.

'That was a good meal,' Jimmy said, pushing back his chair. 'I could just go a nice walk to work it off a bit. Does anyone else want to come?'

Amy looked up at him, then looked away quickly to hide her surprise at his open invitation. *Doesn't he want us to be alone?*

'Oh, yes, I think that would be very nice,' said Susannah. 'I'll go for a little walk with you.'

'Yes, you and I haven't had a walk together in a long time,' Jack put in. 'We'll take the little fellows, that'll help them sleep a bit better.'

'Oh. I was going to leave them with Amy.'

'Amy can come with us.'

'I thought she could do the dishes, I'm rather tired this evening.'

'Leave the dishes, Amy, we're all going for a walk,' Jack said firmly.

'They'll still be there when we get back.'

'All' did not include John and Harry, who showed no disappointment at being left behind. Jack carried little George, and Amy led Thomas by the hand, while Susannah looped her arm through Jimmy's. They walked down to the Waituhi, then a short way along its bank until they reached the spot where the Waimarama ran into the larger stream.

'It's such a clear day,' Jimmy said, looking up at a sky guiltless of clouds. 'There must be a wonderful view from there.' He pointed to a bush-clad hill that rose away from the right-hand bank of the Waimarama.

'Haven't you been up there yet?' Jack asked. 'Amy, I thought you'd shown Jimmy round the place.'

'Not up there, Pa. I've only taken him to a few places, really.'

'That's the best view on the farm. We'll go up there right now, you won't get a better day for it.'

'Oh, no, Jack,' Susannah protested. 'It looks terribly steep, and I'm so tired.'

'It's not as steep as all that, Susannah,' Jack said. 'We could take our time. Are you really tired?' He looked puzzled.

'I'm always tired!' Susannah snapped at him. 'You know perfectly well I'm worn out from having to feed this baby, and I'm not very well anyway. James, wouldn't you like to go back now?'

'Well, I really would like to see that view,' Jimmy said. 'But if you're not feeling up to it—'

'If you don't feel well, I'll take you home now,' Jack cut in. 'You young people go on by yourselves.'

'Perhaps I should—' Jimmy tried.

'You should go and look at that view,' Jack said. 'Take your time. Come on, Susannah.' He tucked George into one arm and attempted to take Susannah's arm, but she snatched it away and started walking in the direction of the house. Jack held Thomas's hand and set off after her.

'Well!' Amy said when Jack and Susannah were safely out of earshot. 'You're not going to be very popular with Susannah now.'

Jimmy shrugged. 'It doesn't matter. I'll make it up to her. Come on, my girl, do as your father tells you—let's see this wonderful view.'

They stayed a discreet distance apart until they were among the trees, then slipped their arms around each other's waists and walked on, more slowly but more companionably. A fantail flitted back and forth across their path as they walked.

'Wasn't that lucky, Susannah wanting to go home just then?' Amy said. 'I thought we weren't going to get the chance to be alone.'

'Lucky? You didn't really think Susannah would want to walk far, did you? I knew she'd want to go back as soon as the going got rough.'

Amy stopped in her tracks. 'You mean you planned all that, about coming up here and Pa taking Susannah back by himself?'

'Yes.' He smiled smugly

'Oh. You really are very clever, aren't you? At getting people to do what you want, I mean.'

'Am I? Will you do what I want?'

'You want to see this view, don't you?' Amy smiled mischievously, and tugged at his hand until he started walking again.

'The baby seems all right now,' Jimmy said.

'Yes, Georgie's fine. The doctor must have been right. Susannah's not very pleased, though, she doesn't like feeding him that way.'

'She's strange sometimes. Well, I'm glad the little fellow's well, but I don't think I'll sit him on my lap again. I haven't got all that many shirts.'

'You should, really, Jimmy, he is your nephew. He's a lovely baby.'

Jimmy pulled a face, then smiled at her. 'You're very fond of Susannah's children, aren't you?'

'Well, they're my little brothers, you know.'

'And my nephews.'

'Oh!' Amy stopped suddenly as a dreadful thought struck her. 'Oh, Jimmy, do you think it's all right for us to get married?'

Jimmy laughed softly and pulled her close to him. 'You're a funny little thing, aren't you? Most people, my darling, would say it's not only "all right", it's just about compulsory—not to mention overdue. What are you going on about?'

'No, listen—we're sort of related, because Susannah's your sister and she's my stepmother.'

'Hmm, I hadn't thought of that.' Jimmy looked pensive for a moment. 'No, I'm sure it's all right. There was a fuss a few years ago over whether a man should be allowed to marry his wife's sister if his wife dies. They changed the law to make that legal, and that's much closer than you and I are. So it must be all right for us to get married.'

Amy gave a sigh of relief. 'That's good. I got a terrible fright for a minute.' She laughed. 'Isn't it complicated, though? Susannah's my stepmother, but when we get married she'll be my sister-in-law.'

'And your father will be my father-in-law as well as my brother-in-law.'

'Tommy and Georgie will be your...' she stopped to work it out 'Your brothers-in-law as well as your nephews. Does that mean they'll be my nephews, too? Oh, and our children will be Susannah's nephews and her grand-children! Or will they? No, that's too complicated.'

'You know what else it means, though, Amy?'

'What?'

'I'm your uncle!' He laughed. 'You'd better do as your Uncle Jimmy says, my girl, or you'll get in trouble.' He wagged his finger at her.

Amy wriggled out from his grasp and pulled a face at him. 'I don't think I like you as an uncle. You're too bossy. I think I'll just have you as a husband.'

She squealed as he made a lunge at her. She hitched up her skirts to run faster, but he caught her in a few strides. He swung an arm around her waist and picked her up off the ground, then he sat down suddenly and Amy found herself upside down across his lap. 'What are you doing?' she gasped out through her giggles.

'Teaching you a bit of respect for your elders,' Jimmy said sternly. He lifted her skirts and gave her buttocks a slap, making Amy shriek, then giggle even harder.

'You're a horrible uncle!'

Jimmy rolled her over till she was lying on her back beside him. 'I don't think I can do this to my niece, so you'd better just be my wife. You still have to do as I say, though.'

'I might say you have to wait till we're married,' Amy teased.

'Humph! You could try.' He lifted her skirts with a flourish. 'Mmm, these are fancy.' He fingered the lace on her drawers.

You noticed! Amy thought in delight, then she felt a stab of guilt. 'Jimmy, do you think I'm shameless?'

'Oh, completely shameless—that's why I love you so much.' Jimmy was undoing his trouser buttons as he spoke.

Amy's face crumpled. 'Do you really think that?'

'Hey, don't cry, little one—I was joking!' He reached out to caress her face. 'Amy, do you think I'd rather you were like Susannah? She shoves her husband away every time he gets within two feet of her. But you—you love me, and you show me you do.' He took her hand and kissed it.

'I do love you, Jimmy. I love you more than anything.'

'Show me, Amy. Show me.'

Amy lay in Jimmy's arms, feeling so delightfully languorous that she would have slept if she had let herself. Her body tingled with remembered pleasure as she lay and listened to a bellbird singing a song of ecstasy in a branch above her. When she opened her eyes she could see the sky through a tracery of leaves; it was a darker blue now.

'The sun's getting low,' she said. 'If you still want to see this view we'd better get a move on.'

'I'd rather stay here,' Jimmy said. 'But I might go to sleep if I do.' He stretched luxuriously.

Amy sat up. 'I think you did drop off for a minute. You were very quiet.'

'No, I didn't. You just wore me out, that's all. I was recovering.'

'Wore you out! What nonsense.'

Jimmy sat up and put a hand on each of Amy's arms, then looked intently into her face. 'Amy, if I ask you a question, will you promise to tell me the truth?'

'Of course I will. What do you want to know?'

'It's important.' He sounded very solemn, and Amy stared back at him, wondering what was so momentous. 'Amy, do you snore?'

'What? Do I snore?' She dissolved in a fit of helpless laughter. 'What a silly question! I thought you were serious.'

'I'm deadly serious,' Jimmy said, but then gave the lie to his assertion by grinning. 'Your brother snores terribly, I thought it might run in the family. I've hardly had a decent night's sleep since I got here.'

'Well, I've slept with Lizzie quite a lot, and she's never complained. I'm sure she would if I snored.'

'*That's* a relief. Do you think maybe I could swap beds?'

'Sleep with Harry instead, you mean?'

'No, with *you*. I thought I might just casually ask if I could. You know, something like "Jack, how about I move across the passage and start sleeping with your daughter instead of your son?" Do you think he'd mind?'

'You could try,' Amy laughed. 'You'd soon find out.' She stood up and shook her dress out. 'Oh, I wish you could, though. This ground gets very hard.'

'It's all right for me,' Jimmy said, standing up and stretching. 'I've got something nice and soft to lie on.'

'That's right! It's not very fair.'

He laughed. 'No, it's not, is it? Oh, I don't know if I feel up to much more walking, shall we just go back now?'

'You lazy thing! What are you going to say when Pa asks you what you thought of the view?'

'Now who's being clever about managing people?'

'I must be learning it from you. Come on.' She tugged at his arm.

'Wait a minute, you've got twigs and things in your hair.' He carefully teased the bits out from her curls, then slipped his arm around her waist. 'Couldn't I just tell your father all the view I wanted to see was in his daughter's beautiful blue eyes? No?' He looked crestfallen. 'Maybe you're right. All right, slave driver, lead the way.'

Amy wound her arm around Jimmy's waist and snuggled against his side as they walked on up the steep hill.

'Amy,' he said softly, 'you really enjoyed that, didn't you?'

Amy looked at the ground in front of her feet. 'Yes. It was nice. Is that all right?' she appealed, looking up at his face for approval.

'All right? It's wonderful! You are the most wonderful girl in the world.' He stopped and kissed her. 'Don't you ever go aloof on me because you think that's how a "lady" behaves.'

'I won't,' she assured him. They started walking again. 'Oh, I do wish we were already married.'

'It won't be long.'

'It *seems* such a long time to wait. I wish I could tell Lizzie we're engaged.'

'Amy, you know it's got to be a secret, don't you? What if your father found out from someone else?'

'Lizzie wouldn't tell anyone—not if I told her it was a secret.'

'She wouldn't mean to, but it might slip out. It's safer not to tell her.'

'I know, but it's hard, Jimmy. She keeps asking me things, and she gets hurt when I brush her off.'

Jimmy looked serious. 'Is she really prying? You haven't told her anything, have you?'

'No! She'd make a terrible fuss if she knew about what we've been doing. Lizzie wouldn't understand how it's all right, really, because we're going to get married as soon as we can.'

'So what have you said to her?' Jimmy pressed.

'Well, she sort of guessed you'd kissed me, and I told her we love each other—that was all right, wasn't it?'

'Don't tell her anything else, Amy. You're right, she wouldn't understand.' He smiled again. 'Frank's a nice chap, but I get the feeling he's not exactly... well, I can't think of a nice way of putting it.'

'He's not very exciting,' Amy volunteered. 'But you're right, he is nice, and Lizzie likes him. He's not a bit like you.' She smiled at a memory.

'What's so funny?'

'Oh, I was just thinking about one time Lizzie was all proud because Frank had taken her for a walk.'

'How romantic. A moonlight stroll under the trees? Maybe he's smarter than I gave him credit for.'

'No,' Amy said, and now she had difficulty getting words out through her laughter. 'No, nothing like that. They took the slops bucket down to the pigs!'

'What?' Jimmy was silent for a moment, then he roared with laughter. 'Amy,' he said when he had recovered himself enough to speak, 'how on earth did a place like this ever produce a girl like you?' Amy smiled and shrugged. 'The sooner I get you out of here and up to Auckland the better,' he said firmly, and Amy could only agree.

22

March 1884

Now that a precedent had been set, Amy took Jimmy on evening walks whenever the day was fine and the household was calm enough for Jimmy to neglect Susannah for an hour or two. They soon discovered a favourite place, in a patch of bush just over the hill from the farmhouse. It was only ten minutes' walk from the house, but the bush was dense and trackless, offering little danger of being disturbed, with a clearing large enough for two bodies to lie entwined. The ferns pressed close around them as they spoke in whispers or cried out in shared delight.

Amy looked out her bedroom window on the first Monday in March, to be greeted by a clear blue sky. She dressed quickly, eager to see Jimmy as soon as she could. When she brushed her hair she found a few of the tiny twigs that were becoming a familiar sight.

As she turned away from her dressing table her calendar caught her eye, and she realised she had not marked off the days for several weeks. A smile crept over her face at the sight of the boldly circled '8'. That was the night he had asked her to marry him. Amy determined to celebrate the eighth of February for ever after. And the night they had first done that thing. She had thought it was terrible then; now she thought it was wonderful. She was quite sure it would be even more wonderful when they were married.

Amy noticed that the day numbered '28' had a cross above it; she puzzled over why she had marked it. She gave up and went out to the kitchen, and it was only when she had started making breakfast that she remembered the significance of the marked date: it was when her monthly bleeding had been due to start.

So the last few times she and Jimmy had lain together had been a gift from the tardiness of her bleeding. *I'm so lucky. The weather's staying nice, and now the bleeding's late.* She knew that when it did start it would leave a yawning gap in their lives for a few days.

By Thursday the bleeding was a whole week late, and Amy was puzzled. She had been regular for almost a year now; why should things suddenly change? It occurred to her that perhaps her abrupt entry into womanhood had thrown her cycle out of balance. That seemed a good enough explanation for a few days' delay.

On the following Monday evening she and Jimmy were about to set off for one of their walks when Susannah spoke.

'James, I don't feel terribly well this evening, I've had to do all that washing in this heat.'

Jimmy exchanged a quick glance with Amy. She could see in his face that he was resigning himself to having to sit with Susannah instead of making love with Amy. 'You poor thing,' he said. 'You do look rather pale.'

'I know. And George has taken to waking up very early in the morning lately. Do you think you could take him and Thomas with you? It might tire them out a little, then they'd sleep better.'

'Oh. That's a good idea,' Jimmy said, managing to hide his lack of enthusiasm from Susannah if not from Amy.

So Amy and Jimmy found themselves with two unexpected companions that evening. Amy led Thomas by the hand and Jimmy carried George rather gingerly.

'I hope he won't be sick on me,' said Jimmy.

'I'm sure he won't. This isn't going to be much fun, is it?'

'It's not exactly what I had in mind for the evening. Does Tommy talk much?'

'A little bit. He repeats words you say.'

'Then I'd better be careful what I say to you, hadn't I? I don't want him giving away any of our secrets.'

As if on cue, Thomas said 'Sec-rets' quite distinctly. Amy and Jimmy looked at one another, then shared a rueful laugh.

'I'll just tell you about the view and the farm and things tonight, I think,' Amy said.

They managed to tire out the two little boys successfully, but she and Jimmy returned to the house with much more energy than either of them had wished.

When her bleeding had still not started by that Thursday, Amy began to wonder if she might be ill. She felt as well as ever, but two weeks late seemed very strange. She toyed briefly with the idea of asking Susannah's advice, but sharing such intimate details with her did not appeal. Amy decided that if the bleeding had not started in another week she would pluck up her courage to ask her Aunt Edie if anything could be wrong.

The image of her aunt struck a chord in her memory. She struggled for the elusive thought. It was something Aunt Edie had said once. Something about the bleeding; what was it? For some mysterious reason the memory that refused to be a memory gave her a vague feeling of uneasiness.

Having to take the little boys on the walk had been a minor irritation, as well as being rather funny. When she realised that Susannah had now

216

decided this was to happen every evening, Amy was alarmed.

'Can't you talk her out of it?' she asked the next night. Thomas had decided he was too tired to walk any further, so Jimmy had to carry him while Amy carried George. 'You're good at managing her.'

'I'm trying to think how,' said Jimmy. 'The trouble is, it's a perfectly reasonable thing for her to suggest. I mean, all we want to do is walk, isn't it? Why not take the little boys with us? I'm already taking Jack's "little girl" for a walk, I might as well take my own nephews as well.'

They sat down with their backs against a large tawa and looked out over the valley. The late afternoon sunlight was deepening the velvet folds of the hills and giving a rich golden tinge to all the shades of green. Jimmy stood Thomas in front of him and looked hard at the little boy.

'Now listen here, Tommy. Let's have a man-to-man talk,' he said very seriously, and Thomas laughed at him. 'I want to give your big sister a cuddle, but I don't want you telling your Mama.'

'You can't, Jimmy,' Amy protested through her own laughter as she bounced George on her lap. 'It wouldn't feel right, not with the little ones watching.'

'You hear that, Tommy?' Jimmy demanded. 'You're stopping me from giving Amy a cuddle.'

'Cuddle Amy,' Thomas said. He threw himself against her, demanding to be hugged. Amy put one arm around him and squeezed, while she held George with the other arm. Thomas climbed onto her lap; she managed to accommodate both children with difficulty. She kissed them both.

'Ugh, you two give such sloppy kisses.' She laughed as she tried to free one hand to wipe her mouth.

'You've got a lot to learn, boys,' Jimmy said. 'Watch this.' He edged his face in between the two children and kissed Amy carefully, putting his arms around all three of them as he did so. 'Hmm, interesting,' he said, disengaging his arms and sitting back to look at them. 'You do look very sweet together. I think I prefer kissing you by yourself, though.'

'They get in the way, don't they? I think Georgie's a bit damp, too,' Amy said, feeling the patch on her dress where the baby was sitting. 'I'll have to change him, we'd better take them back.'

'Maybe tomorrow we could take them down to the swamp and drop them in?' Jimmy suggested as they started back.

'Why would you want to do that? They're a nuisance, but I don't want to drown them!'

'I don't mean drown them, just get them really filthy. Then maybe Susannah wouldn't let us take them out any more.'

'Oh, yes, and I'd get in terrible trouble for not looking after them. It's all right for you, Susannah never growls at you.'

'Well, I was only trying. I suppose it wasn't much of an idea. I'll keep thinking about it.'

'How's the letter to your father going?'

'It's not very long yet. I'm a bit stuck, Amy. It's really hard to know just what to say.'

'You're good with words, you shouldn't have any trouble.'

'I'm good at talking, but I'm not much good at writing. It's just so hard to think of the right way to put it so Father will understand. I keep crossing things out, then it gets so messy I have to start again.'

'Do you want me to help you?'

He smiled at her. 'I'm sure you'd make a very pretty job of it, but Father would be able to tell I hadn't written it myself. I don't want him thinking some cunning girl's got me in her clutches.'

Amy hesitated, not wanting to nag him, then went on carefully. 'I do wish we could get things organised, Jimmy. I know you're doing your best, but it's taking a long time.'

'I know, I'm being stupid about it. Amy, I'm beginning to think maybe I should talk to Father face-to-face. It'd be a lot easier, I'm sure.'

'But then you'd have to go away!'

'It wouldn't be for long. Only a week or two, while I got things arranged with Father, then I'd come back and impress your father with my brilliant prospects. You'd be married and on that boat back to Auckland with me before you knew it.'

Amy chewed her lip thoughtfully. 'Maybe that's what you should do then. I'd miss you terribly, but it's worth it if it means things would go faster.'

'I'll think about it. I'll also try and think of some way we can get out together without these delightful little boys!'

'I've had an idea!' Jimmy said to Amy that Sunday morning. 'Why don't we go visiting this afternoon?'

'You and me? Where do you want to go?'

'I've never been to your aunt and uncle's house, we could pop over and have afternoon tea with them.'

'If you really want to,' Amy said, wondering what attraction her uncle's house suddenly held.

'You don't see why?' Jimmy smiled knowingly. 'Susannah won't expect us to cart the children all that way.'

'Oh! So we can be alone and talk on the way there and back. That's a good idea. I wish we could… well, you know.'

'Why can't we? Who says we have to rush straight back here afterwards?' Jimmy grinned at her, and Amy felt a thrill of excitement.

She revelled in the luxury of having Jimmy to herself and being able to talk freely with him again on the walk over the paddocks. She looped her arm through his as soon as they were out of sight of the house.

'This is so nice,' she said, laying her head against his chest for a moment. 'It's going to be wonderful when we can be together all the time.'

'Not quite all the time, darling. I will have to go out and work sometimes, you know.'

'We'll still be together lots, though. I'll love living in Auckland, too.'

'You might get a bit tired of it after a while. I was starting to get bored there last year.'

'How could you get bored in Auckland?' Amy asked in disbelief.

'Well, you seem to see the same people all the time. Things are dull there in the business, too. There's still plenty to live on, but it could be better.'

'Are you worried about money, Jimmy?' Amy asked hesitantly.

'No, not a bit! Like I said, there's plenty to live on. But now I'm going to have this beautiful wife to show off, it's made me think more. I want to give you lots and lots of nice things, and I mightn't be able to do that at first. It's going to take all I can earn just to get a little house for us to live in.'

'Maybe I could help.'

Jimmy smiled tenderly at her. 'Of course you'll help, sweetheart, but I don't expect a dowry or anything! I can see your father doesn't have a lot of cash to throw around.'

'No, I didn't mean that. I thought maybe I could earn a little bit of money.' She went on quickly before he could interrupt. 'I've heard of women taking in a few pupils and teaching them things. I'm quite good at school work, I could do that.'

'And a lovely job you'd make of it, too. But I can support you, Amy— I wouldn't have asked you to marry me if I didn't think I could earn enough to provide for you.'

'But I want to!' Amy protested. 'Jimmy, I've always wanted to be a teacher, and if it meant I could help you it would be even better.'

'If you want it that much then of course you can. I don't think I could turn you down on anything you wanted, little one.' He stopped walking, and they wasted a few moments in kissing before they set off and he spoke again.

'What I was really talking about was an idea I had a while ago. Falling in love with you has made me remember it. Amy, have you ever thought about going to live in Australia?'

'Australia?' Amy repeated. It was as though he had asked her if she wanted to live on the moon. 'That's so far away!'

'Not as far as all that. It only takes a few days to get there. Melbourne's the place to go, especially in the building trade. It's really thriving, there's piles of money to be made. I've heard of lots of people going there from Auckland. It's a much bigger place than Auckland, too—I could take you to more shows and things.'

'I wouldn't be able to see Pa and the boys, or Lizzie either. Still, I suppose I won't see them much when we're in Auckland, anyway.' She smiled up at him. 'I'll go wherever you want, and I'll be happy if you're there.'

'I think you'd love it in Melbourne. Don't look so worried, Amy, we wouldn't be going there for a while, anyway. I'd better get you used to living in Auckland before I rush you off to Australia.'

Edie made them very welcome, bustling about carrying cups of tea and cakes into the parlour with Lizzie's help. Lizzie was rather quiet, and she stared at Jimmy in a way that Amy found disconcerting. Little Ernie helped himself liberally to the cakes, dropping crumbs which he then trod into the rug, and Amy was glad she would not have to clean it.

After the second cup of tea Arthur invited Jimmy to have a look around the farm. Ernie trotted off at his father's heels, struggling to keep up.

'It's so nice of you to bring Jimmy over,' Edie said. 'I never thought to ask him up to the house when he was helping with the haymaking. I like having visitors—Lizzie, why didn't Frank come today?'

'Because Pa didn't ask him.'

'Oh, he shouldn't wait to be asked! You tell him to just come whenever he wants.'

'Maybe you should tell him that, Ma.'

'But he's your young man, Lizzie.' Edie seemed oblivious to the fact that her daughter was staring at her in open-mouthed astonishment. 'Now, Amy, you bring Jimmy over here again soon. I like him.'

'I'll try, Aunt Edie, but I think he might be going back to Auckland soon.' Amy rose from her chair. 'We'd better be getting home, I'll have to think about making dinner. I'll just go and find Jimmy.'

Lizzie went out with Amy to see her off. 'Did you hear what Ma said?' she demanded. 'My "young man". I thought she hadn't noticed, and she comes out with that!'

'She sounded pleased about it. Aunt Edie's not going to give you any trouble when you want to get married. All you have to do now is persuade Frank to ask you.'

'He'll ask me, don't you worry.'

'He might need a push.'

'So I'll give him one. What about you?'

'I don't want to marry you, thanks, Lizzie.'

'Ha ha. You know what I mean—what's this about Jimmy going back to Auckland?'

'It's where he lives, you know. He only came down for the summer, and it's March now.'

'But what about the two of you? I thought you were in love.'

'He'll be back,' Amy said with a knowing smile. 'Then I'll tell you all about it.' *Well, not all about it. The parts you'll understand.* 'Oh, there's Jimmy by the horse paddock. I've got to go, Lizzie, I'll see you later.' She rushed away before Lizzie could question her further.

'Well, I've done my duty,' said Jimmy. 'I've learned all about breaking in farms and keeping horses and growing maize. It's a pity I'd already heard most of it from your father.'

'Poor thing,' said Amy.

'Are you going to make it up to me?'

'Of course.' She smiled back at him. 'What about a romantic walk under the trees?'

'That sounds perfect.'

And it was perfect, Amy reflected as she lay nestled against him some minutes later. The soaring notes of a nearby tui echoed her own happiness. She knew she would cheerfully follow Jimmy to the ends of the earth.

He stirred next to her. 'We'd better go back,' he said. 'I think I like visiting after all.'

'I thought it was boring?' Amy said with an expression of innocent surprise.

'The one thing you are not, little one, is boring.' Jimmy leant over to plant a gentle kiss on her mouth. 'Let's get going, I can't lie here all day with you, much as I'd like to.' He got to his feet and stretched. 'I'm surprised they can't see it on my face after I've been with you, but no one ever seems to notice.'

'They'll notice if you don't do that up,' Amy said, pointing to his gaping trouser buttons.

'Whoops, nearly forgot. What about you, anyway, with your hair all wild?'

221

Amy produced a comb from her pocket with a smug smile. 'I'm prepared this time.'

Jimmy helped comb her hair, making her squeal when he pulled at the knots, then they walked back to the farmhouse.

'Aunt Edie likes you,' Amy said as they went through the gate in the hedge. 'She said she wanted me to bring you over again.'

'She's a nice lady. She seems fond of you, and I can't help but like anyone who's nice to you. That Ernie's a handful, isn't he? Arthur's quite patient with him, really.'

'He was much worse when he was younger. Now he's old enough to hang around Uncle Arthur it's easier on Aunt Edie—on Lizzie, too, she used to have to look after him a lot. She was worried Aunt Edie might have another one.'

'She's a bit old for that, isn't she?'

'Yes, I think she is now.'

They parted at the back door, with Jimmy going off to the cow shed while Amy went into the house to start preparing dinner. She recalled the panic-stricken look on Lizzie's face when the two girls had overheard Edie tell Susannah and the other women that she had thought she might be having another baby. Amy frowned in concentration, trying to think of exactly what her aunt had said.

Suddenly she recalled it clearly. A shudder went through her as the words dropped into her awareness like a pronouncement of doom. Aunt Edie had thought she was having a baby because her bleeding was late. Because it was two weeks late.

It can't be—I can't be going to have a baby! But I'm two and a half weeks late now. She looked down at her flat abdomen, and fought a losing battle against believing what had happened to her. *I must be. What are we going to do?*

23

March – April 1884

Amy went through the motions of her work scarcely knowing what she did; when Susannah joined her, Amy did whatever she said without comment.

'You're very quiet,' Susannah said as Amy set the table. 'What's wrong with you?'

'I... I don't feel very well,' Amy said, in a tone she hoped would discourage further questions.

'Oh. You look well enough, just a bit flushed.'

Dinner seemed to go on interminably. Amy caught Jimmy's eye a few times; he looked puzzled by her stricken expression, but she avoided meeting his gaze when she found it was difficult for her to hold back tears.

An evening in the parlour would be unbearable. After she had done the dishes and set the bread dough in front of the range, she went into the other room for just long enough to make her excuses.

'I'm going to bed now.' She crossed the room to give her father a kiss. 'I feel a bit tired. Good night.' She brushed cheeks with Susannah. As she left the room she saw Jimmy looking at her in concern. She managed to reach her bedroom and close the door before she broke down.

Amy had a long, troubled night. She got up the next morning feeling more tired than when she had gone to bed. Her face in the mirror was red and puffy with crying. She splashed it with cold water till she looked more presentable, dressed, and went out to the kitchen.

Jimmy soon joined her. 'What's wrong, sweetheart?' he asked, enfolding her in his arms. 'You looked so unhappy last evening, now you look as though you hadn't slept all night.'

Amy tried to take comfort from his touch, but when she started to speak all she could do was sob.

'What is it, Amy? Did Susannah say something horrible to you? Come on, tell me all about it.'

'It's... it's terrible,' she choked out before her words disappeared into weeping.

'You mustn't let her upset you.' Jimmy stroked her hair as he held her close. 'What did she say?'

'It's nothing to do with Susannah. It's us.' Amy made an effort to calm herself, then looked up into Jimmy's face. 'I realised yesterday when we got home. Jimmy, I think—no, I'm almost sure—I'm going to have a baby.'

Jimmy's face took on an expression of utter horror. On seeing it Amy lost all her slender self-control in a moment. Her face crumpled and tears welled in her eyes.

'Please don't be angry with me. Oh, what are we going to do?' she wailed.

'Shh,' Jimmy said, pressing her to him. 'I'm sorry I looked at you like that, I got a shock hearing the news so suddenly. Let's sit down.' He helped her to a chair and sat next to her, holding her hand between both of his.

They sat in silence for a while, then Jimmy gave his head a small shake. 'Well, I didn't expect that. That was stupid of me, I know, but I just didn't.'

'What are we going to do?' Amy pleaded. She felt a little calmer now that Jimmy no longer looked terrified.

'We're going to do the decent thing and get married, of course! Don't you see, Amy, it's wonderful news, really.'

'Is it? Why?'

'Because we'll be able to get married. My father won't try and stop us now. Oh, he'll lecture me about being stupid and irresponsible, but he'll want to see us tidily married as soon as possible. He'll soon forgive me when he meets you, anyway. It's a good thing he's going to like you— we'll have to live with them for a little while.'

'Will we?' Amy asked fearfully. 'Why?'

'Because I'm not going to have enough money to get us anywhere to live at first. It won't be for long, darling—I certainly don't want to see us still living in my bedroom when the baby arrives.' He shuddered at the thought.

'As long as you think they'll accept me. What do you think Pa will say?'

Jimmy smiled ruefully. 'Your father will want to have my hide, and who could blame him? As long as I can persuade him not to tell your brothers what I've done, I'll get through it in one piece. But after he's got that over and done with he'll march us down to the church, maybe with a shotgun to hurry me along. You, my darling, are going to be Mrs Taylor before you know it. There, that's better,' he said, seeing her smile.

'I feel much better now I've told you. What shall we do, then? Will you tell Pa today?'

'No, I still think it's a better idea to tell my father first. I want to get you away as soon as possible after we're married, and if I've got things sorted out with Father that'll be much simpler. I'd better go up to Auckland straight away—this week if I can get a passage.'

'I'll miss you.'

'I'll miss you too. It won't be for long, though.'

Amy saw Jimmy riding off down the road as she was hanging out a load of washing later that morning. She smiled; everything would soon be all right.

That evening she felt brave enough to sit in the parlour with the others, hemming a gown for George. It was almost time for the family to retire when Jimmy spoke.

'I went into town today. The *Staffa*'s sailing on Thursday, I booked myself on it.'

'Oh, no, James,' Susannah said. 'You're not going already, are you?'

'Well, March is more than half over now, Susannah, I've been here three and a half months. I've already stayed longer than I meant to because I've been enjoying myself so much. It's time I went home and did some work again.'

'Couldn't you stay with me a bit longer? Jack, tell him to stay.'

'You're welcome to stay as long as you like, lad,' said Jack. 'You've been earning your keep. But if your pa wants you back I suppose you've got to go. You can always come again next summer if you want.'

'Thank you, Jack, you've been more than hospitable. I really do have to go home now, though.'

'What am I going to do?' Susannah demanded. 'Having you here this last summer has been the only thing that's kept me going. James, I don't think I can bear being left here alone again.'

'Hey, Susannah, don't talk like that,' Jack protested. 'How can you say you're alone with all of us?'

'I might as well be alone—I wish I was!' Susannah flashed at him. '*They* all hate me.' She took in Amy and her older brothers with a wave of her arm. 'And as for you,' she turned on Jack, 'all you want is—'

'Susannah,' Jimmy broke in. 'Don't say anything silly. You'll only regret it later if you do.'

'Oh, James, *please* don't leave me alone down here,' Susannah begged. 'I can't stand it, I know I can't. I think I'll go mad if I have to live through another winter here.'

'Susannah,' Jack said, reaching out towards her arm.

'Don't *touch* me,' she screamed, slapping his hand away before it reached her. 'Leave me alone.'

'Oh, for God's sake,' Harry said in disgust. 'Why don't you take her back to Auckland with you?'

'You keep out of it, boy,' Jack growled.

Susannah turned on Harry. 'Do you think I wouldn't go like a shot if I could? Do you think I enjoy living here?'

'I know none of us have had any chance to enjoy it since you arrived,' Harry said, ignoring the warning hand John placed on his arm.

'Will you take me?' Susannah said, turning a wild-eyed face to Jimmy. 'Will you take me and the little ones?'

'Susannah, you mustn't talk like that,' Jimmy said, looking helplessly at his sister. 'You don't mean any of those things, and you're going to wish you hadn't said them when you calm down. You don't really want to leave, you know you don't.'

'I do, I do! I hate it here!'

'Stop it, Susannah,' Jack said. 'You're carrying on like a child. Stop making a fool of me in front of my own children.' He reached out and put his hand on her wrist.

'Don't touch me.' Susannah tried to shake his hand off, but Jack held it firmly. Amy could see his knuckles whitening from the force of his grip.

'I will touch you, and you will do what I say,' Jack said coldly. 'And I say you're staying here with me, and you're not taking my little ones away, either. And right now you're coming to bed so we can talk about all this nonsense in private, instead of you screaming like a fishwife. Come on.'

He pulled on her wrist, and Susannah fought him, tugging at his arm with her free hand. But Jack was much stronger. He put both hands on her wrist and jerked her out of her chair, only saving her from flying into the wall by the firmness of his grip.

'You're hurting me!'

'Stop struggling, then. Do you want me to pick you up and carry you over my shoulder?'

Susannah subsided at that threat. She let him drag her from the room and across the passage, weeping as she went.

Amy stared wide-eyed after them, then turned to Jimmy, who looked equally stunned.

'Pa's never done anything like that before,' she said. 'He must be really angry.'

'It's high time he did,' said Jimmy. 'That's half the trouble with my sister, your father's too soft on her.'

'I don't suppose you could take her?' Harry asked.

'I'm afraid not, Harry,' Jimmy said with a smile. 'Even if I wanted to, your father seems to want to keep her.'

'More fool him,' Harry muttered.

Amy and Jimmy made the most of their time over the next few days, though it was confined to breakfasting together and evening walks accompanied by the little boys, with the consequently limited conversations.

On Wednesday afternoon Amy went to a grove of fruit trees around the side of the hill from the house. She was picking peaches for jam when Jimmy arrived.

'There you are,' he said. 'I've been looking all over for you, and trying to avoid Susannah at the same time.'

'I thought you'd be busy this afternoon.'

'I told your father I was going to pack, but I haven't got much, so I'll get it done tonight. This is the last chance we'll have to be alone for a while, and I didn't want to waste it. Come on, we're going for a walk.' He took her hand and pulled.

'But I'm picking these peaches,' Amy protested.

'I'll give you a hand later, then you'll get all the peaches you need. Don't you want to be alone with me?'

'Of course I do.'

She abandoned her baskets and walked with him to their favourite glade, where their bodies were soon entwined. The knowledge that this would be the last time they would lie together till Jimmy's return made Amy respond to him with a passion that surprised them both, and left them panting and sweaty.

'How am I going to do without you?' Jimmy whispered in her ear as she lay in his arms afterwards.

'You'll have to hurry back to me.'

'Oh, I will. As fast as I can.' He got to his knees to do up his trousers, while Amy lay with her head propped on one arm.

When he made to stand, Amy rose to her knees and put her hands either side of his face. 'Wait,' she said quietly. 'I want to stay here a little bit longer.'

'I can't manage again that quickly, Amy, much as I'd like to.'

'I don't mean that. I want to print your face in my memory, so I'll be able to see it every day we're apart. Let me look.' She stared intently, tracing the line of his mouth and the neatly-trimmed moustache with her fingers and studying the way his dark hair framed his face, then let her hands drop. 'There, I've done it.'

'It won't be as long as all that, sweetheart,' Jimmy said. He sounded shaken by the solemnity of her tone.

'I know. It's going to seem a long time to me, though, even if it's only a few days.'

Jimmy was quiet for some time as they walked back to the orchard. When he spoke he sounded pensive.

'Amy, I'm going to come back as soon as I can, but it might have to be a little while. I mean, I can't just walk into the house and say "Hello, Father, how have you been the last few months, by the way I've got Susannah's stepdaughter with child, can I go back tomorrow and marry her?" I'll have to get him in a good mood first, hear all his boring news and all that. Especially since I'm going to want him to give me some money.'

'Oh. Yes, I see that. How long do you think it'll be?'

'I don't know, maybe a week or two—it shouldn't be any longer than that. But listen, Amy, I don't want you to tell your father you're having a baby. That's my responsibility, I'll do it when I get back.'

'I don't want to tell him. But I'm going to be with you when you do.'

'That's not a very good idea, Amy.'

'I don't care. It's not fair if you get in trouble with Pa when it's something we did together. He can go crook at us both. I'm not going to let him hit you, either.'

He smiled at her. 'Don't worry about me, I can look after myself. But I'm a little bit worried about you, sweetheart.'

'Why?'

'Well, like I said, I don't want you to tell your father. But if I'm away a couple of weeks, I suppose it's just possible he'll find out. I don't know, Susannah might notice something, she must know a lot about having babies by now. Amy, if he does find out while I'm not here to protect you, what do you think will happen? Will he beat you?'

'Oh, no, Pa never beats me. One time I was rude to Susannah and she made him give me a hiding, but even then he didn't do it properly like she wanted—you know, so I wouldn't be able to sit down. He just strapped my hand—oh, that's a secret, Jimmy, you must never tell Susannah. But he's never really beaten me.' She smiled ruefully. 'Of course, I've never done anything like this before.' She thought hard, her brow creased in concentration. 'No, I'm almost sure he won't beat me. It wouldn't do any good, would it? Don't worry about me.'

'That's my brave girl.' He gave her a squeeze. 'That's a weight off my mind. I think you're right—your father's terribly fond of you, anyone can see that.'

The two of them working together quickly filled Amy's baskets with peaches, then Jimmy carried them back to the house for her.

'I'm not going to come and see you off tomorrow, Jimmy,' Amy said. 'I'd only get upset and give our secret away.'

'That's probably sensible, I might make a fool of myself if you did. Can I have something to remember you by?'

'Haven't I just given you that?' Amy asked, smiling at him.

'Oh, I'll remember that, all right. I meant something to look at. I know, what about a lock of your hair?'

'That's a lovely idea.'

That evening when Amy was getting ready for bed, she cut off a long tress from low on her head where it would not show. She tied it with a piece of narrow silk ribbon.

Next morning when Jimmy joined her for breakfast she slipped it into his hand. He kissed the hair softly and tucked it into the pocket of his jacket. He took Amy in his arms and they shared a long, lingering kiss. 'There, that'll have to last you for a while,' he said, smiling tenderly down at her.

'I love you, Jimmy.' She clung to him.

'And I love you.'

Amy's father and brothers came in then, ending the conversation abruptly.

Susannah came out for breakfast a few minutes later, dressed ready for town. 'When are we leaving?' she asked.

'As soon as I've had breakfast and got changed. One of you boys can catch the horses and get them harnessed. Now, Susannah,' Jack spoke firmly, 'you remember what we talked about last night? You can only come and see Jimmy off if you're not going to get upset about it.'

'You won't stop me saying goodbye to my own brother, will you?' Susannah said, her lower lip quivering.

'I don't want to stop you. But I don't want you making a fool of yourself in front of the whole town, either, screaming abuse at me on the wharf. Can you control yourself or not?'

'You're being horrible to me.' Tears were forming in Susannah's eyes.

'Are you getting upset, Susannah? You can stay home if you are.'

Susannah's eyes dried as if by magic, and she folded her hands neatly in her lap.

'Of course I'm not upset. I'm quite calm. I just want to see James off, and you didn't seem to want me to.'

'That's all right then. Amy, would you like to come for the ride?'

'No, thank you, Pa. I've got a lot to do here.'

'Why would she want to come?' Susannah said. 'What's it to do with

229

her?' Amy glanced at Jimmy and they shared a secret smile.

Jack and Susannah drove off with Jimmy, Susannah holding George on her lap. Amy stood on the verandah, lifting Thomas so he could wave until they were out of sight. Then she let the tears fall unchecked down her cheeks.

'Amy crying,' Thomas said, touching her tears in wonder.

'Amy's being silly.' She wiped her hand across her cheeks. 'Uncle Jimmy's coming back soon. Come on, Tommy, you can help me do some baking.'

Jimmy's departure left a huge gap in Amy's life, and she tried to fill it by keeping herself busy. She made jam and bottled fruit until the shelves in the kitchen and the larder were packed full, and she tended the vegetable and flower gardens in her spare moments. But she found it lonely preparing breakfast in the empty kitchen, and her early-morning sessions in the dairy dragged interminably now Jimmy was no longer there to share her thoughts with.

Susannah received a letter from her mother a week after Jimmy's departure. Amy hovered around her as she read, trying not to seem overly inquisitive.

'Did Jimmy get home safely?' Amy asked.

'Yes. Mother says he's been closeted with Father ever since he arrived, but they won't tell her what they're talking about. At least they're getting on well now.'

'Oh, good!' Amy said with deep satisfaction.

'Why are you suddenly so interested in my family?'

'Well, it's just nice when families get on, isn't it?'

'I suppose it is. I used to get on well with mine.' Susannah sighed deeply, and Amy took herself off before her stepmother could decide to get upset.

Every day Amy waited eagerly for news of Jimmy's return. She marked the days off on her calendar, counting each morning how long he had been away and trying to work out how soon she could expect him back. Every time she heard of the steamer arriving she wondered if Jimmy would be on it.

Lizzie came over one morning when Jimmy had been gone for almost two weeks. When she found Amy weeding the garden she joined her in the task.

'You seem all right,' Lizzie said. 'You're not pining for Jimmy now he's gone?'

'He'll be back, I've told you that.'

'Next summer, you mean? That's a long time to wait if you're as keen on him as you seemed to be.'

'Maybe sooner than you think. Don't pry, Lizzie, you'll find out in good time.'

'How can he come back so soon? I thought he could only come down for the summer.'

'I told you not to pry, Lizzie.'

'Doesn't he ever have to do any work in Auckland?' Lizzie persisted. 'It seems a funny arrangement he's got with his father.'

'I warned you, Lizzie.' Amy threw a large, freshly uprooted dandelion, making her cousin duck.

'There's no need to be violent! You've got awfully secretive since you met him. Ah, well.' Lizzie gave an exaggerated sigh, 'I can't do anything about it, I suppose.'

'No, you can't,' Amy agreed. 'You'll just have to be patient. I thought you'd be busy enough organising Frank without poking your nose into my affairs.'

'Oh, Frank's coming along nicely. Last Sunday when he thanked Ma for having him for lunch he asked her if he could come again this week! Just like that. I didn't even have to prime him to do it.'

'That's good. I suppose Aunt Edie said yes?'

'She said she wanted him to come every Sunday from now on. I didn't know Ma had that much sense.' Lizzie shook her head over the mysteriousness of parents. 'I wish we could get more time to talk, though. Everyone's there at lunch, there's no privacy.'

'Why don't you go for a walk in the bush?' Amy asked, then mentally kicked herself for her carelessness.

'That doesn't seem quite right,' Lizzie said, frowning. 'That's a bit *too* private. I want to be out of sight, but not too far away from—Amy, have you been doing that?' she asked. 'Have you been wandering off into the bush with Jimmy?'

'Never you mind. I don't want to talk about it.'

'You have! I wish I'd known that.' Lizzie stared at her as if trying to read her thoughts, and Amy made herself stare back boldly. 'I hope you know what you're doing,' Lizzie said at last. 'Ah, well, he's gone now, so there's no need to worry, I suppose.'

'No,' Amy said with a confident smile. 'There's no need to worry about anything.' *He's coming back.*

On the morning that marked three weeks since Jimmy had left, Amy stood in front of her mirror, pressing her dress across her abdomen and anxiously studying her reflection to see if there was any bulge. But her

231

profile was as flat as ever. She tried to remember how long before the babies had arrived Susannah had started to swell. Jimmy was sure to be back before she needed to worry about that, anyway. He would probably be back any day now. A week or two, he had said. Surely he had had time to arrange things with his father by now?

'Do you want to come into town with me?' Harry asked Amy when he was about to go in to collect the supplies. 'The *Staffa*'s in this morning,' he added. 'There might be some news.'

There'll be the mail from Auckland. 'All right, I'd like to,' Amy said.

'I thought you might like a break from Her Ladyship,' Harry said as they drove along the beach. 'She's been scratchier than ever since Jimmy went.'

'She's been a bit better with Pa lately—not with me, though. You're right, it's good to have a rest from her. I'll be in a rush catching up later, but it's worth it. Susannah likes to have a lie-down in the afternoon, anyway, so I'll have some peace.'

There were a few strangers in town, passengers off the *Staffa*. Amy peered along the street, looking for a tall, dark-haired figure, but there was no one who even vaguely reminded her of Jimmy.

She rushed over to the Post and Telegraph Office to collect the mail while Harry loaded up the buggy. 'There's a letter from Auckland for Susannah!' she called to Harry when she saw him crossing the road to join her.

'So what?'

'Oh… nothing.' Amy was glad Harry did not have an inquisitive nature.

The trip home seemed very long, and Amy almost regretted having gone into town. She sat with the letter on her lap, wondering what would be in it. Would Jimmy have written a note himself to go with it? Or would he just have told his mother to write? Would it say he was going to marry her, or just that he was coming down again? She hugged herself in anticipation.

'Good, you're back,' Susannah said when they got home. 'I was beginning to think I'd have to make lunch by myself.'

'I'll make it,' Amy said, nearly out of breath from running to the house. 'You sit down and read your letter.'

'A letter from Mother? Oh, good.' Susannah sat at the table and opened the letter.

Harry came in the back door with a sack of flour, and Jack followed close on his heels. 'Was there any mail today?' Jack asked.

'Only for her,' Harry said, waving vaguely in Susannah's direction.

'From Mother.' Susannah looked up as Jack sat beside her.

Get on and read it, for goodness sake, Amy thought as she made herself busy at the bench.

Susannah unfolded the letter and started reading. 'Oh,' she said almost at once. 'Oh, I never thought he'd do that.' She read on intently.

'Is it bad news?' Jack asked.

'It's come as a shock to Mother. James and Father didn't discuss it with her till it was all settled.'

'What? What's happened?' Jack asked. Amy crept closer to the table, careful not to make any noise.

'James is far too young to do something like that—whatever does Father mean by letting him?' Susannah laid the letter flat on the table and looked over at her husband.

'Letting him do what? What's he doing?' Jack asked.

Amy was almost peering over Susannah's shoulder now in her eagerness to see the letter. *He's not too young. His father must have had the sense to see that. When's he coming? When's he coming?*

'He's persuaded Father into giving him some money to start out on his own.' Susannah glanced down at the letter for a moment. 'It all happened just last week—Saturday he left.' She looked back at her husband.

'James has gone to Australia!'

24

April – June 1884

Amy looked up at the sea of faces around her and wondered why they were swimming in and out of focus. She felt hot, and her chest was tight. It was hard to breathe properly.

'Amy?' Her father gave her shoulder a small shake. 'Are you all right, girl?'

'I… I think so, Pa,' Amy said, struggling to sit up. Her father slipped his arm under her shoulders and helped her into a sitting position. Her head felt full of cotton wool, and her thoughts would not form clearly.

'Get her a drink of water, Harry,' said Jack. Harry rushed out the back door with a cup, which he soon brought back filled from the rain barrel.

Amy gulped at the water while Harry held the cup to her lips. The cold water helped clear her head, and for a moment she was relieved at being able to think properly again. Then the memory forced its way in to her awareness.

He's gone to Australia. He's left me here alone. I'm going to have a baby.

She gave a groan, and her father held her more firmly. 'Are you going to faint again?' he asked anxiously.

'N-no. No, I'm all right now, Pa.' She tried to stand, but her legs were too weak to bear her.

'You're not all right at all. You'd better have a lie-down.' He swept her easily into his arms and carried her to her room. Amy was vaguely aware of Susannah and Harry following a short distance behind. 'There's not much of you to lift,' Jack said as he laid her down on her bed. 'Susannah, what do you think's wrong with her?'

'I don't know,' Susannah said, pushing past him to stand beside the bed. 'She's very pale, but that's because she fainted. What's wrong with you, Amy? Do you have a pain somewhere?'

'I feel a bit sick,' Amy said. 'I'll be all right, I'd just like to be by myself for a while.'

'You two leave us alone for a minute,' Susannah ordered. 'I'll have a look at her.' She watched as Jack and Harry left the room, then she turned back to Amy. 'Now,' Susannah said briskly, 'what brought that on?' Amy was silent, struggling for words. 'Is it something to do with your bleeding?' Susannah asked.

'What?'

'Is your bleeding due? I know young girls sometimes feel faint at that time of the month. I'm sure I used to when I was your age. Is that the problem?'

'It… it is sort of due.' *Overdue.*

'That's probably it, then. Do you have a stomach ache?'

'No. I just feel sick. I really would like to be by myself.' It was harder with every word to keep her voice steady.

'Have a rest, then. You'd better take this dress off. Here, I'll help you.' Susannah started to lift Amy's pinafore, and at first Amy lay limp and let her do it. Then she remembered the brooch on her chemise.

'No,' she said, pushing at Susannah's hands. 'I'll do it by myself.'

'I don't know what you've got to be so shy about. Suit yourself, then.' Susannah stood up. 'I suppose I'll have to make lunch by myself now. Will you get up for it?'

'No. I don't want anything to eat, thank you. I just want to be by myself.' The last word came out raggedly as she began to lose the battle to stay calm.

'All right.' Susannah went out, closing the door behind her.

Amy took off her dress and unpinned the brooch from her chemise. She climbed under the covers and held the brooch tightly in her hand until the sharp edges of the 'A' bit into her flesh. She stared at the ceiling with dry eyes. Now that she was alone in the silence of her room the tears refused to come.

Why, Jimmy? Why have you left me? Why did you run away from me? Did I do something wrong? Did I upset you? I tried to do what you wanted. I thought I was pleasing you. You always seemed happy. Why don't you want me any more? What am I going to do now? The empty room held no answer.

An hour later Amy heard the door open quietly, and she closed her eyes. 'She's asleep,' she heard Susannah say. 'Leave her alone, she'll feel better when she's had a rest.'

'It's not like Amy to take to her bed,' said Jack. 'She must feel really crook.'

'Young girls get like this. I used to have terrible problems at her age. Don't worry about her, she'll be all right. Don't disturb her, Jack.'

Amy recognised her father's heavy tread as he tried to cross the floor on tiptoe. She sensed him leaning over her, then he planted the softest of kisses on her cheek. 'Poor little thing,' he murmured. 'I don't like to see her feeling bad.' He retraced his steps to the passage. They closed the door and left her alone once again.

Hot tears welled up in her eyes and fell down her cheeks at the concern and affection in her father's voice. *What'll Pa say when I tell him what I've done? Maybe he won't love me any more. Jimmy doesn't love me any more. What am I going to do?* She sobbed into her pillow until she was weak and ill from weeping, then lay quietly till she had gathered enough strength to weep again. Amy had never in her short life even imagined that she could feel so alone and frightened.

She again pretended to be asleep when Susannah came to call her for dinner, knowing that her face would betray her misery. Susannah closed the drapes and left her in peace. In the middle of the night, when the house was silent, Amy got out of bed and made her way to her dressing table by the small amount of moonlight that crept through cracks between the drapes. Her reflection in the mirror was no more than a pattern of shadows. She opened a drawer and fumbled in it until she felt the softness of her blue velvet ribbon. She nestled the brooch into the ribbon and closed the drawer on it. Her hand was tender where the brooch had dug into it.

I've got to tell Pa. I'll tell him soon. I'll tell him when it's the right time.

Amy shivered from the chill of the June morning as she stood in front of the mirror, looking anxiously at her profile. She had swollen noticeably in the two months since learning of Jimmy's desertion. She now left off all but one petticoat to reduce her bulk, and the fullness of her pinafore gave good camouflage. When she had to put on a good dress to go to church she complained of the cold and kept her cloak wound around her, but she knew her smart dress (last winter's one, serving an extra term) would not fit for much longer. The blue silk gown, with its figure-hugging lines, hung undisturbed in her wardrobe; she had fobbed Susannah off by saying the dress was too beautiful to be worn every Sunday.

As she did each morning, she silently rehearsed various ways of breaking the news to her father. None of them ever seemed right. *Would today be a good time to tell Pa? No, he seemed so tired last night, and Susannah was grumpy about Tommy getting his clothes all muddy. She's probably been growling to Pa about it. I'll tell him soon. Maybe tomorrow.* Then she steeled herself to face the world for another day with a calm face.

Jack had commented on Amy's silence for the first week or so, but now he hardly seemed to notice that his daughter rarely said more than a word or two at any meal. Little Thomas babbled away freely, making mealtimes noisy enough without any contribution from Amy.

The heavy work of scrubbing was becoming difficult, now that bending over needed extra care. She struggled her way through it, then went out of the house to sit on a stump, out of sight of the house and Susannah's prying eyes. It was the safest way to spend the rest of the morning until it was time to start making lunch. The only drawback was that it gave her too much time to think. Thinking meant seeing Jimmy's face again, smiling at her; hearing his voice again, saying he loved her; feeling his touch, remembering once again how that had made her respond.

'There you are!' Lizzie's voice broke into her thoughts. 'Fancy sitting outside in this cold weather. I think it's going to rain later, too.'

'It's fine right now. I like being by myself.'

'You're not reading.'

'No. I don't read much any more. I can't seem to concentrate properly.'

'Why not?'

'I don't know. I just can't.'

'Oh. Reading's a waste of time, anyway. Are you all right, Amy?'

'Of course I am. Don't talk about me, what have you been doing?'

'You've got so quiet lately. Ever since Jimmy left—no, more recent than that,' Lizzie said thoughtfully. 'You were fine for a while, then you went funny.'

'I'm not funny. I don't want to talk about me, I'm not very interesting. How's Frank?'

'What is it, Amy? Why don't you want to talk about Jimmy any more? Don't you like him now?'

Amy choked back a sob and turned it into a cough. 'I don't want to talk about it.'

'You said you'd tell me. You said he'd come back, then you'd tell me all about it. Amy, I stopped asking questions about what you were doing with him because you got funny about it—'

'Don't start again. I won't tell you.'

'No, I am going to ask you. I've said nothing about it for months, just watched you get quieter and quieter. At first you seemed so sure he was coming back and everything would be all right. I thought you must be going to get married.'

'So did I.' Amy was suddenly too weary to fight back the tears.

Lizzie sat down and slipped her arm around Amy. 'And now he's not going to?'

Amy shook her head. She held herself rigid within the curve of Lizzie's arm, trying to keep hold of her remaining shreds of self-control. 'He's gone. He's gone away and left me. He doesn't want me any more.' When the words were out her strength seemed to go with them. She let Lizzie put both arms around her and hold her close as her body shook with sobs.

Lizzie held her in silence until the sobs had died down into quieter weeping. 'So he had his little romance, and now he's gone back to the city, eh? And he made you think he wanted to marry you. I never did trust him. I never thought he was good enough for you.' She leaned forward till she was looking into Amy's face, but Amy looked down at her lap, refusing to meet her cousin's eyes. 'You'll just have to forget about him, Amy.'

'No. I can't.'

'Yes you can. Pretend you never met him. He's hurt you, but it's all over now.'

'No it's not, Lizzie. It's not over.' The burden of her secret was intolerably heavy, and she ached to share it. She raised her eyes. 'I'm going to have a baby.'

She felt Lizzie's body jolt against hers. 'You're what?'

'I'm going to have a baby.' She studied Lizzie's face, half expecting to see disgust. Instead, she saw disbelief turning into anger.

'Did he know?' Lizzie asked. Amy nodded. 'And that's why he ran away. That snake! How could he do that to you?' Amy had no answer to that question; she had asked it of herself many times. 'Well, aren't they going to bring him back and make him marry you? Auckland's not as far away as all that—they must know where he lives. Of course they do, it's Susannah's family.'

'He's not in Auckland. He's gone to Australia.'

'Australia! That's much too far for anyone to go and get him!' Lizzie fell silent, absorbing the momentous news. 'I've been so stupid,' she said at last.

'You? You haven't done anything wrong, Lizzie.'

'Yes I have. I never trusted him, but I let that go on under my nose and did nothing about it. I should have noticed. I should have stopped it.'

'It's my fault, not yours.'

'Of course it's not your fault!' Lizzie rounded on her, eyes flashing. 'He was so clever and charming, he had you wrapped around his little finger in five minutes. I couldn't expect you to see through him. I should have seen what he was up to.'

'How could you see it when you don't know anything about what goes on between men and women?'

'I should have enough sense to know a villain when I see one.' Lizzie shook her head in disgust. 'Well, I didn't. What did your pa say?'

'He doesn't know.'

'What?' She looked closely at Amy's abdomen, stretching the dress flat

238

over the flesh. 'But you're starting to get big. I must have been blind as well as stupid not to notice. Amy, you've got to tell him.'

'I know. I will, I just haven't found the right time yet.'

'You're frightened to, aren't you? But you're going to make it worse the longer you leave it.'

'It's hard, Lizzie. Pa's going to be so hurt.'

'Do you want me to come with you? If it's too hard for you, I'll tell him myself. Would that be better? You can just stand there and listen, or you can stay out here if you want.'

'No. Thank you, Lizzie, you're being lovely to me. Much better than I deserve. But it's my responsibility, I've got to do it myself.'

'Do it soon, Amy. It'll be worse if they just notice. Susannah's had babies, she's sure to notice before long.'

'I'll tell them soon. Maybe tomorrow.'

'Why not today?'

'Not today. It doesn't feel like the right time. Maybe tomorrow.' Amy rose from the stump and shook the creases out of her dress. 'I've got to go and make lunch now. You'd better go home.'

'Wash your face first, it's all red from crying. Shall I come and see you tomorrow? Oh, I can't—Frank's coming for lunch.' She frowned. 'Maybe I could come anyway.'

'No, you mustn't spoil your day with Frank. I've done enough harm without that. You enjoy your lunch and forget about me.'

'I won't be able to forget about you. I might come the next day. Amy, please tell Uncle Jack soon.'

'I will.' *As soon as it's the right time.*

It was an unusually thoughtful Lizzie who returned to her own home that morning, and she was still subdued when Frank arrived for lunch the next day.

'Cat got your tongue, Lizzie?' her father asked, helping himself to more potatoes.

'What? Oh, I was just thinking.'

'Makes a change from talking. Watch out, Frank, my daughter's plotting something.' Lizzie was too wrapped up in her thoughts to take any notice of his attempts at humour.

'Jessie's had a foal, Frank,' Bill said when they had finished eating. 'Do you want to come and see it? They're in the paddock across the creek.'

'All right,' Frank said. His eyes met Lizzie's, and cast a questioning look.

'I'll come too,' Lizzie said. 'I haven't seen that foal yet. Leave those dishes, Ma, I'll help you with them when I get back.'

Bill stopped when the three of them were halfway between the house and the Waituhi stream. 'You know where it is, Lizzie, why don't I let you show Frank yourself? I'll just be having a look at the turnips in the next paddock, give me a yell if you want me for anything.'

'Thanks, Bill,' Lizzie said. She knew her honour was safe with Frank, but she was grateful for her brother's solicitude.

'I meant if Frank wanted me,' Bill said with a grin, ignoring Lizzie's indignant scowl as he strolled away from them. Well, it didn't matter if Bill was making fun of them, he had done her a favour anyway. A chance to be alone with Frank was just what she wanted.

Frank walked beside her, wondering what he could have done to make Lizzie so quiet. Had he said something stupid? He always seemed to be saying something stupid; at least, people always seemed to be laughing at him, which was just as bad. Maybe she was getting tired of that. 'Lizzie,' he said, 'do you want me to stop coming around so much?'

'What?' Lizzie jerked her head around as though she had forgotten he was there. 'Of course I don't. Why do you say that?'

'Well, you're so quiet today. I thought you might be annoyed… or just bored with me.'

'Bored? Of course I'm not bored. Don't be stupid, Frank, do you think I want someone like… I mean… Oh, forget it.'

'So you still want me to come around?'

'Yes, I do.' She gave him a sidelong glance. 'I think Pa's getting a bit worried, though.'

'Why?'

'Oh, he said something about you coming around so much without making your intentions clear. I'm not sure what he meant exactly.'

Frank's heart sank as he pictured Arthur questioning him over those 'intentions'. What would he say if Arthur asked what he wanted from Lizzie? He liked being with her. She was fun, and she made him feel good. Her father mightn't think that was enough.

'Still, he hasn't stopped me seeing you yet,' Lizzie said. 'Perhaps he won't. I just wish we could get more time alone. We're with other people all the time.'

That gave Frank a warm feeling. They crossed the stream where it ran over some rocks, and it seemed natural for him to take Lizzie's hand to help her across. Somehow it didn't seem necessary to let go of her hand afterwards. They were well out of sight of the house, and Bill was a dim figure in the next paddock. He had his back to them, anyway.

Jessie had a roan filly, a miniature copy of herself, standing beside her. The filly was skittish, and when they tried to approach she shied away. They left mother and daughter in peace and walked a little way along the creek bed to where there was a flat stone large enough for the two of them to sit on. They were now below the level of the paddocks, and out of sight of Bill.

'Lizzie, is it all right if I…' Frank began, then her face was suddenly so close to his that he knew he did not need to ask permission. He put his arms around her very carefully and pressed his lips to hers. She smelt deliciously of soap and roast meat.

'Don't you wish we could do this more?' Lizzie said when they stopped to take a breath.

'I sure do.' Frank moved to kiss her again, but Lizzie spoke just as he was about to, making him jerk his head away at the last moment.

'We hardly ever get any time alone. This is the first time we've had the chance to do this since the dance.'

'I know,' Frank said, wondering why she wanted to waste the chance by talking. He reached for her again, but once again Lizzie spoiled the moment.

'I hope you don't think I'm awful, Frank.'

'What?' he said in confusion. 'Why would I think that?'

'Because I'm letting you kiss me without knowing what your intentions are.'

'You're not exactly letting me right now, Lizzie,' he said, trying once more to kiss her.

'Do you? Do you think I'm awful? Do you think I'm a loose woman?' she demanded.

'No! I think you're really, really nice.'

'That's because I'm letting you do this.' She sounded close to tears. 'I've heard of men who take advantage of girls and kiss them and things, then after they've ruined the girl's reputation they go off with someone else. You wouldn't do that to me, would you?'

'Of course I wouldn't. I don't want anyone else, Lizzie.'

'How can I know that? Oh, Pa would be so upset if he knew I've let you kiss me when you've never said anything. I'd better go back to the house now.' She rose abruptly. 'I don't know when I'll see you again, Frank—alone like this, I mean. Maybe I'd better not see you.'

Frank wasn't sure exactly how it had happened, but he knew he had upset her. And Lizzie was always so nice; she was warm and soft, and she seemed to like being with him. She never laughed at him, no matter how much anyone else did. Now she didn't want to see him any more;

no, she did want to, but she was worrying over whether he really cared about her.

Suddenly Frank realised he did care; Lizzie mattered more to him than anything had for a very long time. He had to find some way of showing her that. If he let her walk away now he knew he might never have this chance again. 'Wait, Lizzie,' he said, standing up and taking her by the hand. She turned to face him, and he could see tears in her eyes. 'Maybe... maybe we should get married.'

Lizzie's eyes grew wide. 'Oh, yes, Frank! Yes, I'd love to!' She flung her arms around his neck and kissed him soundly. They stood locked in each other's arms, blissfully unaware of Bill, smiling broadly as he watched them from the next paddock.

25

June – July 1884

'Sitting out here by yourself again,' Lizzie said when she found Amy on the stump next morning. 'At least I know where to find you now.'

Amy straightened a little from her hunched position. 'I come out here most mornings. It's nice and quiet.'

Lizzie was about to sit down beside her when she stopped, reached out and touched the top of the stump. 'Amy, that's damp where you're sitting! It rained last night and it's too cold today to dry things out.'

'It's only a tiny bit damp. It's drier than the ground, anyway.' Amy managed to suppress a small cough.

'Come on, up you get. We'll go for a little walk instead.' Lizzie took her arm. 'Are you shivering?' she asked when they had walked a few steps.

'A little bit. I feel warmer now I'm not sitting still.' This time a cough slipped out despite her efforts, and Lizzie looked at her anxiously.

'You should take care of yourself better. You don't want to get ill. Have you got a flannel petticoat on?'

'No,' Amy admitted.

'How many petticoats are you wearing?'

'Just one. My dress is a bit tight if I wear more than one.'

'Amy, you'll freeze! You need a flannel petticoat in this weather.'

'I know. I'll see if I can let this dress out tonight.'

Lizzie pursed her lips. 'So you still haven't told Uncle Jack?'

'Not yet. It didn't work out this morning, he seemed busy. Maybe I'll tell him tomorrow.'

'I don't think you're going to tell him.'

'I am, I am!' Amy said, trying to sound confident. 'I know I've got to. It has to be the right time, though. It's got to be a day when he's not too busy, and Susannah's not grumpy, and when I feel...'

'When you feel what?'

'When I feel brave enough.' Amy shut her eyes tightly for a moment to keep the tears at bay.

'Are you sure you don't want me to tell him?'

'Yes. It's my job to.' Amy could see from Lizzie's face that her cousin was working herself up to a decision. 'Lizzie, you mustn't say anything to Pa.'

'I think I'd better tell Ma,' Lizzie said. 'I'll tell her, then she can tell Pa, and he'll tell Uncle Jack.'

'No! No, Lizzie, you mustn't.'

Lizzie continued as if Amy had not spoken. 'Yes, that's the best way. It'd be better for your pa to hear it from a man. It'll be easier for me to tell Ma than Uncle Jack, anyway.'

'No, please don't tell Aunt Edie. Please.' Amy's hand clutched convulsively at Lizzie's sleeve. 'I've got to tell Pa myself. I've got to be there to try and explain it to him. He won't understand if someone else tells him.' Amy could picture her uncle breaking the news to her father; she was quite sure he would be incapable of softening the blow. 'I have to do it myself. You mustn't. You mustn't.' Her lungs seemed incapable of delivering all the air she needed. She broke into a small burst of coughing as her chest heaved.

'Well, if you think it's better to do it yourself, maybe you're right,' Lizzie said doubtfully.

'I am right. Promise me you won't tell, Lizzie.'

'All right then, I won't.'

'Promise. Promise!' her voice was almost a scream.

'Hey, please don't get so upset, Amy. I promise. I promise I won't tell anyone unless you say I can.'

Amy closed her eyes until her breathing had slowed to normal. 'Good,' she said at last. 'I'll tell him soon.'

When she felt calm enough, she spoke again. 'How did your lunch with Frank go?'

Lizzie did not answer immediately, as if she were reluctant. 'That's the main reason I came over,' she said after a moment. 'It went really well.' She looked away from Amy. 'Frank's asked me to marry him.'

'Oh. That's good, Lizzie, it's really good. I'm happy for you.' She knew her voice did not sound happy, but it was the best she could manage.

'He hasn't asked Pa yet, but he's coming over again on Sunday, so he can do it then.'

'Why hasn't he asked Uncle Arthur?' Amy said, suddenly alarmed.

'I told him to wait until I'd seen you.'

'Me? Why did you do that?'

Lizzie looked at her with her face twisted oddly, and Amy knew that her cousin was close to tears. 'I didn't want you to hear it from anyone but me. I... I thought it would upset you.'

There was silence between them for a long moment. 'That was kind of you, Lizzie,' Amy said at last. 'You're always kind to me.' She bit her lip to hold back a sob, then with an effort she dragged her thoughts away from her own ill-fated proposal. 'Who knows Frank's asked you?'

'Just me and Frank, and now you. I don't want to tell anyone else till he's asked Pa, or there'll be a fuss when Pa finds out.'

'And he's going to ask him on Sunday?'

'Yes, when he comes for lunch. I just said that.'

Amy took hold of both Lizzie's arms and looked earnestly into her face. 'Make sure he does. Make him ask, Lizzie.'

'He'll ask, don't worry.'

'Make him. You mustn't have a secret engagement.'

'Of course I won't. I'm not stupid, you know. What's the point of a secret engagement?'

Amy dropped her hands and looked away. 'There's no point. You're right, Lizzie, you're not stupid. I'm going inside now.' She started a little unsteadily back towards the house.

'Amy, I'm sorry,' Lizzie called after her. 'I shouldn't have said that, I wasn't thinking. Come back.' But Amy walked on, ignoring Lizzie's voice.

'Are you coming for lunch again today, Frank?' Arthur asked after church that Sunday.

'Ah, yes, Mr Leith. Is that all right with you?'

'Humph! It doesn't seem to matter what I think, those women arrange it between themselves,' Arthur said, turning away in apparent disgust and leaving Frank feeling anxious.

'Maybe I shouldn't come today,' he said to Lizzie as she walked with him to the horse paddock.

'Of course you should,' she said. 'Don't take any notice of Pa, he doesn't mean it. You've got to come today, you're going to ask Pa if you can marry me.'

'Well, maybe it's not such a good day to ask him after all. Your pa doesn't seem in a very good mood.'

'It's a perfect day. You won't have any trouble with Pa, he likes you really. You just remember those things we talked about the other day.'

'Next week might be better,' Frank tried. 'He might be in a better mood.'

Lizzie's eyes narrowed. 'You're not trying to back out of it, are you? I thought you meant it. I thought you wanted to marry me. That's why I let you kiss me again. I *trusted* you. You did mean it, didn't you?'

'Yes, of course I meant it.' Frank took a deep breath. 'All right, I'll ask him today.'

'Oh, *good*. I'll see you later, then.' Lizzie flashed him a brilliant smile, and Frank felt braver.

He no longer felt brave when Arthur rose from the table after lunch. In fact he felt ill. But Lizzie smiled encouragingly at him across the table, and gestured towards her father with her eyes.

'I'm going to have a walk around the cows,' Arthur announced. 'You coming, Bill?'

'Be with you in a minute,' Bill said, taking a last gulp at his cup of tea.

Lizzie nudged Frank's leg with her foot, and he scraped his chair back. 'I'll,' Frank began, and heard his voice shake disconcertingly. He cleared his throat and tried again. 'I'll come with you, Mr Leith—if that's all right?' Arthur grunted something that might have been agreement as he went out the door. Frank quickened his step to catch up.

Lizzie moved around the table to sit beside her brother, and placed a hand on his arm as he made to rise. 'Bill,' she said, too quietly for her mother or younger brothers to hear, 'do you think you could give Frank a chance to talk to Pa by himself?'

Bill looked at her with affectionate amusement in his eyes. 'So he's going to ask, is he? Now, why should I be so keen to help Frank take my sister away?'

'Shh!' Lizzie hissed. 'It's not funny. It's serious.'

Bill chuckled. 'Don't get in a flurry. I'll take Alf and Ernie off somewhere. Are you sure Frank won't need protecting, though? Maybe I should stay in earshot?' Lizzie pulled a face at him, but gave his arm a grateful squeeze.

Frank trudged along beside Arthur, running through various approaches in his head. He had to talk about his farm, Lizzie had been insistent on that. He had to remind Arthur that it was almost as big as Arthur's own. He had to say something about admiring Arthur. What else had she said? He wished Lizzie could do the asking herself, though he knew that wouldn't be right.

'Do you think they look all right?' Arthur asked abruptly.

'What?' Frank said, startled out of his thoughts.

'These cows we're looking at, Frank.' He waved the stick he was carrying in a gesture that took in most of the paddock. 'Do you think they look all right?'

'Ah, yes, they look good. Your stock always looks healthy.'

'Well, when you've been farming as long as I have, you'll probably have a few more clues yourself, Frank. I hope so, anyway.'

'Aw, I don't know if I'll ever be as good at it as you are, Mr Leith. I've always admired the way you do things.' Frank warmed to his subject. 'I think you must be the best farmer around here—maybe the best farmer in the whole Bay of Plenty.'

Arthur looked at him sideways. 'Don't lay it on too thick, Frank,' he said, frowning. Frank subsided, wondering what he had said wrong.

'I like coming here,' Frank tried again. 'It's good of you to have me around so much.'

'I can tell you like coming, all right,' Arthur said. 'You seem to be here every five minutes.'

Arthur really didn't seem in a very good mood with him. How was he going to react when Frank asked him for Lizzie? Maybe he should leave it for another day. But then he would have to tell Lizzie he hadn't asked. He weighed up the alternatives, trying to decide which was the more unpleasant. Lizzie won.

'It's good that your farm's so close to our place, isn't it?' That was another thing Lizzie had said he was to mention: that she wouldn't have to move far away if her father let her marry Frank.

'What's so good about it?' Arthur demanded.

'Well, it's really handy for visits. I mean, if I lived miles away it wouldn't be very easy for someone at my place to come and see you.'

'You think that would be a bad thing, do you?'

'Well, it would mean... it's better than if... well, you know, if someone wanted to move away from home but they didn't want to move too far, my place isn't very far.'

'Frank, that's one of the most stupid things I've ever heard you come out with—and that's saying something. What the hell are you going on about?'

'I just meant we wouldn't be able to visit you much if I didn't live so close.'

' "We"?' Arthur repeated suspiciously. 'Who's "we"?'

'It's... I meant "I".'

'You're not going to start bringing your brother as well to eat me out of house and home? I seem to be feeding you half the time lately.'

'No, no, Ben doesn't like visiting, even if I wanted him to. I'd miss being able to come and see you if it wasn't so handy.'

'But Frank,' Arthur said, in the tone of one explaining things to a very stupid child, 'if you didn't live close you wouldn't know me, would you? You would never have started hanging around my place. So you wouldn't miss it, would you?'

'No, that's true. It's lucky really, isn't it? I learn a lot from talking to you. It's really good.'

Arthur stopped walking for a moment. 'Frank,' he said, shaking his head, 'you might think I'm old, but I'm not stupid.'

'I don't think you're stupid. Ah, I don't think you're old, either,' he added hastily.

'I know I'm not the attraction, Frank. You're after something, all right, but it's not my advice.' He started walking again.

Frank knew that was an opening. 'I… I did want to ask you something,' he plunged in, then his courage failed him.

'What do you want to ask?'

'I wondered if… how much hay do you feed out at this time of year?'

'What sort of a question is that? It depends on the weather, if the grass is growing or not, not to mention how many cows I've got.'

'Oh. Yes, I see. Thanks.'

'Do you think my cows don't look as though I feed them enough?' Arthur demanded.

'No, I mean yes, of course they do. I just wondered.'

Arthur grunted. 'If you think I don't know what I'm doing, I'd appreciate it if you said so outright instead of dropping hints. Then I could *argue* about it,' he said, fixing Frank with a steady gaze.

Frank considered again whether Lizzie's wrath would be harder to face than her father's. Lizzie might cry. Yes, she would cry. That would be worse. Maybe.

'I think you know what you're doing. I'm sure you know,' he amended miserably. This was not going well. 'I wanted to ask you something else,' he said, wishing his voice would not quaver so alarmingly.

'Some more advice, you mean.'

'Yes. No. Yes,' he said, giving in to his fear again. 'About, um, fencing. Yes, that was it, fencing.' Frank knew fencing was the wrong subject to pick as soon as he had said it.

'I've already told you all I know about fencing. If you choose not to take any notice of what I say, that's your look-out.'

'No, I didn't mean fencing. I meant—'

'Don't expect me to waste any more of my time telling you things if you don't take any notice. You'd learn more by getting on and doing a bit of work around your farm instead of hanging around here all the time.'

'I do—I've been getting a lot done lately. I just like coming here, too.'

'I'll have to start charging you board if you keep coming for meals.'

'Mrs Leith said I could.' That was the wrong thing to say, too, Frank knew.

'So you think my wife rules me, do you? Or are you trying to make trouble between me and her? Well, you're wrong, Frank. I run this house, even if those women think they do. Understand?'

'No, I didn't mean it like that. I just sort of thought it was all right with you, too. Is it all right?' he added, dreading the answer.

'Oh, you're asking me now, are you? A bit late, isn't it?' Arthur knocked the top off a thistle with a vicious swing of his stick. 'I suppose it is. Especially since my womenfolk seem to enjoy your company so much.'

Frank said nothing, and they walked on in silence for a few minutes.

'You've gone very quiet all of a sudden, Frank. You had plenty to say for yourself before. Haven't you got any more questions? No one else in your family who needs feeding up?'

'Well... there was one more thing, Mr Leith.' If he could only pluck up his courage to say it. He tried to ignore Arthur's stick. It was a particularly sturdy looking stick.

'Spit it out, then. Not another stupid question, I hope.'

Why did it have to be today? He had never seen Arthur as grumpy as he seemed to be this afternoon. Would Lizzie really be upset if he left it for another day? Yes, she would. She'd be terribly upset, and she wouldn't trust him any more.

Frank shut his eyes for a moment and fixed in his mind the picture of Lizzie beaming at him in delight. The way she had looked when he had asked her to marry him. Before the momentary burst of courage that gave him could fail, he blurted out, 'I want to marry Lizzie.'

'What?' Arthur sounded thunderstruck. Frank took a step backwards out of his range. 'You want to marry my daughter?'

It was too late to deny it. 'Yes,' Frank said.

'What can you offer her?'

Frank felt on surer ground now. 'Well, I've got a half-share in the farm. Pa left it to Ben and me equally. Our farm's four hundred acres.'

'What did it earn last year?'

'Eh?'

'Your farm—what were your income and outgoings last year?'

'Oh.' Frank got a sinking feeling. 'I couldn't say, just like that. But... but there's always plenty to eat. I could keep her all right.'

'Keep her? I want more for my daughter than living on bread and butter. Could you provide for her properly?'

'I... I think so.' What was 'properly'? he wondered.

'What if I say Lizzie's better off staying home? Why should I let you take her?'

'I'm very fond of her.' Frank wished that didn't sound so feeble.

'Fond? Fond!' Arthur scoffed. ' "Fond" won't give you a full belly, will it?'

'No.' Frank looked at his feet. 'Lizzie wants to,' he tried.

'You asked her first, did you?' Arthur pounced. 'Before you asked me?'

'Yes,' Frank confessed. 'But I'm asking you now.' Arthur didn't answer. 'I guess you're going to say no,' Frank said resignedly, wondering how he was going to tell Lizzie. At least he had tried. At least Arthur hadn't hit him.

'Even if you could provide for her, she's too young,' Arthur said, startling Frank with his sudden shift of argument. 'How old are you, anyway?'

'I'm twenty-two.'

'That's barely old enough to know your own mind. You're not trifling with my daughter, are you? What have you been up to with her?'

'Trifling? No! I think a lot of Lizzie.' He steeled himself for one last attempt, and made himself look Arthur in the face as he spoke. 'Mr Leith, I want to marry your daughter. I want to do the best I can for her. It mightn't be much, but I want to do it. Will you let me?'

'Lizzie's only seventeen. That's too young to get married. She thinks she's a grown woman, but she's not.'

This seemed to Frank a much weaker argument. He thought Arthur sounded less fierce now. 'She won't be seventeen for ever,' he said carefully.

'No, she won't,' Arthur agreed. Frank almost thought there was the hint of a smile playing around the edges of Arthur's mouth. 'You can have her when she's eighteen.'

'I can?' Frank stared at Arthur until he realised his mouth was hanging open. 'I... thank you, Mr Leith, thank you!' he said, almost breathless with relief. He grinned broadly as he shook Arthur by the hand.

'You'd better go and tell her you didn't make a complete hash of it,' Arthur said. 'Go on, she'll want a full report.'

Frank nodded, and he turned to run up to the house.

'Oh, Frank,' Arthur said, stopping Frank in his tracks. Had Arthur changed his mind again so quickly?

'Yes, Mr Leith?'

Arthur sighed and shook his head. 'I thought you were never going to ask.'

Amy carried the last dish of vegetables to the table and sat down quickly, anxious to get her guilty bulge under the shelter of the overhanging tablecloth. The exertion had brought on a coughing fit, which she smothered as well as she could. She wished her seat was not so close to Susannah's.

'Well, I can't get over Arthur letting Lizzie get married,' Jack said as he helped himself to the food. 'She's only a child.'

'I do wish you'd stop going on about that girl, Jack,' said Susannah. 'You've hardly talked of anything else the last three weeks. Can't we eat our dinner in peace?'

'I just can't get over it, that's all. She's only sixteen—'

'Seventeen, Pa. Lizzie's seventeen,' Amy put in. She regretted having spoken as soon as she saw the eyes of her family on her. She concentrated on her food until she sensed they had looked away.

'Is she? I thought she was sixteen. Anyway, that's still too young.'

'She's not getting married till next year,' Susannah said. 'Do we have to hear about it every day between now and April? What does it matter, anyway?'

'She's too young to know her own mind.'

Susannah pursed her lips. 'That girl has always struck me as knowing her mind quite well. Anyway, what difference does it make to her? She's going to move a couple of miles down this horrible valley to another draughty house. It's not as if she knows any better life.' She glared at her husband.

'I'd forgotten she was that much older than you, Amy,' Jack said. Seeing his eyes on her made Amy nervous, and she coughed again. Although she tried to muffle it with her hand, her father looked anxious. 'You've got a nasty cough there, girl,' he said, frowning.

'It's just a tickle in my throat.'

'It doesn't sound like just a tickle. It sounds like a real hacking cough. Susannah, can't you look after her better?'

'What am I supposed to do?' Susannah demanded. 'I'm not a nurse. Haven't I got enough to do, running this house and looking after the children? She's got a cough, it's nothing to make a fuss about.'

'I hate hearing that noise, like you're struggling for breath.'

'Amy, try and make less noise,' Susannah said with heavy sarcasm. 'You're annoying your father.'

'I'm sorry.' She smothered the next cough.

'Can I have some more butter?' John asked. Amy fetched it from the bench, then hurried back to her chair and the cover of the tablecloth. Susannah was looking at her with a puzzled expression.

'I suppose she'll want you to be a bridesmaid, Amy,' Jack said. Amy looked at him in alarm.

'I don't think so, Pa.'

'Why not? You've always been like sisters.'

'I… I don't know. Maybe she will.'

Jack smiled affectionately at her. 'At least I'm not going to lose you for a long time, am I? I know you're too young to be interested in getting married.' Amy said nothing as she struggled against both tears and another cough.

'Stop talking like that, Jack,' Susannah complained. 'Really, you do talk a lot of nonsense to Amy. No wonder she's so difficult for me to manage.'

'I'm just saying I'm glad she won't be rushing off getting married for years yet,' said Jack.

Amy felt a sob rising up in her throat. It came out as a cough. 'I... I'm not very hungry tonight,' she said. 'I don't think I want any more of my dinner.'

'Can I have yours?' Harry said promptly.

Amy pushed her plate over to her brother, then stood up. 'I'll just go and do some sewing for a while, I'll come out and do the dishes later.' *When you've all gone into the parlour.*

'You should eat your dinner, girl,' Jack said. 'You need your food, especially when you're not well.'

'But I'm not hungry, Pa.' She longed to escape from the room, but she couldn't walk away while her father was speaking to her.

'Don't force her to eat if she doesn't want to,' Susannah said. 'It wouldn't hurt you to cut down on your food, Amy. You've been putting on weight lately.' Amy felt a stab of alarm, and her head swivelled towards Susannah.

'Don't say that, Susannah,' Jack protested. 'Amy could do with putting on a bit of flesh, she's always been a bit too thin.'

'She's not thin now. She's getting quite plump. That dress looks tight on you, Amy. Do you need a new one?' Susannah reached out to twitch at Amy's skirt.

'No!' Amy slapped at Susannah's hand, fighting a rising tide of panic. 'This dress is all right, you leave me alone.' *I should have told Pa before.*

'What's wrong with you?' Susannah sounded affronted. 'Jack, see what happens when I try to look after her?'

'Amy, watch your tongue,' Jack said. 'There's no need to talk to your ma like that.'

'She shouldn't say I'm fat. I can't help it.'

'Look at you—your dress is cutting in under your arms. You'll have to get a new one. Why ever have you put on so much weight?' Susannah again reached out towards Amy's dress.

'Leave me *alone*,' Amy screamed. Her distress brought on another fit of coughing. She doubled over from the force of it.

'Susannah, she's really sick,' Jack said, rising from his chair and moving towards Amy. Susannah also stood up and advanced on her. Amy looked from one to the other of them in fear.

'I'm not sick,' she said, taking a step backwards. 'I'm a bit tired. I'll have a lie-down. Leave me alone.'

'Stop carrying on so stupidly,' Susannah said. 'Just because I said you've put on weight, there's no need to make such a fuss. Let me look at your dress—it's so tight, that's probably making your cough worse.' Two more strides brought her within inches of Amy. She took hold of Amy's arm with a firm grip, while her other hand reached out towards Amy's bodice.

Susannah looked down at Amy from her height advantage of eight inches, and her hand wavered. Her glance shifted lower. She flashed a look of disbelief at Amy's face before her eyes shot back to the girl's abdomen. Amy tried to twist out of Susannah's grip, but her arm was being held too tightly. Susannah's free hand snaked out and grasped the firm bulge of Amy's belly. Her eyes grew wide.

'Oh, God,' she said, her voice shrill with alarm. 'Oh, God!'

26

Without another word, Susannah dragged Amy by one arm out of the kitchen and down the passage.

'Let go, you're hurting me,' Amy said. But Susannah kept hold of her arm until they were in Amy's bedroom, Jack following at their heels.

'What's wrong with her?' he asked. 'Susannah, what's wrong with Amy?'

'Get out,' Susannah said, not turning her head away from Amy.

'But—'

'Get *out* of here,' Susannah roared. Jack went as if he had been kicked. Susannah followed him to the door and closed it firmly behind him, then turned to Amy. 'Take your dress off,' she ordered.

'No.' Amy's voice trembled as she spoke.

'Do you want me to take it off for you? I will if you don't do as I say.' She made to reach for the buttons of Amy's bodice; Amy turned away to undo them herself. She pulled her dress off over her head and stood shivering in her chemise and petticoat while Susannah looked her up and down in silence.

At last Susannah spoke, in tones of utter disgust. 'You silly little bitch. You've really done it now, haven't you?'

Amy looked at the floor, biting her lip to try and keep back tears, but they spilled from her eyes despite her efforts.

'Whose is it?' Susannah asked.

'What do you mean?'

'Who's fathered it? Do you know? Or could it be just about anyone's?'

Amy looked at Susannah in astonishment. 'Of course I know whose it is! It couldn't be anyone else's. It was Jimmy.'

She took a step backwards as Susannah flew at her, took hold of her shoulders and shook her. 'Don't you *dare* say that! Don't you dare tell lies about him! You sly little devil, don't think you can blame it on my brother. I won't let you.'

'It's true, it's true,' Amy jerked the words out between shakes.

'It's *not!*' Susannah gave her another vicious shake. Her fingers dug into Amy's shoulders so harshly that Amy cried out in pain.

'Stop it, you're hurting me.'

'Admit you're lying. Tell me who it really was.'

'It was Jimmy. It was *Jimmy*,' Amy sobbed. She screamed as Susannah's nails bit at the thin flesh of her shoulders.

The door was flung open to admit Jack, startling Susannah into releasing her grip. Amy backed away from her and snatched up her dress. She fumbled as she turned it right way out again, trying to shield her modesty with her arms at the same time. Jack took in his daughter's half-dressed state and looked away quickly. 'What's going on? What's all the yelling about? For God's sake, Susannah, tell me what's wrong with Amy. Should I send for the doctor, or what?'

'The doctor won't be able to do anything for her. Use your eyes, man, it's quite obvious. *Look* at her.' Susannah strode over to Amy and took hold of the girl's arms, wrenching them down to her sides so that Amy's belly was exposed. 'She must be nearly six months gone.'

'What are you saying?' There was a dawning fear in Jack's eyes.

'She's with child.'

Jack's mouth dropped open. He stared dumbly at Amy. 'She can't be,' he said at last. 'It's not possible.'

'What do you call *that*, then?' Susannah demanded, jabbing at Amy's bulge with one finger. As soon as Susannah released her, Amy scrambled into her dress and clasped her hands over her chest, rubbing at her sore shoulders.

'Amy, is it true?' Jack asked, his voice shaking.

Amy saw the distress in her father's face as he took in her state, and felt her own misery as a stabbing pain in her chest. 'I was going to tell you, Pa. I... I couldn't find the right way to. I was scared.'

'You should have thought of *that* before you got into this state,' Susannah cut in. 'Haven't I told you, Jack? Haven't I always said this girl needed correcting? God knows I never thought she'd prove me right like this, but I always knew she was willful. You've spoiled her all her life, and this is how she's repaid you.'

Jack did not seem to hear Susannah's tirade. He continued to stare at Amy, his face full of confusion. Then he shook his head, as though to clear his thoughts. 'Who did it to you?'

'She doesn't know,' Susannah put in quickly. She looked menacingly at Amy, daring the girl to argue, but Amy refused to meet her eyes. Instead she made herself look at her father.

'I do know, Pa, honestly I do. It was Jimmy.'

'She's lying!' Susannah cried.

'I'm not, Pa, I'm not. It couldn't have been anyone else.' She gazed at her father, pleading with her eyes for him to believe her.

'Jimmy?' he echoed. 'You mean I invited him into my house and he's done this to you?'

'You mustn't believe her! She's lying—she's doing it to shelter someone else.'

'Are you telling me the truth, Amy?'

'Yes, Pa. I promise it's true. No one else has ever touched me.'

'And I say she's lying!' Susannah said. 'Are you going to believe her over me?'

Jack looked from his daughter to his wife. 'Yes,' he said. 'I believe Amy.'

'Why? What have I done to deserve being called a liar?' Susannah demanded.

'She's my daughter, and she's never lied to me. I'm not saying you're lying, Susannah. I'm saying Amy's the only one here who knows, and I believe she's telling the truth.'

'She's not! She's trying to blame it on James to cause trouble. She's always hated me, now she's trying to get back at me.'

'Don't talk rubbish. Are you saying the girl's got herself into this state to annoy you? For God's sake, woman, I invited your brother down here to make you happy. Because you wanted it. All I seem to have done the last three years is try and make you happy.'

'So it's my fault, is it? You see—that's why she's saying it was James—so you'll blame me. She's a little slut.'

'Shut up!' Jack yelled so loudly that Susannah took a step back in fright. He walked to Amy and reached out towards her, then let his hand drop as if he were reluctant to touch her. 'Amy, I want you to answer me honestly. Did he force you?'

'So you're saying he's a rapist now?' Susannah snapped, but Jack ignored her. All his attention was on Amy.

Amy looked up at her father. He was wincing as if the sight of her hurt him, but she sensed he desperately wanted her to say yes. She knew that if she said she had been forced, she would in a moment be enfolded in her father's arms to be soothed and comforted.

'No, Pa. He didn't force me.' She closed her eyes to shut out the sight of her father's pain.

'Force her?' Susannah broke in. 'Of course he didn't force her. Even she doesn't have the audacity to pretend he did. She led him on, the little bitch.' Her eyes glittered as the idea took hold. 'Yes, that's how it happened. She threw herself at him, and he didn't know what he was doing. James was never even interested in girls till he came here. Then she was so shameless that she took him in.'

'Took him in? How could she take him in? She's a child and he's a grown man. She's a *child*,' Jack repeated. 'I asked your bloody brother down here. "Make yourself at home", I said. He repays me by shaming my daughter.'

'She shamed herself! You taught her to be bold—look at the way she's always talked to me. I could never do anything with her.'

'I wanted you to be a mother to her. I thought you'd tell her about that sort of thing. I thought you'd look after her. You begged me to let that bastard come here—why didn't you watch her with him?'

'That's what you married me for, isn't it? To be a nursemaid to that spoiled little bitch. Not to mention an unpaid servant to you and those other brutes. You should have hired a servant—no, that wouldn't have done you, would it? You wanted more than that, and you could never have *forced* yourself on a servant.'

'When have I ever forced you?'

'*Every* time,' Susannah spat at him.

Jack stared at his wife, his eyes narrowed. Amy knew they were saying things to one another that should never have been said, even in the privacy of their bedroom. Things that could never be unsaid.

'It's been a bloody long while since the last time—I'm surprised you even remember it.'

'Oh, you made sure it wasn't easily forgotten,' Susannah shot back.

'Stop your gutter talk in front of the girl.'

'Humph! She's the one who's chosen to wallow in the muck. It's a bit late to try and keep her pure and innocent, isn't it?'

'That's because of your bloody brother!' Jack roared.

'It's because she's a *slut!* Susannah shouted back. 'She's a cunning little whore!' She screamed as Jack slapped her across the face. 'How dare you? How dare you hit me?'

'Don't you ever call my daughter a whore!'

'My father would kill you if he knew you'd hit me!'

'He'd tell me I was a fool not to have done it years ago.' Jack's shoulders slumped. 'And I am a fool. I'm an old fool who can't look after his own daughter. I can't even make that fellow do the right thing by her, now he's taken himself off to Australia.'

'I wish I'd never come here. I wish I was dead,' Susannah sobbed.

'You're here, and you're alive and well. And you're no more miserable than anyone else in this place.' He reached out an arm towards Susannah. She screamed again.

'Don't you touch me! Don't you hit me again,' she said, flailing her arms wildly. 'I hate you!'

'I'm not feeling very fond of myself, if it's any comfort to you. I shouldn't have hit you, and I won't do it again. You drove me too far.

Come on.' He took hold of Susannah's arm.

'What are you doing? Let go of me.'

'Taking you out of here. There's no need for Amy to hear all this. Go to bed, Amy.' He led Susannah from the room. As he closed Amy's door he looked across at her. Amy searched for a spark of understanding in his gaze, but all she saw was hurt and bewilderment coupled with a deep weariness.

She heard muffled shouting through the wall till far into the night. Even when she resorted to putting her head under the blankets the noise still penetrated. When one or other of the little boys woke and cried the shouts would stop for a time. Finally both children wailed in chorus, and the adult voices subsided into an uneasy silence.

Amy thought she would never get to sleep, but when she woke to see the pre-dawn lightening of the sky she realised she had nodded off sometime in the early hours of the morning. It was time for her to get up and make breakfast. She knew the men would be looking for their food soon; the day started later for them at this time of year when there were only the house cows to milk, but they would still want to be fed and out of the house by eight.

She lay in bed trying to screw up the courage to get up and face them all. Her father would look at her as though she were a stranger. Susannah would call her those terrible names again. Perhaps her father and Susannah would have another dreadful fight. She wondered what John and Harry would say when they found out about her. Maybe they'd think she was those things Susannah had called her: *slut* and *whore*.

Amy knew she had to face them all soon; perhaps she should get it over with now. She pushed back the blankets and started to sit up, then scrambled right under the covers and hid in the warm darkness. *I can't do it yet. I'm scared.*

She heard a door opening across the passage; it must be John going out to the kitchen. A few minutes later another door opened, and she recognised her father's heavy tread in the passage. He went into the kitchen, but soon came out again. Amy held her breath as she heard him approach her door, but he walked past it towards his own bedroom. Amy heard him call from the passage.

'Susannah. Get out here and make breakfast.' There was a muffled response with a questioning note in it. 'She hasn't got up yet.' Another muffled sentence. 'No, I'm not going to get her up. You can do it for once.'

Susannah's response obviously satisfied Jack, because Amy heard him go back into the kitchen. When Susannah had not emerged a few minutes later, she heard Jack open the kitchen door and shout down the passage. 'Susannah! Hurry up!'

'All right, all right,' came Susannah's voice. 'I can't get dressed in two minutes.' She grumbled her way into the kitchen and out of Amy's hearing.

When it became too stuffy under the covers, Amy emerged. *I've got to get up soon. Maybe I should now.* But that would mean walking into the kitchen when the others were already sitting at the table. They would all turn to look at her. No, that would be too hard. *Pa doesn't want to see me, I know he doesn't.*

Amy jumped when her door opened half an hour later to admit Susannah. 'Here's something for you to wear,' Susannah said curtly. She flung two dresses onto the bed. Amy recognised them as the ones she had made for Susannah when she had been carrying Thomas. 'They'll be far too long for you, but you can cut off as much as you need to.'

'I'll... I'll take a deep hem,' Amy said, trying to match Susannah's casual tone. 'I don't want to spoil them for you.'

Susannah shrugged. 'It doesn't worry me. I won't need them again. Do whatever you like with them.' She crossed to the window and drew the drapes, letting in daylight. 'Are you going to get up this morning, or just lie in bed all day?'

'I'll get up now.' Amy got out of bed and picked up the blue dress, then took up her sewing box and searched for the scissors to unpick the existing hem.

'Your nightdress still fits, I see,' said Susannah. 'It's not too tight over the bosom?' She came closer to examine the gathered yoke.

'No,' Amy said, turning away from Susannah's inquisitive fingers. 'Leave me alone, please. I don't want to be fiddled with.'

'There's no use taking that attitude with me. You're going to learn, my girl, that there's not much dignity involved in having a child. Let me look.' Amy submitted, and Susannah twitched at the yoke. 'No, that's quite loose, really. That should do you until your time.'

Amy kept her eyes on her sewing, willing Susannah to go away, but her stepmother seemed in no hurry to leave. Instead she sat down on the bed.

'When's the child due?' she asked.

'I... I don't know.'

'You stupid girl. Well, when did it happen?'

'When did what happen?'

'It's no use trying to pretend you don't understand what I'm saying, sitting there with a great belly like that. When did you shame yourself?'

Shame myself. A large tear dropped onto the blue dress, and Amy rubbed it into the fabric with her hand. 'It happened lots of times,' she said quietly.

'You are a little whore, aren't you? And you try to drag everyone around you down to the same level. I'm not going to talk about that filth any more than I have to. When did you last have your bleeding, then?'

'It was at the end of January.'

Susannah counted on her fingers. 'November then, I think. Early in the month. I was right, you're nearly six months gone—five and a half, anyway.' To Amy's relief, Susannah stood up and made to leave the room. 'So we've got three months to decide what to do about you,' she said as she walked out.

When she had finished hemming it, Amy put on the sack-like blue dress over half a dozen petticoats. At least she felt warm, for the first time in weeks. She caught a glimpse of her reflection in the mirror and turned away from the ugly sight, then went out to the kitchen. If she kept busy enough, perhaps she would not have time to think. 'Decide what to do about you.' *What does that mean?*

Susannah raised her eyebrows at the sight of Amy in the shapeless dress. 'Well, you needed that, didn't you? You wouldn't have been able to squeeze into your old dresses much longer. How long did you think you could get away with not telling me?'

'I was going to tell you soon.' Amy picked up a duster and started on the dresser so that she would not have to look at Susannah.

'Oh, yes,' Susannah said. 'You'd come out one morning with a brat in your arms and tell me then.'

Jack came in by himself at lunch-time. He sat down heavily, glanced at Amy in her baggy dress, then looked at the wall. 'Now, listen to me, both of you. There were things said last night that shouldn't have been. I'm going to forget they were ever said, and I want you to do the same. Susannah, I expect you to do what's needful for Amy. You know about such things, and the girl's your responsibility. Understand?'

'Of course I do,' Susannah said. 'I'm already looking after her.'

'Good. It's about time you started—it would have been better if you'd started six months ago. You've dressed her properly, I see.'

Amy walked slowly up to her father, but her courage failed when she was still a table length away from him. 'Pa, I wanted to tell you before, but it was never the right time. I wanted to try and explain it.'

'Never mind all that now. It's no use talking about it, what's done is done.'

'I'm sorry, Pa.'

'It's too late to be sorry,' Susannah said.

Amy closed her eyes against the tears. 'I know it is. But I'm still sorry. Pa, I never wanted to cause all this trouble. I didn't think it would be like this. Please, Pa, can—'

'That's enough,' Jack interrupted. 'There's no use dragging it all out. You just do as your ma says, she knows what you'll need. Where's my lunch?'

After being dismissed so abruptly, Amy did not dare try to ask her question out loud again. She looked at her father, repeating it silently. *Please, Pa, can you forgive me?* But he did not meet her eyes.

'Where's your brother?' Jack asked when John came in by himself a few minutes later. John looked at Amy, then looked away quickly. She saw embarrassment in his face. *So he knows, too.*

'I don't know, Pa,' John said, looking worried. 'He... he got a bit wild, and he went off somewhere. He wouldn't tell me where he was going, but I saw him heading off down the road.'

'Silly young fool,' Jack muttered. 'Well, I'm not waiting my lunch for him. He can go hungry. What have you got such a long face on you for, John?'

'Well, Harry was in a really bad mood, Pa. And he took his gun.'

Amy could see that gave her father a jolt, but he soon looked resigned. 'He's not likely to do anyone much harm. I'd be more worried if he was here in the house with it.' He glanced at Susannah. She looked affronted, then alarmed. 'He'll come back when he's cooled off,' said Jack.

They ate their meal in a silence interrupted only by Amy's occasional muffled coughs. 'You want to do some of that fencing over the hill?' John asked when they had finished.

'You start on it,' Jack said. 'I'll join you later. I'm going to Arthur's for a bit.' John nodded and went out.

'Jack, do you need to tell them?' Susannah asked. 'You don't want the whole town to know.'

'I'm not telling the whole town, I'm telling my brother,' Jack said. 'I'm no keener than you are for anyone else to find out what's going on.'

'It reflects on us all, you know,' Susannah said to Amy as soon as Jack had left the house. 'You've brought shame on the whole family, not just yourself.'

'I know,' Amy said miserably.

'You've driven your brother away already. And look at the state your father's in,' Susannah went on relentlessly. 'At his age, too, to get a shock like this. Especially when he's always doted on you so ridiculously. He can't bear to look at you now.'

'I *know*,' Amy sobbed.

Lizzie thought nothing of it when she saw her uncle talking with her father out in the paddocks; he often popped over for a chat. But when her father strode back to the house looking grim, she knew something was up.

'Go outside,' he ordered Lizzie. 'I want to talk to your ma.'

Lizzie pressed her ear to the door, but her parents were speaking so quietly that she caught nothing except an exclamation of shock from her mother. When her father finally opened the door again, her mother was dabbing at her eyes with her apron and her father looked grimmer than ever. Lizzie looked from one to the other, and her mouth set in a firm line. So they had found out at last. She bent to put her boots on.

'Where do you think you're going?' Arthur said.

'Next door to see Amy. I'm bringing her back here to stay the night.'

'No you're not.'

'Why not?' Lizzie demanded.

'Don't take that tone with me, girl.' He stared closely at her, his eyes narrowed in anger. 'You already knew about this, didn't you? Why didn't you tell anyone?'

'It wasn't my secret to tell. I'm going to get Amy.' She looked mutinously at her father.

'I say you're not leaving this house!' Arthur shouted. 'Are you defying me, girl?' The red tint of rage slowly mounted in his face. 'You'd better not be.'

Lizzie stared back at him, coolly weighing her options. If she did defy him he would make her mother give her a beating, something that hadn't happened to Lizzie for many years. He would probably stand in the bedroom doorway and make sure her mother made a proper job of it, too. If she got him angry enough he might even do it himself.

What mattered far more was that she would not stand a chance of getting off the farm against her father's will. Even if she took to her heels, trousers could beat skirts without even trying.

'All right,' she said, glowering at her father. 'I'll do as you say.' She slumped down in a chair and watched him regain his calm.

'Good,' he said. 'I'm only thinking of you, girl.'

'What do you mean?'

Arthur made a noise of exasperation. 'Isn't it obvious? You're not going to that house, and you're not going to talk to that girl.'

'Arthur,' Edie protested feebly.

'Don't argue. Either of you. She's shamed herself, and I'm not having my daughter mixing with her. That's that, I won't listen to any arguments. And *you*,' he stabbed a finger at Lizzie, 'you don't leave this farm again till I say you can. Understand?'

'Yes,' Lizzie muttered, looking at the floor.

'Just you remember it. You watch yourself with that Frank Kelly, too.'

'What's that supposed to mean?' Lizzie asked indignantly.

'I don't want the same thing happening to you.'

Lizzie glared at him. 'Do you think Frank is the sort of man who'd do *that* and then run away?'

'Frank'd have a bit more trouble running away, wouldn't he? Anyway, he knows I'd kill him if he tried. You just watch yourself.'

'I don't need to be told that.'

'I'm telling you anyway,' Arthur shouted. For a moment Lizzie thought he was going to hit her. She braced herself for the blow. But instead he turned away. 'Get to your room. You can stay there till you've remembered your manners.'

Lizzie went without a word. She stared out her window for a long time in the direction of Amy's house, pounding her hands on the sill in frustration at her own powerlessness.

27

July – August 1884

John again came into the house alone and some time after his father that evening, but this time he looked calmer.

'I saw Harry,' he said.

'Where is he?' Jack asked, looking over John's shoulder as if he expected to see Harry there.

'He's gone next door. He said he wanted to be away from...' John glanced at Susannah, 'people for a while. He went up in the bush—he said he felt like killing something, so he shot a few pheasants.'

'When's he coming back?' Jack demanded.

'I don't know, he didn't say.'

'He'd better be back here tomorrow morning or I'll go and get him,' Jack growled. 'He needn't think he's sloping off like that.'

Jack was not forced to go and fetch his wayward son. Next morning when Amy was carrying the rugs out to the clothesline to beat them, she saw Harry walking across the paddock to join his father and brother. She gave a sigh of relief.

Amy tried to find a way of scrubbing the kitchen floor that stopped her bulge getting in the way so much, but her arms banged against it every time she pulled the brush towards her. She was concentrating so hard on the task that she did not even look up when the back door opened, though she recognised her father's tread.

'Leave that,' Jack said brusquely.

'But... but today's my day for doing the floors, Pa. I'm only half finished.'

'It doesn't matter. I don't want to see you doing that heavy work. Where's your ma?'

'She's in the bedroom, getting the little ones dressed.'

Jack stomped out of the room and up the passage, and Amy carried her bucket of dirty water outside to empty it. She looked anxiously at the half-washed floor when she brought the bucket back in, but she could not disobey her father.

An indignant Susannah came into the kitchen a few minutes later at Jack's side.

'I don't see that it'll do her any harm,' she said. 'Just a bit of scrubbing.'

'I didn't notice you doing it when you were with child.'

'That's different. I was so ill most of the time. Amy's in perfect health—a bit of exercise is good for women in that state if they're well enough.'

'She can go for a walk if she needs exercise. I told you to look after her, and I don't want her doing that heavy work. Understand?'

'Yes,' Susannah muttered. But she made no move to finish the scrubbing when Jack had left the house.

That evening's meal was even more awkward than the previous one. Harry glared across the table at Susannah.

Susannah glared back. 'What's wrong with you?' Harry lowered his brows even further, but said nothing. 'Jack, he's not answering me when I speak to him,' Susannah complained.

'I can't make him talk to you,' said Jack. 'You're better off if he doesn't, anyway. I don't think you'd like to hear what he'd have to say.' Susannah looked affronted, but Amy noticed she avoided meeting Harry's eyes after that.

Now that she was no longer allowed to do the heavy work, Amy found herself with an unwelcome amount of time on her hands. Free time meant time to think.

Amy missed Lizzie badly. She pined for her cousin's ready sympathy now that she had no kind words or soft looks from anyone else. When the rest of the family returned from church the first Sunday after the revelation, an awkward-looking John spoke quietly to Amy as she stood at the bench serving up lunch.

'Lizzie asked me to say sorry she hasn't come to see you,' he said. Amy's head swung to him in surprise at even being spoken to by her brother. He avoided her eyes. 'She said she wanted to, but her pa won't let her.'

'Oh. Thank you, John.' Tears pricked at her eyes. *Uncle Arthur thinks I'm too bad for Lizzie to be allowed to talk to.* She felt lonelier than ever.

Amy adjusted her days to avoid seeing the others any more than she had to. Her father and brothers hardly spoke to her; when they did she could see that she embarrassed them. Susannah's company gave no pleasure to either of them.

So Amy rose early to prepare breakfast, and ate her own before the men got up. When she had served their food she carried Susannah's cup of tea in to her and took the little boys off to play in the parlour while Susannah finished waking up, drank her tea and dressed.

After she heard the men go out, Amy did the dishes and whatever work was light enough for her to manage. She did all of the cooking now, while a grumbling Susannah did the heavy cleaning; or at least the portion of the cleaning that could not be ignored.

Amy could not avoid eating lunch and dinner with the family, but as soon as she finished her evening meal she took herself off into her bedroom and worked at her sewing until she heard the family go into the parlour. With the kitchen to herself she washed the dishes, prepared the bread dough for the next morning, then went early to bed to toss and turn the night away.

That still left much of the day to be filled, and Amy took to wandering about on the farm. When she came back from the first of these long walks, Susannah accosted her. 'Don't you go near the road,' she admonished. 'Someone might see you. You don't want the whole town talking about us, do you?'

Amy did not want that, so she kept well away from the road. She also avoided the places where she and Jimmy had walked arm in arm, and most of all those where they had lain together. That left many parts of the farm where she could trudge across the paddocks or, even better, slip into the peace and loneliness of the bush. Walking up the steep hills got more difficult every day as her bulk increased, but she welcomed the weariness it brought. It meant she could sleep at night.

Jack lay in bed looking at his wife's back as she undressed and put on her nightdress. He had found her attractive once. Damn it, he still did. But there was a limit to how much humiliation a man could take. The sheet was twisted uncomfortably under him. He wished Susannah would make the bed more often than once a week, when she changed the sheets. It didn't seem worth arguing about, though. There had been more than enough arguing lately.

The sight of Susannah gave him no pleasure, only irritation. He turned instead to look at his two small sons, cherub-like in sleep. It was good to have little ones around again. Especially now they both slept through the night. Susannah had given him the young fellows, anyway, albeit grudgingly.

Susannah turned off the lamp and climbed into bed beside him, though each of them now slept on the extreme edges of the bed to avoid touching one another.

'Jack,' she said quietly a few minutes later. 'Are you awake? We need to talk about Amy.'

That jolted him into alertness. 'What's wrong with her? Is she ill?'

'No, no, I've been taking care of her, she's quite well. In her body, that is.'

'What's that supposed to mean?'

266

Susannah gave a deep sigh. 'She's very miserable.'

'She hasn't got much to be cheerful about, has she?'

'No, poor girl. What are we going to do about her?'

Jack grunted. 'Nothing much we can do. The time for doing things was months ago. That's when you should have been taking care of her.'

'You're never going to forgive me for that, are you?' Susannah said, a catch in her voice. 'I did my best, really I did. I don't know anything about looking after girls of her age, and girls in the country grow up so much faster. I never meant this to happen.'

She was obviously near tears. 'Don't go on about it,' Jack said. 'There's no use talking about whose fault it all was. It's done now, we've got to make the best of it.'

'That's what I want,' Susannah snatched at his words. 'I want the best for Amy. I don't think we should give the baby to anyone in Ruatane, I think it should go further away. Auckland might be best. We should start arranging it soon, we've only got a few months now.'

Jack let her run on while he tried to absorb her meaning. 'What are you talking about?' he asked finally. 'Who said we were going to give it away?'

He heard Susannah catch her breath. 'You don't mean we should keep it here?'

'Of course we're going to keep it. That's my grandchild you're talking about. Not to mention your niece or nephew,' he added bitterly.

'Haven't I got enough to cope with, looking after two babies under two years old? However would I manage another one?'

'How would you manage three children? The same way thousands of women do. Amy'd look after her own baby, anyway.'

'But Jack, think of Amy. Now she's soiled it's doubtful any man will ever want her, so she's not going to have much of a life, is she?' She went on, not giving Jack time to answer. 'It just seems too much for her to have the child of her shame before her eyes all the time. The poor girl, she'll never cope with it.'

'She'll cope. She'll have to.'

'Think of her life, Jack! Never to have a home of her own, and to have to bring up a child alone.'

'She's got a home. You're probably right, she won't find a husband now, but her home's here. If she never gets another one, well, I can't do anything about that. And you'll help her bring up the child.'

'But Jack—'

'That's enough.' He rolled noisily onto his side, feeling the crumpled sheet ruck up under him as he did, to let her know the conversation was

267

over. To his surprised relief, Susannah lapsed into silence.

Amy put a blanket over the bread dough and rose awkwardly to turn out the lamp. She jumped when the door opened from the passage and her father came in, carrying his account book as well as pen and ink.

'I was just going to bed, Pa. I'll be out of your way in a minute.'

'Amy,' Jack said, reaching out an arm to stop her, then letting it drop without actually touching her, 'I... I wondered if you could give me a hand with this. You're better with numbers than I am.'

Amy felt a small surge of pleasure at being asked. 'I'd like to do that, Pa.' In the past she had often helped her father with his accounts, which without her assistance involved many crossings-out and ink-blots, and a quantity of bad language.

Jack pulled out a chair for her and they sat side by side at the table. Amy wrote down amounts as he called them out, and they talked in low voices.

'What a lot of butter I made over the summer,' Amy said. 'The cows were producing well.'

'It's high time they started that cheese factory they've been on about for years.'

'We had a good crop of potatoes, didn't we?'

'Mmm. Not a bad price, either. I might put another paddock into spuds next year.'

Amy could tell that her father had put her state out of his mind for the moment. She deliberately lingered over the accounts, taking longer than necessary over writing down each figure and working out the totals. She knew it could not be for very long, but while it lasted she basked in the warmth of their companionship.

It lasted a shorter time than she had expected. Amy was adding up one of the columns of figures when the passage door opened. They both looked up to see Susannah in her dressing-gown, holding a candlestick.

'What are you doing out here at this time of night?' Susannah asked.

'Just doing the accounts,' Jack said. 'I thought you'd gone to bed.'

'I've been writing a letter to Constance. I never seem to get any time during the day. Amy, you should be in bed.'

'She's helping me. Amy's good with numbers, and I always seem to get in a muddle if I do them by myself.'

'Oh yes, she's very clever,' Susannah said. 'But you shouldn't keep her up so late, Jack. She's only fifteen, you know, and she needs her sleep. Especially at the moment. Come along, Amy,' she said, holding the door open.

'I'm all right, I'm not very tired tonight. Can't I stay up a bit longer and help you, Pa?' Amy pleaded.

'No, you do as your ma says, she knows best about these things. She's right, I shouldn't be keeping you from your bed. You're not quite over that cough yet, either. Off you go, I'll manage without you.'

Susannah stood in the doorway and watched as Amy went meekly off to bed. Amy wondered briefly why Susannah bothered writing to her sister when she knew they didn't get on; in fact she could never remember Susannah's having written to her before. But her mind was too full of yet another disappointment to spare much interest for whatever Susannah might be up to. She managed to get the bedroom door safely closed behind her before the tears came.

Frank watched Lizzie carry the dirty dishes to the bench. He caught her eye across the table when she turned back towards him. She gave a small nod, Frank rose to join her, and they started towards the door. Frank had his hand on the door knob when Arthur spoke, making him jump.

'Where do you think you're going?'

Lizzie answered while Frank was still recovering from the rush of guilt that had assailed him. 'We're just going for a little walk across the paddocks. Maybe down to the creek, no further. There's nothing wrong with that, is there?'

Arthur looked at them suspiciously. 'You keep out of the bush. I don't want you going out of sight of the house. Understand?'

'Yes, Pa,' Lizzie said.

'I'll be keeping an eye on you. If I look out of this house and I can't see you...' Arthur let the threat remain implicit. 'You hear me, Frank?'

'Y-yes, I do,' Frank assured him. 'We won't go far.'

'You'd better not.'

Frank glanced over his shoulder when they were a short distance from the house; sure enough, Arthur was standing on the verandah watching them. Frank felt too shy to take Lizzie's hand with such a disapproving audience.

'What's up with your pa?' he asked. 'He's been really funny lately.'

'Oh, Pa's got a lot on his mind.'

'He hasn't sort of... well, changed his mind, has he? About us, I mean.'

'Of course he hasn't. Don't talk rubbish.'

'Well, he doesn't seem as though he likes me very much any more. He was really friendly for a while, after he said I could have you. Now he looks like he wants to hit me or something.'

'He won't hit you. It's nothing you've done.' Lizzie looked thoughtful. 'Actually, I think he'd almost like us to get married sooner than next April, but he's said we're to wait and he won't back down on that.'

They walked for a few minutes, and Frank looked up at the house again. It was still in sight, but too far away for anyone watching to see how close he and Lizzie were. He reached out and took her hand. 'I wish we didn't have to wait till then.'

'So do I. Pa's been so bossy lately, I'm fed up with him.'

Frank snaked his arm around her waist and squeezed. It gave him less satisfaction than he had hoped; Lizzie had gone into adult clothes since her engagement, and she felt stiff to his touch. He missed the sight of her ankles and calves, too, now that she wore long dresses. For a moment he allowed his imagination to wander up from those calves and into the forbidden realms above her knees, but that gave him an uncomfortably tight feeling in his trousers. It also made him see Arthur's face in his mind instead of Lizzie's. He let his arm drop to his side.

'You've been sort of quiet lately,' Frank said, thinking how uncharacteristic this was.

'Have I? That's because Pa's so grumpy. I miss Amy, too.'

'She's been crook for ages now. Lizzie,' he said awkwardly, 'she is... Amy is going to get better, isn't she?'

'I hope so. Oh, I didn't mean it like that,' Lizzie said, seeing Frank's expression. 'She's going to get better. It's just going to take a long time.'

Frank sensed that Amy's illness was not something to be spoken of freely, at least in front of men. 'Is it anything catching?' he asked, hoping he wasn't prying too rudely.

'Pa thinks it is. That's why he won't let me see her any more.'

She looked sad, and Frank reached for her hand again. He was rewarded with a smile.

'I suppose sitting down right beside the creek counts as out of sight from the house?' Frank asked when they had reached the bank of the Waituhi.

Lizzie glanced back in the direction they had come. 'I think it does. We could sit here on the bank, though. We'll just look like two dots from up there.'

'Let's cross over first and sit on the other bank,' Frank said. If a vengeful Arthur was going to bear down on him from the house, Frank wanted a chance of seeing him first. He helped Lizzie across the stepping stones and they sat very close together on the far bank, with their arms around each other's waists.

'Have you told Ben about us yet?' Lizzie asked, bringing Frank back down to earth with a jolt.

'No, I haven't quite got around to it.' He waited for Lizzie to scold him, but she looked unconcerned.

'Oh, well, you'll have to sooner or later.'

'I know.' He studied her carefully. 'I thought you'd go crook at me because I haven't told him,' he admitted.

'Why should I? It's not my problem. You don't have to get your brother's permission to get married, and you've already got Pa's for me.'

'Ben's not going to like it, Lizzie.'

Lizzie shrugged. 'He'll get used to it. He'll have to, once I move in. He might even find he likes having a woman around the house.' Frank was sure it would not be that simple, but he said nothing. 'He won't have to eat out of a saucepan because you've got no clean dishes left once I'm there,' Lizzie said.

'I would have tidied up that day if I'd known you were coming,' Frank protested. 'It doesn't always look that bad, you know.'

'Doesn't it?' She grinned at him. 'Those dishes looked as though they were growing things.'

'They did not! We do them once a week at least, when we boil up the water for washing the clothes.'

'Or when you run out?' Lizzie teased mercilessly. To silence her he kissed her soundly.

They had got better at kissing; there were no more nose collisions now. Frank could concentrate on enjoying himself. He put both arms around Lizzie's waist and held her close, trying to ignore the unpleasant feel of whalebone. He wondered how high the stays came up her body. One hand wandered up from Lizzie's waist until he found the top edge of her corset. A few inches higher and he had a handful of something deliciously soft. He pressed his mouth harder on hers as a thrill of excitement rushed through him, but a moment later he felt Lizzie's hand tugging at his wrist and she twisted her face away from his.

'What do you think you're doing?' she demanded, her face flushed with anger. Frank had always thought Lizzie looked like her mother; right now she could have been a female version of her father at his most fierce.

'What's wrong? It's all right, isn't it? I mean, we're engaged.'

'Yes, that's all we are,' Lizzie flashed at him. 'Engaged, that's all. We're not married yet.'

'But… but I thought you'd let me touch you a little bit, Lizzie. That's all I want to do, I won't try anything else, honest I won't.'

'You won't try *that* again either. You can do what you like once we're married, but until then you can just control yourself.' She glared at Frank.

Frank fought down his irritation at Lizzie's abrupt change of mood. 'What's the point in being engaged if we can't do anything we couldn't do before?'

'Being engaged means we're promised to each other and we've told everyone. It doesn't mean you can take liberties with me.'

'You're always going on about "liberties",' Frank grumbled. 'Anyone would think I was a real ratbag. What's wrong with you, anyway?'

'Nothing's wrong with me. Just because I want to keep myself decent, you're trying to make out I'm strange.'

'I don't see what's so scandalous about letting your intended give you a cuddle.'

'Well, you *should*,' Lizzie flung back at him. 'That was more than a cuddle you were trying, Frank Kelly.'

Frank smothered a curse in time for it to come out as an unintelligible grunt. 'What with you deciding I'm some sort of rogue and your pa looking as though he'd like to kick me all the way down the road, I don't know why I bother coming here. I might as well go home.'

'Go on, then. Don't let me stop you.' She turned away from him.

'All right then, I will.' Frank rose to his feet.

'I suppose it's my fault,' Lizzie said, still facing in the other direction. Was that a catch in her voice? Frank wondered. 'I must have behaved badly if you thought I'd let you do that. Yes, it must be my fault,' she said pensively. 'I wish I knew what I'd done wrong.' Her shoulders heaved as though she were bravely smothering a sob. Frank felt a rush of affection and guilt.

'Aw, Lizzie, don't cry,' he begged, dropping to one knee and putting an arm round her shoulder. 'You haven't done anything wrong. It's my fault, you were right, I shouldn't have done that.'

Lizzie laid her head on his shoulder. 'You sounded so angry with me,' she murmured. 'I thought you didn't love me any more.' Her breath tickled his ear as she spoke.

'Of course I love you. I wouldn't have asked you to marry me if I didn't. I just wish we didn't have to wait so long.'

'Oh, Frank!' Lizzie's eyes were shining. 'You've never said you love me before.'

'Haven't I?' Frank said, surprised. 'Well, I do. I guess I just thought you already knew. Hey, you've never said it to me, either.'

'I couldn't till you did.'

'I've said it now.' Frank grinned at her.

'So you have.' She smiled back at him. 'I love you, Frank.'

There was only one way to seal such a moment. Frank wasted no time in taking Lizzie in his arms and kissing her.

The hill that dropped from Jack's house down to the flat paddocks by the creek was not steep, but it was thickly covered with stumps. Amy had to concentrate on placing her feet carefully as she walked, so that she would not trip over. It was even harder now that she could not see where each step was about to land without peering over the top of her bulge.

When she reached the bottom of the hill the going was easier, and she lengthened her stride. The day was grey and cold. A light mist still lingered over the trees on the far side of the valley. That part of the bush was out of bounds to her. Susannah had repeatedly stressed that she must stay away from the road. She was too shameful for anyone to see.

The forbidden trees looked beautiful to Amy, especially the patch of bush directly opposite where she stood. She longed to stroke the rough trunks; to look up at the sky through the leaves. There was plenty of bush on her side of the road, but none of it held the same fascination as that stand of trees.

But she knew she would never be able to bear to enter it, even when she was once again allowed to wander freely on the farm. That patch was where she had led Jimmy the night of the dance. The place where he had asked her to marry him. Where they had lain together for the first time. She could picture every tree; she could feel the hard ground under her and hear his voice murmuring words of love in her ear. His face so close to hers was clear in her mind, the way he had looked on their last day together when she had held his face in her hands and printed it in her memory. Her hand went involuntarily to the place between her breasts where his brooch had been fastened; but the brooch had lain in her drawer, nestled in the blue velvet ribbon, ever since the day she had learned he was not going to come back to her. She no longer felt any desire to wear it, now that she knew the words that went with the gift had been untrue.

Her eyes blurred with tears, and she hardly noticed that the ground had become rougher. She glanced down in front of her and was surprised to see water lapping over the toes of her boots; she had wandered right down to the creek. *I'd better get out.*

But instead of backing out, she took a step forward. The water, muddy green under the pale grey sky, held a fascination for her. The

273

creek was running at its higher winter level, and it swirled and eddied with the extra burden of water. It was quite opaque; even near the edge where the water was only a few inches deep the creek bed was invisible. Amy watched a small branch tumble along the surface and out of sight around a bend in the stream.

She took another step, and the water came over the tops of her feet. She felt it seep into her boots around the laces. A few more steps and it would reach the hem of her dress, muddy green water touching the dark green of the thick woollen fabric. The water would clutch at her, drawing her into its embrace. Would she sink right away? Or would she float until she reached the sea? No, the heavy dress would drag her down as soon as the water was deep enough.

What does drowning feel like? Maybe it hurts. But it wouldn't hurt for long. Pa might be sad for a while, but everyone would be nice to him. They'd say how sad it was his daughter drowned. No one would have to know about how bad I am. He wouldn't have to look at me any more. She had moved further into the creek without realising it. The hem of her dress was splashed with water. She leaned forward slowly, drawn towards the changing patterns of tiny whirlpools.

A loud rattle caught her attention. She stood up straight and looked across the creek. It was the noise of the buggy coming along the road; her father and Susannah had come home from town with the supplies and the mail.

Amy looked down at the water again, but now it looked frightening instead of inviting. *Pa would know I'd done it on purpose, and he'd feel bad. Even worse than he does now. I mustn't kill the baby—the baby's not bad, only me.* She backed carefully out on to dry ground, then turned and squelched in her wet boots alongside the creek, careful not to look at the water.

When she struck a fence she turned again and walked parallel to it, too clumsy in her bulkiness to want to climb it. She had been following the fence line for some time before she realised it was the boundary fence that separated her father's farm from Charlie Stewart's. *It's a good thing I didn't climb over.*

The ground started to rise, and walking took all her attention as she once more entered an area thickly dotted with stumps. She was so busy concentrating on where to put her feet that it was some time before she sensed someone was watching her. She stopped abruptly and looked around. With a sinking heart she saw Charlie standing just across the fence, barely a dozen feet away. He was staring fixedly at her.

Amy looked at him in horror, hoping desperately that he had not noticed her bulge. But his eyes were on her belly. He lifted his gaze to her face, and Amy tried to think of something, anything, to say that would break the spell of the moment. Instead she gave in to her fear, gathered up her heavy skirts and turned away from him.

She hurried up the hill as fast as her bulk would allow, and was puffing by the time Charlie was out of sight. *That was stupid of me. I kept away from the road, but I forgot about the boundary. But Charlie never talks to anyone, so he won't gossip about me.*

It was too early for her to go home and start making lunch; in any case, she wanted the tell-tale patches of water to dry out of her hem before she faced Susannah, and in this cold weather that would take some time. She climbed right to the top of the hill behind the house, then looked down the valley and out to sea. It was little more than a habit now; whatever Susannah had meant about what they were going to do with her, Amy knew it would not include making any of her old dreams of seeing the world outside the valley come true.

All those things I was going to do. I was going to be a teacher. I was going to live in Auckland. I even believed Jimmy when he said he'd take me to Australia. Plays to see, fancy clothes to wear. None of it's going to happen now. She turned her back on the sea and sat down on a convenient stump to wait for her dress to dry. A tiny rifleman fluttered about in the grass near her feet, hunting for the insects Amy had disturbed.

Half an hour later she saw a man coming up the track to her house. He was nearly at the farmhouse gate before she recognised the tall, slightly stooped figure of Charlie Stewart. Her heart gave a lurch. It would take something serious to make Charlie visit her father; she could not remember his ever coming to the house before. *He must be really annoyed about me. I'll be in trouble now.* For a moment her heart beat faster, then she shook her head over her own foolishness. *It doesn't matter. Things couldn't get any worse than they already are.*

28

August 1884

When the food stores had been put away, Jack waited while Susannah poured tea for them both and sat down opposite him.

'You haven't read the letter from your ma yet,' he said, gesturing to the unopened envelope that lay near her hand.

'It's not from Mother, it's from Constance. I don't like reading in the buggy, it's so bumpy.' She opened the envelope and read quickly. Jack saw a small smile of satisfaction on her face. She folded the closely-written pages and put them back in the envelope.

'Good news?' he asked.

'Yes, I think it might be. I'll have to wait and see.'

Jack had too little interest in the doings of Susannah's sister to bother pressing for a less evasive answer. He helped himself to a biscuit from one of Amy's cake tins and slurped at his tea.

They both looked up startled at a heavy rap on the door. 'I didn't hear anyone ride up,' Susannah said as she went to open the door. When Charlie was revealed in the doorway, Jack was more surprised than ever. 'Oh. Good morning, Mr Stewart,' Susannah said. 'Can I do something for you?'

'It's your husband I want to see, not you,' Charlie said stiffly. He still had a Scottish accent despite having spent all his adult life far from Scotland, and his voice had an oddly rusty sound, as if from lack of use.

'I'm here,' Jack said. He got to his feet, wondering what Charlie had come to complain about. Some nonsense about wandering stock or suchlike, no doubt. As if he didn't have enough worries over his womenfolk without Charlie annoying him.

When Jack reached the doorway Susannah moved a little to one side. Jack knew she was trying to leave the room as quickly as possible without being too obviously rude.

'It's about your girl,' Charlie said. Susannah stopped in her tracks and flashed a look of alarm at Jack.

'What about Amy?' Jack asked, a warning note in his voice.

'I saw her this morning, by my boundary fence. It wasn't hard to see the state she's in.'

'I told her not to let anyone see her,' Susannah said to Jack. 'It's not my fault.'

'She's not got a husband, has she?' Charlie asked, ignoring Susannah.

'I'll thank you to keep your nose out of my family troubles,' Jack said coldly.

'And she's not likely to get one, not in that state.'

'What's it to do with you?' Jack growled.

'I'll take her.'

There was absolute silence in the room while Jack wondered if he had imagined what Charlie had just said. 'What?' he said at last.

'I'll marry your girl, if you want. I'll give her a home and a decent name. I'll not take the bas—bairn,' he corrected himself, 'I'm not giving another man's child my name. But I'll take her.'

'You?' Jack said in amazement. 'You think I'd give Amy to you? I'd sooner—'

'Jack, dear, don't be hasty,' Susannah cut in. 'Mr Stewart has made a perfectly reasonable suggestion, the least you can do is be polite to him. Won't you come in, Mr Stewart, and have a cup of tea with us?'

'No, I won't,' said Charlie. 'I've said what I came to say. I'll come back tomorrow morning when you've had time to think about it and hear your answer.'

'You don't need to wait till then to hear what I think of it.'

'Jack,' Susannah said warningly, putting her hand on his arm. 'We'll see you tomorrow, then, Mr Stewart.' Charlie nodded to them, looked thoughtful for a moment, then as though he had just dredged some recollection of polite behaviour from deep in his memory he tipped his hat to Susannah. She closed the door on the sight of his retreating back.

'Did you ever hear such cheek?' Jack said in disgust. 'He thought I'd give my daughter to him. Him! What did you bother being so polite to him for?'

'Because I think you should consider things properly before you fly off the handle. No, be quiet and listen for a minute,' she said, raising a hand to silence his exclamation. 'I know he's not the sort of husband you hoped Amy would have, but that was when she was still likely to get one at all. No one will ever want her, we've already discussed that, and then out of the blue she gets a proper marriage proposal. I don't think you should turn it down without giving Amy a chance at some happiness.'

'Happiness? With Charlie?'

'Yes, with Charlie. Why not? He must be prepared to look after her, or he wouldn't offer for her. What's so terrible about the idea?'

'He must be nearly thirty years older than her, for a start. And that farm of his is only a hundred acres, that's barely enough to support himself. Anyway, he's a sour, bad-tempered so-and-so.'

'Right,' Susannah said briskly. 'One thing at a time, then. Of course he can support her, even if his farm's not nearly as big as yours. He must have plenty of food, it's a farm, after all. Amy wouldn't take much keeping.'

'What about nice things for her? I always hoped she'd marry someone with a good, big farm so she could have a decent life, not wear herself out like her ma did. A man of twenty-five or so, with his farm well established and a good house on it. Charlie'll never buy her nice dresses and things.'

'But she's not going to marry someone like that, is she?' Susannah said in a tone of utter reasonableness. 'A man like that doesn't need to take a wife who's been soiled, he can pick and choose. It's only someone like Charlie, whom no one's got much time for, who'd consider her. And I don't think he's as sour as you make him out to be. He's not a good mixer, that's all. With a sweet little wife like Amy, I think you'd be surprised at the change in him. He must be fond of her already, to offer for her. And you'd like Amy to live close to you, wouldn't you? If she'd married properly, she might have to go and live miles away. I miss my parents dreadfully, I'm sure Amy would miss you, too.'

She made it sound so convincing that Jack could feel his certainty slipping away. 'He's still thirty years older than her,' he tried.

'I'd say it's nearer twenty-five years.' Susannah smiled rather wistfully at him. 'Jack, that's only a little more than the gap between you and I. I know we've had our differences lately, but I've never, ever thought you were too old for me.'

Jack cleared his throat to cover the conflicting emotions Susannah's last remark aroused. 'I never thought of it that way,' he admitted. 'I suppose he's not as old as all that.' He frowned. 'I still don't like it. I'd rather keep her here.'

'And deny her the only chance she's ever going to have to be mistress of her own home? She's always resented me for taking over this house, and I suppose I can't blame her, really. She was only a child then, but she thought she was running it herself. What do you think will happen when you and I are gone? It'll be John's house then, and John's wife running things. No one will take much notice of Amy. She'll just be the one who couldn't get a husband because she'd been shamed. It seems a hard thing to condemn a girl of fifteen to, just because the man who proposes to her isn't as fine as you wanted.'

Jack was moved by the bleakness of the picture Susannah had created. 'That would be hard on a woman,' he admitted. He fastened on the missing piece of the jigsaw. 'What about the child, though? He says he won't take the child.'

278

Susannah gave a deep sigh. 'Yes, that's sad. It would all be perfect if he'd accept the baby. But you can't really expect him to, can you? The law would say it was his child. If it's a boy, Charlie would have to see the farm he's sweated and slaved over go to another man's son. That's not fair, is it?'

Jack mulled this over. 'There's sense in that, I suppose. One more child wouldn't make any difference here, anyway.'

'What do you mean, Jack?' Susannah asked, her eyes suddenly wide.

'Well, we'd say it was ours. No one would think anything of it, you've got two little ones already. If you stayed home from now until the child comes the nurse is the only one outside the family who'd need to know it was Amy's and not yours.'

'Jack!' Susannah looked at him in horror. 'How could you even think of something so cruel?'

'Don't start that nonsense. It's not cruel to ask you to look after three children. I know you're not keen on having babies, but you don't have to bear this one, just bring it up.'

'No, I don't mean that.' Susannah was still looking at him as though he had said something monstrous. 'How do you think Amy would feel, having to pretend her own child was only her brother or sister? Living next door, she'd see it every week, but she'd never be able to claim it as her own. To hear her child call me mother instead of her? I think that would break her heart.'

'Wouldn't it be even harder for her never to see the child at all?'

Susannah smiled at him. 'That's a strange thing for a farmer to say. I remember when I first came here, the cows were bellowing for their calves. They sounded so miserable, I was quite upset. But you told me they'd forget about the calf after a few days as long as it was out of sight, then they'd have another one next year and be as happy as ever. It's the same for Amy. She can't keep this baby if she marries Charlie, so the best thing in the world would be to send it away so she'll never see it, then for her to have another baby as soon as possible. A baby she could be proud of instead of ashamed. That's the only way you're ever going to see her happy again. You want her to be happy, don't you?'

'Of course I do. If that's what would make her happy... I don't know. It doesn't seem right, somehow.'

'What about giving her the chance to decide? Let her choose whether she wants to accept Charlie or not. I think she has the right to know she's been offered for.'

Jack tugged absently at a corner of his beard. Put that way, what Susannah said was inarguable. Girls all wanted to get married, he knew

279

that. Amy must know she no longer had any chance of making a good marriage; perhaps that was one reason she was looking so miserable all the time. She might jump at the chance of a husband, even if Charlie couldn't possibly be any girl's dream.

The more he thought about it, the more sensible it seemed. It was such a tidy idea. Amy would be respectably married, and she could hold her head high again. She would be just next door, so he could see as much of her as he wanted. She might fret over the baby for a while, but Susannah was right: as soon as she had another child she would forget about it.

'All right,' he said at last. 'Let her decide for herself. If she wants to marry him, I won't stand in her way.'

Susannah smiled approvingly. 'I'm sure you've made the right decision. I think you'll find Amy's pleased about it when she's had a chance to think it over.'

Amy waited until Charlie had disappeared from sight before she got up from the stump and went down to the house. Jack and Susannah were sitting at the table, looking more companionable than Amy could ever remember having seen them. Her father even smiled at Amy. Susannah had a letter near her hand; she fingered it absently.

'Here she is!' said Jack.

'Let me tell her,' Susannah said quickly, but Jack brushed her aside.

'I'll tell her myself. Well, Amy, you've had a proposal. What do you think of that?'

Amy looked at him in disbelief, then a happiness so intense that it hurt flooded through her. *Jimmy hasn't left me. It's just been some terrible misunderstanding. He still loves me! Oh, and I haven't been wearing his brooch. I'll have to confess that to him. I nearly threw myself in the creek! I don't think I'll ever be unhappy again once Jimmy's with me.*

'Well, *that's* cheered her up,' Jack said. 'Look at her, Susannah, beaming all over that pretty little face.'

'When did you hear? Just this morning? Did he write to you?' Amy could hardly get the questions out fast enough.

'Write?' Jack let out a laugh. 'What would he write for? He walked up the road.'

Amy looked around the room in confusion, wondering if Jimmy was in some corner unseen. 'But… where is he now?'

'Back in his own house, of course.'

'Amy doesn't know who you're talking about, Jack,' Susannah put in. Amy looked at her in bewilderment. *Of course I know who Pa's talking about.*

Jack slapped his hand against his forehead. 'So she doesn't. I forgot all about that. Amy, you've been asked to become Mrs Stewart.'

She must have misunderstood him, so she struggled to unravel his meaning. But there was no way of misunderstanding. 'Ch... Charlie?' she said, fear clutching at her. 'Are you saying Charlie's asked to marry me?'

'Don't say anything hasty, Amy,' Susannah said. 'You just have a little think before you answer your father.'

'Now, I won't pretend it's what I would have wished for you,' Jack said. 'Not if everything was as it should be. But the more I think about it, the more sensible it seems. Well? What do you have to say about it?'

Amy looked at Susannah smiling smugly, then at Jack's complacent expression. She ran to her father and knelt before him with her hands on his lap, her bulk making the movement awkward. 'Please, Pa, don't make me marry him. I'll be good, I promise I will. I'll do anything you say. I'll never do anything bad again, ever. Please don't make me marry Charlie.' Her voice cracked on the last word.

'Hey, hey, who said anything about making you?' Jack said, shaken. 'I thought you'd be pleased about it. Susannah, you said she'd be pleased.'

'It's a surprise for her, that's all. Let her calm down—'

'You!' Amy flung at Susannah. 'It's your idea. You want to get rid of me. Pa, please don't let her make me.'

'Your ma's only thinking of you, girl.'

Amy cast a tormented look at her father. *He wants me to! He wants me to marry Charlie! I can't, I can't.* She gave a sob and rushed from the room.

Jack looked after her in confusion. 'She didn't take it very well,' he said to Susannah. 'I thought you said she'd be pleased.'

'You put it to her too abruptly, that's all. It gave her a shock. I'll have a talk with her.' She rose from her chair.

'I won't have her forced, Susannah.'

'Of course not. No one's going to force her. I'll just have a little talk with her, that's all. I want to help her think it through properly. Don't you worry about it.'

Amy lay on her bed facing away from the door. When she heard it open, she rolled onto her back in time to see Susannah enter.

'Go away.'

'I will not go away.' Susannah crossed the room to stand beside Amy, looking down on her. 'You're going to listen to what I have to say.'

'I won't.' Amy put her hands over her ears.

Susannah clutched at one of Amy's hands and forced it down. 'Oh, yes you will, my girl. You won't like it, but you're going to listen.' Before Amy could cry out, Susannah's other hand was pressed hard on her mouth. 'No, you don't. You're not going to get your father running in here wondering what I'm doing to his little girl.'

Susannah's hand was half-covering Amy's nose as well, so that she could hardly breathe. She made a muffled noise of distress. 'Will you keep quiet if I take my hand away?' Susannah asked. Amy nodded. 'Do you promise?' When Amy again nodded, Susannah lifted her hand. 'That's better, now you're being sensible. Let's see if you can carry on being sensible.'

'I don't want to marry Charlie,' Amy said in a small voice. 'You can't make me.'

Susannah sat down on the bed and leaned over till her face was close to Amy's. 'Of course you don't want to marry him. What girl would want a man like that? But you're not in a position to pick and choose, are you? You have to take what you can get.'

'You can't make me,' Amy repeated as though the words were a talisman.

Susannah ignored the feeble protest. 'No one else will ever want you—you do know that, don't you? Why would any man with the chance of a decent wife take a girl who's been soiled? The only man who'd take a girl like you—a *dirty* girl—is the sort no decent girl would look at. Someone like Charlie. Past middle age, poor, and bad-tempered with it. He's no oil painting, is he? And from the smell of him he doesn't even bother with a bath every week.'

'I won't marry him. I won't.'

'You set your sights higher than that, didn't you? Oh, you set them far too high. You wanted to catch a man like my brother—yes, I know you thought your father was talking about him just now.' Amy could not hold back a sob at this thrust. 'You'd better put him out of your little head. He got out of your clutches in time, you'll never see James again. And neither will I! I'll probably never see my brother again, and it's all your fault.' Susannah's voice became shrill, then she modulated it once more into smoothness. 'You're not going to get a man like him. You're not even going to get some yokel like your cousin's managed to hook. At least Frank Kelly's young and not bad looking.'

'I don't want anyone. I don't want to get married.'

'Not now your Prince Charming's seen you for what you are and dumped you? How could you even think you had the right to a man like him? You silly little bitch. You don't deserve a man like James. Do you know what you deserve?'

'Nothing. Nothing!'

'You deserve Charlie. That's just what you deserve. He's perfect for you.'

'You can't make me.'

'You're not only a little slut, you're completely selfish, aren't you? Don't you ever think about anyone but yourself? Don't you know you broke your father's heart when you shamed yourself? Don't you know that?'

'Yes, I know,' Amy said miserably.

'He aged ten years overnight when he found out his "dear little girl" was no better than a whore. Every time he looked at you it was as though he was in pain,' Susannah went on relentlessly. 'You made trouble between him and I—serious trouble. You caused fights between him and his sons. You nearly drove Harry away altogether, and he still refuses to say a word to me. But did you see your father's face when you came in just now?'

Amy saw in her mind the smile that had so startled her, while Susannah's voice went on inexorably. 'Suddenly he saw a chance of making everything right again. His daughter a respectable married woman. "This is my daughter, Mrs Stewart" instead of "This is my daughter, the little whore who's brought shame on the family". He thought he could be proud of you again. But you won't do that for him, will you? Oh, no, you're too high-and-mighty to lower yourself. You! As if you could get any lower. Your father dotes on you, and you don't care a bit about him.'

'I love Pa. I love him more than anything in the world.' Amy felt tears running down her face, but she was too mesmerised by Susannah's words to wipe them away.

'Humph! Words are easy, aren't they? When you get a chance to do something for him, something to make up for a little bit of the pain you've given him, you refuse.'

Would it really make it up to Pa? 'I can't. I'm scared of Charlie.'

'Scared?' Susannah looked astonished. 'What do you think he'll do? Eat you?'

'I don't know what he'll do. I'm scared.'

'You've already got far more idea of what goes on between husband and wife than a decent girl would.' Susannah suddenly sat up straighter so that her face was no longer only inches away from Amy's. 'You don't have to marry him, of course. No one's going to force you.'

'Don't I?' Amy said in confusion. 'I mean, no, I don't. I don't want to.'

'No, it's up to you,' Susannah said in a matter-of-fact voice. 'You're perfectly free to spend the rest of your life in this house. You'll have to do what I say, of course, and I'll be keeping a tighter rein on you than I did before, now that I know what you're like. Your father's going to be very upset that you're turning Charlie's offer down, but you're not worried about that, are you?'

'Pa said he wouldn't make me.'

'No, and he means it, too. You've a very soft-hearted father. He's prepared to give up a lot to try and please you—it's a pity you refuse to make any sacrifices for his happiness, but that's your decision. No one will ever come and visit us once they all find out what you are, but I expect we'll get used to that. You realise Arthur won't let that girl see you because you've been shamed? I'm surprised you don't miss her, you always seemed rather fond of her. You'll have to get used to people staring at you on the street and giggling behind their hands.'

'People won't know about me, will they?'

'Yes, they will. It'll be hard on your brothers, too, once they start courting. A lot of fathers wouldn't want their daughters marrying into a family with a girl like you in it.' She stopped and seemed to consider for a moment. 'I suppose it won't be quite so bad for John and Harry. They're already grown-up, people know them for themselves. It'll be worse for my little boys, they'll never remember a time when you hadn't brought shame on the family. I don't suppose you're worried about Thomas and George, though, they're only your half-brothers.'

'But… but I thought it was going to be kept secret. I thought that was why you didn't want anyone to see me.'

'I wanted it to be secret, but your father thinks differently. He says if you don't get married the child's to stay here, and you'll have to bring it up yourself.'

'It… it is my responsibility,' Amy said. 'I'll look after the baby.'

'Then it won't be a secret, will it?' Susannah said in a terribly reasonable voice. 'Everyone will know when they see you walking around with a baby.' She sighed. 'Things will be hard enough for your father and brothers with you in the house, but as for that child you're carrying…' Her voice trailed away.

'What? What about the baby?' Amy asked.

'What sort of life do you think it's going to have? Oh, everyone will be very kind to it, of course—at home, that is. You'll do your best. But the whole town will call it "Amy Leith's bastard". That's a heavy burden for a child to carry through life. Imagine how the other children at school talk to a child like that. You know how cruel children can be. Then when it grows up—bad enough if it's a boy, with no prospects unless your father gives him money that should have gone to your brothers, but what if it's a girl?' She leaned closer to Amy again. 'A girl whose mother was no better than a whore? What chance will she have in life? She's certainly not going to find a husband. So another girl would end up living here as an old maid all her life, having to be supported by your father then your brothers. There's a difference, of course. You brought this on yourself. Your child won't have a choice about having the sins of its mother visited upon it.'

'That's not fair,' Amy whispered.

'No, it's not, is it? But it's your decision.'

Amy closed her eyes to shut out the sight of Susannah looking so calm and reasonable. Instead she saw a frightened little girl, surrounded by bullying children and censorious adults. She opened her eyes again. 'Why would it be different if I got married?' she asked quietly.

'Charlie doesn't want the child. Your father and I have talked about it, and we agree I should find a home for the baby if you marry Charlie. We don't think it would be right for you to have your own child living next door but not acknowledged as yours. People would think it was my baby, you see. You'd never be allowed to think of it as your child.'

'I wouldn't like that.' Amy chewed at her lip. 'What would you do with it instead—if I got married, I mean?'

'Ah,' Susannah smiled. 'The child would have quite a different life. You see, there are lots of people who want to have babies but they can't, for one reason or another. People who love children, and want to pour out that love on a child of their own. I'd find a couple like that, and they'd adopt the baby. It would have their name then, no one could ever call it bastard.' She gave a little laugh. 'I think the worst danger for a child like that would be getting terribly spoiled!'

'And... and they'd love it? The people who adopted it?'

'Oh, I think people like that love their babies even more than natural parents do. People who think they're never going to have a child. A baby is a real gift to them, not just a part of marriage that can't be avoided. Or a bastard like you're having,' she added casually. 'Still, there's not much use talking about it, is there? You're going to say no to Charlie, and you're never going to get another offer.' She stood up. 'Shall I tell your father you've made up your mind to refuse? It might be easier for you if I break the news.'

'No, don't tell him that. I... can I think about it a little bit longer?'

Susannah patted her on the arm. 'I think that would be a very good idea. It's a big decision, whether or not to turn down your only chance...

285

no, we've talked enough about that, haven't we? You stay here as long as you want, I'll make lunch. I'll bring yours in to you.'

'Well?' Jack said when Susannah came back out to the kitchen.

'She's thinking about it. I tried to point out some of the advantages, but I made it clear to her that it's her decision, and no one's going to force her.'

'That's right.' Jack sighed. 'I think it would be the best thing for her, though.'

'I'm sure it would. Amy's a sensible girl underneath it all, I think you'll find she sees that for herself if we just leave her alone.' Susannah hummed to herself as she prepared the meal.

'You're being very good about all this, Susannah,' Jack said.

'I'm trying to make it up to you for not looking after Amy.' She tilted her head to one side and gazed at Jack. 'Am I? Am I making up for it?'

'There's no need to talk about making up for things,' Jack said gruffly. 'But… I appreciate what you're doing.'

Amy got up from her bed and sat in front of her dressing table. She studied the photograph in its silver frame, staring intently at the expression of love pouring from her mother's eyes. *I do love Pa. I love John and Harry too, and Tommy and Georgie. That must mean I want to make things right for them, make up for the bad things I've done. Pa wants me to get married. I want the best for the baby, too. It's not the baby's fault. I wish I wasn't so scared. Why does it have to be Charlie?* She lowered her eyes from the photograph. *Because no one else wants me. I'm too bad for anyone else.*

She was still sitting there when Susannah brought her lunch in on a tray. 'Thank you. I don't think I've ever had lunch in my bedroom before.'

'It's not every day a girl gets a proposal. I want you to have time to think it over properly, without any distractions.' Susannah put the tray down on the dressing table and made to leave.

'Susannah?'

Her stepmother turned back to her. 'Yes?'

'Would it really make Pa happy if I said I'd marry Charlie?'

'He'd be beside himself. He thinks it's at least partly his fault, you know, that you were soiled. If he could see you settled happily he'd be his old self again.'

'I don't think I would be settled happily, though. Not with Charlie.' Amy gave an involuntary shudder.

Susannah sat down on the bed. 'Well, I wouldn't be too hasty about thinking that. I think perhaps we're all a little unjust to Charlie, including me.'

'What do you mean?'

'It's not easy for a man to live all by himself, trying to run a house as well as a farm. No wonder he seems rather abrupt in his manner. He's probably very lonely.'

'Lonely? Charlie?' Amy struggled with the concept.

'Yes. That's why he wants a wife, I expect. To keep him company, and help him around the house.'

'But you said he was bad-tempered.'

'He *seems* bad-tempered. That's because he's not good at mixing with people. You know, I think you might just be able to sweeten him up if you tried hard enough. I know he's old, but old men are easier to manage than young ones. They're more grateful for the attention.'

'Charlie never seems to like anyone. Do you think he'd like me?'

'He must like you already, or he wouldn't ask for your hand, would he?' Susannah said. 'No one's making him get married. He must want to.'

'I hadn't thought of it like that.'

'He's not a wealthy man, but he's offering to share what he has with you. He wants to make you the mistress of his house. You'd like to have a house of your own to run, wouldn't you? Instead of just doing what I say all the time.'

'Yes,' Amy admitted. 'But... do you think he'll be kind to me?' she pleaded.

'If you please him, I don't see why not. He mightn't be easy to please, but I think you could do it. Men think you're pretty, that should help you charm him. You're more than halfway there already, now he's proposed to you.'

Susannah left the room, and Amy mulled over her words. She ate her lunch without noticing what it was, then sat very still, her hands curled into tight fists on her lap. She stood up and took a few deep breaths until she felt brave enough to do what she had to. When she unclenched her fists she saw red arcs left by her nails in the flesh of her palms.

Her brothers had had their lunch and left, but Jack and Susannah were still sitting at the table in front of their empty plates when Amy walked into the room.

'I've decided, Pa,' Amy said, hoping her father would not notice the quaver in her voice. 'I'll do it. I'll marry Charlie.'

'That's my girl!' Jack almost knocked over his chair as he rose to embrace her. For a moment Amy lost herself in his hug, the first time she had felt his arms around her since he had found out about her disgrace. He put his hands on her shoulders and looked down into her face. 'You're sure you want to? I won't force you, you know.'

'I know. I want to.' *It's not really a lie. I sort of want to. More than I don't want to, anyway.*

Jack frowned. 'You're quite sure? You don't look very cheerful about it.'

'It's all been such a surprise, that's all.' Amy concentrated hard, trying to persuade her mouth to shape itself into a smile. It was badly out of practice, but she felt the corners rise at last.

'That's better,' Jack said. If Amy's smile had a trembling look about it, her father did not seem to notice.

29

'Don't go wandering off, Amy,' Susannah said after breakfast the next morning, when the men had gone. 'I want you to be here when Charlie comes.'

'Why? I thought you'd want me to keep out of the way.'

'Don't be silly. You can't tell him you accept his proposal if you're not here.'

'Do I have to tell him myself? I thought you and Pa would talk to him about it.'

'There's not much point being shy of him when you'll be married to the man before long, is there? Of course you have to tell him yourself. I don't want anyone saying you were forced into it.'

'Oh. All right, then.' Amy spent the next few hours doing all the light housework she could think of, and trying hard not to think about Charlie.

Jack came in late in the morning. 'I've just seen him on his way up the road,' he said. 'I had to spin a yarn to the boys about why Charlie's come over two days in a row—you're sure I shouldn't tell them yet?' he asked Susannah.

'Quite sure. Not till it's all settled. You know what a fuss Harry makes about things. You can tell him after Charlie goes if you like, it'll all be decided then.'

Susannah rushed to open the door as soon as they heard a knock. Her voice exuded enthusiasm as she welcomed Charlie. 'Mr Stewart, come in. We're all here and waiting for you.'

Charlie looked past Susannah, seeking Jack. He seemed surprised to see Amy sitting at the table beside her father, carefully resisting the urge to clutch at Jack's hand. He walked into the middle of the room and stood holding his hat in one hand. 'Well?' he said to Jack. 'What's your answer?'

'Amy can tell you herself,' Jack said. 'I've let her make her own decision.' Charlie raised his eyebrows at this, then turned his gaze on Amy.

She had seen him staring at her many times over the years, and it had always made her nervous. Now she had to promise herself to him. Amy grasped at Susannah's encouraging words: Charlie was awkward with people, that was why he seemed bad-tempered. He must already like her if he wanted to marry her. He would be kind to her if she pleased him.

Amy dropped her eyes and stared at her hands as they twined around each other in her lap. She knew she was taking too long to answer, but the words stuck in her throat.

'Come on, Amy.' Jack nudged her arm with his elbow. 'Don't keep Charlie waiting. What have you got to say for yourself?' He smiled encouragingly at her.

With an effort, Amy raised her eyes to look straight into Charlie's. 'Yes, I will marry you,' she heard herself say. 'Thank you for asking me,' she added, feeling that something else was necessary. Now the thing was said, her pent-up tension came out in a small fit of coughing that she tried to muffle with her hand.

'Well, you've got your answer,' Jack said. 'It's what she wants, and I give her my blessing. She'll make you a good wife, Charlie. A very good wife. I hope you'll appreciate her.'

Charlie looked dubiously at Amy as she smothered another cough. 'Is she healthy?'

Jack frowned. 'Of course she is. Don't talk about my daughter as if she was a mare for sale.'

'Amy had a bad cough for a while,' Susannah came in smoothly. 'She got a little run down early in the winter. She's much better now, that cough will be gone altogether soon.'

'Good,' Charlie said. 'We'd best be getting things settled, then.'

Amy could see that she had played her own small part; now they were all talking as though she were not there. 'Can I go now, please?' she asked, rising from her chair. 'You don't need me any more, do you?'

'No, I don't think we do,' Susannah agreed. 'Off you go, then. Now, the first thing to decide is when the wedding's to be,' Amy heard Susannah say just before she closed the door on the three people who were deciding her life for her.

Lizzie walked into the middle of a conversation between her parents when she entered the kitchen that afternoon.

'But don't you think he's a bit old for her?' she heard her mother ask.

'Is she going to get a better offer?' Arthur said. He turned and saw Lizzie. 'Well, you haven't heard the news yet, have you?'

'What news?' Lizzie asked, a sinking feeling in her stomach. 'Is it something about Amy?'

'It looks like you're not going to be the first one to the altar after all. Amy's managed to find a husband—her pa's found one for her, anyway.'

'Who? It's not Jimmy.' It was a statement, not a question.

'Humph! You'd believe in fairy tales if you believe that. Not quite as glamorous, but he'll do the job. She's going to marry Charlie.'

'What!' Lizzie was at a loss for words. 'Are you serious?' she asked when she got her tongue back.

'It's not much of a joke, is it? No, Charlie says he wants her, and your Uncle Jack's said he can have her.'

'Why?' Lizzie asked, completely mystified.

'Because he wants things sorted out for her. Charlie's no great catch, but Amy can be respectable again once she's properly married. It'll be as though all this trouble never happened. You let that be a lesson to you, my girl—fathers have the right to do as they see fit with their daughters.'

Lizzie ignored her father's pompous speech. 'If she's so respectable now, can I go and see her again?' she asked.

Arthur considered. 'All right,' he said. 'Go over tomorrow if you want. Try not to gloat over her too much. Frank must seem a pretty good catch compared to what she's got.'

Amy was alone in the kitchen preparing dinner when Harry stormed into the house, with John right behind him. 'Amy, they're not going to make you do it,' Harry said. 'They can't force you, and we're not going to let them try.'

'That's right, Amy,' John said. 'You don't deserve that.'

They stood there looking solid and dependable, and Amy wanted to shelter in their strength. But she would be hurting them, too, if she stayed at home in her shame. Susannah had said it reflected on them all. That wouldn't be fair to her brothers, especially when they were trying to be so kind.

'They're not—' she started to say. Her father came in, puffing from having rushed up to the house.

'Don't upset her, for God's sake,' said Jack. 'Amy's happy about it, you just ask her.'

'Are you trying to tell me Amy wants to marry that old b—that old so-and-so?' Harry demanded.

'I don't believe it, Pa,' John said. 'And I'm not going to see her forced into it just because you think she's an embarrassment.'

'Amy wants to! I just want to see her settled and happy.'

'Happy! With Charlie! Don't talk crap,' Harry said in disgust.

'Watch your language in front of your sister.'

'You want to put her in Charlie Stewart's bed and you're drivelling on about language? Shit!'

'I told you—'

'What's going on?' Susannah said from the passage doorway. 'What's all the shouting about?'

'It's her idea, isn't it?' Harry cast a look of disgust at Susannah. 'It's not enough for her that her bastard of a brother did that to my sister. Now the bitch has talked you into giving Amy to Charlie. You're not going to do it. I'm not having that old bugger pawing my sister. Don't,' he said warningly as Jack advanced on him with his fist upraised. He lifted his own fists almost casually, and stared his father down until Jack lowered his arm in defeat.

Amy waited for Susannah to erupt into hysterics, but instead she stood in icy stillness until everyone else fell silent. Then she spoke very calmly. 'Amy, why don't you tell your brothers what you want, since they're so worried about you?'

All other eyes in the room turned on her, and Amy looked at the floor rather than face them. 'I want to get married,' she said quietly. She lifted her head. 'They're not forcing me, really they're not. I've said I'll marry him, and I'll go through with it. It'll be better for everyone.' She saw John and Harry staring disbelievingly at her. 'Please don't fight over me.' *I've caused enough trouble.* 'I'll be all right.' *Maybe he'll be kind to me.* She tried hard to shut out Harry's picture of being pawed by Charlie.

'You see?' Susannah said, still very calm. 'You can't blame me for this. It's what Amy wants herself.'

Harry ignored her. 'You swear that's true?' he demanded of Amy. 'You swear she hasn't threatened you or anything?'

'It's true. Charlie asked, and I said yes. No one's forcing me.'

Harry glowered at Susannah and opened his mouth to say something to her, then turned away. 'If I hadn't sworn never to talk to that bitch again,' he spat out to the room in general. 'All right, she's not forcing you, but she's still talked you into it somehow.'

'It's nothing to do with you, Harry,' Susannah said sweetly. 'It's Amy's decision.'

'Shit!' Harry swung his arm out wildly and knocked over a chair, making Susannah give a little cry, then he swept out of the house, slamming the door after him.

John crossed the room to stand close to Amy. 'You can still change your mind, Amy. If you do, you just tell me. No one can make you go through with it, remember that.'

'I'm not going to change my mind. I've said I'll do it, and I will. Thank you for worrying about me, John.' *Even though I'm not worth it.*

'Well, if you do…' He trailed off into silence, then he, too, left the room, casting an worried glance over his shoulder before he closed the door.

'At one time I would have been quite upset over being abused in such filthy language,' Susannah said in a detached tone. 'That's one thing I've learned from living here, anyway, not to take any notice of brutes. I might as well worry about what the pigs think of me.' She turned to Jack. 'Of course you don't try to support me, do you?'

'They take no notice of me these days,' Jack grumbled.

'Perhaps they would if you showed a bit of authority. Why don't you—'

'Shut up, Susannah.' Jack stomped out of the room.

Susannah watched as he left. 'He's too old to make them take notice,' she said thoughtfully. 'Those two are going to get worse, not better.' She turned to Amy. 'Ah well, they'll forget all this nonsense as soon as you're safely married off. I must say you were very sensible about all that, Amy. I thought you might make a fuss and start crying or some such foolishness.'

'Why would I do that?' Amy answered, in a voice that almost matched Susannah's for calmness. 'There's nothing to make a fuss over. I've said I'll marry Charlie, and I'm going to go through with it.'

'So you are,' Susannah looked approvingly at her. 'So you are.' It was only after Susannah had disappeared back up the passage that Amy allowed herself to indulge in the 'foolishness' of crying.

Amy rounded a hill and almost walked into her cousin. 'Lizzie!' she cried in delight. The girls hugged each other. 'I thought you weren't allowed to see me any more,' Amy said, disentangling herself. 'Did you sneak off? Don't go getting in trouble over me.'

'Pa said I could come.' Lizzie frowned, and shook her head. 'I think the old people have all gone stupid. What's this rubbish about you getting married?' In a flash Amy's happiness was clouded.

'It's true. Charlie's asked for me, and I've said yes.'

Lizzie took hold of her arm. 'You mustn't, Amy. They can't make you do it.'

'No one's making me! Why does everyone think Pa's forcing me?'

'Because you'd never do it of your own free will, you're not that stupid. Amy, just think about it. Marry Charlie? You've always been scared of even talking to him, and now you're going to spend the rest of your life living with him? You can't do it.'

Amy tried to recapture the calm tone she had used with Susannah. 'I know I've always been scared of him, but you used to tell me I was silly to be like that. You were right, I see that now. There's nothing to be frightened of, Charlie's just not much good at mixing with people. I'll be all right with him.'

'No, you won't,' Lizzie said fervently. 'I only said you shouldn't be scared of him because he couldn't do anything to you. If you marry him he can do whatever he likes.'

'Don't talk like that, Lizzie,' Amy said, turning her face away to hide her expression. 'You're only making it harder when I'm trying to get used to it all. I've said I'll do it, and I've got to stick to it. It's for the best, really it is.'

'Why? Why is it for the best for you to marry a man you don't want?'

'It's not just me. There's Pa and the others to think about. I brought shame on them all, and I can make it right by getting married. Then I'll be respectable again.'

'That's too hard, Amy,' Lizzie said. Her voice shook.

'No, it's not. It's my duty to make things right again—as right as I can, anyway. It's the best for the baby, too.'

'For Charlie to be its father, you mean?'

'No. He doesn't want the baby. But it'll be all right, Susannah's arranging it all. She's going to give the baby to someone else, someone who can give it a good home. That's much better than me trying to look after it, isn't it? Everyone would be horrible to it because it's a...' The word *bastard* was too cruel; she left it unsaid.

'I can see the sense in that—about the baby, I mean. But it's a stupid idea for you to marry Charlie. Couldn't you give the baby away and just... I don't know, carry on as if it never happened?'

'But it has happened, Lizzie. You're saying I should stay here and work for Susannah all my life, watching Pa get older and greyer every day he has to look at me? With John and Harry feeling sorry for me, when they weren't wishing I was out of the way? None of them would ever be able to forget what I've done if I was always under their noses. They'd all be fighting about me half the time, anyway. At least I get a home of my own this way. I thought you wanted that for me.'

'Of course I do, but not with him! Why does it have to be Charlie?'

'Because no one else wants me. How many men do you think would even look at a girl in this state?' She pointed to her big belly.

'You won't be in that state forever—not for much longer. It's only two or three months now, isn't it?'

'I'll still be soiled. No one wants a girl who's been shamed. No one who can get a decent girl, anyway. Men like to be the first—or so I'm told.'

'But Amy, you don't have to wear a sign around your neck saying what happened—and stop using those names for yourself. Listen—no one outside the family knows about it—well, except Charlie, and he never talks to anyone. Everyone wants to keep it a secret—I don't know if Pa's even told Bill. If you wait a while, maybe a year or two, you'll meet someone else. Someone good enough for you,' she said fiercely.

'Meet someone wonderful and fall in love again, you mean? And then watch him run away when he finds out what I am? That's not a sensible idea, Lizzie, even if I could fall in love again. Even if I wanted to.'

'Would… would you really have to tell him?' Lizzie asked hesitantly. 'I mean, why tell if it would cause trouble? What someone doesn't know can't hurt them.'

Amy shook her head. 'He'd soon notice something was missing once we got married.' She saw the mystified look on Lizzie's face. 'Oh, I'm sorry, Lizzie, sometimes I forget you don't really know anything about it. It wouldn't be right for me to talk to you about that sort of thing, anyway. Just take my word for it, men know whether they're the first or not.'

'Oh.' Lizzie looked crestfallen. 'Well, what about teaching, then?' she said, animated again. 'You always wanted to do that. If you're really sure you won't get a real husband, couldn't you do that instead? You'd be sort of independent then. You could get your own house to live in.'

Amy shut her eyes against a new wave of grief and loss. 'Lizzie, what sort of parents do you think would let a girl like me teach their children? No, don't say I could keep it a secret. I'm not going to lie to make people trust me with their little ones. That's gone forever. I'm never going to be a teacher now.'

'Maybe that's true, but I still don't want you to marry Charlie. You'll hate it—you know you will.'

'Stop making it harder, Lizzie. It's either stay here and make everyone miserable, or take my chances with Charlie. Maybe things won't be as bad as you think with him. I know how bad they'll be here.'

'But Amy—'

'Stop it! Go away, Lizzie. Leave me alone.' She turned, and when she looked back over her shoulder Lizzie was disappearing from sight through the trees.

Jack watched as Susannah replaced the covers Thomas had kicked off before she put out the lamp and climbed into bed. 'It'll be September soon, Amy's only got a little over two months to go now,' she said. 'She'd better go to Auckland soon.'

'Well, you've been writing all these letters, arranging everything. What have you sorted out for her?'

'There's a woman who organises adoptions, Constance has got her name and address for me. And Constance has booked Amy into a small nursing home. She said it's very clean and nice. She won't be able to go there till the child's coming, of course, so she'll have to stay somewhere first.'

'Will your sister have her?'

'Hardly, Jack! You can't expect Constance to have an unmarried girl in that state in her house. What if anyone were to see Amy there? Mother often visits, too.'

'I suppose you haven't told your ma and pa about Amy? Or about their son, come to that,' he added bitterly.

Susannah ignored his reference to Jimmy. 'I haven't *really* told Constance about her,' she admitted. 'She thinks it's your niece she's been arranging things for. I'd never hear the end of it if she knew it was my stepdaughter.'

'Humph! I can see why. Well, where's Amy going to stay, then?'

Susannah said nothing for a few moments, then spoke in a careful tone. 'There's a place that takes girls like her. It's not very far from the nursing home, and she'd be well looked after.'

'What are you talking about, Susannah?' Jack asked suspiciously. 'What do you mean "Girls like her"?'

'Girls who have babies before they're married. Fallen girls. They look after them,' she added quickly. 'The women who run that sort of place are terribly kind people. This one is run by the church.'

'You mean a place for whores, don't you? You want to send my daughter to a home for whores.'

'Reformed whores, Jack.'

'I'm not having Amy living with whores! She's just a child. Don't you ever make a suggestion like that again.'

'Shh! You'll wake the children.' She gave a sigh. 'Well, if you're going to take that attitude she'll have to stay in a boarding house. I'll see if Constance can find one near the nursing home.'

'That sister of yours doesn't waste any time, does she? She's sorted all this out pretty fast. You only let her know a couple of weeks ago, when Charlie asked for Amy. Up till then we were going to keep the baby here.'

'There's no time to waste,' Susannah said. Jack wondered why she sounded so defensive. 'Constance knows that, she's been rushing around as a favour to me.'

'I suppose I should be grateful to her. What about this boarding house, then? I want Amy in a decent place, not another home for reformed whores.'

'No, no, it'll be an ordinary boarding house, the sort you might stay in yourself if you went to Auckland.'

'Good. I don't want to hear that other place mentioned again.'

'You realise it will cost quite a lot of money for Amy to stay in a boarding house all that time? She'll probably have to be there two months. That's on top of the money for the nursing home, not to mention her passage to Auckland and back.'

Jack turned towards her in the darkness. 'Do you think I begrudge spending a bit of money on her? I'd gladly spend ten times the amount if I thought it would make things right for Amy.'

'I'm sure you would. I'll write to Constance again tomorrow, then, and ask her to book Amy into a boarding house. You'd better see about getting her a passage on the boat, too. Will you take her yourself or send one of the boys?'

'I've been thinking about that. Amy should have a woman with her, in case she's taken poorly on the boat. You'd better take her. You can't stay with her the whole time, but I want you there the first week or two she's in Auckland, to see that everything's all right.'

He heard a sharp intake of breath from Susannah's side of the bed. 'You mean you'll let me go to Auckland?'

'I don't have much option. You'll have to take the little fellows, too, I can't look after them properly.'

'Oh, I want to take them! Mother and Father have never even seen them—oh, Jack, it'll be wonderful! I'll see my family, and visit all the people I used to know, and do some shopping, too—you will give me some money, won't you? I'll be able to get some decent clothes again at last.'

'I'll give you a bit. You'll stay with your ma and pa, will you?'

'Of course. I could hardly go to Auckland and not stay with them, could I?'

'I suppose not. You make sure you see Amy settled in properly first, though. And I want you to visit this nursing home yourself, to see that it's a fit place.'

'I will. Oh, I can hardly wait!' He felt Susannah give a wriggle of excitement, making the bed shake a little.

'Susannah,' he said. 'I'm trusting you.'

'I know you are. I'll look after Amy, don't worry.'

'That's not what I meant. I'm trusting you to come back again. I don't want to be made a fool of, Susannah. I'd be the laughing-stock of the town if you stayed in Auckland. It's not that long ago you said you wanted to go up there and not come back.'

He felt her roll over to face him, and one of her knees brushed lightly against his leg. He wished he could see her expression. 'I didn't mean it,' she whispered. 'I sometimes say things I don't mean, when I get tired and upset. I'll come back, I promise I will.'

'Good. I'd have to come and get you if you didn't, you know.'

'I know.'

30

September 1884

Amy let the arrangements go on around her as though someone else were being spoken of. She listened with mild interest when told she would be going to Auckland to have the baby. She packed the clothes Susannah told her to pack. On the morning they were to leave she sat in the kitchen, her father's battered old case on the chair beside her, and waited patiently for Susannah to finish getting ready.

She fingered the catch on the case and thought about the two things she had put in that Susannah knew nothing of: Jimmy's brooch, and the velvet ribbon its box was nestled in. She could not wear the brooch, but she couldn't bear to leave it in the drawer for Susannah to find and speculate over, and perhaps to question her about when she came home. And she could not bear to throw it away.

The months that stretched ahead of her were simply an interlude she had to pass through before the next real thing was to happen in her life: she was going to marry Charlie. Before then she would have the baby, but that had no solid meaning for her. 'The baby' was an abstract idea; a creature without a face. She knew she had to do the right thing by this being she had created, but the people around her had decided what the right thing was. Amy's only responsibility was to do as she was told. It would all be over once the baby was born and had been given to the kind people who were waiting for it. Then she would come home and marry Charlie. *Then everyone will be happy. Everyone else, anyway. And I'll be all right. Maybe he'll be kind to me.*

Jack drove them into town and carried their bags onto the boat, and stayed with them until the 'all ashore' call was given. He gave each of his little boys a hug and kissed Amy, putting his arms around her carefully so as not to press too hard against her bulge. He kissed Susannah more as if he thought it was the right thing to do than with any real enthusiasm, then went back up the gangplank to wave to them as the *Staffa* pulled away from the wharf.

There was still just enough child left in Amy for her to feel a small surge of excitement when the boat started moving. This was her great adventure; she was leaving the place where she had spent her entire fifteen years. From now on, every place on the voyage would be somewhere she had never set eyes on before. Even the sounds and smells were new to her: the rumble of the engines, the thrumming of the deck under her boots, the grind of cables, the smell of burning coal. She was travelling. Never in her dreams had she imagined travelling for such a reason as this, but still she was travelling. A wayward thought forced its way into her awareness, and refused to be crushed down. *Jimmy was on this boat six months ago. When he left me.* Amy looked past the wharf at the buildings of Ruatane and the hills behind the town, and knew she was leaving behind everything familiar and safe.

Susannah's voice broke into her thoughts. 'Wrap your cloak around you properly. And you'd better come and sit in the ladies' cabin. Not that the little hutch deserves such a fancy name—I'd forgotten what a horrible little boat this is.'

She took Amy by the arm and led her into a tiny cabin astern of the wheel-house. 'There aren't any other women on the boat and men are blind about that sort of thing, but there's no sense making yourself conspicuous. It's too stuffy in here for the children, I'll be up on the deck with them if you need anything.'

The cabin was almost airless, and what little breeze made its way through the doorway brought the smoke of the engines with it, mixed with a smell of hot oil. Amy soon gave up brushing coal soot from her cloak. At least the dark fabric would not show the cinder smudges too badly. She sat on one of the narrow benches that lined each wall and peered out at the coastline as it slowly slid past the portholes. All she saw was sandy beach with fern or flax behind it, and bush-covered hills in the background. She crossed to the other side of the cabin and tried there. At first it looked exactly the same, but when they crossed the river bar the view changed to one of flat grey sea stretching out to meet grey sky at the horizon. It was too cloudy for a glimpse of White Island.

She went back to the first side, keeping her balance with difficulty in the swell that was now making the little boat pitch and roll. Amy tried to concentrate on the land slipping past, but the hills were rising and dipping in a disconcerting way, and her stomach seemed to want to imitate their motion. It was not long before she made her first grab at the bucket someone had conveniently placed beside the bench, and emptied her breakfast into it.

Susannah came down to see her early in the afternoon, her face tinged with green. 'Do you want anything to eat?' she asked. Amy lay on the bench and groaned. 'No, I'm not surprised. The Captain says this is a calm trip—I'd hate to be on a rough one, I'm ill enough as it is. Thomas has been sick, too, I can't get any food into him. George hasn't, though, I suppose that's something. You're sure you don't want this?' She thrust a package of sandwiches towards Amy. Amy pushed them away and leaned over the bucket once more. 'You're even worse than me,'

Susannah said. She left, and Amy was again alone in the cabin.

In the evening there was a pause in her misery when the boat pulled into harbour. Susannah came to the cabin to fetch her; much to Amy's disappointment, this was not the end of the voyage.

'Wh-why are we catching another boat?' Amy asked groggily, her mouth feeling as if it were full of rancid cotton wool. 'Isn't this one horrible enough?'

'The *Staffa* doesn't go to Auckland, you know that. Don't be so silly. We have to change here, we'll be on the *Wellington* for the rest of the way.'

'I'd forgotten that. So this isn't Auckland yet?' Amy peered through the darkness as she made her way unsteadily down the gangplank, trying to make out the shape of the town by the lights that stretched a short distance either side of the wharf.

'This?' Susannah said scornfully. 'This place isn't all that much bigger than Ruatane—well, not compared to Auckland, anyway. This is Tauranga. Now, I must see that those men get our luggage moved properly. Stand here out of the way.'

When their luggage had been safely stowed Amy found herself being bustled into a much larger ladies' cabin that, with its padded leather couches and heavy drapes, was positively luxurious after the *Staffa's*. She was vaguely aware of a stewardess approaching her and being brushed aside by Susannah, then her stepmother led her to a little bunk and helped her remove her boots and stockings. She lay down gratefully, and in the hour or two before the *Wellington* sailed she dropped off into a blissful sleep. *If I'm asleep I won't be sick*, she thought drowsily as she drifted off.

In the early hours of the morning the motion of the ship woke her, and Amy found that nausea was more insistent than sleep. At first she tried to vomit quietly, so as not to wake Susannah and the few other women in the cabin, but soon nothing mattered except getting to the bucket in time. It was a very long night.

When daylight had come at last, Susannah leaned over her. 'I'm taking the children up on deck for some fresh air. We're in the gulf and it's not so rough now. Were you ill in the night?'

'Yes,' Amy muttered miserably into her pillow.

'You stay here. Shall I bring you breakfast?'

'No,' Amy groaned.

'You'd feel better if you had something, you know. You won't be sick again, not now we're out of the open sea.' Amy proved her wrong at that point. 'Oh. Perhaps you'd better not have breakfast, then. You're a terrible traveller, aren't you? I thought I was bad enough—none of my family are good sailors. But you're much worse than me.'

'Susannah,' Amy said weakly, 'could I come up on deck with you? The fresh air might make me feel a little bit better.'

'No, I want you out of sight. You don't want people staring at you, do you?' Susannah moved out of Amy's field of vision, and Amy tried without success not to notice how stale the air in the cabin was. It smelt of bodies overdue for a bath, of small children who had soiled their clothes, and of sickly-sweet perfume, with engine fumes overlaying the whole mélange. She reached for the stinking bucket again.

But Susannah was right; the water was calmer now. After another hour or so, Amy could bear to look out the porthole at little bays slipping by. They passed several islands, and she wondered what their names were. Finally she saw a large wharf, lined with stacks of firewood, come into view, and felt the engines slow down. Amy could just manage to get her stockings and boots on, though her bulk made it difficult to see what she was doing, and by the time Susannah came back into the cabin to fetch her she was sitting up on the bunk with her cloak wrapped around her.

Amy was vaguely aware of noise and bustle all around her as sailors made the boat fast, passengers retrieved their baggage, and dock workers started unloading the cargo. Susannah hurried Amy ahead of her down the gangplank, at the same time leading Thomas by the hand and carrying George.

'The ground's still swaying!' Amy said in dismay when she was safely on the wharf.

'No, it's not. You only think it is,' Susannah said, and Amy soon found that her stomach believed it, even if her head did not. Susannah made Amy stand by a pile of flax bales and hold Thomas and George by the hand while she organised their baggage, then she retrieved her charges and shepherded them along briskly.

When they walked around the flax and started up the long wharf, Amy saw the city spread out before her. She stopped in her tracks and stared open-mouthed at the sight. There were huge buildings in either direction; some of them were three storeys high, and many of them were made of bricks, not wood. There were more buggies, carts, and carriages of various types than Amy had ever imagined the world could hold, and most of them seemed to be going at a breakneck pace. And people. Everywhere there were people. From the men unloading the cargo, to smartly-dressed men and women strolling along the broad pavements, to small boys rushing about on mysterious errands.

'So many people,' she breathed.

'Twenty-five thousand,' Susannah said proudly. 'So Father said before I left—it might even be more now. You're not in the country now, girl. Hurry up, I want to get a cab. There're always plenty in Customs Street. Leave that,' she said when she saw Amy reaching for her bag. 'Hi, you,' she hailed an eager-looking boy of about ten. 'Carry my luggage for me and I'll give you threepence.' The boy did not need to be asked twice, and Amy soon found herself standing on the edge of a busy road. Suddenly she felt nauseated all over again.

'Pooh!' she exclaimed. 'It smells terrible!'

'What are you talking about? Nothing smells worse than farms.' Susannah sniffed the air. 'Actually it does smell a bit, I suppose it must be all the horses.' Piles of horse dung littered the street, and as each vehicle rattled along its wheels went through the noisome heaps, disturbing colonies of flies. 'There's the Ligar Canal as well, it empties into the harbour, and it can be quite strong in the warm weather. I'd forgotten the smell,' Susannah said in surprise. 'Maybe it's got worse the last three years. Never mind, we'll soon be out of it. Cabby!' she called, waving her arm vigorously when she spotted a black hansom cab coming in their direction.

The cabby stowed their luggage and held the door open until they were safely inside. 'Grafton Road first,' Susannah instructed. 'Then Parnell.' The cab started up a broad avenue, and they were soon going past a building site. 'That's where they're going to build the new railway station,' Susannah said, as proudly as though she were erecting it herself. 'It's going to be a huge place. It's all reclaimed land, you know. When I was a girl Customs Street wasn't here, it was sea up to Fort Street.'

Amy looked out the window, but there was nothing more interesting than piles of dirt and rocks on the left of the cab, with what seemed to be hundreds of workmen moving the dirt around in wheelbarrows and carts.

'Is it always like this?' she asked. 'All these people building things, and nothing properly finished?'

'Well, there're always new buildings going up—that's how Father makes his money. But I must say it doesn't usually look quite as... well, confused as this. Except for around Point Britomart, of course, they'd already been slicing that away for two years before I got married. That's where they got the rocks from to make this new land. It'll be wonderful when the new station's ready, trains right to the bottom of Queen Street.'

Amy looked at the buildings on the other side of the road, trying to make out the signs in their windows as the cab rattled past. The buildings petered out into ordinary-looking houses, and she glanced back to the left hand side. She gave a shriek as she saw a black monster hurtling towards them, belching a cloud of dark smoke.

'What's wrong with you? Haven't you ever seen a train before?'

'No, only pictures of them. It just gave me a fright.' Amy looked with interest at the monster as it disappeared past the cab. It seemed an unbelievably rapid way to travel.

The little boys were restless after having been confined for so long. 'Do stop squirming, Thomas,' Susannah said. 'Sit up properly.'

'Want to sit on Amy,' Thomas said. He wriggled out of Susannah's grasp and clambered onto the seat beside Amy. 'Cuddle me.'

'There's not much room on me, Tommy. How about you just snuggle up?' Amy put her arm around the toddler and held him close.

'Want a lap!' Thomas insisted. 'Make a lap.'

'I can't make a lap. Sit on Mama's lap.'

'No, he'll crease my dress,' Susannah said automatically, then she gave a snort. 'What am I talking about? This dress couldn't possibly get more creased than it already is. Come and sit on me then, Thomas, if you're so desperate for a lap.'

'No! Want Amy!'

'All right, Tommy, I think I can fit you. Come on.' Amy managed to perch Thomas on what was left of her lap.

George apparently felt left out, and he, too, slithered over to Amy. 'You want a cuddle as well?' she said. 'Make room for your brother, Tommy. Oh, you want a kiss, Georgie?' The little boy thrust his face at her.

'Kiss, Amy,' Thomas demanded.

'I'll kiss you both. There. Oh, you two give such sloppy kisses, you really have got a lot to learn.' Amy fell silent, recalling those same words from Jimmy. She turned her face away from Susannah and surreptitiously wiped her tears on her sleeve.

'You've stopped those two grizzling, anyway. Now,' Susannah said briskly, 'I'll get you sorted out first. You understand what's happening? I'm taking you to the boarding house, and I'll see you settled in there. Oh, by the way, the landlady thinks your name's Elizabeth.'

'Why does she think that?' Amy asked, confused.

'Because she thinks you're my niece, not my stepdaughter. After I've done that—'

'You shouldn't have used Lizzie's name like that,' Amy said in distress. 'It's like saying she's been bad.'

'Don't talk nonsense. No one in Auckland has even heard of your precious Lizzie. Don't interrupt, we haven't much time. After that I'll go to the nursing home and see everything's all right. Your father wants me to inspect it, though I hardly think that's necessary. I'll tell them your real name there, it's probably for the best, just in case anything… well, just in case. Then I'm going home to Parnell.' Her face lit up at the words. 'Now, I'll leave my address with the landlady, so if you need me you just ask her to get in touch with me. I'll be staying there for two weeks, then I have to go back to the farm.' Susannah grimaced. 'When your time comes the landlady will take you to the nursing home, and when you're well again you'll come home. Do you understand all that?'

'Yes.' In this strange place, all the talk of nursing homes suddenly took on an unpleasant reality. 'Susannah,' Amy asked, 'what… what's going to happen when… when the time comes?'

'Didn't I just tell you that?' Susannah said impatiently. 'The landlady will take you to the nursing home. Weren't you listening?'

'Yes. I meant… I don't know what it will be like. When the baby starts coming.'

'Baby coming?' Thomas looked around the cab, obviously searching for the baby someone had hidden there. He wriggled on Amy's lap and tried to look behind the seat back.

'Stop that, Thomas—here, look out the window at the horses,' Susannah said. Thomas obediently looked for a few seconds, but horses held no novelty for him. 'I can't discuss that sort of thing on the street,' Susannah said, her lips pursed. 'Not in front of him, anyway. He picks up everything you say and parrots it. He'll be repeating things to Mother if I'm not careful. Don't talk about it.'

'No, I see. I'm sorry.' Amy shrank against the seat and tried to take an interest in the scene outside the cab window. A large tear rolled down one cheek.

'Don't go getting in a state,' Susannah said. 'There's nothing to be upset about. They'll give you something to put you out, and you won't know anything about it. You've no need to be frightened.'

'Oh. Thank you.' Amy tried to take some comfort from Susannah's words.

The cabby pulled up before a two-storied wooden building, and waited while Susannah led the way up the path. They were greeted at the door by the landlady, a grey-haired woman in her fifties who announced herself as Mrs Kirkham. She nodded to Susannah and looked rather disapprovingly at Amy. Amy wrapped herself more tightly in her cloak and tried to look inconspicuous.

Susannah opened her purse and counted off a wad of notes. 'That should be the correct amount, I believe,' she said. 'There's extra for your trouble in taking the girl to the nursing home, and I've put in enough for any cables you might have to send me.'

Mrs Kirkham counted the money quickly and nodded. She gave Susannah a frosty smile. 'I'll show Miss Leith to her room,' she said. 'Do you want to settle her in, Mrs Leith?'

'No, I don't think that's necessary. This is my address for the next two weeks if there's anything serious.' She handed a sheet of notepaper to Mrs Kirkham. 'And my husband's name, in case you have any call to cable us in Ruatane after I've left Auckland. I must be on my way now.'

'As you wish. I'll be in the hall.' Mrs Kirkham went inside, leaving Amy alone with Susannah and the little boys.

'You're costing your father a lot of money, I hope you realise that,' Susannah said.

'I'm sorry.'

'Ten pounds for you to stay here! And we have to give pounds and pounds to the woman who'll sort out the adoption. Then there's the nursing home, not to mention the boat. I hope you're grateful.' Amy said nothing.

'Well, you're all organised. I'll be off, then. Come along, boys.' Susannah tried to take hold of her sons' hands, but they clung to Amy's cloak.

'Amy come too,' Thomas protested.

'No, I have to stay here, Tommy. You go with Mama now.'

'No! Want Amy!'

'Amy!' George echoed.

'Stop being so naughty, you two,' Susannah scolded. 'I'll tell Papa you were bad, and he'll smack you.'

'Papa! Want Papa!' Thomas cried.

'Papa!' George chimed in.

'Papa's not here,' Susannah said. 'Just do as you're told.'

'Amy! Come on, Amy.' Thomas tugged at her.

'No, Tommy, I can't.' Amy carefully lowered herself to the little boys' level and put an arm around each of them. 'Listen, Tommy, and you too, Georgie. You're going to go and see your granny. You'll like that. Granny will be kind to you. She's probably got some nice cakes for you to eat.'

'Cakes?' Thomas looked more hopeful.

'You'll stay with your granny for a little while, and I'll stay here, then we'll all go home and see Papa. Now, off you go with Mama. Mama's waiting for you.'

'Amy come and have cakes too,' Thomas insisted.

'Oh, for goodness sake,' Susannah said irritably. 'Come *on.*' She snatched the fabric of Amy's cloak out of George's little fist and scooped him up onto one of her hips, then took hold of Thomas' wrist and yanked.

'Amy!' Thomas wailed as his mother half-dragged him down the path. He squealed when Susannah gave him a hard slap on the buttocks, and he was still yelling loudly when the cab pulled away. Amy stood and watched till the cab had disappeared around a corner, carrying with it the last of the people she knew. Now, for the first time in her life, she was among strangers.

She turned and went into the passage, where Mrs Kirkham was waiting with Amy's bag at her feet. 'I've given you a room on the ground floor, you don't look as though you're too good at stairs at the moment,' she said. 'Early November, isn't it?'

'What? Oh, yes, I think so.'

'Hmm. Two months. Come through here.' She led Amy down the passage and into a small room on the side of the house. There was a bed with a green coverlet, a small wardrobe with two drawers, a chair against one wall, and a washstand with jug and basin. Dark green drapes and a faded rug on the varnished wood of the floor completed the furnishings. The room smelt faintly of polish.

'You should have everything you need in here,' Mrs Kirkham said, putting Amy's bag down on the bed. 'You'll be hungry, I expect?'

'A little bit,' Amy admitted. Her stomach grumbled loudly at the suggestion of food after having been empty so long.

'Lunch will be in half an hour. I'll bring it in to you.'

'Oh, don't go to any trouble—I can come out for it.'

'I'd rather you didn't,' Mrs Kirkham said. 'I'd prefer to bring your meals to you. In fact, I'd be grateful if you didn't show yourself any more than you have to. The other guests, you understand. This is a decent house.' She looked meaningfully down at Amy's belly then went out, closing the door behind her.

Amy sank onto the bed and looked around at the four walls. *Do I have to stay in this room for the next two months?*

31

Jack stood on the wharf and watched the *Staffa* come in. As soon as the boat was close enough for him to make out individual figures, he saw Susannah standing beside Thomas on the deck, holding George and pointing towards the shore. When she saw Jack she smiled broadly, waved, and encouraged the little boys to wave too.

So she was pleased to see him. That surprised Jack; he could not remember Susannah's having shown any pleasure in his company for a long time. He looked at the three of them on the deck and thought of the one who was missing: Amy. It was unpleasant to think of the girl's being left among strangers, and even worse to think about the reason she had to be.

Still, it would all be put right soon. Amy would be a respectable married woman, and before too long she'd have another baby to take her mind off this one. A pity he couldn't have got a better man for her, but Susannah was right: not many men would take a girl who'd been shamed. And Amy seemed happy enough about it all, now she'd got used to the idea.

Thomas made a rush at Jack when he went onto the boat, winding his arms around his father's legs. 'Papa!' he cried in delight. Jack hoisted him in the air and sat the little boy on his shoulders before giving Susannah a chaste peck on the cheek and gathering up her luggage.

'Oh, Jack, I've had *such* a lovely time,' Susannah said animatedly, looking around to see that Jack had not missed anything before she followed him down the gangplank. She balanced George on one hip while she juggled two packages on her other arm. 'Everyone's been so nice.'

'I been sick,' Thomas announced.

'Yes, we've all been sick, Thomas—well, except George, he's quite a good sailor for some reason—that's nothing to boast about. That's the only trouble with going to Auckland.'

'So everything went all right?' Jack asked when he had settled them in the buggy.

'Just perfect. It was lovely to see Mother and Father again, and all my old friends. Every day I seemed to be going to someone's house for afternoon tea or they came to ours. We went to the theatre twice, too. And the shops—oh, it was wonderful to see real shops again.'

'You've bought plenty, I see,' Jack said, grimacing at the weight of one of Susannah's cases as he hefted it into the back of the buggy. He climbed in himself and flicked the reins.

'Well, a few things. I don't know how long it'll be before I get the chance to go back.'

'You must have made the money go a long way. I didn't give you all that much.'

Susannah's face took on a defensive look. 'Father gave me a little to spend. Oh, I *knew* you'd be awkward about that,' she said, seeing Jack's expression.

'Have you been telling your pa I don't keep you properly?'

'No, of course I haven't. I didn't ask him, it was Mother's idea, and I couldn't turn him down, could I? He hasn't had the chance to give me anything since I got married. Mother thought I was looking a little dowdy, and I had to humour her. Oh, don't be bad-tempered with me, Jack, I've been so looking forward to seeing you and telling you all about my holiday.'

Jack grunted. 'All right, don't get upset. I suppose there's no real harm in it, as long as you didn't go complaining about me.'

'Why would I do that? Oh, everyone was asking after you, they all sent their regards. They were all so impressed with my boys, too. Just think of it—Constance's son is nearly a year older than Thomas—well, eight months, anyway—and Thomas is a good inch taller than him! And Mother says George looks closer to eighteen months than thirteen. They all said it must be the healthy life in the country, all the clean air and good food.' She looked about her. 'The air certainly is fresh here, isn't it?'

'They're fine boys, all right,' Jack said, smiling fondly at his little sons.

'And Constance has another one coming!' Susannah said on a note of triumph. 'She's nearly three months gone. That'll be her fourth. She's got terribly matronly-looking—no wonder. Really, no one would think she's two years younger than me now.'

'Perhaps she's fond of children. Perhaps she's fond of her husband, come to that.'

'Jack, there's no need to talk like that, especially in front of the children. Actually, I thought Henry seemed rather irritable—I expect he gets tired of broken nights all the time. It's different for Constance, anyway—she has a nursemaid in the daytime, and a general servant to do the rough work.'

'I know. You've told me that before. How's my girl?'

'What?' Susannah seemed taken aback for a moment. 'Oh, she's all right.'

'Did you see her yesterday?'

'No, I was busy packing and saying goodbye to everyone.'

'Well, when did you last see her, then?'

'It's a very nice place where she's staying, I'm sure she's fine, she's a healthy girl.'

'When did you last see her, Susannah?'

Susannah seemed reluctant to meet his eyes. 'I saw her settled in all right the day we arrived. I've been busy ever since.'

'You mean you haven't been back to see her since the first day?' Jack demanded.

'How could I? Constance thought it was only your niece, and Mother and Father don't know anything about it—they thought I'd just come to see them and show them the children. I couldn't go wandering off by myself all the time, could I? It's quite a long way from Parnell, too, I would've had to take the phaeton, and Mother would've wanted to come too.'

'I thought you'd keep an eye on her. That's why I sent you—and why I let you stay two weeks.'

'Do you begrudge me a holiday after three years? I did what I could, I went to see the nursing home, and the woman who'll arrange the adoption. And I left my address with the landlady, she would have contacted me if there'd been any trouble.'

'I wanted you to check up on Amy.'

'Shh,' Susannah hissed, but it was too late.

'Amy?' Thomas said, looking around. 'Where Amy gone? Want Amy.'

'Now you've done it,' Susannah said. 'He grizzled for Amy the first few days until I managed to take his mind off her—Mother thought it was quite strange for him to be pining so much for his sister. I had a lot of trouble getting him off to sleep at night. Amy's not here, Thomas, do be quiet.'

'Want Amy!' Thomas complained, and George joined in. 'Amy!' the two little boys chorused.

'Stop it!' Susannah snapped. 'Papa will smack you if you don't be quiet.'

'Settle down,' Jack warned them, but he made no move to hit either child. He had no intention of punishing them for missing Amy as much as he did. 'Here, I got them some lollies in town.' He passed a paper bag to Susannah. She looked rather disapprovingly at the toffees, then sighed and gave the little boys one each. They were soon sticky-faced and happy.

'So now we just have to wait, do we?' Jack said when they had turned

310

off the road and on to the beach.

'Yes. The nursing home will send us a cable when it's all over.'

Jack grimaced. 'I wish she didn't have to be left with strangers. I don't know if this Auckland thing was such a good idea.'

'She'll be all right. The landlady seemed quite a motherly type, she'll take Amy under her wing.'

Jack was lost in his thoughts as they drove along the beach, with Susannah quieting the children every few minutes by giving them another toffee. He hardly noticed when he turned the buggy away from the beach and up the familiar valley road.

Susannah looked around the farm with a new awareness when they reached the boundary. 'Five hundred acres really is quite big, isn't it? All Father's friends seemed very impressed.'

'It's the same size it's always been,' Jack said shortly, his mind still on Amy.

'I know, but I hadn't really thought about it. I suppose I'd got used to it. It's only when you're talking to people, and you say "five hundred acres" and see how impressed they look, that you realise what a big farm it is. Some of my friends said they'd like to come down for a visit.'

'Tell them not to bother. I haven't got any more daughters to be ruined.'

'Jack! What a terrible mood you're in. You're not a bit pleased to see me, are you?' Her voice trembled a little, and Jack wavered between guilt and irritation.

'I'm pleased to see you,' he said gruffly. 'I'm just thinking about my girl, that's all.'

'Don't worry about her, I'm sure she'll be just fine.'

'I hope so,' Jack muttered, more to himself than to her.

'Well, I suppose I'd better start getting dinner on,' Susannah said when she had unpacked and tidied herself and the children up. 'I'm quite hungry after that long trip. How has that girl been managing? Has she been feeding you properly?'

'Yes, Lizzie's not a bad cook. She talks too much, but she gets a good feed on the table.' Jack mused on the last two weeks. It had been something like the old days, when Lizzie had often come to stay with Amy. No Susannah, no dark silences from Harry. No little boys, either, though he had missed them. Yes, a lot like the old days. Except that Amy was missing.

'She doesn't seem to have done any cleaning,' Susannah said, running a finger along the dresser and wrinkling her nose at the dust she picked up.

'I suppose she had her own work to do at home. She still had to help her ma, and it was good of Edie to spare her at all to get the meals on for us. She took our washing home with her on Sundays and brought it back ironed.'

'Humph! I'll have a lot of catching up to do, getting things straight again.' She sighed heavily.

Susannah was sleeping soundly when Jack woke next morning. He dressed quietly so as not to disturb her, before joining his sons in the cow shed.

The three of them worked up their usual hearty appetites. When they walked into the kitchen Jack looked around the empty room in confusion, wondering why there was no welcoming aroma of bacon and eggs. But the range was cold and the pans were empty; there was nothing but a pile of last night's unwashed dishes on the bench.

'There's no breakfast,' John said in amazement.

'She's still in bed,' Harry added in disgust.

'She must have slept in a bit,' Jack said, trying to hide his annoyance. 'She's probably just coming now.'

He stomped down the passage and into his bedroom, to find Susannah sound asleep. He shook her shoulder, not roughly but enough to make her stir.

'Ohh, go away,' Susannah said drowsily. 'I'm so tired.'

'Susannah, wake up.' Jack gave her another shake. 'There's no breakfast! The range hasn't even been lit.'

'It's so *early*. I'm still asleep. Can't you do it?' She tried to pull the sheet over her head, but Jack tugged it out of her hand. He swept the covers right off, revealing Susannah's legs up to the thighs where her nightdress had ridden up.

That got a reaction. 'What are you doing?' She pulled her nightdress down over her legs and cast a resentful look at Jack through half-closed eyes.

'Helping you wake up. For goodness sake, Susannah, you've got three hungry men in the house waiting for you. We've been up and working for a couple of hours already—you can't lie in bed all day.'

'But I'm so tired after that long trip. And I'm not used to getting up so early—no one gets up before eight at home in Parnell.'

'I expect that servant you're always on about gets up earlier than that. And you're not in Parnell now. Hurry up and get dressed.' He sat down on the bed and waited.

'I wish I was still there,' Susannah muttered, but she clambered out of bed and staggered over to the wardrobe. 'Do you have to sit there?' she

312

asked, poised to unbutton her nightdress.

'I don't want you going back to sleep.' Jack did not add that he had no wish to face his sons with the news that they would have to wait for Susannah to get dressed before even the preparations for breakfast could start. 'I can sit in my own bedroom, can't I?'

'You're putting me off, looking at me like that,' Susannah complained, making no move to take off her nightdress.

'I won't look, then.' Jack turned his face towards the window, and wondered how a woman who had borne him two children could still behave as though she had never lain with a man. Well, he had no intention of ever again giving her the chance to accuse him of forcing her. He tried not to think about those smooth, white thighs of hers, or her breasts, surprisingly full for a woman as thin as Susannah.

There were black looks from John and Harry when Jack at last brought Susannah out to the kitchen, but Harry still maintained his stony silence towards his stepmother. The bacon was a little underdone when the meal was finally set before the men, but by that time they were all so hungry that they were grateful for anything. After the bacon and eggs they devoured one of the loaves Lizzie had brought over the previous day, along with some of Amy's marmalade. Then the men went off to get on with their much-delayed work while Susannah took herself back to the bedroom to do her hair and get her sons up.

Susannah's cheerful mood had not survived her return by many hours, and Jack felt a slight regret at its loss, but he shrugged it off. She had her work to do, and it was no use her making a fuss about it.

Lunch and dinner appeared on the table at the proper times, but Jack was not going to risk a repeat of the first morning's performance. Next day he made no attempt to get up quietly, and as soon as he had dressed he gave Susannah a firm shake.

'I'm going out now,' he said. 'You'd better get breakfast on soon.' Susannah gave a grunt and rolled further away. 'Susannah!' he said more sharply. 'Wake up.'

Susannah opened her eyes a fraction. 'But it's not even light yet,' she protested. 'I don't need to start for ages.'

'If I leave you lying in bed you'll go back to sleep. I want to see you sitting up before I leave this room.'

'It's a ridiculous time to wake up.' Susannah sat up in bed and glared at him. 'I'm awake. Are you satisfied?'

'I'll be satisfied if you've got breakfast on the table when we've finished milking.'

To his relief, breakfast was ready for them when they came back, and this time it was well-cooked. It was only when the bacon and eggs had been eaten that he realised something was missing from the table.

'Where's the bread?' he asked.

'There doesn't seem to be any,' Susannah said. 'I think you ate the last of it with dinner yesterday.'

'But… but I want some bread,' John said, frowning in confusion. There had always been bread before.

'Well, you can't have any, can you?' said Susannah. 'Goodness me, you've had plenty to eat without filling up on bread.'

'There's no bread, Pa,' Harry said, looking accusingly at Susannah.

'I know that,' Jack said shortly. 'Shut up about it.'

But when his sons went out, Jack remained behind. 'Why isn't there any bread?' he asked.

'I don't know, I just didn't think of it. Anyway, when did I have the time for that sort of thing yesterday?'

'You should have done it last night. You haven't done the dinner dishes, either,' he added, looking at the greasy pile on the bench.

'If you're going to make me get up before daybreak I've got to go to bed early, haven't I? You can't expect me to sit up half the night doing dishes and baking. And I'm busy all day looking after the children.'

'Well, you'd better get on and bake some now. We'll want it with lunch.'

'No,' Susannah said, her lower lip protruding slightly.

'What do you mean, "No"?'

'I can't bake it.'

'Why not? You can't be as busy as all that.'

'Because I don't know how. Don't look at me like that.'

'Are you telling me you've never baked a loaf of bread in your life?'

'I never had to. We always bought it at home. The baker's boy came to the door.'

Jack stared at her in amazement. 'You mean that in the three years you've lived here you've never so much as once made the bread?'

'Amy always did it. I had plenty of other things to do, looking after the children and cooking meals.'

'Cooking? You never cooked breakfast, did you? You always left that for Amy as well. I thought you were running the house. Damn it, I gave you authority over things—the lady of the house, I called you. I put you in charge of Amy. And all the time she was doing the work. She's been making the bread every day, and I never even noticed!' Jack shook his head over his own obtuseness.

'Do you begrudge the bit of help Amy gave me? I was with child all during the first two years, how could I manage all that work as well?'

'You're not with child now, I know that for a fact. And you'd better get some bread made.'

'I can't! I don't know how!' Tears were welling in Susannah's eyes, but Jack refused to be moved.

'You'll have to learn, then. Go over and see Edie, she'll show you how. There can't be that much to it.' He glanced at the bench, where flies were crawling over the dirty dishes. 'You'd better do those dishes first.'

Susannah glared at him. 'Don't talk to me as though I was a servant.'

'Servant? Yes, that's what you accused me of wanting, isn't it? A nursemaid for Amy—well, she'll be off your hands altogether soon enough. You won't have her help then, either.'

'She's always been more trouble than help.'

'Has she? Then you won't mind managing without her. What was it? A nursemaid, an unpaid servant, and what else? Something else unpaid?'

'Don't bring all that up again, Jack.'

'Listen to me, Susannah. I'll tell you what I do expect of you. I expect you to keep the place decent and get reasonable meals on the table. That and look after the little fellows. That's all I ask of you. Understand? Nothing else. That's not too much to ask, is it?'

'It's enough,' Susannah muttered.

'Maybe. But it's not too much. So get on with it.'

Amy hoped the days would start going faster when she had got used to her life in the boarding house. But even after weeks had passed, there still seemed to be the same number of hours in each day, and each of her waking hours dragged.

She came to know the room intimately, from the details of the pattern on the rug down to the tiny nicks in the paint of the windowsill. The window looked onto the blank wall of a house much the same as the one she was in. If she opened it and leaned out, all she could see was a hedge behind the boarding house in one direction, with the barest glimpse of a large windmill beyond it, and the front fence in the other.

There was absolutely nothing she needed to do. That was the hardest thing of all to get used to. Mrs Kirkham brought her meals in on a tray, and collected the tray when she had finished. That was the only time Amy saw another human being. If she had wanted, there was nothing to stop her lying in bed all day. But although getting out of bed became more and more of an exertion, she made herself get up, get dressed and tidy the bed. At least it filled in the first ten minutes of the day, and let her feel a tiny bit useful.

At first Amy tried to keep track of the days, but each was so much like the one before that she had to give up the attempt. She knew when it was a Sunday, because she could hear church bells ringing, but she lost count of Sundays after the first few. She wished she could write to Lizzie, but that would have meant begging paper and money for postage from Mrs Kirkham. She could tell the landlady was reluctant to have any more to do with her than she had to.

Even walking around the room became an effort, as her bulk increased and her muscles grew weaker from lack of use. For a time Amy tried to count out ten circuits of the room every morning and afternoon, but gradually it began to seem a better idea to spend the day just sitting by the window, looking at the wall or the hedge or the fence.

Amy was watching the shifting patterns of sunlight on the blank wall one day when Mrs Kirkham came in with her lunch. She still felt awkward at being waited on, but that was a tiny part of her discomfort.

Mrs Kirkham, as usual, made a small effort at conversation. 'It's getting warmer lately.'

'Yes,' Amy agreed.

'Not long till summer, really. It'll be November before long.'

'November—will it? What's the date today, Mrs Kirkham?'

'The sixteenth.'

'Of October?'

'Yes. It's Thursday.' She looked anxiously at Amy. 'There's nothing special about the date, is there? I thought you weren't due till November. Around the tenth of November, your aunt said.'

'Yes, that's right—that's what she told me, anyway. No, it's just that...' She trailed off. She was quite sure Mrs Kirkham would not be interested in knowing that Amy had turned sixteen three days before.

'Didn't you even know what month it was?' Mrs Kirkham asked, frowning slightly.

'No. Every day's the same, you see.' Amy tried to smile.

'Would you like a paper to read?'

'Yes, please!' Amy said, hoping she didn't sound too eager.

Mrs Kirkham disappeared, and was soon back with a *New Zealand Herald*. 'It's yesterday's, I'm afraid. Still, I expect you're not too worried about that.'

Amy would have been happy with a paper ten years old. She devoured the newspaper from cover to cover, even reading all the tiny advertisements for grazing and stock feed. It was the happiest waking half-hour she had spent since she had arrived in Auckland.

After that Mrs Kirkham brought her a newspaper with breakfast every day, along with an occasional ladies' paper. Amy only wished she could have had more than an hour or so's worth of reading to help the day along. The chair became too uncomfortable after another week or two, and she took to sitting on the bed all day, though she still made the effort to get dressed every morning.

Amy woke early on the first of November, and was annoyed when she realised it was barely sunrise. That meant it was only about five o'clock, so it would be two hours or more before Mrs Kirkham came in with her breakfast. Two hours to lie in bed, too uncomfortable even to toss and turn.

She felt more uncomfortable than usual this morning, with a dull ache low in her back. When she twisted around to try and find a better way to lie, the discomfort seemed to spread out. The pain became sharp for a few seconds, then to Amy's relief it faded away. She lay very still, hoping to drift back to sleep, and she had managed to fall into a light doze when the ache returned. Again it lasted barely a minute, but Amy was thoroughly awake by now. It was no use even trying to sleep if she was going to be disturbed every few minutes. The baby had chosen an awkward time to be active this morning.

She got up, put on the green dress, and made the bed, interrupted in the task by another wave of pain. Then she drew the curtains and sat by the window in the sunshine to re-read one of Mrs Kirkham's magazines. She almost knew the articles off by heart now.

But it was hard to concentrate when every twenty minutes or so the ache would spread across her back again. Each pain did not last long, but while it was there it took all her attention. She put the magazine down in disgust, and by the time Mrs Kirkham brought her breakfast Amy was pacing the floor, her hands braced against her back.

Mrs Kirkham took one look at her and put the tray down on the washstand. 'Where does it hurt?'

'Oh, it's nothing much, only a bit of backache. It's just a bit worse than what I've had up till now.'

'Low in your back? And spreading across towards your hips?'

'Yes.'

'And is it coming and going?'

'Well, yes, it is. It lasts a minute or so, then it goes away for... oh, I don't know, maybe quarter of an hour.'

'It's started. You won't want this,' Mrs Kirkham said, glancing at the breakfast tray. 'I'll pack your things.' She opened the wardrobe and pulled out Amy's case and her other dress.

'What's started? What are you doing?'

'The child's coming.' She lifted Amy's underwear in a heap from the drawer and shoved it into the case, then looked around the room to see if she had missed anything.

'But it's not time yet,' Amy protested. 'Not for another week at least.'

'Babies come when they're ready, not when you are. My first was two weeks ahead of time. You wait there, I'll run out and find a cab.' She darted out of the room, leaving Amy wide-eyed and trembling.

So it had started, and she had been too stupid to notice. She wished she knew just what was going to happen. She had seen enough calves being born to know that the baby was going to come out from between her legs, though it was hard to believe there was enough room for it. She remembered hearing Susannah cry out through the wall before the chloroform had silenced her, but Aunt Edie had said that wasn't real pain. Susannah had told her she wouldn't have to know what was happening, because the chloroform would make her sleep, but Susannah had said it was terrible when she had Thomas and George. Of course Susannah always made an awful fuss about everything; maybe it wouldn't be too bad. And the chloroform would take away the pain before it was too hard to bear.

Mrs Kirkham was soon back, and she helped Amy on with her cloak. 'We'll be on our way, then. Oh, just one thing, Miss Leith.' She pulled a piece of paper from her apron pocket; Amy saw that it was a ten-shilling note. 'Your aunt left extra money in case I needed to cable her, and you're leaving me a week earlier than I expected, anyway. I don't want money I'm not entitled to.' She slipped the note into the bottom of Amy's case, then helped her outside to the waiting cab.

The nursing home was only a few minutes' drive away. Mrs Kirkham was soon leading Amy up a short flight of steps and through an open door. They went a little way down an echoing corridor and into a room where a severe-looking woman with her hair scraped under a white cap sat behind a desk, writing in a large notebook. She looked up from her writing when Amy and Mrs Kirkham walked in.

'I've a patient for you,' Mrs Kirkham said. 'I believe she's booked in, though it's a week or so early. Miss Leith.'

'Miss?' the woman at the desk echoed. She looked disapprovingly at Amy.

'Yes. Miss Elizabeth Leith.'

The woman glanced down at her book and flipped over a page. 'I have an Amy Leith written down.'

'That's me,' Amy put in. 'My name's Amy.'

Mrs Kirkham looked at her in surprise. 'Your aunt told me your name was Elizabeth.'

'It's not. It's Amy.' *And she's not my aunt.*

'Her pains have started?' the nurse asked Mrs Kirkham.

'Yes. This morning, I believe.' As if on cue, Amy felt another pain. She grimaced at it.

'Right, we'll soon have you sorted out.' The nurse rose from her chair, picked up the suitcase, took Amy's arm and propelled her down the corridor. When Amy turned to thank Mrs Kirkham, the landlady had already gone.

The nurse led Amy into a small room that contained an iron bedstead and little else. 'I'm Sister Prescott,' she said. 'Get undressed.' It was obvious from her voice that she was not used to being disobeyed. Amy slipped off her cloak and unbuttoned her dress as quickly as she could. 'You're not married,' Sister Prescott said.

'No,' Amy admitted, her voice muffled through the fabric of her dress as she pulled it over her head.

The nurse made a noise of disgust. 'I don't particularly like having young whores in my nursing home.'

'I'm not a whore,' Amy protested feebly. She was not sure exactly what a whore was, but from her father's reaction when Susannah had called her that name she knew it must be a very wicked sort of girl.

'What do you call yourself, then? You're not a decent married woman, are you?' Amy said nothing. 'Come on, take the rest of your things off, then put this on.' She pointed to a long robe that lay across the end of the bed, then watched as Amy removed her underwear. It was hard to strip under Sister Prescott's gaze, but she knew it would be no use asking the nurse to look away. She snatched at the gown and pulled it on quickly, the coarse linen rasping at her flesh.

The nurse pulled back the sheet and made Amy lie down. She washed her hands at a basin in one corner of the room and came back to the bed. She pushed Amy's knees up and out, so that the girl was lying with her legs sprawled wide apart, and started prodding at Amy's abdomen. Sister Prescott's touch was rough, and Amy cried out in shock.

'What are you doing to me?'

'Seeing if the child's lying right. Now I want to see how far along you are. Quiet.' Amy could not see what the nurse was doing, but she felt hands probing between her thighs. She managed to smother a cry of distress when the probing became more painful. 'Only two fingers dilated,' she heard the nurse mutter, but it meant nothing to Amy.

'Nothing's going to happen before evening,' Sister Prescott said, withdrawing her hands and wiping them on a cloth.

Another wave of pain spread out from Amy's back; this time it was sharper, and seemed to spread out further. 'Sister,' she said timidly when the wave had passed, 'it hurts a bit when the pains come.'

'I know it does. It's the worst pain a woman can endure. That's nothing, what you're feeling now. Come evening, you'll know what pain is.'

'When will you give me something?'

'What are you talking about?'

'Something to take the pain away. Chloroform.'

'I don't waste chloroform on bad girls like you. That's for easing the pain of respectable women.'

Fear gripped Amy like a hand clutching at her heart. 'But... but it'll get really bad later, won't it?'

'Yes, it will. I want you to remember it afterwards. I don't want to see you back here in twelve months carrying another bastard. That's what happens when things are made too easy for bad girls.'

Amy was too frightened for tears, but her voice trembled as she spoke. 'But what if I can't bear it?'

The nurse leaned over her and spoke quietly. 'You'll have to bear it, won't you? And you should have thought about that before you lay with a man who wasn't your husband.' She went out, shutting the door behind her with a slam that rang against the bare walls of the room. Amy felt the noise echoing inside her head like a throbbing pain.

32

November 1884

Amy lay on the hard bed waiting for each new wave of pain. At first she tried to be brave and tell herself it wasn't too bad, she could bear this, but as the day wore on the pains became stronger and more persistent. When each one came she tensed against it. Her clenched jaw soon ached, a discomfort that remained steady as the sharper pain waxed and waned.

Every hour or so a nurse would look in on her, either Sister Prescott or another, slightly younger, woman whom Sister Prescott called Nurse Julian. She was no gentler than the other nurse when she probed Amy to check the progress of her labour. Amy had no pride left to make her try and hide her tears, but weeping gave no relief.

She measured the passing of the hours by the changing faces around her. Nurse Julian took over in the afternoon, then disappeared to be replaced by Sister Prescott. When Amy opened her eyes from one particularly severe contraction she saw that the room was dimmer. The day was nearly over.

There seemed to be nothing left of her but the pain. The waves that squeezed her like a giant fist came every few minutes now, and left her whimpering and shaking.

When all the daylight had gone and the lamps had been lit for hours, Nurse Julian came back. The two women stood over Amy and discussed her.

'Still not fully dilated,' Sister Prescott said, after probing Amy once more. 'She's going to be a long while yet.'

'She's going to have a hard time of it,' Nurse Julian said. 'She doesn't seem very strong.'

'Too much sitting around, that's her trouble. Her muscles have gone. There's nothing to be done here for now, come and have a cup of tea.' They left her alone again.

The lamps seemed unnaturally bright. Amy squeezed her eyes shut against them and saw red shapes as the light flickered. She wondered how long 'a long while' was, when she had been labouring since the early hours. The pain clutched at her again, even stronger now. She bit on her fist to stop herself from crying out.

Hours later she saw blood on her hand from the bites, but she had no attention to spare for that. The pains were too intense for her to keep silent any longer. She screamed, and found it gave a tiny scrap of relief.

She half-expected the nurses to come running, but she was left alone to scream as pain gripped her. Amy felt a warm wetness flooding out from her; she wondered if it was blood. *Maybe I'm going to bleed to death.* The thought carried no fear. Death would bring relief from the pain.

When the women did come back, Amy did not even feel Sister Prescott's rough handling, so tuned was her body to the greater pain. 'Good, the waters have burst and she's fully dilated at last,' Sister Prescott said. 'Nearly midnight, too. Now the real pain starts,' she said, addressing Amy for the first time since that morning.

Amy felt an irresistible urge to push, although pushing seemed to make the pain even worse. She pushed and screamed, pushed and screamed. It went on and on, and nothing seemed to change except that the pain racked her with ever-increasing intensity. Her whole body was soon drenched with perspiration. Sweat ran off her forehead and into her eyes, making them sting.

'She's taking a long time.' That was Nurse Julian's voice. 'How long are you going to let her try?'

'Another couple of hours won't matter,' Sister Prescott said. 'Leave her to yell her head off for a bit.'

The door closed, and Amy knew she was alone again. She screamed, but screaming no longer gave any relief. And she was so tired. Her head was trying to tell her to push, but her body rebelled. *Why do I have to push? Maybe if I lie very, very still it won't hurt so much. I have to push. I can't push any more.* She pushed and screamed, then she lay limp. *Yes, that doesn't hurt as much.* Her body pushed feebly, but the urge was weaker. It grew weaker still, and Amy let exhaustion wash over her. The slight lessening of pain was like pleasure. *Oh, yes, that's much better.* Her jaw unclenched and her eyes closed.

Amy did not know how much later it was when the nurses returned.

'She's going out of labour!' she heard Nurse Julian say.

'Come on, push again, you lazy girl,' Sister Prescott said, shaking Amy's shoulders roughly.

'I can't,' Amy murmured. 'I can't push.'

'Forceps?' Nurse Julian asked.

'That means getting a doctor, and it's after three in the morning.' Sister Prescott leaned close to Amy. 'Listen, girl. Do you want me to get a doctor to you? He'll stick his instruments up inside you to rip the baby out. Do you want that?'

'Leave me alone,' Amy mumbled.

'I won't leave you alone. Either I get the doctor in with his butcher's tools—then you'll think your insides are being ripped out—or you start pushing again. What's it to be?'

Her words slowly penetrated, and Amy roused herself enough to give a feeble push. The pain brought her back to full consciousness, and for a moment she tried to resist the urge, but she knew that the terrible woman meant it. If Amy didn't push, then a man would come and pull her apart with bits of metal. She pushed harder and screamed.

'That's better!' Sister Prescott said with satisfaction.

There was no longer a rest between bursts of pain. Now it was all one long scream. The screams seemed to come when she breathed in as well as when she exhaled, so that there was no break in the wailing noise that echoed round and round the bare walls of the room.

She felt her body being ripped. *I'm going to die. There's no room. The baby can't get out because there's no room.* Still she pushed, even though she knew it was tearing her apart. *How long before I die? I hope it's not long.* There was a tearing pain, even worse than all that had gone before, and a scream that seemed to take the top of her head off, then she lay flat and unresponsive. It was over. She had no more to give. It didn't matter if the butcher-man came to rip her apart; she had already been torn in half.

Through the silence that replaced her screams she heard a strange mewling sound. Sister Prescott took a step back from the bed, holding aloft a tiny, bloodied creature. 'It's a girl,' she announced.

Amy slowly became aware that the horror was over and she was not dead. The searing agony was replaced by rhythmic throbbing that gradually subsided to a background discomfort. Every few moments her body was racked by a fresh wave of trembling. She felt bruised all over.

Sister Prescott disappeared from the room with the little creature, leaving Nurse Julian to deliver the afterbirth. The nurse massaged Amy's abdomen firmly, making Amy cry out with the pain of it. 'Be quiet,' Nurse Julian ordered. 'I've got to do this if you don't want to bleed to death.' She continued until she was satisfied with the results. 'You're not really made for childbearing,' the nurse told Amy as she cleaned the blood and mucus from her loins. Amy's flesh burned and stung at the nurse's touch; she whimpered at it. 'You're too small. Especially if the father was a big man.'

The door opened again. 'Prop her up a bit,' Sister Prescott said, advancing on the bed. Nurse Julian slipped pillows behind Amy and helped her sit up. It hurt, but she was beyond complaining. If the pain would only weaken a little, she would fall asleep in spite of it. 'We'll get her to suckle it for a minute to help the milk come in.'

Nurse Julian undid the buttons of Amy's bodice and peeled it open. She took a small, blanket-wrapped bundle from Sister Prescott and placed it on Amy's chest.

Amy looked down to see a tiny creature lying in her arms. It had a little rosebud mouth and huge, blue-grey eyes. The eyes, though unfocussed, studied her with a strangely knowing expression. Its head was covered with a thick, black mop of hair. Nurse Julian nudged the baby on to one of Amy's breasts and its mouth nuzzled at her, exploring the flesh before it began to suckle.

A rush of emotion flooded through Amy as the baby pulled at her breast. She looked at the child in wonder. *My baby. I made you. You're perfect.* Her fingers brushed against the baby's face, feeling the softness of her skin. 'Little one,' she murmured close to the tiny ear. 'My little one.'

She looked up at the unmoved faces of the two women. 'She's beautiful.'

'All mothers think their babies are beautiful,' Sister Prescott scoffed. 'But I think that one is going to be pretty, once her head gets to its proper shape. She'll look like you. I hope she turns out better.'

Nurse Julian fetched a cradle and placed it beside the bed, while Sister Prescott put the baby to Amy's other breast. After what seemed only moments, Sister Prescott took her from Amy and placed her in the cradle, ignoring Amy's feeble attempts to push the nurse's hands away. She found that if she leaned over the edge of the bed, ignoring the pain moving brought, she could just see the baby's face.

'She'll sleep now,' Sister Prescott said. 'You will, too.' Both women left the room.

Amy was sure she would not sleep. All she wanted to do was lie and watch her baby, fascinated by each tiny movement of the head, each little grimace on that beautiful little face. But it was not long before weariness overwhelmed her elation. She closed her eyes and dropped into an exhausted sleep.

All Amy's waking moments now centred on her baby. As soon as she opened her eyes she would check the cradle. Sometimes it was empty, and she knew that one of the nurses had taken the baby away to wash her or change her. Sometimes the little girl was asleep, and Amy would watch her making tiny movements while her eyes stayed tight shut, listening to the strange little snuffling noises the baby's breathing made. And sometimes she was awake, and those were the best times of all. Amy would lie and watch the baby turning her head from one side to the other as though she were trying to comprehend her surroundings, and wait until hunger led to the little mewling cries that would summon a nurse to lift her into Amy's arms.

Amy's milk came in on the second day. Feeding was the only time she was allowed to hold her baby, and the hours between each one dragged. When a nurse lifted the baby into her arms Amy kissed her and held her close, whispering her love into the little girl's shell-like ears. She tried to prolong these precious moments as much as she could, but one of the nurses would always come back into the room and take the baby away much too soon.

In the afternoon of the day her baby turned one week old, Amy looked up from the child in her arms to see Sister Prescott standing close beside the bed.

'Is that child still feeding?' the nurse asked suspiciously.

'Yes,' Amy said, sneaking a nipple back into the slack mouth. *Suck, little one,* she begged. As if she understood, the baby began sucking vigorously. 'You see?' Amy said, smiling at her baby's cleverness.

'Hmm. She's a slow feeder, then. She's still feeding every two hours, too, she shouldn't take that long over it.' She looked at Amy through narrowed eyes. 'Don't you go getting too fond of that child. You know you have to give her away.'

'I know,' Amy said, holding her baby tighter.

When they were alone again, Amy whispered to her. 'I have to give you away, little one. Your father doesn't want us, and I can't keep you on my own. I hope you'll understand when you grow up. I love you, that's why I have to give you away. It's best for you. You'll have people to look after you properly, and no one will call you horrible names.' A tear dropped onto the baby's face, and Amy kissed it away carefully. The baby stared up at her with bright eyes, as though she understood every word.

A week later Sister Prescott told Amy, 'You're having a visitor this afternoon.'

'A visitor? Who? I don't know anyone in Auckland.'

'You'll see.'

That afternoon Amy was feeding her baby when Sister Prescott came in with a short, plump woman who looked to be in her late forties. She wore a straw hat covered with some unlikely-looking fruit, jammed onto a thatch of brown hair streaked with grey. Her mouth and cheeks seemed unnaturally red, and Amy stared curiously at her until she realised that here, perhaps, was one of those women who *painted*. She noticed Sister Prescott giving the woman a disapproving glance as she left. Amy could not help but feel more positive towards the visitor.

The woman pulled the one chair that the room contained close to Amy's bed and sat down, panting a little as though the effort had taken all her energy. 'I'm Mrs Crossley. You're Miss Leith, aren't you?' Amy nodded, wondering what this woman had to do with her. 'Mrs Leith visited me a little while ago,' Mrs Crossley said. 'I only live a few streets away from here, so I thought I'd pop down to see you today.'

Amy gripped her baby more tightly; the little girl let out a small whimper of surprise. 'You've come to take my baby away.'

'Not just yet. But yes, your stepmother asked me to arrange an adoption for the child. You did know that, didn't you?' Mrs Crossley asked, a little uncertainly.

Amy looked down at the baby until she felt her face was under control. 'Yes, I know. When are you going to take her away?'

'The baby's too young just yet, it won't be for... oh, another week or two. It's too hard to rear them without their mother's milk if they're too tiny.' Mrs Crossley looked at the baby suckling, then looked away as if the sight bothered her.

'Good,' Amy whispered. 'They will be good people, won't they? The people you give my baby to?'

'Oh, yes. I get a very nice class of people coming to me for babies. Always well-set up types, often businessmen and suchlike, people who can't have children of their own.'

'Will they be kind to her? Do you think they'll love her?' Without giving the woman time to answer, Amy rushed on. 'She's pretty, isn't she? That might help the people like her. And she's going to be clever, I think. See the way she watches things? So knowing. And look at this.' She held her finger a few inches from the baby's face and moved it slowly; the little girl's eyes followed the movement. 'She's been doing that since she was only two days old. My little brothers were nearly a week old before they did that. She's always taking notice of noises and things, too.'

'She's a fine little girl,' said Mrs Crossley.

'Will they love her?' Amy pleaded. 'Will they be kind to her? I want them to be kind to her.'

'I'm sure they will. Remember, these are people who may have longed for a little girl of their own for years. They'll make a great fuss of this one.'

'I hope so,' Amy murmured.

She looked up from the baby and saw that Mrs Crossley was staring at her, her mouth twisted oddly. 'You're very young,' the woman said quietly. Then her face took on a bland expression. 'Now,' she said briskly, 'I want to register the little girl so she'll have a birth certificate. I'll have to ask you a few questions.' She pulled a dog-eared notebook and a pencil from a large bag she carried.

'She was born on the second of November, wasn't she? That's what the nurse told me.'

'I think that's right. Sister Prescott knows the date better than me. Yes, it was the second.'

'All right. Now I need her name. What are you calling her?'

'Oh. I haven't given her a name yet. I just call her...' *Little one. That's what I call you. That's what your father used to call me.* 'I haven't given her one yet.'

'Well, what do you think you'd like to call her?' Amy chewed her lip thoughtfully. 'Would you like to give her your mother's name?' Mrs Crossley prompted. 'Lots of girls do that.'

'Yes,' Amy grasped at the suggestion. 'Yes, I'll call her Ann. My mother was called Ann.'

'Ann.' Mrs Crossley wrote in her book. 'Just Ann? Or do you want to give her a second name? Perhaps your own name?'

'No, she mustn't have my name. People might think she's like me.' Amy struggled to think of a name good enough for her little girl. 'I know. I want her to be Ann Elizabeth. Those are good names, aren't they?'

'Very good names. Ann Elizabeth Leith. Very nice. And your full name?'

'Amy Louisa Leith. Why doesn't she have her father's surname?'

'Because you're not married to him. How old are you?'

'Fifteen—no, I'm sixteen,' she corrected herself.

'And where were you born?'

'Ruatane. It's in the Bay of Plenty,' she added, seeing the blank expression on Mrs Crossley's face. 'But I'm not exactly sure... her father's probably twenty-one now, but he might still be twenty. And I don't know for sure that he was born in Auckland. I think he was, though.'

Mrs Crossley held up a hand to interrupt the flow. 'I don't need to know those things.'

'But don't they have to go on her birth certificate? Why do you need to know things about me and not her father?'

'There won't be anything about her father on the certificate. It'll just say "Illegitimate", and the place where the father's details should go will be left blank.'

'No,' Amy breathed. 'You can't do that! That would make it look as though I didn't know who her father was. I do know who he is, I do! Why can't it be on her birth certificate?'

'It's just the way these things are done when a child's illegitimate. You see, otherwise you could say any name you wanted, and the man wouldn't be able to defend himself.'

'I wouldn't do that.'

Mrs Crossley studied her thoughtfully. 'No, I don't think you would. But I'm afraid some girls would, so that's why it's the rule.'

'She'll hate me,' Amy whispered. 'She'll hate me when she sees a big blank space on her birth certificate. She'll think I was a…' *whore*.

'Now come along, it's nothing to get upset over,' Mrs Crossley said. 'There's no need to go talking about anyone hating anyone else. The child won't be told anything about you until she's old enough to understand how things were, and by that time it'll all be so long ago that she probably won't even be very interested.' She shut her notebook with a snap and put it back in her bag.

'Won't she?' Amy said wistfully. 'No, I suppose she won't.' She studied the baby in her arms and stroked her hair. An idea struck her. 'Mrs Crossley, can I give her something?'

'What do you mean, dear?'

'Could I give you something to look after for her? Then you could give it to the people who take her.'

'All right.'

Amy craned her neck to see her case, leaning against the wall under the window. 'Please would you bring my case over here? I'm not allowed up yet.'

Mrs Crossley laid the case on the bed. Amy fumbled the catch open, then reached around inside. She had to dislodge Ann from her breast to free her hands, but the little girl lay contentedly nestled in one arm while Amy rummaged, only the working of her mouth showing that she was still hungry.

Amy pulled the small box and the tangle of ribbon that surrounded it from the case. She opened the box and took out the brooch. For a moment she studied it as it lay in her palm. She reached out and traced the outline of the 'A' with one finger. Then she held her hand out towards Mrs Crossley. 'I want her to have this.'

Mrs Crossley reached for the brooch, then stopped and looked doubtfully at Amy. 'This looks rather valuable. Are you sure it's all right for you to give it away?'

'Yes. It's mine to give.'

'You're quite sure?' Mrs Crossley pressed.

'Yes. I don't want it any more.'

'Did your father give it to you?'

'No.' *It was* her *father who did.* 'I want Ann to have it. Her name begins with A, the same as mine, so she'll be able to wear it when she's older.' Amy closed her eyes and remembered the day Jimmy had given her the brooch. She felt again the touch of his mouth, soft against her lips. Her fingers started to close around the brooch. With an effort, she uncurled them and opened her eyes. 'It's right for her to have it. It belongs to her more than it does to me.'

'Well, I suppose it's all right.' Mrs Crossley lifted the brooch carefully from Amy's hand and put it back in the box.

'Take the ribbon too, please. It sort of goes with the brooch.'

Mrs Crossley tucked ribbon and box into her bag before returning Amy's case to its place by the wall. 'Don't you worry, I'll keep it safe until she's adopted, then I'll give it to her new mother.'

Her new mother. The words were a knife thrust through Amy. She turned away, and did not look up again until the woman had gone.

'You've got a name now, little one,' she murmured when she was alone with her baby once more. 'You're called Ann. Ann Elizabeth.' The little girl seemed much too small for such a grand name.

Amy nudged the baby on to her other breast. 'Maybe you won't want to know anything about me when you grow up. Maybe your new... the woman who takes you won't even tell you about me. She might think it's better if you don't know. But if she does tell you... please don't hate me, Ann,' she whispered. 'Please don't hate me.' She looked down at the baby pulling at her breast. It was impossible to imagine that solemn little creature ever feeling so harsh an emotion as hate.

'I hope she'll let you wear the brooch. Your father gave it to me, you see. I thought it meant he loved me. But it's not really mine any more, because he doesn't want me now. But he's still your father. Running away from me doesn't change that. So it's right that you have something that belonged to him and belonged to me, too.' A tear fell on Ann's blanket. 'Anyway, I haven't got anything else to give you.'

The baby let go of Amy's nipple and lay very still, staring up alertly at her mother. Amy smiled down at her and brushed a finger over the softness of the baby's cheek. 'You're going to fall asleep in a minute, aren't you, Ann? Maybe those women will forget about us a bit longer and we can have a cuddle. They'll growl at me for not calling out to tell them you've finished. I don't care.'

A week or two, Mrs Crossley had said. Maybe seven days, maybe fourteen. That meant every hour was precious, and Amy determined to waste none of them. She grudged even sleeping, when it was time she could have spent watching her baby.

'I wish I could explain things to you, Ann,' Amy said to the little girl one day. 'About why I did wrong with your father. If I tell you… maybe it'll sort of go into your mind, and when you're old enough you'll remember it in a way. I suppose that's silly. But you might.' She tried to recall the way Jimmy had made her feel, the soft words of love he had used. It was becoming harder to dredge up the memories; harder to think about anything but her baby. 'I will tell you, little one. I'll tell you before I say goodbye.'

Three days after Mrs Crossley's visit, Amy woke from a morning nap with a heavy feeling in her breasts. When she stirred, she found they were painfully swollen. Ann must be overdue for a feed. She leaned over to look in the cradle, but it was empty. *Those nurses must have her. I hope they bring her back soon. She'll be hungry.* Her breasts leaked a little at the thought.

She lay back against the pillows and tried to wait patiently. But time dragged on and her breasts became more tender. She twisted around on the bed trying to get comfortable, then lay very still and listened for any sound of her baby. Amy was sure that by now Ann must have missed two feeds, and she began to be anxious. *Is she ill? What are those women doing with her?* She had a sudden picture of Sister Prescott touching Ann with the same rough handling she used on Amy.

Amy pushed back the covers and sat on the edge of the bed, then stood up. She had to grasp the bed end to stay upright against the wave of weakness that assailed her. *I've almost forgotten how to walk.* Her bare feet made no sound as she padded out of the room and down the corridor.

The first door she tried opened onto an empty room. The next seemed to be a storeroom of some sort. The last door on the left stood open; when she peered into it she saw that it was the kitchen. Amy had just turned away to try the doors on the other side when an angry voice came down the corridor.

'What do you think you're doing? Who said you could get out of bed?'

Amy turned to see Sister Prescott bearing down on her. 'Where's my baby?'

'You get right back in that room,' Sister Prescott ordered. 'Do you want to do yourself some injury and make more work for me?' She took hold of Amy's arm and propelled her along the corridor. Amy had to struggle to match the nurse's stride; she stumbled as she walked.

'But I was looking for my baby. She's not in my room. Where is she?'

Sister Prescott pushed her onto the bed. 'There. You just stay in here until I tell you you can get up. Do you understand me?'

'She must be hungry. I don't know how many feeds she's missed now, but she must be really hungry. I can't hear her crying anywhere. Where is she? What have you done with my baby?'

'She's gone,' the nurse said flatly.

'Wh-what? Where's she gone?'

'That Crossley woman collected her this morning. Now, don't you go making a fuss, girl.'

'But... but she said she wouldn't take my baby away for a week at least. I thought I'd have her for a little bit longer.'

'Well, you haven't. Mrs Crossley thought you were going to be silly about giving the child up—she said you'd gone and got attached to it. I told you not to, you stupid girl.'

'Ann's gone?' Amy whispered. 'But I never said goodbye to her. I wanted to say goodbye. I wanted to tell her things.' She felt tears sliding down her cheeks.

'Stop it!' Sister Prescott's broad palm snaked out and slapped Amy. 'Don't you dare make a fuss. You knew you had to give that baby away, there's no reason for you to carry on silly now.'

Amy's shoulders heaved with suppressed sobs. *She's gone. My baby's gone.* Her breasts ached from their load of milk. 'It hurts here,' she said, pointing at them.

'You're full of milk, that's why.' The nurse fetched a broad band of cloth and wound it tightly around Amy's breasts. 'They'll be sore for a few days, then the milk will go away.'

My milk will go away. Like my baby's gone away. Amy laid her face against the pillow to let her tears soak into it. 'When can I go home?' she asked quietly.

'You'll be fit to travel in a few days. I'll send Mrs Leith a cable to tell her to come and fetch you.' The nurse glanced down at the floor beside the bed. 'You don't need this in here any more.' She picked up the cradle and carried it out of the room, closing the door on Amy.

Amy lay with her breasts throbbing against their constricting band. *My baby's gone. She's gone away, and I never said goodbye to her. I'll never see her again.* She pressed her face into the pillow to try and muffle her sobs, but the noise of her weeping mounted until it filled the room. 'My baby's gone,' she wailed aloud. She expected an angry nurse to burst in on her. But she was left alone to cry until her throat was too raw for any sound to escape.

The next few days ran meaninglessly into one another until one evening, when she brought in Amy's dinner, Sister Prescott lingered for a moment. 'You're being collected tomorrow,' she said. 'Some time tomorrow morning.'

'Oh. Good,' Amy said, toying absently with her food.

Next morning she rose early and dressed herself. The green maternity frock was badly creased when she pulled it out of her case, but it didn't seem important. Her cloak would cover it, anyway. She sat on the hard chair and stared at the spot where the cradle had been. She ignored her breakfast when Sister Prescott brought it in, and ignored the nurse's scolding when she returned to find the food untouched and cold.

Her hand went absently to the place on her chest where the brooch had once hung. The worst of the pain had gone from her breasts, along with the milk, but they were still swollen and tender. She stared fixedly at the floor, thinking she could see a mark where the cradle had scratched a board. *It's all gone, Jimmy. All the things you gave me. The ribbon, the brooch, and now my baby. There's nothing left. Nothing.*

She closed her eyes to conjure Jimmy's face. But all she could see was the face of a tiny baby, staring up at her. *I can't see you any more, Jimmy. Even the pictures of you have gone.*

Amy kept her eyes closed to hold the picture of Ann before her. It was better than staring at the space a cradle had left. *I've never seen you smile, Ann. You might start smiling about now, I think you're just old enough. I hope you have lots of things to smile about.*

She heard the door open. 'Here she is,' Sister Prescott said brightly. 'Sitting up and all ready to go. What a good girl.'

Amy steeled herself to meet Susannah's disapproving gaze. She opened her eyes and took one last look at the spot where the cradle had rested, then turned to face the door.

Her eyes opened wide. She sprang from her chair and launched herself at the smiling figure standing there with his arms open. 'Pa!' she gasped. She buried herself in her father's arms and sobbed against his chest.

33

November 1884

'I d-didn't th-think it would be you,' Amy sobbed. 'I didn't think you'd c-come and fetch me.'

'Shh,' Jack soothed, holding her close. 'I missed you, so I thought why shouldn't I come up myself? Anyway, I wanted to see you were properly looked after coming home.'

'I'm glad,' Amy murmured.

'Thank you for getting her right,' Jack said to the nurse.

'Oh, she's been no trouble,' Sister Prescott said. 'Such an easy patient! Quite a pleasure to have, really.'

'She's a good girl, aren't you?' He gave Amy a squeeze. 'Well, there's no need to hang around here any longer, I've got a cab waiting. Let's be on our way. Where's your luggage?'

'Here you are,' Sister Prescott said, handing Amy's case to Jack.

'Thank you. Amy, aren't you going to thank the lady for taking care of you while you weren't well?'

Amy turned to look at the nurse. Sister Prescott's teeth were bared in a smile that did not reach her eyes. 'No,' Amy said quietly. She hid her face against her father's chest again.

'Amy!' Jack sounded shocked. 'Where are your manners?'

'Don't worry about it,' Sister Prescott put in smoothly. 'She's overcome, seeing you again after all this time. She's been rather homesick, poor little thing. Off you go with your father, dear.' She saw them to the doorstep, then disappeared back inside the nursing home while Jack helped Amy down the path and into the cab.

Amy snuggled against her father in the cab, reluctant to miss a moment's contact with him. 'When did you get here, Pa?'

'Just this morning.' He pulled out his watch and checked it. 'Less than an hour ago.' He smiled at Amy. 'I didn't want to waste any time coming to see you. We're going home on the evening sailing.'

'You've just come up and you're going straight back? Pa, you must be really tired, spending all that time on the boat.'

'It wasn't so bad. I came up on the *Minerva*—that's Connolly's sailing boat, remember? Had to sleep in the hold on a load of sacks, but it suited me to get a ride with him. It was lucky he was bringing it up this week—you know the *Staffa* doesn't go every day, and I wanted to work it out so I could bring you straight home.'

'I've been a terrible nuisance to you, haven't I, Pa?' Amy felt tears welling up.

'No, you haven't,' Jack said briskly. 'There's been a bit of trouble, but it's all coming right now. Don't you go upsetting yourself over anything.'

'Thank you.' Amy squeezed his arm. 'How's everyone at home?' she asked, trying to sound bright. 'Have you seen Lizzie lately? I suppose Tommy and Georgie will have grown, I've been away so long.'

'Lizzie looked after the place while your M—while *Susannah*,' he amended, 'was having her holiday. Lizzie's as bossy as ever, going on about Frank whenever she gets the chance.'

Amy smiled at the picture he conjured up. 'She must be well, then.'

'The little fellows are good, Georgie's talking a bit now. Tom's been missing you.'

'Has he? It'll be good to see them all again. Is everyone... well, getting on all right together?'

Jack snorted. 'Susannah wasn't too pleased about being left at home this time.' He flashed a wicked grin at Amy. 'What do you think, girl? Do you reckon I'll still have a wife when we get home?'

Amy surprised herself with a little laugh. 'Pa, what a terrible thing to say! They'll be all right, John will keep Harry and Susannah apart.'

'Mmm, as long as she gets the meals on the table she'll be all right. What do you think of the big city, anyway? All these shops and things people go on about.'

'I don't really know. I haven't seen anything of Auckland.' Amy thought for a moment. 'Do you know, this is only the second time I've been outside since the day I arrived?'

'What? In three months?'

'Yes. Susannah took me straight to Mrs Kirkham's, then Mrs Kirkham took me to the nursing home. And now you've collected me.' She smiled at her father.

'Well, we'll have to do something about that.' Jack leaned out the window and attracted the cabby's attention. 'Hey, you can drop us off in what-do-you-call-it, Princes Street. Near the park.'

The cabby turned down a street lined with elegant two-storied houses, and Amy peered at them through the young trees that edged the footpath. 'That's where the nobs live,' Jack said. 'Rich businessmen, that sort of thing. I think there're a few more houses than last time I saw this place. Here we are,' he said as the cab drew to a halt.

He helped Amy to the ground. When Amy saw him fiddling for money, she remembered her own little store. 'I've got ten shillings!' she announced. She opened her case and fished the note from a corner. 'It's left over from the money Susannah gave Mrs Kirkham.'

'Humph! That was lucky—if Susannah had got it, it would have been spent by now.'

'Oh, it's pretty,' Amy exclaimed, looking around at the flower beds and tree-studded lawns that spread before her. 'Look at all these lovely flowers.'

'Mmm. Looks even better since they got rid of the old barracks that used to be here. Let's take a stroll.' He held out his arm, and Amy linked her own through it. They had not gone far before she was short of breath.

'I'm sorry, Pa, I have to stop,' she said, leaning more heavily against him.

'What's wrong? Don't you feel well?'

'I don't feel sick, but I'm really tired. I don't seem to have any strength since...'

'You've been ill, so it's no wonder. You'll have to take it easy for a while. Come on, we can sit down.' He led her to a bench, and Amy sank on to it gratefully.

They sat in companionable silence for some time, looking around them. On this weekday morning there were few other people in the park. Men dressed for business hurried past, perhaps on their way to meetings, and pairs of middle-aged women strolled along the paths.

Amy enjoyed watching the people until she saw a young woman walking towards them, pushing a baby carriage of cane with a fringed awning. Amy turned away and stared at the fountain, but the woman stopped at their bench and sat down beside them. Amy's eyes were drawn irresistibly towards the baby carriage. She peeped into it and saw a baby of about six months old, with a mop of dark hair, chortling and waving its arms at its mother.

That's what you might look like in a few months, Ann. I wish you were coming home with me and Pa. She choked back a sob and looked away from the baby. When she met her father's eyes she saw concern there. 'Can we go somewhere else now, please?' she asked. 'I'm getting a bit hot in the sun.'

Jack nodded. 'I've had enough, too.' He helped Amy to her feet, and she looped her arm through his again. 'It brings back a few memories, this place,' he said. He gave a snort. 'Silly reason to come here, though.'

'What memories, Pa?' Amy asked, glad of the distraction.

'Oh, I brought Susannah here a few times when we were courting. Not that we courted for long. But she liked walking around here on my arm, and I enjoyed showing her off. She was a fine-looking woman—still is, come to that. This is the place for couples to wander around showing themselves off. Especially on a Sunday.'

'Is it? What's this park called?' Amy asked, already sure of the answer.

'It's Albert Park.'

Amy was silent for a few moments. 'Oh. I've heard of Albert Park.' *So this is where you were going to take me walking, Jimmy. After we were married. Did you ever mean anything you said to me?*

Tears filled her eyes, and she would have stumbled on the steep path if her father had not taken her arm more tightly. 'You all right, girl? Not feeling faint or anything?'

'I... I'm very hot,' Amy said, aware of the sun beating down on her dark cloak.

Jack's hand brushed her forehead. 'You feel hotter than you should, and you're sweating a bit. No wonder, that great big woollen cloak over a heavy dress like that. Here, I'll help you off with it. I can carry it for you.'

'No!' Amy pulled the cloak around her more closely.

'Why not? You don't really want it on, do you?'

Amy looked around at the passers by, then stood on tiptoe to whisper into her father's ear. 'I'm scared people will stare at me, because my dress is so baggy.'

'Is it that bad?' Jack asked. Amy nodded. 'And you haven't got any others with you?'

'One other, but it's just as bad.'

Jack fumbled in his jacket pocket. 'Do you want me to buy you another one? I've brought a bit of cash with me, I could run to a plain sort of dress.'

'No, you mustn't do that. Don't worry, Pa, I'll be all right. I'll just keep my cloak on and stay out of the sun.'

'I don't know, girl, your colour's pretty high. I don't want you fainting.'

'I won't faint,' Amy assured him, then wondered if perhaps she just might. As the sun mounted, the day was getting hotter and hotter. 'Maybe... maybe if you could buy me a sash? Then this dress wouldn't look so awful.'

'All right, I'll take you to Milne and Choyce—Susannah's always going on about what a wonderful place it is. She must have just about bought their stock out when she came up with you, but I expect they still run to a girl's sash.'

It was a downhill walk from the park to where Wellesley Street met Queen Street, but even so Amy had to lean heavily on her father's arm. They waited for a horse tram to pass along the dusty road before they could cross. Amy stared with interest at the huge carriage. Another tram crossed Queen Street and stopped at the foot of the steep hill to have a massive Clydesdale harnessed in front of the other two horses.

'They didn't have all these trams last time I came up here—of course it was three years ago,' Jack remarked. 'Watch your step,' he warned as they stepped off the footpath. Amy stopped just in time to avoid standing in a pile of horse dung.

She sheltered against her father as they walked through the crowds milling around the busy corner, then Jack guided her through a heavy door. 'Here we are,' he said. 'Now, where do you think they'd have sashes?'

Amy was lost for words as she gazed around the magical place her father had brought her to. Gas lights made the store startlingly bright, illuminating all the goods on display. Counters stretched out in every direction. Amy felt her head spinning as she tried to see a pattern in the layout of the store. 'So many things!' she breathed when she had her voice back at last. 'It's so big, how do people find anything?'

'I expect they learn their way around—or maybe they just ask someone. Miss,' he hailed one of the dozens of young women, all attired in dark dresses, who were standing behind counters or bustling about on messages. 'Where can my daughter get a sash?'

'All the way down the back of the shop, sir, on the left hand side,' the assistant said, pointing the direction.

'It would be,' Jack muttered as he and Amy began to weave their way through the complicated series of aisles. Amy held on tightly to his arm, fearful of getting lost forever amongst the frenetic activity all around them.

She glanced at the counter they were passing, let go of her father's arm and stood stock still, transfixed by what she saw. The counter was covered with babies' clothes: little jackets, bonnets and shawls. But what had caught her eye was a tiny dress of white lawn trimmed with delicate lace. Narrow ribbon in the palest of pinks was threaded through the lace at the hem and neck edges, and the ribbon was drawn into a little bow at the front of the yoke.

Amy stared at the dress. *It's beautiful. Beautiful enough for you, Ann. I hope the people who take you will buy you lovely things. What would you look like in a pretty dress like this instead of that horrible old flannel thing Sister Prescott put you in? I wish I could see you.*

The little bow was perfect; it fascinated Amy. Without thinking what she was doing, she reached out to finger it. She had almost touched it when her hand was grasped and gently pulled away from the dress. Her father had taken it in his own.

'Don't look at those things, Amy. You'll only go upsetting yourself. That's all over now, you just put it out of your head.'

'I'm sorry, Pa.' Amy felt tears pricking at her eyes. She fought them back, determined not to embarrass her father in front of all these strangers.

Amy chose the plainest sash the assistant showed them. It was pale grey, and she thought it would look reasonable against the green dress. She put the sash on, trying to ignore the stares of the young women lining the counters when she revealed her ill-fitting dress, then with relief she pulled off her heavy cloak. Jack took it from her and draped it over his arm.

'I've loaded you down, haven't I?' Amy smiled at her father. 'You've got my case, and now that great big cloak.'

'It doesn't weigh much,' Jack said stoutly. 'It's a good thing I got my own stuff on the boat first thing, though. No, let's go out a different way,' he said, taking hold of Amy's hand when she made to retrace their steps. 'You can see the rest of the shop.' But Amy knew it was to avoid taking her past the baby clothes again.

She deliberately studied each counter as they walked back to the front of the store, trying to forget that little dress. But the first few had such mundane items as sheets, towels, and men's shirts, and Amy found it impossible to feel any interest in them.

Then they rounded a corner into the hat department, and Amy stared about her in wonder. 'Aren't they gorgeous? So many, and they're all so beautiful. Oh, no wonder Susannah loves this shop. Can I look at them for a minute, Pa?'

'Of course you can—take all the time you want. We're in no hurry.'

'You'd almost think those were real cherries,' Amy said, studying a delicate arrangement of fruit on a straw hat. 'And aren't the flowers on this one pretty?' she said of a grey felt hat with a cluster of daisies around the brim. She glanced at the other end of the counter and saw the loveliest hat of all. 'Oh, look at this one,' she gasped. It was pale blue felt, with a ribbon in a darker blue around the crown. The broad brim tilted up at a saucy angle, revealing a blue velvet lining. Tiny dark blue roses had been sewn onto the ribbon and the exposed lining. The finishing touch was a small ostrich feather dyed the same dark blue and tucked in behind the tilted brim. 'What a beautiful, beautiful thing,' Amy said, gazing reverently at the hat.

'Can I help you, dear?' A middle-aged woman stepped behind the counter. 'Do you want to try on one of the hats?'

'Oh, no,' Amy said, taking a step back in confusion. 'I'm sorry, I was just looking at them because they're so pretty.'

'Yes, she does want to,' said Jack. 'She wants to try on that blue one, and I want to buy it for her.'

'Pa, you can't!' Amy protested. 'I don't need a hat. And it looks awfully expensive,' she added quietly.

'Try it on,' Jack said firmly. 'I want to see it on you.'

Amy gave in. She nodded shyly at the assistant. The woman carefully lifted the hat from its stand and placed it on Amy's head, smoothing a few stray strands of hair out of the way as she did so. 'Very pretty,' she said. 'Perhaps a little grown-up for you, but if Papa likes this one?' She looked questioningly at Jack.

'Let's see you, girl.' Amy turned to her father, and saw his face break into a broad smile.

'That looks good on you. You look prettier than ever in that.'

'Take a look yourself, dear,' the woman invited. She led Amy to a full-length mirror. Amy saw herself for the first time since she had left the farm. She grimaced at the drawn-faced figure staring back at her. Her eyes seemed unnaturally large in a face that had lost the last softness of childhood, and the dark blue shadows under them looked like bruises. She tried to ignore her face and concentrate on the hat.

'It's lovely. But… I really don't need it, Pa,' she said, reluctantly pulling off the hat.

'That's enough arguing. Wrap that hat up, please,' her father instructed the assistant.

'Certainly, sir.'

The hat was soon safely in a box. Jack was about to add it to his burdens, but Amy insisted on carrying the precious parcel herself.

'Thank you, Pa,' she said as they made their way out of the store. 'It's just beautiful. It was awfully dear, though.'

'I've never spent a guinea better,' Jack insisted. 'It's worth every penny to see you smiling again.'

'You're so kind to me.' Amy felt her lower lip tremble.

'Hey, I said I wanted to see you smile.'

'I'm sorry.' Amy smiled at him again. 'Is that better?'

'Much better. Anyway, you'll need a fancy hat.'

'Why?'

'For your wedding, of course! That looks just the sort of hat to get married in.'

Amy was silent for a time. 'I'd sort of forgotten,' she said at last.

'That's a funny sort of thing to forget,' Jack snorted. 'Of course, you've been ill. I expect that put it out of your head.'

'Yes, it did. When is it going to happen, Pa?'

'Have you forgotten that as well?'

'I don't think I ever knew.'

'Didn't we tell you? I suppose we didn't. Well, we decided New Year would be a good time. Susannah told me you wouldn't be… well, ready till then. Charlie's been over once or twice to ask when you were coming back, he's pretty keen to see you.'

'I see.' A little over a month. Far enough away that there was no need to think about it. 'Maybe you should buy Susannah a present while we're here.'

'I won't bother. She bought herself plenty of things when she came up.'

'She might be hurt, Pa. Especially when she sees my lovely hat.'

'She won't be hurt. She might be annoyed, but that's just too bad.' He pulled out his watch and glanced at it. 'It's after one o'clock! My stomach thinks my throat's been cut. Tell you what, we'll have a bite to eat in a tea room, then I'll buy you a slap-up dinner before we sail. How does that sound?'

'It's probably a waste. I expect I'll bring it all up again on the boat.'

'Do you get seasick? I don't, except when it's really rough. Never mind, you'll enjoy it while you eat it.'

'But won't it cost—'

'Stop going on about money. I can give my daughter a treat, can't I?'

Amy put her arms around him and squeezed. 'It's enough of a treat that you came to fetch me.'

They negotiated their way back across the busy road and upstairs into a small tea room, where they were soon drinking tea and munching through a pile of sandwiches, followed by little cakes.

The tea room was almost empty, but two smartly-dressed women in their early forties came in and sat at the next table. The women talked animatedly, ignoring their tea for some time. Amy stared at them in mild interest, wondering if they would remember the tea before it had cooled completely.

'A little girl!' one of the women said. 'You must be so excited, Helen.'

The one called Helen nodded, setting her heavy pearl necklace bobbing. 'After so long, we'd almost given up. At my age, I thought perhaps it was silly, perhaps I wouldn't be strong enough to look after a baby, but I don't regret it now. Although it hasn't been easy for Fred to get used to a baby waking him up at all hours—nor for me!' She laughed.

'One does get out of the way of those sleepless nights,' her companion agreed.

'Yes, Maurice is nearly ten, it's a long time since we had a baby around. Oh, I hate to leave her, even for a moment! This is almost the first time I've left the house since she arrived—the nurse we've engaged is excellent, but I still feel I should be there myself. I'm so looking forward to taking her out and about, but I can't disturb her when she finally gets off to sleep. Nurse says the cow's milk's been disagreeing with her, and of course I haven't any of my own this time. She's just beginning to thrive, though, and I'll soon be able to show her off properly. Won't she look sweet in this?'

A cold wave of shock went through Amy when the woman opened a paper parcel and pulled out the baby's dress that had so entranced her in the store. *That's Ann's dress!* she wanted to cry out. *You're too old to have a baby—you can't even feed a baby—but you're allowed to keep yours. And you've bought Ann's dress!* For a moment Amy felt she hated the woman. But then she saw the look of love in her eyes as she gazed at the dress. *You love your baby too, don't you? I'm glad you can keep her, even if you are old.*

'Are you listening, girl?' Jack's voice broke into her thoughts.

'What?' Amy dragged her gaze from the women, glad that her father could not see them and had not been listening to their conversation. 'I'm sorry, I was thinking about something else. What did you say?'

'I was telling you about that teacher.'

'Miss Evans? What about her?'

'She's left. She came to see you a couple of weeks ago, to say goodbye. She'd heard you were ill, everyone in Ruatane knew you were sick, but she thought maybe you were ready for visitors.'

'Where's she gone, Pa?'

'Said she's got a job near Hamilton, in a bigger school. She seemed pretty pleased about it, but she was sorry to have missed you. I told her you were in Auckland getting well.' He talked so freely of Amy's having been ill that she began to suspect he almost believed it.

'Oh, I wish I'd seen her! You talked to her yourself?'

'Yes, she came looking for me in the cow shed, she never even went to the house. Susannah was quite put out.'

'Susannah was very rude to her once. I expect that's why.'

'I told her you're getting married soon. I thought that would shut her up if she was going to go on about that teaching.'

'What did she say?'

'She seemed surprised. Old maids are always jealous when they hear about someone else getting a husband. It's a good thing you didn't see her, girl.'

'Perhaps it is, Pa.'

'Now,' Jack said when they were on the footpath once more, 'I'll take you to the boat and you can put your stuff away, then we'll have a look around the wharves until it's dinner time. Do you feel strong enough to walk down to the bottom of Queen Street, or do you want to go in the tram? It's a fair step.'

'I'll walk,' Amy assured him, anxious to avoid making him spend any more money on her. Once or twice during the next few minutes she almost gave in and asked if they could, after all, take the tram, but she managed by leaning more heavily on her father's arm. She was panting by the time they reached the wharves; she did her best to hide it.

Jack saw Amy's case safely stowed on the *Wellington*, though she refused to part with her hat. He looked at Amy's heaving chest.

'You don't really feel up to walking around the wharves, do you?'

'Not really,' Amy admitted.

'Never mind, we'll stay where we are till we get hungry. You can see plenty from here.'

They sat on the deck and watched the activities around them. Carts came and went, loading and unloading crates and sacks. Horses stood and munched contentedly from nosebags while their owners watched cargo being stowed. Steamers and sailing craft shared the wharves, and the tall buildings of the city made a backdrop to the bustling scene.

'That's a load of kauri gum from Northland,' Jack pointed out. 'Those sacks look as though they're full of wheat. Crates of butter over there, of course—that's the other thing I meant to tell you, they've opened a cheese factory next to Forsters' place. Good thing I didn't hold my breath waiting for it, eh? They're taking all the milk we can supply, though.'

Amy sat in the warm sunlight, pressed against her father. The background noises seemed to fade, and his voice took on a droning quality that she found soothing. She closed her eyes to concentrate on the sound.

She was surprised when she felt his hand shaking her shoulder gently. She opened her eyes and wondered how the sun had dropped towards the horizon so quickly.

'Had a good sleep?' Jack smiled at her. 'You must have needed it. Time we went back on dry land for a bit and had something to eat.' He stood and stretched. 'My arm's stiff from keeping it still that long! I didn't want to move and wake you up, you looked so peaceful.'

Amy stood up and waited for her head to clear. 'I had a lovely sleep, Pa. It must be all that walking. It's funny, I used to run all over the farm and not get tired, and now just walking down the street wears me out.'

'That's because you've been ill. Are you going to wear your new hat to dinner?'

'Do you want me to?' Jack nodded.

She went into the ladies' cabin, undid the parcel and put on the hat in front of a small mirror, trying not to notice how odd it looked with her dress. When she came back, Jack gave her a smile that had more than a hint of sadness in it. 'That's nice,' he said. 'You look more like her than ever now.'

'You mean Mama?'

'Mmm.' He fell silent.

'You and Mama were happy, weren't you?' Amy probed. Ever since Susannah's arrival, it had become rare for him to speak of her mother.

'Yes. She was a fine woman. I only wish I'd given her a better life.'

'You loved her, Pa. That's enough.'

'I certainly did.' He cleared his throat noisily. 'Let's go and see about this dinner before you nod off again.'

Jack took her along Customs Street to the Thames Hotel. Amy found herself seated opposite her father at a white-clothed table set with shining silver cutlery. She was too overwhelmed to select from the menu flourished before her, so she let her father choose for them both.

She enjoyed her first experience of dining at a hotel, though she did indeed come close to dozing off again between the roast chicken and the apple charlotte. Jack persuaded her to try a small glass of Madeira, which Amy assumed to be some sort of coloured lemonade and which made her even sleepier.

Her father took her back to the boat well in time for the sailing, and Amy found the fresh breeze from the sea revived her wonderfully. She half-expected her father to hurry her below deck as Susannah had, but Jack showed no sign of wanting to be rid of her. Instead they stood on the deck as the ship slowly made its way out of the harbour on a delightfully flat sea, and Jack told her what he could about the places they passed.

'This bare-looking island's Rangitoto,' he said. 'They say it's a volcano, that's why there's not much growing on it. The one next to it's Motutapu, looks like decent grazing. On the other side we've got Brown's Island. In the summer they take excursion boats out to all these places. I remember Susannah telling me about them when we went up to Waiwera.'

The grassy islands were jewel-bright in the setting sun. Amy looked about her with interest, but she soon grew tired of standing. She leaned more heavily on the rail. Next moment she jerked her head back, and realised that she had very nearly gone to sleep standing up.

Jack slipped his arm around her. 'You're pretty weary, aren't you? I'd better take you to bed.' He guided her to the ladies' cabin and gave her into the care of an attentive stewardess. 'She hasn't been well,' he explained. The motherly-looking woman clucked over Amy.

'Poor little thing,' she said, leading Amy to a bunk. 'You look terribly thin in the face. Never mind, you have a good sleep and you'll feel better in the morning.' She helped Amy undress, and Amy stayed awake just long enough to ask the woman to put her hat away carefully.

Nausea woke Amy in the early hours when the boat was well out of the sheltered Waitemata. She leaned over the familiar bucket, but the sickness was not nearly so violent as on her previous voyage. Once her stomach was empty she managed to drift back to sleep, and the stewardess had to wake her for breakfast. Amy was surprised to find she felt able to eat. She joined her father in the saloon and tucked into a plate of sausages and mashed potatoes. 'I've hardly been sick at all this time,' she said.

'It's a calm trip, especially now we're around the Coromandel. All that fresh air you got before you went to bed probably helped.'

They disembarked at Tauranga and went for a short stroll till Amy again felt too weak to walk, then they sat on the wharf until the *Staffa* was ready to sail. Amy had no intention of sitting in the smelly little ladies' cabin of the small boat this time; instead she stayed on the deck with Jack all day, well away from the engine fumes, breathing deeply of the sea air. She lost her lunch when the *Staffa* rolled its way clumsily across Ruatane's bar, but it didn't seem to matter.

'There's the wharf,' she said as soon as it came into view. A few minutes later she caught sight of John, and pointed him out to her father.

'That's good. I told those boys to make sure one of them was here on time to meet us.' Jack stood up and tried to make out his son. 'Your eyes are younger than mine, I'll take your word for it. Is he by himself?'

'I can't tell yet, there're too many people on the wharf. Why, did you think Harry might come with him? Won't he be busy milking?'

Jack ruffled her curls. 'I thought there might be someone who couldn't wait to see you again.'

'Who's that, Pa? Do you mean Lizzie?'

'I mean your intended, of course!'

'Oh. Charlie.' *I'm going to get married.* Suddenly a month did not seem very long at all.

34

November – December 1884

Charlie Stewart was not waiting on Ruatane Wharf, but John was, nevertheless, accompanied by someone who couldn't wait to see Amy again. As the *Staffa* pulled up to the wharf, Amy saw that a self-conscious looking John was holding Thomas tightly by the hand, despite the little boy's energetic attempts to pull free. As soon as Amy had made her rather unsteady way down the gangplank, Thomas finally broke away from John and launched himself at her, winding his arms around her legs.

'Amy, Amy!' he squealed.

Amy knelt down and gave him a squeeze. 'Hello, Tommy darling. Did you miss me?'

'He heard me say yesterday I was coming in to pick you up,' John said. 'Then he started driving Susannah mad wanting to know when you'd get back, so she asked me to bring him in this afternoon. You've been a brat, haven't you, Tom?'

'Yes,' Thomas said proudly.

John smiled at his little brother. 'Nah, he hasn't been bad, really. He gets on Susannah's nerves, so Harry and me have been letting him hang around with us.'

'I been milking,' Thomas announced.

'Well, you've been in the cow shed a couple of afternoons,' John corrected. He surprised Amy by giving her a hug. 'It's good to see you again, Amy. Are you feeling better now?'

'I'm getting there.' Amy smiled at him.

'She's not very strong yet, but good food and fresh air will soon put her to rights,' said Jack.

'Pick me up, Amy,' Thomas demanded.

'Oh, I don't think I can, Tommy. You're too heavy for me.'

'Pick me up. Please?'

'I'll carry you, boy.' Jack hoisted Thomas onto his shoulders. 'John, you carry our stuff. Take my arm, Amy.'

Amy leaned gratefully on her father. He helped her into the buggy, sat beside her and took up the reins. Thomas squeezed between them, leaving John to sit in the back seat with their bags.

Thomas clambered onto Amy's lap and wound his arms around her neck. 'You got a lap again!' he said in delight.

Amy turned her face away to hide the sudden tears. 'Yes, Tommy, my lap's come back,' she said quietly.

Harry saw them from the paddocks, and rushed to greet them as the buggy pulled up to the house. 'I'm glad you're home, Amy. You're looking well.'

'Thank you, Harry.' *But I haven't been ill. I had a baby.*

'I was going to come in and pick you up, but I took the milk to the factory this morning, so John said he'd go.'

'You *always* take the milk to the factory,' John said, grinning.

'Shut up,' Harry muttered. Amy was puzzled to see a smug expression on his face. She turned to John with a questioning look, and while her father was distracted with lifting Thomas from his seat John leaned close to her.

'Jane Neill's staying with the Forsters again this summer,' he murmured. 'And the factory's right next to their place. Harry gets himself invited over there every morning after he drops the milk off. Pa hasn't noticed yet that Harry takes ages to get home.'

Harry carried their bags into the house while John took the buggy to its shed. Susannah was in the kitchen with George; she greeted Amy with a cool kiss on her cheek. Amy thought Susannah looked rather harassed, and her hair was not quite as neatly pinned as Amy remembered it. 'Here you are at last. How are you, dear?'

'I'm tired,' Amy said, trying unsuccessfully to manage a smile. She saw George hiding behind the table and peeping out. 'Georgie, don't you have a kiss for me? You haven't forgotten me, have you?'

'You've been away nearly three months,' Susannah said. 'It's a long time for a child his age. Don't be silly, George, here's your sister.' She took hold of George's arm and coaxed him away from the security of the table. He gave Amy a shy smile, then let her kiss him.

'I hope you enjoyed your little holiday,' Susannah said to Jack in a voice heavy with sarcasm.

'Humph! If you call sitting on a boat a holiday. I'd sooner have stopped home and slept in my own bed.'

'Well, you know I would have gone if you'd let—'

'I know. I wanted the job done properly this time. Well, we're home now, there's no need to go on about it.'

Susannah gave him a cold look, but let the subject drop. 'I expect you'll both want to get changed. That dress looks a little odd with a sash, Amy—it's very creased from travelling, too. I've dinner keeping warm.'

Amy changed out of the baggy woollen dress and into a cool cotton frock that hugged her newly-slim figure. She hurried back to the kitchen to find the family assembled at the table. Susannah produced generous platefuls of chops and vegetables, but when Amy tried to cut herself a slice of bread she found it too much of a challenge for her weak arms. She poked at the leaden bread dubiously.

'I think this bread's a bit stale—I'm having trouble cutting it.'

'I made it fresh this morning,' Susannah said, looking affronted. 'Don't you start complaining, everyone else does.'

'Susannah's still getting the hang of bread,' said Jack. He pulled the bread towards himself and sawed off several slices, though not without obvious difficulty, then pushed the bread board back to the centre of the table. Amy took a slice, and found it was almost as much of a challenge to her teeth as it had been to her arm. 'You fellows been getting on all right while I've been away?' Jack asked. 'No... trouble?'

'No, no trouble at all,' Susannah said hastily, but the black look she and Harry exchanged gave the lie to her assurance.

'There was no breakfast the first morning,' Harry said darkly.

'Shut up, Harry,' John put in, but Harry ignored him.

'We had to do a bit of waking up. Had to just about break her door down with knocking.'

'Harry said "lazy bitch",' Thomas volunteered eagerly.

Susannah's hand snaked out and slapped him on the side of his head. 'Don't you ever let me hear you using a word like that again, Thomas,' she scolded. 'And don't make such a fuss, either,' she said over Thomas's wail.

'He did! He did say it!' Thomas protested through his sobs.

'There's no need for you to copy your brother's rough habits. Stop that crying. Do you want me to tell Papa all the naughty things you've been doing? He'll give you a strapping if I do.'

'No, don't tell Papa,' Thomas pleaded.

'Why doesn't she leave the kid alone,' Harry muttered.

Susannah turned on him. 'You stay out of it. Teaching my child filthy language!'

Harry glared at her. 'It's true. She is a lazy bitch,' he said to the room at large.

'Do you see the treatment I get?' Susannah demanded of Jack. 'And you left me alone with these two.'

'Shut up, the lot of you,' Jack growled. 'Can't I eat my dinner in peace? Harry, watch your language at the table.'

'That's rather weak, after what he said to me,' Susannah complained.

'You shouldn't have slept in, should you? I told you not to. Stop bawling, Tom, Papa's too tired to give anyone a hiding tonight. I don't want to hear another word out of anyone till I've finished eating.'

Amy was relieved at the silence that followed. It was obvious that the family had been getting on about as badly as possible. At least her father's presence would stop them from being too openly aggressive.

She rose to clear the dishes when the meal was over, but she had only picked up her own plate when Jack spoke.

'Leave those, Amy. You can hardly keep your eyes open, you'd better get off to bed.'

'I don't mind doing the dishes, Pa.'

'I said leave them,' Jack said shortly. He stared at Susannah as if expecting her to argue, but she contented herself with a resentful look down the table at him.

It was blissful to sink into her own familiar bed with its soft sheets. Amy stroked the crocheted bedspread she and her grandmother had worked together, then she lay back enjoying the darkness. Her bedrooms in Auckland had never been completely dark; nor had the nights been as quiet as this one. She could hear the hooting of a morepork in the distance, and the occasional lowing of a wakeful cow, but there was no noise of carriages clattering or people shouting, and no distant hints of gaslight.

Amy woke to find the early morning sun streaming through her window, and realised she had forgotten to close the drapes. She looked around the room to reassure herself that she really was home, then dressed and went out to the kitchen. She was astonished to find Susannah already there, in her dressing-gown and with her hair loose.

'Oh, I thought you'd still be asleep.'

'I'm not allowed much sleep these days,' Susannah grumbled. 'I have to get up at the crack of dawn. I thought you'd sleep in this morning.'

'I want to get strong again, and I won't unless I do some work. I can make breakfast if you want to have a sleep.'

Susannah considered the idea, then shook her head. 'No, I'm awake now. But I wouldn't mind getting dressed if you'd carry on while I'm gone?'

'All right.'

'I'll only be a minute.' Susannah disappeared into the passage.

Amy found everything took her twice as long as she was used to. She had to make repeated trips to take the dishes to the table, now that she did not have the strength to carry many at once. Lifting the leg of bacon down from its hook left her out of breath. She was leaning on the bench trying to recover from the exertion when her father came in.

'What are you doing, girl?' he asked in amazement.

'Getting breakfast on. I'm sorry, I'm a bit slow this morning, but it'll be ready soon.'

Instead of answering, Jack strode to the passage door. 'Susannah!' he roared. 'Get out here.'

'I'll be there in a minute,' Susannah called back. 'I'm just putting my hair up.'

'You get your lazy backside here right now or I'll haul you out by your bloody hair!'

There was a moment's silence, then Susannah practically ran up the passage and into the kitchen. 'What are you screaming at me like that for?' she said indignantly, but Amy noticed that she stayed well out of Jack's reach.

'Pa, I was only helping Susannah,' Amy tried to explain. 'Susannah was up before me this morning, but I wanted—'

'Listen to me, both of you,' Jack interrupted. 'Amy's been ill, Susannah, you know she has. She's still not right, anyone with a bit of sense could see that. And until she's got her strength back I don't want to see her doing any heavy work. That includes hefting great legs of bacon around the kitchen. You just take it easy, Amy, get back into things slowly. You understand me? Both of you?'

'Yes, Pa.'

'You mean I've got to carry on doing everything by myself?' Susannah said.

'That's right. Until the girl's properly well again, it's up to you to look after things. Have you got any complaints to make about that?'

'It wouldn't do any good if I had, would it?'

'No, it wouldn't,' Jack agreed.

After breakfast, Amy sat on the verandah with a book of poems in her lap. She tried to rouse some interest in the story of the Lady of Shalott, but the memory of her little, blanket-wrapped bundle kept intruding. She looked up from the book just in time to see Lizzie striding determinedly towards the kitchen door.

'Lizzie, I'm here,' Amy called. Lizzie changed direction to rush up to the verandah. She dropped onto the seat beside Amy and they embraced.

'I've missed you,' said Lizzie.

'I've missed you, too. I wish I could have written to you, but I just couldn't.'

'I know.' Lizzie studied her closely. 'You look awful.'

Amy gave a little laugh. 'I can rely on you not to spare my feelings, anyway. Everyone else keeps telling me how well I look.'

'No, you're really pale, and you've got thin. You haven't been sleeping very well, have you?'

'Not till last night,' Amy admitted.

'You've got horrible shadows under your eyes. Still,' she said brightly, 'you'll come right now you're home. Of course you look awful, you've been ill.'

'Don't say that,' Amy said fiercely. 'I'm sick of everyone saying I've been ill. I thought I could trust you not to pretend. I haven't been ill. I had a baby. Do you hear me? I had a baby!'

'Shh,' Lizzie warned. 'Someone will hear you.'

'They all know. Even though everyone pretends she never happened. She did happen, Lizzie. Oh, I wish you could have seen her.' Amy closed her eyes to see again that serious little face staring up at her, then opened them to look at Lizzie. 'I had a little girl. The most beautiful baby you've ever seen. My little girl. So tiny, so perfect. She had dark hair, and big, blue eyes that looked as if they knew everything.'

'Amy, you're going to upset yourself, going on like that.'

Amy flashed an angry look at her cousin, and saw that Lizzie was reluctant to meet her eyes. 'I'm embarrassing you, aren't I? I'm sorry, I'll stop. I just thought you'd let me talk about her. No one else will.'

'I think it's better if you don't talk about it, Amy.'

'All right, I won't talk about her.' *They all want to pretend you never happened, Ann. They want me to forget about you. I'll never forget you.* 'We'll talk about whatever you want.'

What Lizzie seemed to want to talk about were the everyday things that had happened during Amy's absence. Amy had soon been brought up-to-date on all the doings of the Waituhi Valley and Orere Beach, as well as much of Ruatane, from the opening of the new cheese factory down to the new ribbons on Martha Carr's bonnet, which were in a shade of pink of which Lizzie did not approve. Lizzie had just launched into the life story of the valley school's new teacher when Amy interrupted her.

'You haven't mentioned Frank much, Lizzie. Nothing's wrong, is it?'

'No, everything's fine. There's nothing new to tell, that's all.'

'Tell me old things, then. I want to hear about Frank. Have you set a date for your wedding yet?'

'Sort of. Well, yes, we have really. We already knew it was going to be April, but I've decided to make it as near my birthday as possible. Pa said we had to wait till I'm eighteen, but I'm not going to wait any longer than I have to.'

'And where are you going to have it? What about your dress?'

'I don't want to go on about all that stuff, Amy.'

'Why not?' Lizzie looked down at the ground and said nothing. 'You're scared of upsetting me, aren't you? Scared you'll remind me I've spoiled my chances of a flash wedding like you're going to have? Don't be. I want to hear about what you're going to do, Lizzie. Don't worry about me. I had my fun.'

'Amy!' Lizzie protested. 'That's an awful thing to say when you're only sixteen.'

'It's true. You always used to be a great one for facing facts, don't look so horrified when I do it.'

'You're still going to go through with it? Marrying Charlie?'

'Of course I am. Lizzie, we've been over all this before and nothing's changed. It's the only way to make things right for everyone, so I won't bring shame on them any more. Pa's so pleased about it, he keeps talking about my "big day" coming up. I've said I'll go through with it, and I'm not going to let him down. I've hurt him enough.'

'You could still change your mind. Especially now you're not... you know.'

'Now I haven't got my baby any more, you mean?' Amy fought back tears with difficulty. 'So it would look as though I'd lied and said I'd marry Charlie just so I'd have an excuse to get rid of her? As if I wanted to get rid of Ann. I gave her your name, you know. Ann Elizabeth, I called her. I suppose you don't like having a bastard named after you.'

Lizzie was quiet for some time. 'I have upset you, haven't I?' she said at last. 'I didn't mean to, Amy. I'm just not very good at talking about all this.'

'I'm easily upset just now. It's because I'm so tired.'

'You'll be better soon, when you feel well again.'

'Yes, that's right, Lizzie. I've been ill, haven't I?'

When Amy woke the next morning, she fretted over whether she should go out to the kitchen to help with breakfast. She decided to wait in her room until she was sure Susannah would have things well under way. An hour after waking, she went out to find her stepmother half-heartedly punching at some bread dough.

'Do you want me to do that?' Amy asked.

'Not if it means your father's going to abuse me over it.'

'I could do it sitting down. Pa wouldn't go crook about that, I don't think.'

'Hmm, that's not a bad idea. Everyone looks down their noses at my bread, anyway.'

'You have to...' Amy began, then thought better of telling Susannah that the bread should have a good fifteen minutes' hard kneading, not the two or three slaps Susannah was obviously making do with. 'What you put into bread is what you get out of it,' her grandmother had always said. Even sitting down, working at the bread soon had Amy's arms trembling with the unaccustomed strain. But the thought of bread that would not wear out her jaw was as appealing as the chance to be of some use.

'Taking it easy, are you?' Jack said when he came in and saw Amy sitting at the table. 'That's good.' He ignored the glare Susannah turned on him.

Later that morning, after helping Susannah with some baking, Amy had just dusted the parlour and was trying to decide what other work was light enough for her to be allowed to do when Susannah came into the room. 'You've a visitor,' she said brightly. She ushered Charlie Stewart through the doorway. 'Now, why don't you take your fiancé out to the verandah, and I'll bring some tea and biscuits out to you. Take your apron off, dear.'

Amy stared dumbly at the stern figure before her. Susannah had to give her a small shove before she responded. 'Yes, come out here,' she said, pulling her apron off and handing it to the waiting Susannah. She led the way through the parlour door and onto the verandah.

Charlie sat down and Amy took the chair opposite him, from where she studied the floorboards rather than meet his eyes. 'I thought I'd come and see how you are,' Charlie said after an awkward silence.

'That was nice of you. Thank you, Mr Stewart.' Amy forced herself to raise her gaze to meet his. He was staring at her in a way that she found disturbing. It reminded her just a little of how Jimmy had looked at her.

'You'd best be calling me by my name,' Charlie said. '"Mr Stewart" will sound foolish from my wife.'

His wife. 'I'll try. It might take me a while to get used to doing that.'

'Your pa says you're not too well yet.'

'I got really worn out in Auckland. I'm getting better now I'm home.'

'Good. You've not got much colour in your cheeks.'

'I've been inside so much, out of the fresh air.'

'Here we are,' Susannah said, bustling out with a tray. 'I'll leave you in peace to have a chat. Now, you must try some of these biscuits, Mr Stewart. Amy made them herself. She's a very good cook.'

Charlie did not comment on the biscuits, but he managed to demolish most of them without any apparent difficulty. 'You don't eat much,' he said, looking at Amy's empty plate.

'I'm not doing much work just now, so I don't get very hungry.'

'That's fair enough.' He looked hard at her. 'You're getting better, you say?'

'Yes, I'll be quite well again soon.'

'Good.' He finished his tea and stood up. 'Well, I'll be on my way.'

'Goodbye, Mr Stewart.' Charlie turned and looked at her. 'I'm sorry, I mean Charlie.'

'Goodbye.'

That wasn't too bad. He was quite nice, really. Well, he wasn't horrible, anyway. Amy tried to ignore the way she was shaking with relief at being alone again.

35

As the days wore on, Amy made slow progress in returning to her old strength. She took short walks every day, and each day she extended her range a little, but it was more than a week before she could get so much as halfway up the hill behind the house. Even then she had to stop partway to sit on a stump.

She managed to get just high enough to see beyond the mouth of the valley and catch a glimpse of the steamer on its way to Tauranga. She stood and watched the little boat. *It's full of people going to Auckland, Ann. I don't suppose I'll ever go there again. I'll never see you again.*

She had to pick her way carefully down the hill with tears blurring her vision, but her eyes were clear again by the time she reached the house. Susannah had started preparing lunch; Amy thought she looked hot and flustered.

'Can I help you with anything, Susannah?'

'Humph! I could certainly do with a bit of help, but I don't seem to count for anything around here. No one cares if I wear myself out trying to do all the work.'

'I want to help, I just get tired.'

'I know. All I hear is "look after Amy, she's still not well." I don't know what would happen if I decided to be ill. I might get ill, too, having to do everything by myself.'

'Please let me help you with something, Susannah. I know, I'll shell these.' Amy picked up a pile of peas and a bowl to put them in. She sat at the table and started on the peas, hoping Susannah would forget her irritation, but her stepmother had warmed to her subject.

'You certainly manage to get a terrible fuss made of you. I didn't have people worrying over me for months after I had my babies. I had to start work again after a couple of weeks. I don't remember your father telling everyone to treat me as if I might break.'

'I don't want people to make a fuss of me. I can't help it if Pa keeps worrying about me. Please stop it, Susannah.' Amy's voice cracked a little.

'It's just ridiculous, the way he goes on about you.' Susannah punctuated her words with the crash of pot lids. 'Anyone would think you were the first girl ever to have a baby. At your age, too, it would have been easier than for a grown woman. Your bones are still soft. Anyway, you had the chloroform to make you sleep, I don't know why you're still carrying on as if you'd really been ill.'

'I didn't!' Amy wailed.

Susannah seemed surprised at the interruption. 'You didn't what? What are you talking about?'

'I didn't have chloroform.'

'No? What did they use, then?'

'Nothing! She wouldn't give me anything.' The words came out in gasps as Amy relived the agony.

'Are you telling me you didn't have anything to stop the pain?' Susannah said slowly.

'She said she wouldn't waste chloroform on me because I'm a bad girl. She wanted me to remember it. So I wouldn't do it again.' Amy's shoulders heaved with dry sobs.

Susannah sank heavily onto the chair beside her. 'I didn't know. Amy, I swear I didn't know they'd do that to you. That woman must be mad. She shouldn't be trusted with girls.'

'I thought I was going to die. The—' Amy stopped and took a gulp of air, 'the baby wouldn't come out. There wasn't room. I had to push and push, and I couldn't any more.' She licked her dry lips to moisten them. 'Then the woman said she'd bring a man to pull my insides out with bits of metal if I didn't push.' She gave a convulsive shudder at the memory. 'So I had to push. I thought I was going to die. I thought I was being ripped in half.'

'Shh, Amy, that's enough. It's a horrible, horrible thing that happened, but it's all over. You should try and forget about it. Talking will bring it all back to you.'

'And then she was there. My baby. My beautiful little girl. All warm and soft and nuzzling up to me. She lay in my arms and trusted me. She trusted me! And I gave her away. They just took her one day. I never said goodbye to her.'

'Oh, God, you got attached to it. I thought they'd take it straight away so that wouldn't happen. It would be a little girl, wouldn't it? Why couldn't you have had an ugly boy?' Susannah placed a hand awkwardly on Amy's shoulder. 'Amy, listen to me.' When Amy made no response, Susannah shook her gently. 'Listen! You gave her away for her own good. Because you wanted her to have a better life. You know that really, don't you?'

Amy turned to look at her, and saw Susannah wince at what she met in Amy's eyes. Susannah's voice shook as she spoke. 'If you hadn't given her away, you'd have to leave her with me when you get married. I'll be honest with you, Amy, I'd have trouble loving your baby. Oh, I'd try to do my best by her, but I don't want three children under three years old to look after. And every time I had a disagreement with your father he'd blame me for the fact that the baby was born at all. It's for the best this way, Amy, really it is.'

'Do you think they'll look after her?' Amy pleaded.

'I'm sure of it. Now, I think you'd better have a lie-down until lunch-time. I don't want your father seeing you like this, he'll think I've upset you. Come on.' Susannah helped Amy from her chair and into her bedroom. 'You just stay here quietly for a while—read a book or something.' She looked hard at Amy. 'You're really not very well yet, are you?'

'I just seem to get so tired, that's all,' Amy said, searching in a drawer for a clean handkerchief.

'Hmm. It's going to take you a little while to come right, I think.' Susannah made to leave, then turned back. 'Amy, your father doesn't know, does he? About how cruel that woman was to you?'

'No.'

'Don't tell him, please. He'd only blame me for it. He's quite difficult enough these days, since he got so bossy, without him having that to abuse me with. Anyway, it would only upset him.'

'I won't tell him. What's the use?'

Susannah closed the door on Amy and returned to the kitchen. She was shelling Amy's abandoned peas when Jack came in.

'Where's the girl?' he asked, looking around the room.

'She's having a lie-down. I told her she should.'

'So you're taking a bit of care of her at last. That's good.'

'Don't be so nasty to me all the time, Jack. Sit down and listen for a minute.'

Jack sat at the table and fiddled idly with an empty pea pod, wondering what Susannah was going to complain about now. Though she didn't look as though she wanted to moan about anything. In fact she looked as though something had genuinely upset her. 'What do you want to tell me?'

'Amy... well, I suppose you could say she unburdened herself to me just now. She had quite a hard time of it, bearing that child. I don't think she's going to be strong again for a while yet.'

'Do you think there's been damage done to her?'

'Oh, no, I shouldn't think so. I'm sure she'll still be a good breeder, if that's what you're getting at. She should be her old self again in a couple of months. But I do think it will take another two months, Jack. She's

356

not going to be ready to get married in the New Year.'

'Charlie won't be too pleased about that.'

'I expect not. Does that matter?'

'Of course it doesn't, not if it's the best for Amy. I'll tell him he's got to wait till February. Do you think that's why she looks so miserable all the time? Because she's still a bit crook?'

'That's part of it.'

'She's pining for the child, isn't she?'

'I'm afraid so. She got attached to it.'

'I thought as much. She couldn't so much as look at a baby in Auckland without getting weepy. It's hard on her, Susannah.'

'Well, there's only one way she's going to get over it. As soon as she's got another baby she'll be fine again—she'll forget this one for good.'

Jack sighed. 'I expect you're right. I hope he can give her one quickly, then.'

Susannah gave a little laugh. 'What a silly thing to say! We had two babies in two years, and you could give Charlie a few years.'

'That's true enough. Oh well, I'll go over this afternoon and see him. Early February, you think? Will she be well enough by then?'

'Early February should be just right. It'll give me more time to get her clothes organised, too.'

'What clothes? She's got plenty of clothes, hasn't she?'

'Women's clothes, of course. She can hardly wear pinafores any more, can she? She can probably let down some of her dresses, but I'll have to get her properly fitted for a corset.'

'Grown-up clothes.' Jack was silent while he wondered how it could all have happened so quickly. 'She's grown up too fast.'

'Now, Jack, please don't start on about that sort of thing again. Not when we've got everything sorted out so well for Amy.'

Amy woke on the fourth of February and wondered what was different about this day. She could see the sunshine through cracks in her drapes, and she could hear birds singing. So why did she have such a feeling of foreboding? Awareness rushed in on her. Today she was going to get married.

She rose and dressed, struggling with the laces of her uncomfortable new corset. She still found it difficult to lace herself in, but she was determined to manage by herself. From today Susannah would not be there to pull the laces tight, and the thought of asking Charlie to help with them left Amy cold.

She was torn between wanting the day to be over as quickly as possible and wishing the afternoon would never come. She looked around her family at the breakfast table, and felt as if she were never going to see them again. *That's silly. I'll only be next door. I'll be able to come and see them whenever I want.* But she was unable to shake off a deep sense of loss.

Jack was at his most hearty. 'So the big day's come at last,' he said. 'Getting excited, girl?'

'Sort of, Pa,' Amy said, wondering if the fluttering in her stomach counted as excitement.

'Now, don't got on about it, Jack,' Susannah reproved. 'Amy's probably a little nervous. All young brides are. I remember I was.'

Harry muttered something under his breath that might have been a curse. 'What was that, boy?' Jack asked.

'Nothing. I'd better go and get that milk to the factory.'

'Don't be all day about it, either,' Jack said. 'We've got to get some work done before lunch, what with us all going into town this afternoon for the wedding.'

'I'm not coming.'

'What do you mean, you're not coming? It's your sister's wedding!'

'I'm not going to pretend I'm happy about Amy being given to that... I'm sorry, Amy, I'm not coming.'

Amy looked at her plate. 'That's all right, Harry. Don't come if you don't want to.'

'Funny way for a brother to carry on,' Jack muttered.

The morning dragged wearily on. Amy tried to keep herself occupied with cooking and cleaning, but her thoughts kept returning to the thing that was to happen that afternoon. When Lizzie called in, Amy was unsure whether to be grateful for the distraction or wary of what her cousin might have to say.

'Come for a little walk,' Lizzie coaxed. 'Just for a few minutes.' She persuaded Amy out of the kitchen and away from Susannah's wary gaze.

'Lizzie, don't say anything silly,' Amy said when they were safely away from the house. 'I'm glad you came, because I mightn't be able to see you again for a while. I expect I'll be busy getting used to everything. So let's just have a nice little time together.'

'All right,' Lizzie agreed reluctantly. 'Amy, are you sure you don't want me to come to your wedding?'

'I've already told you, it's not the sort of wedding people come to. We'll just be saying a few words in the courthouse, that's all. Even Harry's not coming. You don't think it's anything to celebrate, anyway.'

'I don't think it's fair you're only having a courthouse wedding. Why can't you have a proper wedding with a minister and everything?'

Amy sighed. 'No one's exactly said why. Pa just said it's for the best. But I think it's because bad girls like me aren't meant to mock the church by getting married in front of the altar.'

'It's not fair. What about that Tilly Carr? She was nearly bursting out of her dress, she was that far gone when she got married.'

'That's different. She didn't let her man get away, did she?'

'Yes she did! Mr Carr had to go chasing off to Tauranga to catch him and bring him back.'

'Oh, I'd forgotten that. So he did. Well, Tilly didn't let him get away very far, then.'

'Humph! It's the only way she could get a husband at all.'

'It doesn't matter, Lizzie. I'd rather have it this way, with no fuss. It'll all be over much faster.'

'Amy, I know you don't want to hear this, but I'm going to say it anyway. It's the last chance I'll have. You don't have to go through with this. No, shut up and listen for a minute. I want you to remember when you're standing there, until you say "I will", or whatever you say at courthouse weddings, you're not married. And no one can make you say it. Remember that, Amy.'

Amy was quiet for some time. 'You've said what you wanted to, Lizzie,' she answered at last. 'Now let's talk about something else.'

Susannah helped Amy into the blue silk dress, its hem newly lowered, then piled her hair into a heavy mass on the back of her head. 'Your hair is so thick,' Susannah remarked. 'It's quite hard to pin.' She placed Amy's beautiful Auckland hat on top of the tamed curls and stood back to see the effect. 'Lovely,' she pronounced. 'You are going to make a very pretty bride. Look at yourself.' She pointed Amy towards the mirror.

Amy stared at her reflection. With her hair pinned up and the new angles her face had developed in the last few months, her image no longer looked familiar. And yet in a way it did. Her eyes drifted from the mirror to the photograph beside it, and she realised where the familiarity came from. She had her mother's face now. The only thing missing was her mother's smile.

As soon as she saw her father's expression, Amy knew he could see the resemblance, too. 'Beautiful,' he said in a voice that shook. 'You're beautiful.' He recovered himself. 'Well, we'd better get moving. We don't want to keep your intended waiting too long—not that it'll hurt him to wait a bit! Are you coming, John?' he asked, quite unnecessarily as John was already wearing his suit. 'You're not wandering off in a huff like your brother did?'

'I'm coming,' John said.

John took the reins and Amy sat beside him, while Jack and Susannah settled onto the back seat with their children squashed between them. Amy was glad the tide meant they had to take the inland track. Today she did not want to see the ocean holding out its false promises of escape.

'The *Staffa*'s just got in,' Jack commented when they crossed the bridge into Ruatane. 'There're a few strangers about.'

The courthouse was on the road that led from the bridge to the wharf, and Amy could see that the town was busier than usual. She looked at the people milling about without any real interest. For a moment she thought she caught a glimpse of a familiar tall, lean figure, but when she looked again there was no one but a middle-aged couple from the steamer. Her imagination was playing cruel tricks.

Charlie's grey gelding was tied to the hitching rail outside the courthouse. John tethered their own horses before the Leiths made their way into the small, wooden building. He caught Amy's arm at the foot of the steps up to the doorway, and pulled her aside for a moment.

'Amy,' he said in a low voice, 'I didn't want to come today any more than Harry did. But I came anyway.'

'Thank you, John. I'm glad you did, it's nicer for Pa.'

'That's not why I came. I just wanted to tell you…' He stared earnestly at Amy. 'If you change your mind—even at the last minute—just remember I'm here. No one can make you go through with this, you know.'

'John, don't make me cry,' Amy begged. On an impulse, she kissed him on the cheek. 'Stop worrying about me. This is what I want.'

Jack and Susannah were standing in the porch waiting for them. Amy knew they must be wondering why she and John were taking so long. She hurried up the steps to her father's side.

'Take my arm,' Jack said. 'We'll do this properly.' Amy slipped her arm through her father's, leaving Susannah to shepherd her children, with John in the rear of the little party. They walked in the door, through a small anteroom, and into the office of Ruatane's Resident Magistrate.

Mr Leveston was sitting behind his desk, while Charlie stood against one wall turning his hat around between his hands. Both men looked up at their approach, and Mr Leveston smiled warmly.

'So the bride has arrived—and a particularly beautiful bride, if I may say so.'

'Didn't keep you waiting too long, did we, Charlie?' Jack asked.

'No.' Charlie stared at Amy, and she had to turn away from the intensity of his gaze. It made her feel as though she were not wearing anything.

'Now, Mr Stewart has brought the licence, and everything seems in order.' Mr Leveston scanned the piece of paper in front of him as he spoke. 'Yes, I see you've signed your permission, Mr Leith, as your daughter is under age.' He glanced up at Amy for a moment. 'Well under age,' he murmured, his eyes flicking briefly to Charlie then back to Amy. A puzzled expression flitted across his face. He cleared his throat and continued.

'Mr Stewart, Miss Leith, if you'd both stand in front of me?'

Amy let go of her father's arm and walked across the room to stand beside Charlie as Mr Leveston picked up a small book from his desk.

'First of all, I must ask all those present if they know of any impediment to this marriage's taking place.'

Mr Leveston looked around the room at them all for a long few seconds, until Amy wanted to shout at him to get on with it. The longer she had to wait, the more clearly a forbidden picture formed in her mind: a vision of Jimmy rushing in the door and saying it had all been a terrible mistake, gathering her in his arms and taking her away to fetch their baby. *I mustn't think about another man when I'm getting married. It's wicked.* But when there was a noise at the door, Amy could not suppress a small cry of excitement. Mr Leveston glanced at her in surprise, then spoke briefly to the clerk who had just brought the mail in to him.

'I must apologise for that interruption,' Mr Leveston said when the clerk left. 'I'm afraid the bride was a little alarmed.' He picked up his book once more and continued.

'Charles Alexander Stewart, do you take this woman as your lawful wife?'

'I do.'

'Amy Louisa Leith, do you take this man as your lawful husband?'

'I do,' Amy heard herself say in a tiny voice.

'Then by the authority vested in me, I declare you to be lawfully married.' Mr Leveston put down his book and smiled at them, and Amy realised that the ceremony was over. It had lasted no more than two or three minutes.

'Mr Stewart, do you have something for your wife?' Mr Leveston prompted.

Amy saw Charlie looking expectantly at her father. Jack stepped over and pressed something into his hand. 'It was your ma's,' he said to Amy.

'I told Charlie I wanted you to have it.'

Charlie held out his hand and waited for Amy to place hers on it. With his other hand, he slid a narrow gold band onto her finger. Amy shivered at the unfamiliar touch, and studied her wedding ring rather than meet his gaze.

Mr Leveston broke in on her concentration. 'I must say what a great deal of pleasure it gives me on the rare occasions when I have the opportunity to join two youn—' He broke off for a moment; one of the two people before him was most definitely not young. He cleared his throat and went on in the same pompous tone. 'Two people together. I'm afraid a good deal of my time is spent passing sentence of justice on miscreants. It's certainly a more pleasant task to bestow a much happier, ah, sentence,' he laughed at his choice of words, 'if I may use the term. Yes, a very happy sentence indeed, and a good thing, too, since it's a life sentence. Congratulations, Mr Stewart, and my very best wishes, Mrs Stewart.'

Mrs Stewart. That's my name now. It sounded strange to Amy's ears. 'Thank you,' she murmured. She turned to look at her new husband.

It's done. I'm married. I belong to him now.

Made in the USA
Charleston, SC
04 April 2013